ANTIGRAVITY DRIVE

The Diary of an Invention

Barry C Cunningham

Copyright © 2015 Barry C Cunningham

All rights reserved.

ISBN: 1501048848
ISBN-13: 978-1501048845

DEDICATION

This book is dedicated to my entire family. Especially my wife, Diane, whose love, patience and support has always been a constant. Also, to my grandson, Josh, a continual source of inspiration and, not least, to my 'Brother from another Mother' Ian. I loved him, unconditionally, as a brother for the 40 years that we were in this existence together.

The people and events in this book are fictional. None of the characters in this book depict real people. Any similarities between them and any person living or dead are merely coincidental, with the exception of Professor Brian Cox who is referred to as the remarkable scientist and public character that he is.

Kindle, Kindle Fire and Kindle Fire HDX are trademarks of Amazon.com Inc. or its affiliates.

CONTENTS

Acknowledgements	i
Diary One – It Begins with a Dream	1
Diary Two – The Return	34
Diary Three - Divergence	89
Diary Four – Building Bridges	157
Addendum – Excerpt from Proceedings	216
Appendix I	223
Appendix II	224
Appendix III	225
Appendix IV	226
Appendix V	227

ACKNOWLEDGMENTS

There are, as always, many people who have supported me in writing this book, chief among those is fellow Sci-Fi nut and brother in law, Vin. He has given constant encouragement and feedback from day one, I may never have completed this book had he not done so. My grandson, Josh, sister, Janet, Friend and Fellow Rotarian, Will and a 'never fails to amaze me' friend, Simon. They have all read and given valuable suggestions and feedback at many different stages in the writing of this book, I cannot thank them enough.

ANTIGRAVITY DRIVE
The Diary of an Invention

DIARY ONE – IT BEGINS WITH A DREAM

Day 1 - 31st May 2016

There I was, fast asleep, dreaming (I think I knew I was dreaming) slumped in my favourite chair, when suddenly it seemed obvious, in my dream-state, that all I had to do was build an antigravity drive, build a vehicle around it, pop into orbit, then clean up all the debris everyone was always banging on about.

I could see that it would be relatively easy, find a mineral, rich in gravitons, refine it, pop it in a mechanism that gave it a controlled squeeze, a really strong, megaton type of squeeze, and somehow it would acquire an opposite (anti) force equivalent to gravity from the biggest mass in the vicinity, for example, the Earth or, if you were near it, the Sun.

The harder the squeeze the more the antigravity. That means, I could pop away from Earth, or fall back towards it, just by squeezing.

It felt like a good idea, if I proved it, built a model, patented it I could literally clean up.

Different sized engines for all sorts of applications, from skateboards without wheels to spacecraft without rockets, I can imagine cars, trains, planes, boats/ships, every sort of transport all whizzing about soundlessly at any height they wished.

What a great invention, all I had to do was invent it.

Day 15 – 14th June 2016

That 'Eureka Moment' was some time ago and I seem to be stuck on something, something fundamental. What is a graviton and what mineral is rich in them?

So not making progress really, well not at all actually, but it still seems like a good idea.

Maybe I should prove it mathematically or something first, yeah that's a good idea, the second good idea I'd had all month.

The internet seemed yet another good idea.

It's amazing how you can get side-tracked when googling!

Day 16 – 15th June 2016

Not sure anybody knows about gravitons so I'm playing around on the internet and googling a bit more.

Bollocks! Looks like someone has already done it, or is it a spoof? The Chinese are going to build one.

Now hang on a minute, it was my dream, can you patent dreams?

Day 20 - 19th June 2016

I've been thinking, not dreaming, thinking.

When I had that dream I felt awake, but it was really clear, as if it was obvious it would work as if I was being told it would work.

What if I was being told it would work, some alien or something psychic, transmitting on my wavelength?

Had I been eating cheese?

My mum always said cheese does funny things to dreams if you eat it before you sleep.

ANTIGRAVITY DRIVE - THE DIARY OF AN INVENTION

Thinking back, I might have had a cheese sandwich.

Hang on I'll just go and eat some cheese and have a nap.

Day 21 – 20th June 2016

Nothing!

Day 23 – 22nd June 2016

Well 2lbs of cheese and an 18 hour sleep and no further on, so much for that experiment. Feel a bit nauseous actually, not doing that again! Think it was all the bread and crackers.

Day 24 – 23rd June 2016

Mouth like the bottom of a baby's pram and a fiery ring (if you know what I mean) not sure Stinking Bishop was a good idea either. If ever I do that again, for the sake of scientific experimentation, I would choose something milder like Wensleydale. After all "Wallace and Grommit" did alright with their inventions.

Day 26 - 25th June 2016

I've been doing some serious thinking again. I need to get some neodymium or other rare earth metal that can be used for super strong magnets.

I am going to squeeze 'like-poles' together (north to north or south to south), really hard, they usually repel each other. Not sure how I came upon this idea but it does have a feel to it.

Not figured out that bit yet. But I'm sure I will, I seem to be having very creative thoughts and for some reason this is gripping my interest.

Day 35 – 4th July 2016

Can you believe it? Those magnets are sold as toys in any novelty store, wrong shape, they are like torpedoes, but at least I've got some.

Day 36 – 5th July 2016

Wow! These magnets are really fun, still not sure what I am going to do with them, but they are fun.

Bollocks, think I've just magnetised my watch!

Day 40 – 9th July 2016

You won't believe this but I've sourced some more, these are much better, they are little ball-bearings that are sold in packs to make 3D shapes, like cubes and things. It's captivating and addictive, making shapes with magnets, this is real fun.

Day 45 – 14th July 2016

Somebody take these magnets away, can't stop making shapes, it really is addictive.

Help!!!

Day 50 – 20th July 2016

There are only so many shapes a person can make, arrghh!

Think I might be over it now and can concentrate on my invention again.

Day 51 – 21st July 2016

So, where to go to from here? These magnets to make cubes are great but they are small and spherical, how can I get the wrong/like poles to connect and stay in place?

My head hurts thinking about it, but never mind, still fun to play with.

Day 55 – 25th July 2016

Had another dream last night, this is getting weird, solving problems and being creative in my dreams, really odd.

Anyway, it's obvious, press like poles together and set them in pairs in a plastic or resin. Going to use those craft kits for making key rings and paper weights and stuff.

Going to make my own moulds, with a magnet sphere in a little plastic cube with the surfaces of the spheres just touching their six cube faces.

Day 56 – 26th July 2016

Ordered a set on the internet, meanwhile, let's make more shapes.

Day 60 – 30th July 2016

Plastic kit arrived, can't wait to get stuck in. Making moulds out of balsa wood, got to be real accurate so that the magnet spheres just fit . Finished an array of 10 x 10 so I can make a hundred in one go, not that I'm impatient or anything.

Need a beer, head hurts.

Day 61 – 31st July 2016

Too many beers, head throbbing, going back to bed, ergh!

Day 62 – 1st August 2016

Right, got my array, got the little magnetic spheres, got the plastic resin components, here we go. Making them on a metal tray, so the magnets all go into their cells with North/South poles vertical. Half fill each cell with resin mix, drop in spheres, top up if needed, place flat sheet on top and wait.

Removed the top plate and there they all are, one hundred full cells of magnetic spheres in clear plastic, can't believe got it right first time.

That's what comes of imagining, dreaming and thinking things through, visualising the end result, well whatever, it's worked.

I've got 100 perfect little cubes of spherical magnets in plastic. Now I just need to get like poles fixed together.

Day 63 – 2nd August 2016

The answer is, I hope, a centrifuge. I've used them before, I know what they are like, but where can I get one, a really fast one, that has got detachable buckets so I can modify them.

I'll start with eBay.

Can you believe it? Hundreds of them from a few 10's of £s to hundreds, wow! Mostly for small samples, like blood, too little for this purpose, need a good size with lots of rpm.

Found one, buy it now £57.00, buyer to collect.

I'm off, got to drive to Leeds.

Day 64 – 3rd August 2016

Wow, what a beauty, four buckets, perfectly balanced, runs with variable speed up to 40k rpm.

Even got a dozen fitted glass tubes.

It's years since I played with one of these, let's get the kitchen scales out and separate a few things.

I set it all up in the garage where accidents might not be too devastating.

I wondered how much water would spin out of the mud in the garden.

Exactly 50g in each, all four buckets with tubes, exactly same weight, here we go, woo-hoo!

What fun, spin for 5 minutes, spin down, auto lock clicks, lift lid and have a look.

Amazing, looks almost a 50:50 separation in those tubes with the heavier solids mostly at the bottom but a few still suspended with just a small amount on the surface of the top layer of water.

Gosh, I'd forgotten how much I enjoyed this sort of stuff. Feel like I ought

ANTIGRAVITY DRIVE - THE DIARY OF AN INVENTION

to do something with the samples, daft I know, but took a picture of them for posterity.

Shall I do more playing, it's tempting, but really should get on with my magnets, how on earth is this going to work?

So what am I aiming for?

I want to make a cube that has 8, 27, 64 or 125 magnets all held in a matrix with like poles touching in one direction, they have to be touching so that I can squeeze them together.

The idea is to take two at a time and force them together whilst spinning at high speed in the centrifuge. Not sure yet what I will use to fuse them together without coating the touching magnet surfaces.

I don't want to waste my little spherical magnetic cubes so lovingly prepared but I can't think of an alternative approach.

I've made a square section tube of balsa wood with another square section inside so the cubes fit in snugly, like a square telescope.

Once in the bucket they're held in place by dry sand. I can use the sand to make sure all four buckets are the same weight. It is really important to balance opposite buckets, otherwise dangerous and damaging vibrations happen that could destroy the centrifuge.

I have decided to coat one surface of each little cube (avoiding the magnet itself) with part one of a two-part adhesive and the prospective other surface with the other part, load into my inner balsa wood sleeve and place some lead shot above that, to give it extra squashing 'umph'. Balance the weight of all four with sand and pop into the centrifuge. Spin up and leave for 20 minutes.

I think that's plenty of time for it to harden. Here we go, all balanced, two magnetic spheres in place with their respective parts of the adhesive, lid closed, spin up, full speed, 20 minutes in the timer.

I trembled slightly with the excitement as I stripped down my little construction.

Minor disaster, the squeezing has forced a little adhesive out and is stuck to the inner balsa sleeve, I hope it's not coated the magnet too. Using a craft knife I carefully removed the balsa.

I will need to do it every time, glad I didn't use metal as I would never get them out.

I think the balsa was inspirational but it's going to be a real faff doing it every time. Never mind if it works it will be worth it. It appears to have worked the surfaces of the spheres seem to be touching and they are like-poles, so that's the first two.

Day 65 – 4th August 2016

Up early, son (Tom) off to meet friends for a game of football, wife (Jane) off to work, I'm at home, jobless and redundant. You might wonder why there is not a lot written here about me and the rest of my family in our daily lives? I suppose it might make this more interesting for another reader, but this diary is just a sort of record about what I'm doing with this antigravity drive thing. (Sometimes I can't believe I'm actually having a go, I don't even know why I'm convinced it will work.) Anyway, this diary is not really intended for others to read, unless it's fabulous and changes the World then I suppose it becomes an important document.

Maybe I should be keeping proper scientific records with lots of exact measurements and detailed data.

Nah! If this little experiment works, I'll keep proper records on the first full scale example. So I decamped into the garage armed with craft knife and balsa, to make more little square telescopes. Got to make plenty, not doing this piecemeal.

Think I will start with a 2x2x2 cube just to test this out. So that's four pairs I need to make.

There was a CRACK! and a POP! What on Earth was it?

I'd heard a distinct crack immediately followed by a little pop.

I've located the source of the noises it was the fused magnetic sphere cubes, they had just fractured and popped apart. Blast it! I thought I had solved that problem, so the process was right but glue wrong.

Maybe they could be clamped straight away, but that would mean that they would be impossible to fiddle about with.

Oh well another problem to solve, I think two part adhesives need mixing together first to go hard so I should think again what to use. Anyway those two cubes are unusable unless I retrieve them from their little plastic cases. I'm going to press on and prepare everything for a 3x3x3 cube instead, all the balsa telescopes.

Just finished laying everything out and realised I can only do this using pairs so can't do a 3x3x3 got to be a 2x2x2 or 4x4x4 or 6x6x6. I am sure the latter is too big for me to play around with so it's a 2 or a 4. I think the 2 is too fiddly so it has to be the 4x4x4.

Well thank goodness I have 98 good magnetic spheres in cubes.

Just got to figure out the adhesive. Super glue I think, a tiny, little dab on each corner of opposing faces and make sure plenty of lead shot in each centrifuge tube.

Doing four pairs at a time, all prepared, here we go. 8 hours later got 32 pairs done, glue seems to be holding and I'm ready for next stage of pairing up the pairs linked with like-poles.

Knackered now, off to bed.

Day 66 – 5th August 2016

Do you know what? I'm getting quite excited with this, it's absorbing and time consuming. Mind you, to anyone else it must look bonkers.

I'm enjoying it, no one else knows what I'm doing, don't think anyone else would think this worthwhile, I suppose it might come to nothing, but just feel I have to give it a go.

Right, same process as before but using pairs of cubes this time and as before the two new fused faces are like-poles. Four at a time all weighed and balanced, super glue in place and spin up. Twenty minutes later have four magnetic sphere rods of four magnets all with touching like-poles.

Just got to repeat another three times.

Well that's that, got sixteen rods, which, to me, look identical and are almost exactly the same weight.

Never thought before but now I have to get them together to form a cube. Easier said than done, because as before, they want to flip over and stick together like proper magnets. I think they are big enough to use clamps or a bench vice.

Taking two rods at a time I used my bench vice to glue them together being extra careful not to get glue on the little magnet faces.

I've made four, 4x4 squares, this is getting really exciting now.

I need to start thinking about how I'm going to squeeze the cube when it's finished.

Day 69 – 8th August 2016

Been a busy weekend in the garden, so here I am, Monday morning, gluing the four squares together. By the end of today should have my perfect cube of little magnets all sat in a matrix of like-pole to like-pole.

It's finished, a real milestone, 64 little neodymium magnets all sat in a matrix of like-poles, in one direction, I can hardly believe it, all that effort and there it is - my perfect little antigravity engine core.

Day 70 – 9th August 2016

Now I'm looking at the cube and realising that squeezing all six faces at the same time with equal force is quite a problem. I need some thinking time.

The cube shows no apparent sign of fracturing, but, if I don't get on with applying this squeeze they might eventually pop apart.

ANTIGRAVITY DRIVE - THE DIARY OF AN INVENTION

Day 80 – 19th August 2016

Nowhere nearer coming up with a squeeze solution and getting more nervous about leaving the fused cube unclamped, if it pops open I might give up. No, I can't give up, done too much, I need to know if it will work or not. Squeezing six directions at once, equally? For me this is a real brain teaser. Can't seem to think of anything practical and accessible to me.

Come on, need inspiration! (Oh no, not cheese again)

Day 85 – 24th August 2016

What about car jacks, little bottle jacks? It might be a good idea, but from six directions and all squeezing the same at the same time.

It's obvious that whatever the solution is it cannot be manual, it will have to be automatic, electrically driven or something.

Will have a search on the internet, going to try googling and eBaying it. I wonder if you can buy little hydraulic piston things that you get in automatic doors, forklifts and stuff like that.

Day 88 – 27th August 2016

Just realised I've been absorbed in this project quite a lot and still no one knows about it, everyone I know would think I was absolutely bonkers, but I just have a feeling this might be interesting in the long run.

I have a magnetic core but no squeezing mechanism. I can visualise the solution:

- Six hydraulic devices, somehow connected to one controller.

- Each "Jack" will be pointing directly at a face of the cube and will need anchoring very strongly to a steel frame cube constructed with internal braces.

- Need to encase the whole structure in a metal mesh or solid plates just in case all that squeezing causes an explosion of some type.

The structure seems to be growing quite large for just a little core. If this works I hope it's not too heavy to make the whole thing impractical. It would have to be miniaturized for skateboards, can't imagine that right now.

Day 90 – 29th August 2016

I'm so excited, found the solution, little hydraulic piston, can even buy them on eBay. Hydraulic ram actually, 200+ ton, and only 25cm tall. (I know it's not megaton, but at least it's a start) Found a used job lot of 10 identical rams for £254. I can't believe it. Have to pick them up in Glasgow. I will need one or more hydraulic pumps, so sourcing them, or it, as soon as I can.

Day 91 – 30th August 2016

One good hydraulic pump with a six way manifold will do the job. Pick that up first from Sheffield and only £350.

Just hit a potential snag, all this money on seemingly strange purchases, nipping off to Sheffield and Glasgow. The time has come to bring my wife and son onboard, not going to be easy, might need to say the device has another more practical purpose that is probably more plausible and consequently believable.

Well I've told them I have thought of a way to automatically Jack lorries when they have flat tyres on motorways and make it possible for drivers to quickly change a wheel. I said it will save haulage companies millions and I need to build a prototype.

Lots of discussion, argument and money limits but she and he are OK. So off we go, all having a day out on Saturday, up to Scotland via Sheffield. Why am I so excited? I suppose it's like one of those obsessive hobbies, like stamp collecting or model trains.

Day 100 – 8th September 2016

Bought some welding gear too and lots of steel, 25mm x 2000mm angle sections, 12.5mm x 2000mm square rods and other odds and ends of steel and welding rods. Garage looks like a proper workshop now with all this gear and materials.

Before I start constructing I am running trials with the hydraulic pump and rams. They have to run simultaneously and exert same force. I also need to make sure they keep pumping and pushing when pushing against each other.

There are pressure gauges on the hydraulic inlet to each ram.

Day 101 – 9th September 2016

Just realised I've been keeping this diary for more than 3 months, amazing how time flies. I'm really struggling to know how to set these rams up and control them, can't seem to set them all off together, even when put on a six gang manifold.

They always appear to be ever so slightly out of phase, maddening! Also, the needles in each of the pressure gauges seem to waver about and are not giving identical readings.

My initial excitement with these rams is waning, not sure I have the skills to crack this problem. Maybe it's important to have them in matched pairs and not all six identical.

Day 105 – 13th September 2016

I've been trying and repeating little experiments and trials for days, but, not really getting anywhere, except that I have become very familiar with all the kit. I am convinced this is the way forward, but, I am sure even small differences in forces exerted in opposite directions would cause problems.

Day 110 – 18th September 2016

What an idiot! After days and days of trials and experimenting and trying to think of elaborate control mechanisms.

It came to me in a flash of stupid realisation, Newton's third law, "For every action there is an equal and opposite reaction", I only need to push in three directions as long as it's pushing against an immovable surface.

What an idiot, I feel like I have wasted days and days and got terribly frustrated in the process.

Day 111 – 19th September 2016

On the plus side I also realised that it is possible to build a control mechanism using an adjustable valve, controlled by a small computer, using data taken from a pressure transducer placed between the ram and the object surface (the cube).

I'm going to use one or more Raspberry Pi computers and some auto valves and pressure transducers obtained from eBay, yet again. I have a good basic knowledge of coding going back thirty or so years, when learning and using several computer languages such as Algol, FORTRAN, Pascal and Basic.

It's amazing when I think how much has happened since I had that weird dream. I'm actually going to build a device that may turn out to be a pile of rubbish and scrap metal.

I don't know why I'm doing it really especially as I have not proven anything, yet, theoretically or physically. I must be mad to keep going, but, for some obscure reason, I remain positive that this will work.

I have also realised that there are now so many things to do that I should start planning what I do each day; I have to work out what is the best sequence of all the things that I need to do.

This is what needs doing : -

1. Learn welding

2. Draw structure

3. Source valves

4. Source 'Raspberry Pi' Computers

5. Source transducers

6. Develop control system

7. Make and test a second/reserve cube

8. Build structure

During list making and thinking, I've realised that most of the equipment I have runs on a normal 240 volt system. So, I think I might as well buy a little generator with the correct voltage output, then I will have a stand-alone system.

If I am linking everything with computers I might as well get other gadgets too, so going to put in a couple of cameras and temperature sensor.

Day 112 – 20th September 2016

I have signed up on a two week welding course for beginners, ordered the Raspberry Pi computers, ordered the valves and started to draw the structure of the cage.

There needs to be a central, 3 faced cube holder. Each face to be braced with a tripod structure behind it, welded to the corresponding larger inside face of the supporting cubic assembly.

The cube holder needs to be perfectly square and aligned accurately in the larger cube. The hydraulic rams also need positioning perfectly square corresponding to each of the magnetic cube faces.

Day 120 – 28th September 2016

Have largely got this welding 'thing' and don't intend to do a perfectly aesthetic structure, so don't need to be a master, consequently, the introductory course is enough.

The challenge is to set the struts and cups in perfect position, as I feel with all this pressure, if it is not in straight lines it would result in buckling and fractures.

Have decided to make concrete jigs using set squares and tack weld to hold things in shape, then a full seal weld to hold each join.

Day 125 – 3rd October 2016

This has turned into an almost full-time obsession, wife going nuts, not doing enough around the house, will have to calm down and restore some balance.

In any case I have made all sorts of jigs from concrete, made in wooden moulds, I think they are going to be essential in getting this structure right.

I have also changed direction slightly with hydraulic control, going for three individual pumps rather than one pump on a manifold. This means that each ram can be controlled separately and minutely to achieve desired results.

Day 126 – 4th October 2016

Started welding, it's very therapeutic, because it needs focused concentration and effort.

Making the six outer cube faces, each face will be 2 metre squares. This will allow plenty of working area inside the supporting frame.

Each outer face and the top will have a hinged steel mesh door for safety, each will have locking mechanisms to keep them secure when squeezing begins.

Day 150 – 28th October 2016

Done six perfect 2 metre squares made from angle steel, don't really need one for the base but I made one, just to be sure I have somewhere to attach the central supports. Done a spot weld on each corner and have a perfect cube. This is getting really exciting now, I can picture the end result easily now.

My wife spotted the structure today and is now unconvinced it's for lorries. I managed to convince her it's the test rig and the cube represents a lorry. I have to keep telling myself, this just might work, but also bear in mind there is, as yet, no evidence to support my ideas. But, as I am incapable of proving this with maths and physics on paper, I have to do it physically, trial and error.

Day 155 – 2nd November 2016

Fabulous progress, got the large cube finished, six sides with supports from the corners of two adjacent sides and the base holding three sides of a small twenty-centimetre cube that will hold the engine core.

Supports from the other corners hold three braces for the hydraulic rams. These are perfectly aligned with the corresponding face of the central cube holder. I know everything is perfect and true as I have used my DIY laser level.

I think I am ready to start the control mechanism. Excitement and anticipation building every day.

Thoughts have crossed my mind to pressure test the rig before a cube goes in, but I don't want to test to destruction, so in a bit of a dilemma, but if it fails at least I would know to make something stronger.

Day 156 – 3rd November 2016

Each of the cage cube faces, except the base, have a full, hinged door made from a slightly smaller square of angle steel and steel mesh. The face doors are hinged at the top, except the top of the rig, which is hinged on one side, when shut all the faces are bolted in position, using large butterfly nuts.

Also, inside one of the sides I have built a steel box for the generator and on another 'ram-side' I have a steel box at chest height to hold the laptop, the Raspberry Pi and other bits of electronics.

I have also mounted three cctv cameras on the ram sides all looking at the central cube. In the view of one camera I have mounted a clock showing date, time and temperature. Attached to the business end of each ram is a pressure transducer pad.

Day 160 – 7th November 2016

I can hardly believe it, I keep popping into the workshop just to have a look, everything is in place, even the magnetic sphere cube. The rams are fixed and ready, along with their transducers, the cameras work, the structure passed my pressure test, the generator works and has a 10 litre fuel tank.

When running with all face doors locked, it will be self-sufficient until I intervene and turn it off.

Meanwhile, I am up in the study writing a little control programme for the rams, hydraulic systems and the transducers providing feedback.

I am making sure that whatever can be logged and stored in data files is done too.

The Raspberry Pi is a fabulous little computer that I am using to control the systems and to store data on my laptop, which is also logging video from the CCTV cameras.

Day 180 – 27th November 2016

Big day today, I am going to run a trial of the whole system, with a solid steel cube in the rig instead of the magnetic cube.

I am writing this in 'real time' as the trial progresses, instead of the end of the day.

Generator running (exhaust to the window with detachable pipe), fueled with 5 litres of petrol, all computers on, cameras on and recording, transducers giving readings, start control programme.

Only the face door at the computer station to close and lock.

It's running, doors locked, I can see through the grille that pressure readings are increasing with a preset gradient with two rams following the output from the vertical ram (this is the main direction of fused like-poles).

All seems OK, have it set to stop and reset when ram 3 reaches 100 tons.

It took 4 hours and 25 minutes to reach pressure and a further 30 minutes to reset to zero.

I'm absolutely knackered observing all that time, I dare not leave it, who knows what might happen?

ANTIGRAVITY DRIVE - THE DIARY OF AN INVENTION

Day 181 – 28th November 2016

Just finished second trial, it went exactly as the first, nothing to see on camera, no temperature change in the rig, ramp up to pressure, exactly the same time and return to zero.

Tomorrow I will start the big squeeze on my magnetic cube.

Day 182 – 29th November 2016

I'm as nervous and excited as Hell, hands trembling I am going through the same procedure, except I have put no limit on pressure so it will run until I stop it.

Again I am writing in 'real time', but with difficulty as I really have the shakes.

One hundred and eighty days of thinking, dreaming, planning and effort, here we go.

I have set it going, with a full fuel tank, it's running and locked.

Watching pressure readings ramping up along the same gradient as the trials.

Not sure what to expect.

I never really thought about how I would know if anything actually happens. Idiot! I could have the rig stood on a transducer to monitor weight, oh well, not done it, too late now.

It's got to an even pressure of 150 tons and it is 11.30 pm, I pressed the button at 10.30 am so it's been running for 13 hours.

I think I can leave it, can't keep eyes open any longer. Off to bed.

Day 183 – 30th November 2016

Bollocks! Bugger! Bollocks! I don't know what to do, it's gone!

The whole rig, even the exhaust tube out of the window, all gone. As I was walking to the garage I couldn't hear the genny, thought it must have stalled or run out of fuel.

I unlocked the side door and was gob-smacked to see the eye boggling emptiness of the garage, with no massive, steel cube dominating the space.

What am I to do? How can I explain it, who do I tell?

I am gutted I feel like someone's died, shocked, tearful actually in physical pain.

I just stood and stared for a full twenty minutes, completely in denial, I even went out and came back in fully expecting it to be there.

I was at a loss, it must have been stolen, but who and how?

The doors were all locked, it weighed a ton, I definitely couldn't lift it, you would need at least four strong men or lifting equipment and what about transport?

Oh no! The window with the exhaust, it was still open, maybe that's how they got in.

Why had no-one heard anything?

What do I do?

Should I start to build another one?

Why would anyone steal it?

Who even knew about it?

Only I knew of its potential purpose and that wasn't proven, to anyone else it's just junk. Maybe that's it, stolen for metal and computers, that's it, that's what's happened. I'm lost for words, annoyed, frustrated, hurt, bloody angry actually!

I felt a tap on my shoulder and nearly filled my pants!

It was Jane, my wife, just going to work.

I tried to look normal, even tried to stop her looking in, but couldn't conceal the absence of the rig. I thought of trying to convince her that I'd had it moved, but realised that was impossible, especially as she'd already noticed my state of distress.

She has called the Police.

ANTIGRAVITY DRIVE - THE DIARY OF AN INVENTION

She assumes it's another one of the spate of burglaries that had been reported in the local press.

The Police are here, will catch up later.

Well that was awkward, it might be easy to report a garage burglary, but one with a steel structure, an invention for lorry maintenance.

Well here comes the awkward bit Jane told them all about it, a device for replacing tyres or wheels on lorries.

The constable was making copious notes and asked if I had drawings or photos as well as a full rundown of events in the morning about the discovery of the theft.

He appeared to notice, with a certain amount of curiosity, the locked doors and the fact that power tools and all sorts of expensive gear had been left alone by the thief, or thieves. He also noted the open window, I had to admit I had left it open all night.

The really awkward bit is Jane told him I was keeping a detailed diary. I was not even aware that she knew I had one, anyway he took a copy on a borrowed memory stick.

After several hours he departed, saying he would write it up and will call back tomorrow for me to check and sign my statement.

So did you notice the awkward bit?

He was told about a device for lorries, but if he reads the diary he will learn of its real potential purpose.

I am absolutely wracking my brain as to how I am going to handle this tomorrow.

Hang on, someone knocking on the front door.

Day 190 – 7th December 2016

Well that's it, I'm shit-scared, can hardly type. I'm adding this to the diary for completeness, but don't know why I'm bothering to do it.

That knock on the door, the day the rig was stolen?

I opened the door, thinking it might be that nice Constable back with statements to read or something, I was wrong, very wrong.

I was shoved backwards into the house, whipped around by strong hands and pushed against the wall so hard I could hardly breathe, it all happened so quickly, so silently and efficiently.

I was handcuffed, bodily lifted into the air and carried outside and straight into the back of a nondescript silver coloured car, no idea of the make. I could see there were at least four men, dressed, not in black with balaclavas as you might expect, but in ordinary clothing, jeans, chinos, tee shirts, light sweaters that sort of thing, I could see at least two were carrying automatic guns of some type.

I was so scared I am sorry to say I wet my pants, didn't know I had done it until it felt damp in the back of the car, as we sped off down the street.

No squealing tyres, or high revs, just quickly speeding away.

There was one man either side of me, squashed into the back, two in front.

As we were speeding along I was informed that I was under arrest and on my way to a secure unit for questioning. My heart was pounding, I tried to speak but the man on my right just told me to shut it and save it for someone who gives a shit.

I dare not argue, the sheer efficiency of my abduction, or arrest, was totally unbelievable! It was like being in a movie, but so surreal, but very, very, very, scary. I was terrified, thousands of thoughts were crashing around my head, it was difficult to concentrate or even be aware fully what was happening, even now it mostly seems like a blur. I thought I might never be released or, even worse, I might be killed off. What about Jane, where was she? Where is Tom, our boy, did they get them too?

As I am typing this a week after my abduction I am able to record what happened.

Jane heard the knock that I had answered, but nothing else, then moments later she heard another knock. She answered the door to find the friendly

ANTIGRAVITY DRIVE - THE DIARY OF AN INVENTION

bobby, smiling at her, he explained to her that a colleague had just taken me off in a rush to possibly identify the stolen rig, it had apparently been recovered in Glasgow, so I might be a couple of days. We will keep you informed, were his parting words, as he was getting into the passenger side of an unmarked Police car, parked right outside the house.

Consequently, although she thought, it a bit strange, she accepted my absence as being part of the investigation, she even thought I was lucky to be that involved!

So that answers the question for you, all they did was abduct me, nothing else, just efficiently removed me from the house.

Efficiently and silently, no fuss, just removed me without raising any suspicions, no one would miss me, life went on as normal, except it didn't, not for me anyway.

I was so shocked, so terrified, handcuffed, wedged between two huge men, I took almost no notice of the route the car was taking, like I said before it's just a blur. I am not even sure how long I was in the back of the car. I know it wasn't just a few minutes and not hours.

We came to a stop in a car park behind a nondescript, multistoried, 1960's brick building. No idea where or what the building was.

I was taken from the car, I offered no resistance. I was walked arm in arm into the building and along a corridor. Then down a couple of flights of stairs and bustled through an open door to be confronted, almost predictably, with a room having two chairs facing each other across the long sides of a small table placed directly under a single light bulb in the centre of the small, windowless space.

They removed the handcuffs from my wrists, sat me in the chair facing the door and handcuffed each wrist separately, attaching each to a small ring set into the top surface of the table about 25cm apart.

The burly abductors left me in silence, closing the door behind them. There were absolutely no features at all in the room, with the exception of the door and the single light bulb, there was nothing I could see, no switches, cameras, windows, recording equipment, nothing. I have no idea how long I sat there, I could stand up, but not quite upright, I was bursting for the toilet, I had a raging thirst and felt really hungry.

Worst of all I had at least three itches on my head, my back and arm that I couldn't get to, they were driving me mental. On top of all that I was still almost comatose with terror. It was probably the worst thing I could ever imagine, looking back now it almost feels just like I imagined it, like it couldn't possibly have happened, but it did.

Reliving it now has got me sweaty and tense, it really was unbelievable.

I had sat there in my mental tortured state for some interminable amount of time when, suddenly, the door burst open, making me jump out of my skin, I was out of the chair, struggling against the handcuffs.

Only one man stood there, silhouetted against the brightness of the corridor behind him. He ordered me to calm down and sit down, he had an authoritative but distinctive American drawl.

Sitting down I pleaded with him to know where I was and why was I there, who was he and to please release my hands. He curtly replied that he could not release me or answer any questions and that I should just remain calm and cooperate fully answering all questions truthfully.

I whinged and whined that I had done nothing wrong and that I had rights and that he couldn't treat me this way.

He just calmly informed me that what was happening was completely legal, that I had no rights, no say at all in what may or may not happen to me and that whatever they decided to do with me after interrogation remained open, depending how I cooperated.

"So you think lying to the Police is doing nothing wrong?" It was like a stab in the heart.

I felt a bright red blush building from the neck up, I didn't know what to say, I was squirming, uncomfortable and desperate to pee. I tried to talk but only stammered a muffled apology.

ANTIGRAVITY DRIVE - THE DIARY OF AN INVENTION

He appeared to be completely unimpressed and slammed a folder full of papers down between my hands with a loud bang, once again making me jump up with fright, he again demanded that I sit down and calm down.

I protested I had nothing to hide, everything in the diary, my diary, the one the Police had a copy of, explains exactly what happened.

He just silently stared at me, almost appeared disinterested, waiting until I'd finished, he half stood, leaning across the table until our noses almost touched, looking straight into my eyes, he shouted so loud it made my ears ring, Crap! Tell me who you work for? Who is directing you? Where is your device?

He was shouting with such force spittle was splattering my face and his breath smelled of a recently devoured bacon butty, which strangely made my stomach rumble.

I was ravenous, again it seemed unreal, but, how could I think of food at the same time as being terrified?

I could hardly speak, tears were streaming down my cheeks, I began to sob and speak at the same time, sounding like a small child trying to explain how they grazed a knee in a fall. I knew I sounded pathetic, but I couldn't help it, couldn't control it, I was now in some sort of survival mode.

I sobbed my heart out to him, pleading with him to listen, that everything in the diary was the truth.

My white lie to Jane was a cruel and manipulative thing to do and she got everyone confused in her innocence.

He silently and closely observed me all the way though my sobbing soliloquy.

We sat there, for what seemed an age, me sobbing, him watching. Eventually I managed to stop and was trying to wipe my tears on my upper arms, suddenly he stood, gathered his papers, and walked wordlessly out of the room, gently closing the door as he left.

I didn't know whether to feel relieved or more scared, scared of what may happen next. I had become quite calm, still bursting for the toilet, still ravenously hungry and still terrified.

The door opened, this time quietly, and in trooped the four burly abductors. They each stood, arms folded, in separate corners of the room. Once they were in position, another well-built man, dressed in a pin-striped business suit and sporting a red bow tie, ambled in and sat himself opposite me.

He looked calm, self-assured and definitely "in charge".

Clearing his throat, with a half delivered smokers cough, he said, in an Etonian-like English accent, "Here is what we are going to do, Mr. Charles. You will do exactly as we say or next time we pick you up you will be removed from society at large, Mr. Charles, disappeared without trace, Mr. Charles, do you understand, Mr. Charles?" He made each 'Mr. Charles' sound like an insult, something to be ashamed of, sinister to the core.

I wrote that in quotes because it is permanently etched in my memory, every word, every intonation and emphasis, I can hear him saying it now, I'm scared and shuddering at the thought.

All I could do was nod, even that was difficult in my, then, constant state of terror. He proceeded to read a numbered list as follows :-

1. You will be cleaned up and released back to your family.

2. We will confiscate all remaining materials, equipment and software.

3. You will inform anyone that asks that it was not recovered in Glasgow, but it was an interesting trip.

4. You will not try in any way to repeat your experiments.

5. You will not communicate to anyone at any time in any way about your experiments.

6. You will not divulge to anyone the events or conversations since your arrest.

7. You will sign a document stating that you are subject to the Official

Secrets Act, and that all that has transpired during your experiments and subsequently your arrest are subject to said act.

8. We will continue to observe and monitor your activities until such time we deem it as not appropriate.

9. Any failure on your part to comply with these requirements will result in your aforementioned disappearance.

After delivering his list, and not speaking again, he thrust a document with an "x" marked near a box for my signature, towards me.

At the same time a pen was placed in my right hand and my handcuff released. I signed, without hesitation. He scooped up the paper and pen, stood, turned on his heels and left the room.

The four burly guys remained and promptly sprang into action. They released me from the table and frog marched me out of the room and along the corridor to a door marked GENTS. I was pushed inside, one of them said that I had 3 minutes. Once I had gathered my wits I relieved myself in the urinal, I almost forgot where I was it was such a blessed relief.

I then washed my hands and face, as I was drying them the door burst open and one of the guys thrust a pair of trousers at me. They were identical to the ones I had on, indicating that I should put them on, he took my soiled pair and exited. There was an electric shaver and comb which I used to further tidy myself up. Feeling a bit refreshed I opened the door to leave. Again I was quickly cuffed and frog marched up and out of the building and straight into the back-seat of a revving car.

It was a dreary evening, with little light and a fine drizzle. We sped along until we were about a 100 yards from my home. The car stopped, they pulled me out of the car, produced a coat, which they helped me put on, they had an umbrella, which was erected and thrust into my right hand and an overnight bag that was thrust into my left. "Courtesy of Her Majesty's Government" said one of the four.

With that they quickly got back in their car and, without any more fuss, sped off. I just stood there, for what seemed like an age, not sure if it was safe to move, I think I was in a state of shock, everything felt unreal as if I was not really there, as if I was in a dream.

I came to my senses and slowly trudged up the street to my door, I was amazed to find my house keys in my newly acquired coat pocket, I let myself in, dropped my bag, hung up my wet coat and eased off my shoes. It was ten thirty in the evening, two days after being forcibly removed.

I have done exactly as requested, except to write this, which, in principle, contravenes the conditions set. I am back safe with my family, the garage has been stripped, by unseen hands, of most traces of my invention, as has my computer in the study. They left my Kindle, they must have thought it was nothing more than for reading e-books.

This should be my last act in this amazing saga. I am finding it difficult to get on with day to day life, constantly reliving my abduction, but worst of all desperate to rebuild the rig and try again. I dare not even buy magnets, never mind purchase steel or any of the other equipment I had. I feel numb, it is like I am grieving for a lost friend. So this is it, the story ends, my last diary entry.

The invention that never was, I suppose I will never know if it worked or not, probably not.

Oh well, life goes on. - Goodnight.

Day 200 – 17th December 2016

I am petrified, can hardly sleep, every knock at the door sends me into a panic.

I rarely go out.

Jane is very understanding but her patience with me is wearing thin. She really does not know why I am behaving this way, I'm sure she thinks it's an overreaction, after all we were only burgled.

When I am out I am always looking for someone following me.

I know I'm paranoid, but my abduction scared me shitless, I'm terrified it may happen again.

I have been to the doctor today for the first time in years, I had to, or my Jane would have dragged me there.

He has prescribed beta blockers, I hope they help.

Day 249 – 2nd February 2017

I'm almost under control, the support from Jane and Tom has been marvelous, I love them very much.

The beta blockers have worked, I am much calmer and as time goes on I have seen no evidence whatsoever of being watched.

I think less and less of my invention and have focused on other things.

Day 280 – 7th March 2017

I feel back to normal, very much involved with Tom and his sports, football and cricket, playing and supporting.

I volunteer with local charities.

Jane and I are enjoying a good social life too, pub, cinema, theatre that sort of thing.

Not had a beta blocker for nearly a month.

Day 368 - 3rd June 2017 - Six months and three days after my abduction

THE RIG IS BACK!!!!!!

IT REALLY IS HERE, IN THE GARAGE!!!!!

BUGGER ME!

LOST FOR WORDS

Barry C Cunningham

DIARY TWO - THE RETURN

Day 368 – 3rd June 2017

I'm so excited I'm beside myself, with a huge, boiling mass of emotions.

Can you believe it?

This morning, a bright sunny summer's day, I unlocked the side garage door to get the lawnmower, stepped briskly inside and "SMACK!" I walked straight into the rig, I think I might get a black eye, my head is pounding. I have a large red lump on my forehead, just above my right eye. It really hurts.

But it's back!

Just like on the day it disappeared, I went out and came back in, fully expecting its absence this time, but the lump on my head cemented the reality, it really is here.

How? Why?

Who brought it?

How did they get it back in?

Where has it been?

Oh, shit! How can I hide this from everyone, particularly those invisible, shady characters, who are supposedly watching my every move?

I stepped back inside and pulled the door shut.

After a lot of head scratching and walking to and fro in the garage, occasionally touching and stroking the rig, I convinced myself that those shadowy characters, who abducted me, somehow removed the rig six months ago and, having discovered that it didn't actually "do" anything, have put it back where they found it.

Why and how they did it mystifies me, but here it is, large as life, seeming to be as fully intact as the last time I saw it.

Having got a coffee, I sat in the garage, staring at the rig, absolutely convinced that if they did actually return it, then they have given me tacit approval to use it again.

ANTIGRAVITY DRIVE - THE DIARY OF AN INVENTION

How the Hell do I explain this to Jane and Tom?

I think I was sat there for over an hour, just staring and thinking when suddenly I noticed the exhaust tube in the window, yes, in the window.

The tube, seamlessly went right through the glass and a small portion of the frame. I could see the tube touching the glass surface and see it protruding out on the other side, it was as if the window had been made around the tube, but perfectly, seamlessly.

Amazing! Fascinating, how on Earth has that happened?

I was completely unable to think of an explanation, it's impossible.

I couldn't pull it out, I went outside to the short end protruding into the garden, picking up a long screwdriver on the way, I inserted the screwdriver into the pipe and, sure enough, the glass was there, on the inside of the tube, continuous, through the tube, as if it had materialised into the glass itself.

Materialised?

Materialised?

Bloody hell!

That would explain a lot. How it disappeared so "tidily" and now reappeared, bloody Hell, impossible, surely impossible? It didn't make sense, how could it? Things like that just do not happen.

I went back into the garage to begin examining the rig more closely.

First of all I unlocked the two sides with the generator and the tech box (the one with controllers and lap top). Immediately it struck me, the genny was still warm, the engine was still hot to the touch.

I looked in the fuel tank, it was empty. So the genny kept going until it ran out of fuel, it has only just, well recently, stopped. Amazing, can't get my head around this.

If that's the case and it could only run for about 24 hours on a full tank, it has literally just stopped, but more than six months have passed!

It didn't make sense at all, how could it make sense?

Lost in a reverie I suddenly snapped back to reality, I remembered the meticulous effort I had put into recording data and video.

I whipped the laptop open, and woke it up, it was still fully charged, having been plugged into the "on-board" electrics.

First of all I checked the data logger for pressure readings. It had ramped all the way to 204.377 tons, taking 16 hours 30 mins, to reach that value, held it there for a further 9 hours 15 mins then a dramatic drop off to 157.55 tons.

This was almost the current reading, it was still decreasing at a steady rate, the drop off started 2 hours 46 mins ago.

So, total time running, according to the readings, was 28 hours and 31 mins!

So it should be that amount of time after 10.30 am (the time I started the run) on the clock.

Oh my giddy aunt! It is, it is!

The time is 15.03 pm of the next day, on my little clock that I mounted inside the rig, the clock had not stopped, it was still running, 15.04 now.

It's impossible, this can't be happening.

I needed to look at the video feed, I selected the log from the camera with the clock and temperature gauge in view.

Nothing appeared to be happening at all, the temperature held steady at around 18 degrees, as far as I could see. The time was just progressing along as it should.

Speeding up the log really showed nothing untoward, the log ended at 15.01 the day after it began!

Something has to be wrong, it just cannot be like this.

I checked the date and time on the laptop, it was 15.27 01/12/2016, exactly 6 months and 3 days ago, except that it was now 10.30 in the morning.

I sat down heavily into my chair, stunned by the facts that had just presented themselves. I must have been sat there a full half hour with all sorts of thoughts and half-baked explanations whizzing round my head, when a thought suddenly occurred to me.

ANTIGRAVITY DRIVE - THE DIARY OF AN INVENTION

I jumped up and replayed the video log from the start at normal speed.

There.

I was right.

I had left the strip light on in the garage for the run, to illuminate the rig.

There it was, as I looked at the image and through the mesh on the opposite side of the rig there were some cans of paint and other odds and ends of stuff on the shelf in the garage, they didn't move, they were there all the time that I was viewing the log. That's the point, the amazing bloody point. I could see them, but the rig had not actually been there at that time!

My head is spinning, still hurting from the bang it received earlier and hurting more from all these revelations. I am totally and utterly dumbfounded.

Another thought suddenly hit me, if the rig had really been here all the time, invisible (mad, mad, mad) then those shady characters did not remove it or replace it.

That means they don't know it's here, that means if they find out, oh shit! I felt nauseous, panicky, frightened actually.

I needed to pull myself together, short of running away, the only alternative was to hide it, disguise it somehow.

Day 368 – 3rd June 2017 - 14.05 pm

After a snatched lunch I decided to examine all three video logs to see if there was anything else I should have noticed.

I put all three on screen at once and played them at 16 times normal speed. Nothing looked out of the ordinary, except I could now see that it really was the garage in the background on all three!

With all three running side by side, during the time when peak pressure had been achieved, I noticed in the feed from camera 3 that it was darker, in more shadow somehow from the strip lights, and that there was a pulsing, flickering effect that wasn't that obvious on the other two feeds, but looking closer I could see the same flicker on all three.

At first I thought it must be a faulty strip light, but then realised it was flickering because of the 16 times speed. I slowed it down, the pulse was still there, but obviously, not as quick. I realised it was a very regular pulse.

On a hunch, I slowed the playback to quarter speed and immediately noticed the flicker or pulse was not an "on-off " type of pulse but one where there was a gradual change from light to dark and dark to light. With a sudden shock I realised that what I was observing might be day/night transitions.

Dawn and dusk. Incredible!

So I calculated how many days it had been missing and with the hours that appeared to have passed in the rig it should give a pulse rate of approx. 20/hr. That's one full pulse every 3 minutes or so when the video runs at normal speed.

Playing back at the beginning it was more like 2 minutes, but as the playback progressed it changed so that when I checked the end of the "missing period" it was nearer 4 minutes, obvious really, the pulse changed with lengthening daylight hours.

That confirmed it for me, the pulse must be day night transitions and unless I bother to calculate more accurately, it seems to correspond to the number of days it was missing.

Thinking through the facts: - apparent disappearance, apparent materialisation (6 months and 3 days later), the exhaust in the window, the apparent passage of time in the rig, correlating pulse to day/night transitions, empty fuel tank, pressure profiles, oh and I forgot to mention, a 2.5 degree temperature drop that happened immediately it reached peak pressure and continued to drop steadily until it's materialisation down to a 3.1 degree drop.

I can only reach the conclusion that when peak pressure was achieved, time passed differently for the rig. In fact there was a period of about 9 hours when there was a light pulse, so 9 hours with time passing differently, but this 9 hours appears as 6 months and 3 days to me outside the rig. When you think about it, it's obvious, you can't see it because as soon as it reached peak pressure, we zoomed off in a torrent of passing time, and left it behind, so it was always there but it was only there in our past. That seems ridiculous but it's the only way I can express it.

No, it can't be, but, that would explain the window and exhaust pipe. The window was open when it disappeared and shut when it came back. This explanation seems to defy any physics that I knew and must be full of all sorts of assumptions and paradoxes. The truth is, it seems to fit the facts as far as I can see them. I cannot deny its disappearance as, equally, I cannot deny its return. I really do not understand at all why it comes back to the 'real' time, can't figure it out, it's beyond my understanding, come to think of it, it all is!

The next revelation hit me in the face liked being slapped with a wet fish, I had done it, made an antigravity drive (or something), on my first bloody attempt.

Well maybe it's not as I thought it might be but it's definitely bloody amazing, not sure how useful it is and I don't even know if it became weightless or anything during its disappearance.

I cried out with sheer joy, wooo-hooooo!

The euphoria didn't last long, I still had this issue of the shady characters and my threatened disappearance if they found this.

Shit, shit, shit what am I to do?

Day 368 – 3rd June 2017 - 16.00 pm

It occurred to me that the only way to prove this was to repeat it, not the whole build, just the disappearance. I also need to do it now.

This time I will only allow it to run for a small amount of time at peak pressure. How long is the right amount?

If it ran 9 hours equivalent to about six months then based on previous calculations a day in normal time is somewhere between 2 and 4 minutes rig time, so 3 minutes or 180 seconds = 1 day (approx), meaning that 1.8 seconds is about a quarter of an hour.

It means that to test this I need it to turn off almost immediately it reaches peak pressure, just so that I can observe the effect without waiting too long for it to return. I also do not intend such a slow ramp up to peak pressure, I am going to risk a gradient taking only 10 minutes! The other reason I am doing this, it also occurred to me, is that it might be the best way to hide it!

Filled up with petrol, start genny, bugger, it will not start, come on!

I twiddled with the genny but no joy, then I felt like a prat when I remembered I have a blocked exhaust (Window glass in the pipe).

I cut the plastic tube at the window, opened it and popped the end out.

Have to remove that window and board it up, can't leave a pipe in it like that. It's actually the whole window opening that needs removing.

I took the window off its hinges and hid it behind a stack of wood.

Anyway back to the genny, after a cough and splutter it started.

I locked that side panel, checked the new settings on the control unit and locked that panel too. I stood back, with my phone taking video, and waited 9 minutes.

Nothing.

Then at exactly 10 minutes the whole rig, including exhaust tube again, just disappeared, there was no sound, no pop, bang or rush of air, nothing, it just was there one instant and gone the next.

No dramatics, nothing. Amazing or what?

I am truly astounded that it did it again. How did I get it so right? (I am so glad I made that back-up cube when I was in the construction phase and hid it in my sock drawer, I am going to test that tomorrow too).

Here it is, back again, bloody amazing, exactly 12 minutes absence. Once again there were no dramatics it was just there.

I can hardly believe it. It's so surreal. It's just doing it like it's sort of "normal". It is definitely not normal.

It's amazing, astounding and unique.

Researchers and professors should be informed about this. I could win a Nobel Prize. I could make a fortune.

Trouble is I'm shit scared of those crazy, shady buggers, I have no idea how I could capitalise on it without putting myself in danger (understatement!!!).

Jane and Tom will be home from their shopping trip soon, so no time for any more messing about. I need it to be gone for 14 hours, so I reset the hold time for 1 minute 50 secs. That will be near enough.

Lock up and wait 10 mins.

Gone! Wow, this is bloody marvelous.

But I need to box clever if I'm going to keep this secret. I boarded up the missing window. I will tell them I broke it, when I was cutting the grass.

Oh Bollocks! I haven't cut the grass yet!

Day 369 – 4th June 2017

As soon as Jane took Tom off to his Sunday League football, I popped out to the garage.

I'd had a thought in the evening as to how unbelievably lucky I had been. I had been thinking about the window and how it materialised "in it" and realised how incredibly fortunate it was that nothing was in the space that the rig materialised in.

What if the car was there, or lawnmower or even a person, would it just "merge" like it did with the window. It was a shocking thought, not knowing it was coming it could have been Tom, Jane or anyone, or anything.

A very sobering thought. What should I do to prevent it happening? No one else knows it's hidden. Nothing can be in that space when it returns!

I quickly removed the boards from the window, at least that will not happen again.

About another hour to wait, not sure exactly when, I'm still being fairly approximate with RVR (rig vs real) time. I'm going to start measuring this accurately each time the rig is HRT (Held in Rig Time). I am curious to know if it is constant or not.

I needed to be here, for safety reasons, making sure the M space (Materialisation space) is clear.

I know all these abbreviations are a bit twee but it helps me with typing and I can be consistent with naming things, I don't think I have been up to now.

Another thing that is grabbing my curiosity is how does it decide what is HRT, I mean why only the rig, why not the garage, or maybe at least the garage floor.

The more I think about it, the more questions pop up, not just physics type of questions, but, sort of, obvious ones like that one. I have to get all scientific and design some simple experiments to investigate the obvious things, they might even help with how I understand and control the rig.

Another thing is really bugging me. What happens to the exhaust fumes? If it is not here, in real time, would the fumes fill the garage in the first few days after it is HRT, if I didn't put the exhaust tube out the window? What I mean is, do they materialise on their own straight after emission?

I think this is important because of the question of what is included when it stays behind in time and how does it define the boundary and how can anything pass through that boundary (exhaust fumes!!!) And if it does pass through what happens to it, does it materialise in real time or stay outside the rig in rig time, or something else entirely?

These questions are giving me cold chills they seem to immediately make my head hurt as there is no obvious answer, how can there be? I think I'm involved with something here where that sort of question has never ever being asked before.

Bloody hell, I just realised I'm a Pioneer!

A shit scared Pioneer, one really spooked Pioneer in fact a Paranoid Pioneer, PP for short. (Hah! Made myself chuckle there, Hah!)

I dare not step in the M space or, in fact, leave anything there either. I think I am right to be cautious, but I will need to check. That will be one of the simpler experiments that I am going to plan.

It's back, 14 hours and 12 minutes, my estimation was not far out.

One of my first experiments will be determine at exactly what pressure the rig departs into HRT. This is because I believe the peak pressure is the maximum my little rams can do, not the actual trigger point for HRT.

I am paranoid about being found with the rig in the workshop, I don't even want to think about the consequences of being discovered by the shady characters that abducted me. I've never seen them since they left me out in the rain that night. All the things they gave me, I took to a charity shop, just in case they were bugged. It used to give me some comfort thinking how confused they might have been, but I suppose they foresaw that I would do that and found other ways to observe and monitor me without my awareness.

Anyway, I think the best way to avoid detection is to keep the rig hidden in HRT, in a controlled way, so that I know when it will materialise and can conduct experiments in the process.

ANTIGRAVITY DRIVE - THE DIARY OF AN INVENTION

I have so many things I want to do, it would make quite a long list. I am keeping all things like that and this diary on the rig laptop so that when it's in HRT all the evidence will be with it, hidden in time.

Wow, what a good title for a book that would be. 'Hidden in Time' , very catchy. I think if ever I get the chance to publish something about this, that's what I might call it.

With the rig in the workshop, I am really at risk. Consequently, all experiments that I plan have to be ready to roll as soon as the rig is available. I discretely made a chalk mark on the garage floor at each corner of the rig. When it is next HRT I am going to replace the chalk with a tiny blob of paint. A different colour for each corner. I have carefully placed a clock, with date and time, on one of the shelves behind the rig, so that it can be observed in the same CCTV log as the onboard clock. I have reset the onboard clock to current date and time and synchronized them both with the laptop.

The rig is now in HRT, for a planned 20 minutes. I have placed an object on each of the four corner blobs of paint, I could have selected any number of things for this experiment but want to observe which materials merge, how they merge, do they become permanently part of the rig if they merge and are there any obvious effects on the object once merged.

The objects are as follows:

- 4 cm piece of 25 mm square cross section of wood .
- 10 cm piece of the angle steel used in the rig construction.
- A small sirloin steak. (Simulating a person, well almost)
- A geranium, flowering, in a pot. (Something living)

Doing experiments like these has really gripped my imagination and curiosity, it is quite difficult to stop thinking about all the possible outcomes, and what each might infer, I need to stay focused and just wait, observe and think about the actual outcome and conclusions that can be made. Maybe that's the difference between a scientist and a dreamer.

It's back, I don't have long to observe and measure, I want it back in HRT as soon as I can with the next experiment onboard.

All four objects are completely merged with the rig on their respective corners, it is really quite creepy to see, although I cannot be certain that the steak is not just crushed, as it appears to be just around the outside edge. I think I could have probably positioned that better. The wood looks much the same it appears to protrude from the metal, but looking just inside the frame I can see some wood inside the angles of the steel, as with the exhaust tube I am unable to pull the wood away from the rig.

It just occurred to me that I could use a scalpel and cut the wood (or steak) at the interface with the rig, I am really curious as to what I might see.

The piece of angle steel appears as if it is part of the rig, a seamless joint, oddly it's quite difficult to look at as the interface forms a perfect 90 degree right angle.

The flowering geranium is the oddest thing to look at, perfectly merged, with all the bits of the pot, compost and plant that are not within the rig steel, sticking out at all sorts of angles, the plant looks perfectly healthy and no obvious signs of drooping. If it stays healthy does that mean all the little tubes in the plant that carry sap are still functioning? Now that would be weird!

I don't have a scalpel to hand, so I put that off until the next reappearance.

The next experiment is one that will lead up to determining if a living creature can survive the experience. I balanced a small glass aquarium, with a mesh lid, on the interior structure. I powered up and locked the rig doors, stood back with my mobile in video mode and waited for the disappearance.

Gone, "SMASH", the aquarium was still here, it fell to the garage floor and smashed! I was really taken aback, but had the presence of mind to hold the phone still and only stop recording once it was over.

Straight afterwards I had a second and more profound shock, all four objects I had placed on the corners where also sat there on the concrete floor, seemingly fully intact, with no apparent damage. But they had been merged, seemingly integral with the steel!

I was at a loss, both of these events were completely unexpected and rendered me paralyzed, not even breathing, for a number of seconds. I looked at the steak first, not a blemish, nothing, the same with the plant and piece of wood. The piece of angle steel, that was so perfectly merged, was also laid on the concrete just as I had placed it. I have to really get my head around this, I don't know where to begin.

ANTIGRAVITY DRIVE - THE DIARY OF AN INVENTION

How on Earth does it do that?

At that moment I had a little epiphany, I jumped up and retrieved the window from behind my stack of wood, the piece of exhaust I had earlier seen merged, was gone! The window was not broken, no marks, nothing.

Now I'm really freaked out. Can't get my head around this at all, no way can this happen.

I had become distracted and lost all track of time. With a sudden and complete lack of anything at all, the rig was back, but right in front of my face, I tried to jump back out of the way and immediately fell backwards, my left foot was merged a third of the way along the generator edge! My whole foot and shoe appeared to be inside the rig.

I cried out in shock and what I thought was pain but in actual fact, I quickly realised, the pain was because my foot was held rigidly and I was on my backside, knee elevated, but my leg was still at a funny angle, I shuffled forward and the pain eased then disappeared altogether. I tried to wiggle my toes with no result, I did not try and pull as I knew that would be futile. There was no pain, no odd sensation, it felt perfectly OK, except that it wasn't, it was merged.

This had been my biggest fear since its return. How? How? How? I can't believe I've been so stupid. I was the one merged. Bollocks! I sat there, numbed, for at least five minutes, I had a tiny crumb of comfort in the fact that the steak and plant appeared to be completely unaffected by the same experience. Fingers crossed it's the same for me.

All I needed to do was send the rig into HRT and everything would be fine. I had no idea why it should be fine but it was almost my only hope. I reached around to the other face, with the control unit inside, and undid the bolt nearest to me, it was a large butterfly nut, so was quite easy to remove.

I tried to reach across to the other butterfly nut, 2 metres away from the one I had undone, I couldn't reach! No matter how hard I tried to reach, stretching with every ounce of energy I had, I was within 10 cm of it, it just felt as if a bit more effort would do it, I was severely restricted by my foot being held rigid, I couldn't bend or twist my left leg. It was impossible, I gave up and sat down.

I had an instant feeling of panic, what the Hell was I to do? The nuts are only finger tight, not difficult, if only I could reach. I looked around the garage to see if there were any tools or objects within reach, nothing.

Nothing of any use anyway.

My toolbox lay half open on the floor, at the other end of the garage, with a pair of pliers laying at an enticingly jaunty angle right on top, taunting me. "Nah, nah, you can't reach me, ha, ha" they said. Well they didn't actually say it, it was me speaking on their behalf, they might as well have said it though. Fuck, bugger, shit, Bollocks! There was nothing within reach that I could use.

I decided to make a mental inventory of what I actually had with me; keys on a keyring, small Swiss army knife(with little blades, scissors, toothpick and a small pair of tweezers), my mobile phone, a handkerchief and the clothes I was wearing. Namely, a fleece jacket, shirt, trousers (with the bottom of the left leg merged), underpants, a sock and a shoe, my other sock and shoe were also merged.

I also had the window I had retrieved just before this happened, well I ought to have, I was holding it when the rig reappeared, I looked around expecting to see it on the floor, nowhere to be seen. I grabbed hold of the protrusion on the rig to pull myself up. Protrusion! There is no protrusion, there it is, one corner of the offending article, the window, I must have been holding one corner when the rig materialised, it was there, merged in the rig, just like my foot. I could also just make out inside the rig, the bit of exhaust was back too, merged in the window, spooky!

I couldn't see that the items in my inventory were any use at all. The most obvious thing to do was call someone on my mobile, but who, who could I trust, what if it was being monitored.

Shit, shit I suddenly felt panicky, a huge knot of fear in my stomach. As a last resort I could ring Jane, I'm sure she would be OK, eventually!! But, I'm certain ringing Jane would alert those shadowy characters, I was so vulnerable, they would probably just cut my foot off and take the rig.

Now I really am shitting myself, well not literally, just bloody scared, really scared. My heart was pounding, I broke out in a sweat, I felt useless and very vulnerable. What the Hell can I do? Well as sure as night follows day, if I sit here long enough, Jane or Tom will find me. So, if I do nothing I will be discovered, if I use my mobile, I will be discovered.

What on Earth can I do?

I was wracking my brain, trying to a force a solution out onto the open, but to no affect. Then it came to me, I have to make use of the things I have and use them to get the pliers.

ANTIGRAVITY DRIVE - THE DIARY OF AN INVENTION

But how? I could see a loose bundle of bamboo canes, used to support pot plants, each cane was a strip of bamboo about 50 cm long, but they were way beyond reach. If I could get them and somehow lash a few together I could make a sort of fishing rod.

I looked around for more inspiration. Nearby was the shelf with small, half used, pots of paint. If I could throw them at the canes they might scatter, allowing me to grab one or two.

I managed to get four of the small paint pots, the first carefully aimed throw missed by miles, the second much closer, the third was a direct hit, scattering the canes in every direction over the garage floor. I stretched and scrabbled and managed to get three of them. I felt elated, just as if I had won a small victory.

Now I got to business, I stripped off my fleece and shirt and used the scissors on my little pen-knife to initiate a tear, I ripped the back of my shirt into strips. I had ten strips. I proceeded to lash the canes together to make a longer 'rod' and with the three together I had a rod just over a metre long. I used this to retrieve more canes and proceeded to extend my first rod. When I had finished I had a rod over two metres long, a bit flimsy, but at least it nearly reached the pliers.

I was just beginning to cut and tear more strips, when it came to me, bloody idiot, fancy thinking of the most convoluted and difficult solution, I put the shirt and bamboos down and picked up the remaining can of paint, I leaned and stretched around the rig and used the paint pot to tap the wing nut around and around, unscrewing it off the bolt, it clinked to the floor. "Bloody Plonker" I said to myself.

The rig is in HRT, the garage is a mess and I have a ripped up shirt. I held on to the window, to prevent it falling, it had now had a complete absence of a bit of exhaust tube!! I had sent the rig into HRT for another 18 hours, got to clean up and gather my thoughts, I need to be more in control from now on.

My foot feels completely unaffected, there was no sensation, apart from being trapped, when it was merged, I felt nothing as I was released and it feels absolutely normal now.

Bloody annoying, but what a relief!

Day 370 – 5th June 2017

I'm sat in the garage waiting for the rig to appear in M Space, the space is absolutely clear, apart from the paint spots, I needed it back no fuss, nice and clean. I've been thinking, reevaluating, trying to get my head around everything.

I didn't realise it that much yesterday, but, I was so very close to total disaster through my lack of concentration and attention to detail. I either need to get very serious about this or give up completely.

I took stock of what has happened since that first dream, it is absolutely bloody astounding, how on Earth has this happened? From one little dream all the way to a total paradox! I do not want to give up, I want to tell the World, but can't, so, no more risks and carelessness, plus I am keeping a real-time log from now on using my Kindle Fire.

Every time I design or actually do stuff I'm going to get it into this diary. This is too bloody important now. I also have the dilemma of spending time on this and not daily chores and stuff. I also do not want to change the things we do as a family, since my abduction, in any case, if I did, might that not draw attention to myself?

So how do I explain this to Jane, should I tell her, or find another decoy story.

I have decided to say I am writing a book and will treat it like almost a full-time job (if she agrees), I will make a little office in the garage, desk and everything, as it gives me inspiration. In actual fact it's the truth, I am, after all, writing this diary.

Another major dilemma is the fact that the more I get back into this, the more I run the risk of being found out by those who abducted me, I know I signed a document that made it easy for them to arrest me, but I signed under duress, any court would agree that, but how would I prove it?

Would they even take any notice of what I think anyway?

Every time I do anything at all with rig I have these nagging paranoid fears tickling the back of my mind and giving me a tiny knot in the pit of my stomach, but the pull of the unknown, the excitement linked to this 'invention' is just too much to miss.

The rig is back.

ANTIGRAVITY DRIVE - THE DIARY OF AN INVENTION

Regardless of anything else I have to try and gain some understanding of merging and what is and what is not included in the rig and how it is included or what makes it included.

I have prepared the piece of steel I used last time by drilling a hole in it to take a nut and bolt. Now the rig is here, I have drilled a similar hole in one of the two rarely used hinged doors and bolted them together. It is now integral to the rig. It is positioned, horizontally, in a way that makes it like a very small shelf. I balanced another small piece of angle steel on the shelf I had just made. I have set the rig to go into HRT and return almost immediately, so it will be away for about 10 minutes.

My mobile is as near to the rig as practicable recording a video of the shelf as the rig goes into HRT.

The rig disappears as usual, but the piece of steel balanced on the little shelf does not, it remains behind and clatters to the floor, the new little shelf has gone with the rig. This is just as I thought, if it is integral to the rig, i.e. fastened/connected, then as part of the rig it goes into HRT, if it is not connected, it remains behind.

It's back with its newly acquired shelf intact. I removed the nut and bolt and placed all three pieces (nut, bolt and shelf) on the floor next to the rig. Again, I set the rig for immediate return. With my mobile's camera focused on the three parts, the rig went into HRT. As I expected, all three, now not connected, disappeared too, just like the small piece of exhaust pipe that is seemingly merged with the window!

This is a phenomenon I can describe but cannot explain, it must be some sort of quantum physics effect, in that if integral to the rig it is part of the rig and is from that point onwards always part of the rig, whether it is then connected or not. This is truly amazing but immediately throws up all sorts of questions in my mind, the most obvious to me is that if I conduct experiments by attaching devices to travel with the rig they will, from then on, always travel with the rig.

This gives me at least two more issues; firstly, I will have to be careful how and where I attach things, particularly if I remove them (They may travel with the rig, always occupying their original position. I can test this by having one of the onboard cameras record something attached and then again detached, just like the shelf), secondly, how could a device like this rig carry a passenger?

If the only way to travel with the rig into HRT is to be integral with the rig, it makes it very awkward for a passenger, particularly in the fact that once a passenger always a passenger once you have been integral with the rig, maybe you could be miles away and every time it popped into HRT, you would too. I think I might have to test that, by placing the shelf components at different locations, various distances from the rig.

Day 370 – 5th June 2017 – 16.00 pm

I was right, separation and distance did not affect the components of the shelf going into HRT. I was too curious about this particular phenomenon, to do other experiments before I knew the answer about separation and distance.

I attached an old car wing mirror, externally, to the same frame door as the shelf and positioned it and an internal CCTV camera, to record what happened to the space where the shelf was previously attached. I took the components on a journey and secreted each one away from public view.

The screw was one mile away, the nut, ten miles away and the angle steel fifty miles away. I came back, sent the rig into HRT, the on-board camera recorded the event (I was tempted to set up remote recording at each location, but decided against it. I might draw attention by being more visibly active and in any case if it is observed on the rig they must have disappeared from their new location).

On the rigs' return I viewed the video log and as I predicted the fully intact shelf was in its original position on the rig the instant it materialised. The shelf and its other components had disappeared.

I retrieved the components from their distant locations and reattached them to the rig, that little shelf might become more useful in future experiments.

I am relieved to know these few but very strange facts about the rig. The fact that it has to be physically attached to travel with the rig and that once it is, or has been, part of the rig it stays part of the rig, probably forever.

The other fact, that it merges with anything in M space, but seemingly in a way that has no effect on the object it merges with (in the short term at least, I have not had prolonged merges, as I keep the rig mostly hidden in time), except that they are held fast and even more curiously continue to function almost normally whilst merged.

Thinking about these facts makes me relieved that I did not secure the rig

ANTIGRAVITY DRIVE - THE DIARY OF AN INVENTION

to the garage floor, can you imagine, the garage would have been in HRT with me included, that means I would have thought nothing happened, oh hang on I went to bed before it went, so the garage would have been gone 6 months.

That would have caused a lot more issues!

But, just a minute, what if I had stayed in the garage and was engrossed with observing the rig I would have thought nothing was happening, it would just be there. No, no it wouldn't I would have immediately noticed the day/night transitions and if I looked out of the window I would see the observable world speeded up, what would have happened if I had opened the door and tried to leave?

The exhaust fumes were leaving, the petrol in the tank was being consumed, that petrol never comes back when in HRT, I keep filling the tank. There is no evidence of too much petrol, like overflows or anything, but it travels into HRT, it's not 'attached' and it gets used up. It's not attached, but, it's contained in something that is attached. But hang on again, if me and the contents of the garage were not attached, would we have been left behind in a heap, or carried off like the petrol?

What a revelation! I rummaged around the garage and found an old tobacco tin with a hinged lid, my father used to roll his own and subsequently keep nails and stuff in them, I have continued to use them myself, they must be sixty years old, anyway it's drilled and attached to the rig near to the little shelf.

I looked around for something to place in the box, something that might provide other answers too. I found a large spider hidden away behind some junk on a shelf, having captured it, it's now imprisoned in the attached tin with the lid firmly closed.

The rig popped off into HRT, no spider was left behind.

The rig is back.

I carefully opened the lid, the spider shot out so quick it almost made me jump, I let it escape, it had answered my question, hang on no it hadn't, I need to know if it suffers the same effect as the shelf components, I watched the spider whizz across the floor and up the garage wall to take refuge under the windowsill. I quickly caught it again and popped it into a jam jar that I had rapidly emptied of its collection of washers all over the bench.

The rig is in HRT, the spider is still here. So it is possible to travel with the rig without being attached and without being forever part of the rig, but whatever travels must be contained fully within something that is attached.

It also appears that a living thing is unharmed by the experience. I let the spider go, it had contributed a huge amount to my understanding and deserved its freedom.

Another thought had aroused my curiosity, it's linked to the petrol being consumed and emitted as it's component molecules, drastically changed but still component. I know the petrol was a sort of 'passenger' now, but what if something like that was attached and then subsequently destroyed?

I found my piece of wood that I had used in the merging experiment, drilled it and attached it to the rig, again near the little shelf. I sent it into HRT with the rig. It's back, I have retrieved it and have completely burned it to destruction on the gas barbecue.

The rig has again been and come back from HRT.

The video log from the camera trained on the wing mirror, shows the piece of wood attached to the rig. It appears fully intact and looks to me completely unharmed. Now that is bloody astounding! That means every molecule, or even every atom, was retrieved from its new location in the barbecue and the atmosphere, reconstituted and put back on the rig in HRT! Even more strange is that when back from HRT, the molecules go back to their incomprehensibly disparate positions in the Universe.

Well, that experiment really is spooky, I am lost for words, I sort of expected it to happen but somehow thought that would prove the theory wrong.

The ramifications from this must be huge, but as yet I am completely unable to grasp what they are. I am, also, still not really sure what happens to the exhaust fumes, what 'time' do they exist in, it seems like it ought to be an obvious answer, however, nothing has been that obvious so far.

It's very late, I must get some sleep.

Day 371 – 6th June 2017

I have decided to send the rig into HRT for 2 weeks, this will give me time to get my head around a few things, clean up the garage, set up my office (Jane has agreed to me writing a book, but she says it had better be good!) and think long and hard about what experiments to do and why do them. It will allow me time to gather a few things together and really do this as properly as I am able.

I started by giving the garage a thorough clean and a good throwing out session, getting rid of stuff I kept just in case one day I might need it. I then placed tool boxes and other useful equipment within easy reach of the paint spots (M Space).

I tried really hard to make it look just like any tidy, organised garage/workshop should look. At the end of the garage, with most natural daylight, I erected a flat-pack desk and brought one of my office chairs down from our family study/computer room. I filled the drawers and surface of the desk with useful items of stationery and installed a computer and printer, also appropriated from the study.

I stood back and surveyed my handiwork, there appeared to be something missing. Lighting, that's what is needed, I needed a good table lamp and some directional spots in the roof structure. A trip to the local DIY depot this afternoon then.

Day 372 – 7th June 2017

The garage rearrangement is complete, all lighting installed and working, computer up and running, I'm sat at my desk twiddling with pencil and paper, trying to get my head around how I should plan my approach and suite of experiments for when the rig returns in 12 days.

I was sat quietly, thinking and doodling for at least an hour, when the door slowly opened and in strolled the man in the pin-striped, business suit, still sporting a red bow-tie. "Good morning, being busy are we?" I jumped out of my skin and leapt to my feet sending my chair scuttling backwards and crashing into the up-and-over door.

"Get a grip Mr. Charles, no need to be like that, just here for a chat." He had that easy, quintessentially English accent, authoritative and very distinct. He strolled over, arm extended in a hand shake gesture, I reciprocated, shakily and with trepidation, his hand-shake was firm and solid, he held my grasp just a little too long.

He said "Don't be nervous Mr. Charles, I only need a little chat." I couldn't help thinking it was more than a little chat he needed. He retrieved my chair and placed it near my desk, indicating that I should sit.

I sat.

I have tried to set down the event and the conversation as it happened as follows;

"So, Mr. Charles, you've been busy I see?" He began, his eyes casting around the garage, "My associates tell me you are very active, almost secretive, difficult to know what you are up to, except that you spend an inordinate amount of time in your garage, very tidy."

He left a long silence, seeming to wait for a response, I held out, didn't speak. "Did you think we had gone away, Mr. Charles?

Well we have not, we are still here, watching your every move, we have unfinished business, Mr. Charles."

He leaned forward placing both palms on my desk, until his face was level with mine. "Where is your device Mr. Charles? It was not stolen, was it Mr. Charles?"

I nodded, "it was" I squeaked.

The way he kept repeating my name was unsettling, belittling and very threatening. I got more and more shaky as time went on, I couldn't believe how fortunate it was that the rig was in HRT for a prolonged period.

He turned and walked towards the door, suddenly he stopped and looked at the concrete floor, he carefully stepped on the little blob of red paint and twisted his foot from side to side, as if he was trying to rub it out. After inspecting the sole of his Saville Row shoe, he looked at the other three, differently coloured, dots, "Hmm" Was all he said, as he continued towards the door. Without looking back, he said "We are watching you Mr. Charles, never forget, we are watching you." He left, closing the door quietly behind him.

It all seemed to be over in a flash, had I had one of my stupid dreams that seem to land me in all sorts of trouble? I don't think so, that was real, very real. I had palpitations, I was sweating and shaking ever so slightly, what was I to do?

I had got complacent about being watched, I suppose I did think they had gone away. The first thing I am going to do is put blinds on all the windows and install a ventilation unit in the wall for exhaust fumes, instead of the open window, which is now repaired.

I know I'm paranoid, but, I checked all around the desk and garage, just in case 'Mr. Pinstripe' had left bugs.

I've found something, right at the top of the back of my chair, embedded in the fabric, it was barely noticeable, I only found it because of how I gripped the top of the chair to move it, I could feel a little bump under my thumb. It is tiny and looks to me like a miniature camera and microphone. What shall I do, they will know I found it if they are watching the live stream. Hah! Covered it with a coat and I will get a radio to have on loud when I'm occupying the garage. Just thought of a better solution, I've swapped it for a different chair from the upstairs study. They can listen to Tom gaming and chatting to his friends on his headset, until they get fed up, I know I would. So off to get blinds and a wall fitted extractor fan, will fit all this afternoon.

Day 373 – 8th June 2017

Well that's that, blinds and fan fitted, hope it appears that it's all part of my setting up a new study in the garage.

I have had a stroll around the area and even, discretely, looked through my binoculars at all nearby houses, I can see no sign whatsoever of anyone watching me, or following me. They must be bloody good at it, because, they are obviously doing it somehow!

I am really worried about being caught now, writing this would even contravene their rules. I just don't know why they are obsessed with what I did, building the rig and everything, you would think anyone would be at least as excited as I am. Why would they want me to stop, why would they suppress it, are they really on our side? British, I mean, Police or one of our secret services.

Do they already know about, antigravity or this other phenomenon, whatever it is, that I am playing around with?

Are they scared more people would find out? I'd not really thought about it that much before, but, why? Why do they not want me to rebuild?

After all, as far as I know, they do not know that the rig came back or all the things that I have discovered since it did reappear.

Or do they?

My diary contained a detailed description of how to build the rig, surely if they are that bothered they would have built one.

Oh my goodness! That's it, they must have built one. Not after reading my diary but, before I did! They must know what had happened to the rig when they 'arrested' me. Is it that they think somehow I'm copying them? No, no it can't be that, my diary is too explicit, too honest, it's obvious I've discovered this by accident.

But, why remove all traces of what I did if they do not know the significance of my little project? I just can't seem to put my finger on it. Why had I not thought about this before? Why had I not realised that they must already know about this area of research, why else would they be so 'sensitive' about it, if they did not already know something? But why let me go? None of it made sense, it seems it ought to be obvious, but then again not. Maybe, they want me to rebuild? Maybe they are waiting for it to come back! Waiting for me to make these discoveries so that they can just walk in and take it all.

No, that's just too ridiculous.

Day 374 – 9th June 2017

Again I'm sat at my new desk, thinking, doodling, it's Saturday morning, a beautiful, sunny summer's day. The garage door is propped open, letting the fresh air in, and some of the heat out.

I'm mulling over my thoughts of yesterday. Suddenly, I heard running footsteps coming towards the garage, the knot in my stomach tightened, someone ran in and slammed the door shut.

To my, short lived, relief, it was Tom, he rushed up to my desk and threw something onto it in a flurry of anger, something small, with a little piece of trailing wire.

It's the bug from the chair.

He appeared to be consumed with rage and demanded to know what I was up to, shouting at me, ranting about invasion of privacy, do I think he is looking at pornography or something, don't I trust him, he demanded to know where my receiver is and what I'd recorded.

I just sat there, in shock, in disbelief, I was at a loss, I didn't know what to do. I stood up and shouted STOP! I retrieved the bug, walked over to my toolbox, took out a hammer and smashed the bug to pieces on the garage floor. I just said sorry you had to find that, it's not me, but I know who did it. In a complete moment of madness, I pushed my tablet computer towards him with my complete diary open. I said read this, it will explain everything.

I felt as if a huge weight was lifted from my shoulders, to share this with a 17 year old was either very brave or incredibly stupid. Surprisingly, he stopped ranting and began to read.

Every now and then, he gasped, and looked at me, then continued reading. When he'd finished, he just smiled and said, so this is your book, it's not bad, gripping but ridiculous, unless you like sci-fi, then maybe it's not so ridiculous.

How does this fantasy explain anything? I protested, saying all of it is true, every word. The rig is held in the past hidden for another eleven days. It's giving me time to get organised. There was something else I could show him, the video clips on my phone, he viewed them all, silently. He stood quietly for a few seconds and the just asked, how on Earth did you get that good at photo-manipulation?

There was nothing else for it, he will not be convinced until it has returned. All I asked of him is that he keeps it to himself, tell no one, not even his mum. Amazingly he agreed.

I asked if he would like to be here when it returns, it will be school holidays, so he will be here. Eleven days' time, approximately 10.30 am.

Day 377 – 12th June 2017

Tom and I have been talking this through for a couple of days, he has asked hundreds of questions and has admitted he is still very skeptical and only if the rig reappears will he really believe the story in the diary.

I have asked him if he would like to help, it would be a great relief if he would agree. He remains noncommittal, until he has hard evidence.

Meanwhile, we both get our thinking caps on and produce quite a lengthy list of experiments that should be carried out. (If it turns out to be true!)

Day 384 – 19th June 2017

Tom and I have been working hard, but discretely, preparing materials and experiments for when the rig returns tomorrow morning.

It's been marvellous, having his help and support, it is a real joy to be working together.

I have taken great care to explain how serious and even dangerous working on this project can be, not only from the dangers with the rig itself but from those shady creeps that are a threat to our continued freedom! I'm particularly anxious since I smashed that bug, surely they know I did it.

Day 385 – 20th June 2017

At last, the day is here when the rig should return. Tom and I have made sure nothing is in M Space, and the window is open.

10.30 arrives, nothing. I can see Tom looking at his watch and looking somewhat disappointedly at me. I just shrugged.

10.33 it's back, as usual no fuss, no dramatics, it's just there.

It is amazing, there are no gradual transitions, no warnings, it just there in an instant, absolutely amazing.

Tom is inanimate, standing, open mouthed, in a state of shock. I think he believed that it wouldn't happen, he must have only been humouring me for the previous eleven days, not really convinced that anything in the diary was really true. Well he has to believe it now, it materialised right before his eyes. Tom reached out and tapped the steel cage with the knuckles of his right fist, "Holy Shit", was all he could say over and over again. "So it was all true", was the first thing he said once he had regained some of his composure, "they really did arrest you and stuff?"

All I said was that everything he read was true and now we need to try and understand what is happening when the rig is in HRT and how it can be utilised safely.

We also need to figure out how we tell the world about this without putting ourselves in danger.

Now the rig is back I showed Tom some of the stored data and video logs. This absolutely convinced him that the rig and its 'time travelling' was real, but also got him so confused that he was scared. Scared, because it was entirely beyond his understanding and it seemed to defy logic and much of the physics that he knew from school. He was also scared because this definitely meant that those shady characters were very real too. He turned to me and said "But, Dad, there must be a reason they are obsessed with this, with you, with antigravity and its potential, it must scare them too"

Out of the mouths of babes and sucklings!

I've been too obsessed with being the victim to notice. That's it, it's antigravity they are interested in, not the effect that is absorbing my interest. It has to be, because that is what I was trying to invent in the first place.

The ramifications of a real, working antigravity drive, are huge and massively important to any government of a country, probably in an enormous variety of ways. When I think about it, I never really knew (and still don't really know) whether it would work or not, it was purely 'suck it and see'.

The effect we see now is not what I set out to do, I still do not know if there is any antigravity effect when it lingers in time (ha, another good title!), maybe, that if it was squeezed harder there might be different effects or maybe that this current effect would be made stronger in that it could slow down even more.

We are a long way from finding out things like that. Tom and I are about to put in place a long string of experiments, sending the rig into HRT quite a number of times over the next few days. We are going to investigate, absolute pressure, HRT trigger value, and most of all we are going to try and solve the mystery of boundaries and the exhaust fumes and what time zone emitted items exist in.

We will also examine more closely the issues of merging and permanent connection, even at a distance. I am going to try out the back-up cube.

We are both really concerned about detection and are doing everything we can to keep a semblance of normality about our daily lives and the comings and goings to the garage.

I'm convinced that the more we do, the more active we are then the more we will draw attention to ourselves. I am resolved to try and think of a way out of this situation so that we have the freedom to communicate with experts.

Day 395 – 30th June 2017

What a busy and exciting time we have had, I have completely broken my promise about writing this in real time. I'm afraid I was so caught up working with Tom, intensely focusing on all the experiments and their outcomes that I put off real-time diary entry.

So here is a catch up to get the diary up to date.

First of all, RVR, I had always used an approximation of 1.8 seconds rig time equals about 15 minutes real time, well after repeatedly measuring each run, that we did for other experiments, we got a very consistent result of 1 second rig time equals 8 minutes, or 1 minute rig time equals 8 hours, or 1 hour rig time equals 20 days.

Therefore, 1 second RIG TIME = 480 seconds REAL TIME.

Amazing and very consistent RVR ratio of 1:480

Just think if I could supply it with enough fuel for a year, it would not reappear for 480 years (give or take a bit for all our calendar approximations).

Astoundingly, if you could manage to stay on board for two years in HRT you would emerge nearly a 1,000 years in the future.

The only sad part about that, is that real time really would be a 1,000 years in the future, you could never come back to when you had set off, never come back to let anyone know what the future is like.

All you could do is let the future people know what it was like in the past, nowhere near as exciting, or is it?

The next value, that we measured on all the runs, was the pressure trigger value (PTV), this is a result that shows how fortunate I have been to see this effect at all. Remember the peak pressure that we always seem to achieve, 204.377 tons, I predicted it was the maximum the rams could achieve, I was right, the trigger point was 204.350 tons.

This is so close to the maximum that I could easily have missed this whole experience, especially as the rams are rated to 200 tons, a value below the trigger point! I have also been thinking about units. Units of pressure that I have been using, because the rams were rated in tons, I acquired transducers to measure tons. I realise I do not know what this means. I am not sure if it easy to convert this to Bar or psi or kilopascals, which are more usual in use for pressure measurement. Will have to look into this and possibly change.

At some point in the future I would like to try larger rams with much higher pressure ratings, I am curious to know if higher pressures change the trigger point and continue to give the 1:480 RVR ratio and if larger pressures would give different ratios. Mind you, I would be a bit scared about the strength of the rig. It's scary enough now! We repeated the attachment/non-attachment experiments a number of times and arrived at exactly the same conclusions as before. Once part of the rig any attachment

ANTIGRAVITY DRIVE - THE DIARY OF AN INVENTION

travels to HRT with the rig and then, regardless of being subsequently attached or not, is permanently a part of the rig even if it is destroyed and/or separated from the rig and is unaffected by large distances. This is such a curious effect I cannot begin to explain it scientifically, nor can I really explain it unscientifically, it just 'is'. A quantum phenomenon if ever I saw one. (Not at all sure what that means, either)

We also established that if an object is not physically attached to the rig, it will never travel into HRT, unless it is completely contained within a closed receptacle that is attached to the rig. Just like fuel for the generator. Curiously, any carried object can be consumed and will never behave as an integral part of the rig. This means that, theoretically, it is possible to carry a passenger, without the risk of future permanent attachment.

We continued to send a variety of things into HRT, contained in the tobacco tin. Whatever was sent appeared to be completely unaffected by the experience.

We also constructed a small mesh cage within the structure, to repeat the tobacco tin experiments, it did not work, the open mesh is an open structure, so is not a closed container, even more weird or what?

Trouble is we now have a small mesh cage that is unusable that will always travel into HRT with the rig even if I detach it! So will keep it attached and try and think of some use.

We also confirmed the temperature drop every time the rig goes into HRT. It is consistently the same on every run, an initial 2.5 degree drop and a slow decrease to reach a drop of 3.1 degrees, if we leave it in HRT long enough. I am completely at a loss to explain this, but Tom says it is like latent heat, I will look this up later.

Now onto the more interesting experiments that we did during the previous 10 days. We now know things can be carried and consumed in a closed system, but what happens to something that is ejected whilst in HRT, just like exhaust fumes. The obvious thing to do was have an automatic device that ejected something from a closed container, we tried to think of something suitable, rejecting all sorts of daft ideas, we finally settled on a simple syringe of water, with a little, fairly loosely fitted plastic cap over the nozzle, a solenoid valve as an actuator, linked to a timer. We trained a camera internally to capture the squirt into the unknown. And a camera looking at the exit point on the rig.

What we captured on video from a series of short trips into HRT was far from easy to interpret, I'm not sure if I fully understand it but here goes; under pressure from the actuator the plastic cap popped off and water ejected from the syringe, it can be seen to travel to an invisible boundary, flush with the outer surface of the rig, where it disappears. There is no visible event at the boundary, it's obviously not got a physical presence, the water-jet just disappears. There was absolutely nothing to see in the video from the external camera. What we do see in real time is a puddle appears on the garage floor, no jet, no splashing, just a puddle.

My interpretation of this is, that the water is ejected into a real time that is still in our past but not the same as rig time. Time is passing 480 times faster outside the rig so, although the garage is visible, nothing moves so it is deceptive to the viewer of the video log, but time is definitely passing 480 times quicker. The water is ejected and forms a puddle during a very fast series of real time events, somehow equivalent to how long it takes the water to leave the rig and splash to the floor and add to the puddle. To us, outside the rig, permanently in real time witness nothing, except the now complete puddle, all ejection and splashing was in the past, we only observe the aftermath of the ejection, the puddle. So this tells me, rightly or wrongly, that there is always a real time outside the rig, that corresponds to a constantly changing Rig Time, that also always remains in our past. Not sure if any of that makes sense at all, but it does mean that something can leave the rig, probably unharmed.

This "probably" applies only to water and exhaust gas and when I think about it they are actually a stream of a collection of separate molecules, that appear as a whole 'thing' but are not. I find this really hard to visualise but it is giving me a nagging doubt about ejecting solid objects or living things.

I sense a bit of a paradox here though, I have found that trying to get my head around some of these "paradoxes" is so hard, it really does make my head hurt! Trying to imagine, that if it was me ejected from the rig then would I be able to meet myself in real time? Too hard, can't visualise it, I give up. Although we did not do it on these runs, I would like to try ejecting a clock and, separately, something living. I have real misgivings about using animals so will not do that yet or until I am sure they will not be harmed.

The final things we looked at on this series of runs, gave very curious results, and if we were a true research establishment, a whole career could be built around this phenomenon. The merge/unmerge effect where anything that merges with the rig on apparent materialisation, seems to be integral with the structure, but continues to function as if the rig does not exist. An effect I have experienced myself with, as yet, no detected side-effects.

ANTIGRAVITY DRIVE - THE DIARY OF AN INVENTION

Knowing that merged objects are left unaffected and functional, but appear integral, we repeated my earlier experiment with a chunk of steak, a block of wood and a plant on three of the corners and on the fourth placed a hosepipe with water flowing.

As before, they all appeared merged and completely integral in the steel structure, the water in the hosepipe was still flowing, with no apparent decrease in flow rate, this time I had sharp knives and a scalpel. First of all we cut the steak and wood at the interface with the steel. Inspection of the cut surface on the piece of steak or wood that I had cut off, showed that everything appeared normal, however, the interface surface at the steel was far from normal, what we saw simply took our breath away.

It was so difficult to look at, difficult, in that at the same time, the exposed interface just looked like steel but at the same time looked like wood, or steak, staring at it didn't make it change, there was no flickering or rippling or anything, no flipping, no switching from one appearance to the other, it was so difficult to resolve it made my eyes ache, I just couldn't tell which it looked like, it just looks like both substances at the same time! It actually makes me feel nauseous. It is beyond description, it's beautiful and horrible at the same time, in fact it even made me tearful.

Both Tom and I were mesmerized by this very strange effect, we found it difficult to stop looking, to stop trying to focus on one appearance or the other, trying to resolve the image, I had to almost forcibly drag myself back to reality, back into action.

We had to take a little time to settle ourselves after such an amazing and eventful few minutes. Eventually I plucked up the courage to cut the hosepipe at the interface, it is quite simply staggeringly beautiful, there is no reason to struggle to look at this, the water appears to emerge from a solid steel surface as if it is emerging from a perfectly round hole, without a hole being there, fabulous!

I turned off the tap and the water stopped flowing. Now it's difficult to look at, just like the wood and the steak, two images at the same time, which I am completely unable to resolve. This is truly amazing, we run experiments and just find more questions. Both Tom and I can only observe, not fully interpret. We would need to be expert physicists to understand and decipher what we have discovered. The more I do, the more captivated I become, but, have an increased sense of inadequacy. This should be shared, an expert or a team of experts should be helping. The trouble is we can't, we just can't it would be too risky.

Tomorrow I am planning to try out the back up cube. I hope it works as I am increasingly concerned we just keep applying pressure, run after run, I have no idea how robust the first cube is.

The truth is, more and more I realise how amateur my approach to this whole thing has been. I've just been playing at it really, cobble stuff together, give it a go, suck it and see, it didn't seem important until I was arrested and even then I had no idea what I had done. Not until now, really.

Day 396 – 1st July 2017

Despite my misgivings we have made real progress, we have found out more and more how this absurd invention of mine works. It has occurred to me that I concentrate our efforts in confirming and observing effects, not on how it works or why it works. I'm a bit surprised it's not been done before, compressing magnets, that is. It seems so simple, but when you think about it, making a cube of little neodymium magnets with all like poles squashed together, compressing as strongly and equally as you can on all six surfaces, it's not that obvious is it, it really is a bit obscure, a bit off the wall, not a natural, or even normal, thing to do.

Anyway, today we did a bit of maintenance and attempted to give the backup cube a run.

We opened up all the sides and propped them up, a truly strange but remarkable sight, 6 metres across in both directions, I knew this double garage was useful, but where would we be without it now?

We cleaned, oiled and greased where appropriate (I've never seen Tom so focused, so active, it's almost all worth it just for this), being extra careful not to get oil in the wrong places and not being too enthusiastic with cleaning near the cube and the rams.

Once done, I disconnected the three rams in turn and carefully balanced and supported them within the rig structure. Having exposed three of the cube surfaces, I used a permanent marker pen to label them T, F and R (Top, Front and Right).

Without moving the cube I examined the three exposed faces as closely as I could. There was nothing obvious, no cracks, no bulges or delamination. It appeared to be just as it was when I first made it.

Very carefully I removed the cube and placed it on a prepared site on the shelf with the paint cans. I took the back-up cube out of my pocket (I

ANTIGRAVITY DRIVE - THE DIARY OF AN INVENTION

know, I know, a bit unscientific, but, when I made these I had no idea what was going to happen, no idea how important to check everything, label everything or anything really).

I had no real idea on the orientation but I assume as we are compressing in all six directions equally it shouldn't matter.

The back-up was in place, all rams repositioned, the rig faces locked, everything running, off we went.

10 minutes, it was still there, nothing had happened.

Pressure was at maximum.

I'm sure everything was as it should be, maybe orientation is important after all. Maybe we have to have the cube correctly aligned, somehow, with Earth's gravitational field. So have to try each face in the top position, until we find which is correct. Having stripped the rig down I labelled each face, consistent with its current position, T, F, R, L, Bo and Ba.

We started a sequence of up to 5 more runs. To determine what the orientation should be. 'F' in top position next, nothing!

Having gone through the sequence again, with the cube positioned with R on top, I was just about to begin the run when Tom shouted for me to stop.

He pointed out that we already knew about the attachment issues, once something is attached it always travels to HRT, what about the original cube, it will be in the same place, or is it that the rig cannot travel without the original cube, but if the back-up does take the rig to HRT, the original cube will try and occupy the same space.

He was right of course, we have to stop trying the back-up in the same rig. We probably just had a lucky escape, the cubes may have been irreparably damaged.

But, I have a sneaking suspicion that it didn't work anyway. I did not know why, but I think the back-up cube will never work.

Day 397 – 2nd July 2017

I am sat here on my own the rig is in HRT from yesterday, the original cube was installed and it worked first time.

I have just had an earful from Jane, spending too much time on that bloody book, apparently. She is right, I almost do nothing else. She has also noticed Tom seems obsessed with helping me. She has demanded to know what is going on, what an uncomfortable situation. She is going to ask Tom what he is up to, when she gets in from her shift. I think the time has come to spill the beans, be completely open and honest.

Oh, here is Tom, will discuss this with him.

Day 397 – 2nd July 2017 - 6.00 pm

Having had a long discussion with Tom about the situation, we are sat in the garage waiting for Jane to arrive home from her shift at the Hospital, the rig is in HRT, it is due back in exactly 25 minutes.

Jane came into the garage at 6.20, still in her uniform, she could see our solemn looks and wanted to know what was wrong, of course nothing was wrong, I asked her to stand next to me, we held hands in silence, she kept trying to speak, Tom and I just asked her to be quiet (nicely of course), I think she must have thought we had found religion or become born again Christians, she squeezed my hand tighter I could see she was beginning to worry something was wrong.

She let go and was just about to say something when, at 6.25 exactly, the rig was back. As usual, no fuss, no dramatics, it's just there.

She, just like Tom when he first saw it, was dumbstruck, I had to tell her to breathe! Jane stepped forward and touched the rig as if trying to convince herself it was really there. She turned to me and demanded to know how we did it, was it a magic trick, like on the telly?

I just said read this, and proffered my Kindle with the diary open, ready to read. She cried, actually cried, said she had no idea, no idea at all what had happened to me. Then she got angry, all the secrets, the deception, the danger it was all too much.

It took quite a while for her to gather herself together, taking deep breaths, sobbing slightly she wanted to know why now, why get her involved at this late stage, all this time not knowing, not involved, except by deception. It was mean, cruel and it felt like I'd had an affair with another woman or something. I had not realised at all that she would see it this way, I had been so wrapped up in the whole thing that I had not taken into account Jane's feelings. What an insensitive and stupid pillock I had been.

All I could do was to say sorry, apologise for everything and hope for forgiveness. I hoped she would see I had kept her at a distance to protect her really, protect her from the worry and the unknown. After some considerable time, discussion, questions and answers between the three of us, it got to trying to decide what we should do next. It was obvious we could not, should not, continue alone. We need help, we need bigger intellects than ours, but who? How? How do we go about involving anyone without breaking the demands in the paper I signed? There is no way to proceed without doing that, without putting my, our, freedom under severe risk. It was Tom who suggested that he did it, that he would approach someone, he had not signed, he had made no such agreements. I insisted that I didn't think it, they, worked like that. They really set their own boundaries and appeared to me to not worry about the consequences.

We all decided to send the rig into HRT for the evening, lock up and discuss over our evening meal.

Day 398 – 3rd July 2017

We had a long, and sometimes heated discussion, over dinner and long into the night, a lot of which was like a question and answer session for Jane. Eventually it was decided that it would be Jane, not Tom, who would make an approach, if that was what was decided, to a carefully selected academic.

We had plenty of suggestions of famous, celebrity type scientists, but no idea how to approach them or to convince them to be involved without them publicising it to the World or something equally as disastrous. We knew we could not risk failure, whoever we approached had to be immediately convinced, but, we couldn't take the rig to them and surely there is nothing we could say to convince them to come and look in our garage. In the end we arrived at the conclusion that the only way to get a celebrity scientist involved was to abduct one ourselves, kidnap them and make them watch the rig going in and out of HRT. Of course this is a ridiculous proposition but after long consideration we decided, that if it was a celebrity we needed, then this was probably the only way.

We also thought of involving an acquaintance of ours who knew someone who actually did know a celebrity scientist, probably a good candidate too, Professor Brian Cox, they were a roadie or something in his pop group days. The trouble with this was the number of people we had to convince, but at the same time trust implicitly. We decided this was just too risky (Sorry, Brian Cox you might have enjoyed this adventure).

We finally agreed that, although we needed someone to help, we could not think of a way to do it, with the guaranteed success that was required. We just had to press on, running experiments and being as covert as possible. The downside is we know we are sort of only playing at it. One of the big reasons for this is the restriction of not being able to purchase things openly to try new things or to build new rigs and stuff.

Today Tom and I intend to revisit two experiments, the first being things in the tobacco tin and the second ejection from the rig. I'm a bit subdued today, I feel so bad about how I have treated Jane, it was very remiss to behave in such a way. I feel like a naughty schoolboy who has been caught cheating in an exam and at the same time I feel guilty for being so unfeeling.

The rig is back, I have modified the mesh box, used silicone sealer and glass sheets (Things I feel I can buy without arousing suspicion) to make a sealed glass box inside the mesh box, allowed the silicone to merge into the mesh and, hopefully, subsequently behaving as attached and integral to the rig.

Before anything is placed in our new glass box it must go into HRT empty first, just in case it does not travel. It would be a waste of a run to send the rig into HRT just for this, so another experiment was set up too.

The tobacco tin has been used to take all sorts of 'passengers' into HRT and back, today I am using it to repeat the spider experiment with a bit more sophistication, well just a video of the spider going in and arriving back. First I needed to make sure the tin is clean.

How strange, I found a small, rectangular piece of grubby white card, 1.5 x 3.0 cm in size, with the word 'STOP' printed on one side, the card was wedged closely inside, tight into one corner, it was the sort of rectangular piece of card that might be part of some literacy game for a small child learning to read. I'm sure we had many of that sort of thing when Tom was learning to read as a 4 or 5 year old. The card must have been there all this time, wedged in the tin, strange how it's not been noticed before. I popped the card into my desk drawer and got on with the job at hand.

The spider survived and is now a video star, the first recorded living thing that has travelled in time. I'm not sure the rig is really traveling in time, but it sounds good. Come to think of it, if the rig is held in the past, when it reappears in the present it must be, sort of, travelling forward in time, to a time it's never been in, so does that mean the future regardless of how far in the future always exists. Oh that's deep, too deep for me, just can't get that at all. But that would mean either only one future, like we are living on a

ANTIGRAVITY DRIVE - THE DIARY OF AN INVENTION

predetermined path, or many futures determined by choices, but there would be millions of choices, so millions of futures, that all exist, millions of parallel universes! Now that is too deep for me, it's making my head hurt thinking about it.

As I removed the spider, or actually, filmed its escape, I noticed the piece of white card with STOP, on it was back in the tin. How curious, I checked the desk drawer, it was not there, so this must be the same piece of card. How odd, it's not really following attachment rules that we have so far observed. I removed it again and this time popped it in my pocket. I secretly thought Tom was playing tricks on me. I'll tackle him later about it.

I have caught a whole range of insects in the garden, they are now contained in the glass/mesh box, with a camera recording every move, the tin contains a small battery powered clock, with date and time synchronized with the on-board laptop.

The rig is back, the insects all survived the experience, and the clock now has its time discrepancy, but is still synchronized with the laptop. This is the one thing that has become tedious, resetting the time after every run on the on-board clocks and computers.

I had checked that the piece of card was in my pocket during the run, it was, so it has not travelled and is not integral. I checked inside the tin on its return, just to be sure. The card was there, the same piece of card, it looked the same, grubby white card, with 'STOP' printed on one side. I checked my pocket, it was still there too!

I now had two identical pieces of card! What on Earth is going on here?

I was just about to show Tom, when we were interrupted by a loud rat-a-tat-tat of knuckles on the side garage door, we froze, didn't breathe, we looked at each other, neither knowing what to do next. The rat-a-tat-tat was louder and more insistent the second time and even louder the third time. We still hadn't moved, or taken a breath. A familiar voice, shouted through the door for us to open up, he knew we were in there, he'd seen us.

I breathed a huge sigh of relief, it was Dave from next door!

We still had a problem, the rig was sat there in the garage. The insects were moving around in the glass box, oblivious to the role they were playing in transforming the future.

The door handle turned and in walked Dave. He stood, stock still and stared open mouthed at the rig, the generator was running and the rig side with the control box was propped open. For the first time, in 40 years, Dave was speechless. We had rendered him incapable of movement, talking or breathing.

Dave was the sort of neighbour, that you either loved or hated, he was affable but oh so competitive. Competitive, that is, with respect to tools, garden implements, gadgets and cars. Dave was always happy to help anyone, as long as it added to the points on his personal crusade of one upmanship.

Ever since he became a widower, 5 years ago, Dave had been keeping track of everything I did, from buying a car to cutting the grass, he always seemed to be one step ahead in everything and went to great lengths to let me know just what I need to do to be on the ball, just like him.

As I said you either love him or hate him, right now I wasn't sure which, all I did know was that he needed to breathe. I shouted his name, he took a very loud sharp intake of breath.

He actually looked a bit shaky, a bit overwhelmed, I placed a stool next to him so he could sit and get his breath. He just waved me away as he set off on an inspection tour of the rig, walking around, in turn touching, standing back and rubbing his chin before setting off again, he repeated this over and over again on his quadruple circumnavigation of the two metre steel cubic rig.

At last he stopped, arms akimbo, head cocked to one side, silently demanding an explanation. Tom and I both started to speak at the same time, with two slightly different explanations, we stopped, took a breath and did it again, this time I shot Tom a stern look for him to shut up. I gave Dave the full Lorry Invention version of the story, that had so conveniently convinced Jane and Tom at the beginning of this adventure.

Dave was having none of it, partly due to the rams all pointing in to the centre but mainly because there was a glass box in a mesh container full of live insects. Me, then Tom, tried to proffer a reasonable explanation, both different, both full of bollocks, Dave, again, would have none of it, he was not convinced, he appeared twitchy and a bit anxious. It became immediately obvious to me he perceived this, whatever it was, to be potentially several points to my advantage in the brinkmanship war.

I held up my hand for Tom to shush. I had an opportunity I just couldn't resist. I said that I was being cagey because it really was a smart invention,

ANTIGRAVITY DRIVE - THE DIARY OF AN INVENTION

something that would be amazing once it hit the marketplace and, jokingly, that if I told him I would have to kill him. He pleaded to know, I refused point blank, but here was the opportunity. He could get involved if he liked, help me out, take a share in the credit. Tom shot me a glance that asked if I was insane. Dave seemed uncertain, I dived deeper into the brinkmanship stakes, if he started helping me now he could be a 40:60 partner, take a huge amount of credit and be the envy of the entire neighbourhood.

He was hooked, all would be revealed at a later date, meanwhile would he sign a confidentiality agreement, you know the usual stuff, inventions, patents that sort of thing. I told him I would get the agreement to him this afternoon, but until then I couldn't reveal anything. I ushered him out of the garage and through our little adjoining garden-gate, that Dave had constructed four years ago.

He was gone, lost in his own ambitions, I rushed back to the garage. Tom was waiting for me, he had a look of complete bewilderment, he was convinced the World would know in precisely 10 seconds. I tried to calm him down and explained my motives. Dave would keep quiet, but we have to keep him involved, keep him interested. I am going to get him to be our supplier of materials and gadgets, spin him some yarn of me keeping secret all activities so suspicions are not aroused anywhere.

We immediately sent the rig into HRT for 2 hours to give ourselves time to gather our thoughts and grab a bite of lunch.

We were about to leave the garage when there was another rat-a-tat-tat, the door opened in mid 'tat', it was Dave again, he was accompanied by a tall, gangly looking young man, looking as if he was a refugee from a fashion disaster, all corduroy and pullovers. Try as I might to not let Dave in, he elbowed his way past me and was lost for words for the second time in 40 years. He demanded to know where it was, we hadn't had time to dismantle or remove it, so where was it? He appeared to be quite cross, as if we had fooled him, played a prank and made him look a fool in front of this gangly stranger.

Dave was not the only one lost for words, I too was at a complete loss, Tom came to my rescue, he told them all would be revealed after lunch and a coffee, if they would care to join us in the kitchen, Dave could start proceedings with introductions.

It turned out the gangly stranger was Robert (Bob), the son of Dave's cousin Sheila, one of his London side of the family. Bob was over here on business and was a physicist (A bloody physicist, can you believe it?), based at Livingston in America on permanent secondment from the University of Birmingham. Either all my prayers were being answered or it was a very suspicious coincidence or even something else. I tried to appear cross with Dave for breaking our agreement, he just shrugged, couldn't see what harm it could do. He's a good lad, a very clever lad, we're all proud of him, was to him a reasonable excuse. I was livid and getting very scared, this was all getting out of hand. I quizzed Bob on his reason for the visit, his reply is now emblazoned on my memory, for all time, word for word. I was so shocked and I could see Tom was too.

Bob was part of a team in the US that was working on a huge laser observatory that had been built to detect gravitational waves, they were having severe calibration issues due to some sort of anomaly or interference emanating from this area in the UK, he said it had taken them a year to pinpoint it to the UK as there were not that many devices that could detect the waves, he went in to some detail that is irrelevant here, so they could not do a classical telemetry exercise. They had, however, built a device that could home in like signal strength detectors, something like a tracker. They were going to set up and start tomorrow, he was really excited as none of the team could even begin to theorise about what the source could be, but until they find it the millions of dollars invested so far would be useless.

I asked how many were in this team over here, two was the reply, him and Gregori, a post-doc, research fellow, from Moscow. Oh, and one other, some sort of government representative, safeguarding their investment or something. I almost fainted, my knees actually buckled, the coincidence was too much to take in and it was screamingly obvious that the rig was going to be the source. There was nothing for it, this moment in time was my one and only chance, I jumped up from my chair and beckoned for them all to follow me to the garage.

Once we were all inside, door shut, all sat in chairs or on stools, Dave and Bob sharing very quizzical looks, I asked them not to move, to be patient and in (I checked my watch) 2 minutes they could ask all the questions they chose.

The rig materialised, Dave screamed loudly, jumped off his stool and headed for the door, Tom barred his way.

Bob, shouted YES! He knew it, knew something like this was going to be the source, it had to be. He turned to me and said, and I quote "Tell me everything".

ANTIGRAVITY DRIVE - THE DIARY OF AN INVENTION

I passed him the Kindle Fire with the most up to date diary.

Day 399 – 4th July 2017

Writing this diary has become second nature to me now, I have several ways of keeping it up to date, I use my mobile to record my immediate observations and other events, I have a tablet to keep the diary file itself and type into that during the day, the main record/diary is on the rig computer, with a backup on a memory stick, which is hidden in the house. I update the diary at least once each day, sometimes less than that if the rig is in HRT. I delete daily files once the diary is up to date and backed up. I have become very disciplined in this respect. It is now too important to do otherwise.

I have noticed a developing style in the diary, brought about by necessity and experience. I feel there is more need to record details as minutely as possible, including conversations and others actions as I am certain this is now becoming an important document. It sometimes reads more like a novel than a diary due to my increasing need to record conversations. I am not skilled enough as a writer, (but I am becoming more experienced) to embellish, exaggerate or to find endless linguistic trickery to make the diary a good academic piece of writing. So I now take this opportunity to all future readers to apologise for changing styles, grammatical and linguistic errors and most of all for possible scientific and experimentation howlers.

Even as I write this I am completely and utterly humbled, by the enormity of what has happened and what has been achieved from such a hobbyist approach to an interesting scientific problem. Furthermore, I am totally at a loss to even begin to comprehend why it has become so dangerous with secret services operating as they are and almost even more amazing is the way we have become involved in International Academia. I have to mentally pinch myself almost hourly to make sure I am awake and all this is actually happening, it has become life changing, not just for me, but for all those involved, particularly, right now, Tom and Jane.

I have just finished getting the diary up to date to include yesterday afternoon, when Bob, my neighbour Dave's cousin Sheila's eldest son, miraculously appeared on the scene, Bob was like a gift, a perfect gift, too good to be true, he was even involved with the effects of the rig before he got here, purely by accident. It seems too much of a coincidence, too good to be true. He has been in the garage with Tom all night, Dave and I retired to our respective abodes and beds at about 1.00 am.

It is 7.30 in the morning. I am showered, dressed and ready for action. Will catch up later, fingers crossed.

I opened the garage door gingerly, popped my head in and looked around, no rig, Tom asleep, slumped in the office chair, Bob asleep too, kneeling beside the desk with his head resting on his arms on the desk-top.

Also on the desk top was a jumble of cards, all similar to the two I had in my pocket. They were all white, not all the same size, a bit dog eared and grubby, with a word or letter printed on one side. It looked as if they had been tipped out of a word game for children.

I coughed loudly as I walked in and shut the door, they both jumped, shocked into wakefulness. I suggested they both pop into the house to freshen up, then we could all have a catch up over coffee. They agreed and left the garage, stretching, yawning and, in Bob's case, farting loudly. On his way out Tom let me know that the rig was due back at 10.00 later this morning.

The jumbled array of cards on the desk was intriguing, I was tempted to pick them up and inspect a few, but I thought I had better wait, just in case they were in some sort of order, that wasn't immediately obvious.

Tom arrived back first, carrying 3 cups of coffee on a tray. He said he was itching to bring me up to date but would wait for Bob, he should be the one to tell me. Bob ambled in, (no Dave, he was in bed) a big grin on his unshaven face, he asked Tom if he'd brought me up to speed, Tom shook his head, he was grinning too. The pair of them looked almost comical, disheveled and grinning like idiots.

Bob, babbling like an excited child, gave me a brief rundown of last night's mad capers (as he called them). Although, everything about the rig and the cube was hugely fascinating and important, the thing that immediately sparked his curiosity was the phenomenon of the white cards, those in my pocket, he said they gave him an immediate mental itch that needed scratching. The way they appeared, almost unnoticed, breaking newly discovered rules, intrigued him.

They apparently did lots of runs, they lost track of how many (this annoyed me ever so slightly, because as a non-academic, even I was keeping better records than that), Bob wanted to see for himself, attachment, non-attachment, merging and water ejection. They repeated many of our experiments, but not with steak, he said he would rather eat it. He particularly enjoyed the merging object interface and even, to my utter amazement, merged his own foot on purpose. He was fascinated by the texture of a merged object interface, it felt just like it looked, neither one nor the other. He found he could stick a scalpel blade into a piece of wood that appeared to be totally inside the steel frame, but if you tapped the same surface with a hammer it gave a metallic ring.

When they did a run they always checked the tobacco tin and to their increasing perplexity, they found cards, the first two had STOP printed on them just like mine, in fact they were identical, they assumed we now had four identical cards. Was it the same card, with this process somehow reproducing it?

Bob had said that this had to be more thoroughly investigated, so they had set about trying to find answers. The first thing they did was put a 'STOP' card in the tin with one character written on the reverse in black marker pen, a '?'. With hindsight, it seems predictable, that on the return of the rig from that run, the tin contained not a STOP card but five smaller square cards, made of the same card, with a single lower case letter on each, **u, u, m, s** and **t**. Easy to decipher - u must - you must. Bob could hardly contain his excitement. This was communication:

Stop. Why? You must.

My immediate thoughts were, who have we communicated with? Where would they be? What time do they exist in? It doesn't make sense, but yet there was something achingly familiar about the cards.

The second STOP card they had, was used next, on the reverse they wrote, 'Y ?'

On the rig's return they eagerly opened the tin to find it crammed full of cards, with a mixture of words and letters, try as they might they could not decipher it, from the jumble of cards they used another STOP card and wrote on the back, WHAT?.

The reply this time was completely unexpected, scrawled on the back of another STOP card, was some spindly looking hand writing using what appeared to be dirty oil and a stick or metal nail, it read '*put cards box*'. This was the last message they had.

As they were explaining this, I looked at the pile of cards on the desk, all were the same construction, but different sizes, they seemed ever so familiar, as if from an Early Learning game or something. Then it hit me, I rushed to the back of the garage, got the step ladders and erected them under a little trapdoor leading to a small loft space used as storage. Rummaging around in the loft I shouted that I'd found it.

The 'it' was a cardboard box filled with old games and toys of Tom's, inside the box, almost at the bottom were two smaller cardboard boxes - Learning to Spell and Phonics - The Learning to Spell box was almost empty, the Phonics box, was full. I brought both boxes down to the garage.

This just has to be the box mentioned in the note. Surely it had been full when stored away. If that was the case then maybe, somehow, these were the cards, those left in the box were of identical construction and condition. It had to be them. How, do they get in the tobacco tin? It is a complete mystery, it has me baffled.

Bob appears to know, but is not saying, he obviously wants confirmation, more evidence or something. We took note of all the cards on the desk and then placed them in the Learn to Spell box.

Did the message mean we had to leave them in the box, or put the box in the rig, we had the mesh/glass container we could use, even though it still contained the insects.

We had until 10.00 for the rig to return, it was now 9.51.

I had just put the lid on the box, the three of us were fully concentrating on what was happening on the desk, when I heard a very slight, but spine tingling, cough, a half delivered smokers cough, I spun round. Standing inside the door was Mr. Pinstripe, attired immaculately, as usual, in a pinstripe suit and red dickie bow tie. He too was sporting a big grin.

He addressed us in his almost perfect Queens English. "Well, well, well, good morning gentleman, what a nice surprise, I see you are already acquainted with Doctor Bob. We are also acquainted with Doctor Bob, is that not so Doctor Bob? We are helping Doctor Bob with his project, are we not Doctor Bob?" (He has this really annoying habit of over using people's names, in a way that is very intimidating) "Have you told them about your project Doctor Bob? Have you told them that we are working together Doctor Bob?"

My heart sank, this was it then, we were discovered, I'd taken the risk but had now revealed everything to them. The gangly shitbag, the snake in the grass, no wonder Dave was lying low, he must have been in on it too, somehow. I knew it was too good to be true.

ANTIGRAVITY DRIVE - THE DIARY OF AN INVENTION

Just then I realised that Mr. Pinstripe had edged forward as he goaded us and was now stood on the red spot, the only rig corner that has not yet been used. I had a sudden rush of adrenalin, my heart was pounding, I looked at my watch. "Expecting someone, are we Mr. Charles?" There were 30 seconds to the return of the rig. I didn't know whether to warn him or encourage him to stand still, the only thing I knew the rig would materialise in about 20 seconds. He stepped forwards away from the spot, my heart skipped a beat, 10 seconds to go. All I could say was a stuttering "I, I..."

Suddenly Bob stepped forward, arm extended, proffering a hand-shake, only it wasn't, he seemed to push Mr. Pinstripe ever so slightly, he took one staggered step backwards, the rig materialised, he was caught in mid-stagger, merged into the rig!

His whole body was in the rig, all that was visible was his head, neck and shoulders, along with his right hand and forearm, which were protruding lower down as was his right foot. He let out a blood curdling scream, his face was a picture of terror, eyes bulging, he went purple, then the colour drained out of him, he went limp, not moving. An eerie silence fell on the garage only broken by the gentle thrumming of the generator.

"Oh fuck, we've killed him"

I didn't know what had shocked me more, the demise of Mr. Pinstripe or Tom swearing.

Bob stepped forward and felt for a pulse on Mr. Pinstripe's neck, there was one, he's not dead, just fainted. He slowly began to come round, groaning and mumbling. He looked up, tried to move, groaned and promptly passed out again. I took the opportunity to launch a sarcastic tirade, congratulating Bob, on tricking me into revealing everything to him, while all the time he was in cahoots with Pinstripe and his cronies. Although I knew we had Pinstripe trapped, I also knew it was, surely, only a matter of time before his men came to find him. When they do, it will all be over. Goodness knows what they will do to me, to Tom and Jane. What will happen to the rig?

Bob appeared to be genuinely shocked, he turned to me with a look of astonishment and hurt, I didn't let him speak, I just continued with my tirade of accusations and self-pity. I came to a sudden halt, when, without warning, the door flew open and in jumped Dave, "Am I missing anyth....." was all he could manage before he too collapsed in a heap beside the rig.

In the midst of all this drama, excitement and danger, the three of us just erupted into laughter, Dave's comedy entrance was priceless, it diffused the situation completely. We were still giggling like idiots as we helped Dave to sit up, "what's so funny?" was all he could manage. A spluttered cough, above my head, brought me sharply back to reality. I stood up, dusted myself down and took a step back to take in the scene before me.

The rig was there in all its glory with Mr. Pinstripe trapped in one corner, slowly coming back to consciousness. Dave, too, was coming back to the land of the living, assisted by Tom and Bob. I could not believe this was all going to come to an end soon, for me at any rate, once Pinstripe and the rest of his team take control.

So what's next Bob? I said in true defeatist style.

Bob really took me aback with his response, he took a few seconds to gather his thoughts, looking first at Pinstripe, then the box of cards, lastly at Dave and Tom.

He took a deep breath then admitted that yes he did know Colonel Smyth (Mr. Pinstripe), that he already knew the source of the effect he was looking for was somewhere in this vicinity, of approximately 5 miles radius, that he too was blown away by the coincidence that Dave (his mother's cousin) lived in this vicinity, he had absolutely no idea that the source was next door to Dave, until I revealed it. He explained that Colonel Smyth had met them at Heathrow Airport the moment they arrived in the UK, making contact with their own government-assigned individual. Apparently Smyth had no idea where they were heading or any details about why they were in the UK at all. He was assigned for International security purposes. Bob went on to say that he believed that Colonel Smyth only managed to put two and two together once he realised that two of his team's assignments had coincided, in a pin-point geographical kind of way. He believed that Smyth was as surprised and amazed as we all were.

Bob continued, the enthusiasm in his voice building with every word. The thing is, what we have here is so important, one of the biggest discoveries in physics in our lifetime, it just has to be investigated properly and openly, it has to be shared with everyone. Don't forget I read your diary I know what Smyth did, I know he wants to suppress this, I, we, cannot let that happen. Right now, at this moment, we have the upper hand, we have him trapped, compromised, but, I don't know how we capitalise on the advantage. Whatever it is, we don't have much time. Oh we do, I replied, we have 480 times more than you think!

I may be foolish, but I have decided again to trust Bob.

ANTIGRAVITY DRIVE - THE DIARY OF AN INVENTION

Day 399 – 4th July 2017 - 11.00 am - 1 Hour after Colonel Smyth was merged.

I estimated that we had a further hour, two at the most, to do whatever it was we decided gave us the best way forward. Bob had said all we need is time. Time to get organised so that we can somehow continue work or find a way to move this rig to a University facility. As I said before, we have plenty of time, it's a matter of how we use it. I knew we could not just send the rig into HRT as Smyth would be instantly released.

Colonel Smyth had become fully conscious and began to show the signs of a panic attack, he opened his mouth wide and a scream began to build, a scream rapidly punctuated by short rasping breaths making him sound like he was practicing a New Zealander's Haka before a rugby match. Bob surprised me yet again, he stepped forward and slapped him, hard, on the right cheek. He stopped breathing altogether for at least 10 seconds and then had a huge intake of breath.

Smyth seemed to come to his senses after the slap and stopped us in our tracks, "SHUT UP, SHUT UP, WHAT ABOUT ME, WHATS GOING ON, GET- ME - OUT - OF - HERE."

Bob, held up his hand for him to be quiet, and tried to calm him by saying that we are trying to find a way to release him. Smyth replied, almost hysterically, that he needs an ambulance, fire brigade to cut him out, his men, call them, phone in pocket. He wanted to know why he wasn't bleeding, why wasn't he in pain, had they anaesthetised him or something?

Smyth turned, as much as he could, to look at me and accused me of having the rig all the time, he said he should have known all along it was not stolen he went so far as to call me a deceitful little piece of worthless shit. I laughed, actually laughed, having the situation completely reversed was even more like a dream than ever. An opportunity not to be missed.

I stepped forward and said, "Right, Colonel Smyth. I am going to show you one or two little video clips, stay quiet, just watch." I showed him some of the clips relevant to attachment and how things stay attached even at a distance, also the clips about merging.

When finished, Smyth had a look of wonderment on his face and said, "So if the rig is sent away I will be released?" I replied that he was right, he had understood correctly, unless I choose to attach him or contain him. I offered him three options of how his immediate future may take shape. He could be released or be held in containment travelling into HRT at my whim or be forever attached wherever he is, whenever the rig is in HRT.

So Colonel Smyth, what do you think we should do? "Release me immediately" was his obvious response. I said I would if I could trust him to support us, to help us, but I couldn't do that, because I knew only too painfully what he would do. I only have two options Colonel, attachment or containment, which do you choose now? He said again, release me at once. If you won't choose, then I will choose for you, Colonel.

I choose attachment, I'm going to pierce your ear, insert a ring with a chain and attach you to the rig. I'm condemning you to a life of travel into HRT with the rig, whenever it travels, wherever you are, even if you escape, you will always travel with the rig, Colonel, always! Colonel Smyth was struck dumb by my statement, Tom, Bob and Dave just stared, open mouthed, at me in astonishment.

I stepped to one side, out of the Colonel's view, and shot a wink and a smile at Tom and Bob, who were still staring at me in astonishment. Bob, understood immediately and joined in, "the only choice, available", he said in support. I beckoned for the others to follow me out of the garage. I explained to them the idea I had had, it was risky but it will give us time to get organised.

The idea I had dreamt up on the spur of the moment, was to pretend to attach Smyth to the rig, but contain him in a wood and polyethylene sheet structure that would be attached, and although it's risky to send him into HRT, he will only be there for a few minutes, rig time. But, he will believe he will always travel, so, when he returns we will release him with conditions, which I had not yet thought of. We had very little time to discuss, but after a very lively and heated discussion, in hushed tones, outside the garage, we decided it was the best of a very limited number of options we could think of.

We very quickly knocked up a wooden frame, from wood I had saved over the years, it only served to surround the Colonel on the corner of the rig, we attached it with G clamps, from my tool box, four of them. All the time we were doing this Smyth was pleading with us to stop, he insisted we were getting deeper into trouble, stop now, he kept repeating. I borrowed some old earrings, with a large hoop, from Jane's jewellery box, they were like clip-ons, but had a screw mechanism just like a miniature G clamp. Back in the garage I put the earring on his right ear lobe, without him being able to see what I was doing, I screwed it very tight, he screamed and begged me to stop, I left it there for some time while I made a show of attaching a chain to the rig and then to his ear. Meanwhile Tom had retrieved, from in the house, a wide roll of opaque polythene sheeting we used when decorating.

We cocooned Smyth inside the wooden frame, stapling the polythene in sheets to the wood, inside and outside the frame, I poked a tube, made of garden hose, from inside the rig, through the polythene sheet and supported it right next to his mouth, as a breathing tube. During this action I carefully took the earring off his ear without him noticing. Smyth continued to berate, threaten and plead with us to stop, we didn't. When we had the last piece of polythene in place I programmed the rig to be away for 24 hours, this should give us plenty of time to decide and organise what we do next and how we deal with Smyth on his return. Smyth would actually only feel he was in HRT for 3 minutes.

The rig has gone, with Smyth onboard, he was screaming to the end, it's a wonder the whole neighbourhood had not turned up to see what the racket was. One of the downsides of taking this action, was that the wood and polythene structure would now always travel with the rig, even if we deconstruct it. We tidied the garage as quickly as we could, in case anyone else turned up unexpectedly.

They did, it was Jane in from work. We turned out the lights, locked the doors and all retired to the kitchen to bring her up to date, there was a lot to tell.

Day 400 – 5th July 2017

It's 9.00 am Tuesday morning, Jane is with the four of us in the garage, sat around the desk discussing options. Jane has pulled a sicky, she rang her boss first thing, before breakfast. It's a strange feeling, five people discussing, well arguing, about what began as an idle fantasy, a pipedream that started out as a one-man secretive hobby that has now got five people actively involved, one other person (held in HRT), two nation's security organisations and two large academic institutions waiting in the wings. In a way I wish that it had not worked then all this would still be a dream and no one would be in danger. After two hours of the discussion going in all sorts of directions, it seemed we only had three viable options:

- Carry on as we are and try and remain "underground"
- Give in to Colonel Smyth and let that route take its course
- Get both academic institutions involved, get the rig moved and hope they can protect us from interference

The first option appeared to have more of pitfalls, difficulties and danger as time went on, the second could mean we will land ourselves in real trouble, so the third seemed the most credible. The plan will be for Bob to contact his colleagues and say that he has found the source, but they must come here to see it. It's up to him to think of a way that will convince and entice his peers and/or his superiors. We do not have the time to wait for more of his colleagues to come from the USA, but the Birmingham people should be able to get here quick. First, he has to get them to agree, without telling them what it is, Then we have to get Gregori on board.

The time for the rig and Smyth's return loomed ever nearer, we were not sure how to deal with the Smyth situation. All we knew was that it had to be over and done with before anyone else turned up. Interestingly, we all thought it very strange that his team have not appeared, even if only to find out why he had gone quiet, we came to a sort of conclusion that they didn't know he was here and that if they are trying to find him, this place is not on their list of possibilities.

It's 11.55 all five of us are sat or stood waiting for the rig to return in 3 minutes, we are still not sure how we will deal with Smyth, it depends on so many things, but in particular his state of mind.

Video and voice recorder on, 10 seconds to go, Bob started a countdown -

8 - 7 - 6 - 5 - 4 - 3 - 2 - 1

It's back, as usual, with a very unsettling, lack of anything at all. In an instant, there it is. There seemed to be no movement behind the opaque polythene, Smyth is not making a noise. Looking closer I could see a large vertical slit in the polythene, sealed with clear adhesive tape, I lurched forward and not very carefully removed the tape opening the slit wide with both hands, which was accompanied by a collective and very loud gasp from all five of us. Smyth was gone, there appeared to be no evidence that he had ever been there at all, apart from the sealed slit.

We rapidly removed the whole of the wooden structure to examine the corner of the rig, where Smyth should be entrapped, not one of us had yet uttered a word. Personally, my thoughts were completely muddled. I was thinking of everything at once, or at least it felt like it. Where is he, what time is he in? Did he actually go? Has he escaped? Did someone, or something, rescue him? Where is he now? When is he now? What do we do about it?

Jane broke the silence, saying that we should look in the tobacco tin. It was

ANTIGRAVITY DRIVE - THE DIARY OF AN INVENTION

empty, I checked the box on the desk, it was almost empty too. There were still only insects in the other container (I made a mental note to get them out as soon as possible). After all the silence, we all started to speak at the same time. There was just complete bewilderment from each of us, I had a sick feeling in the pit of my stomach, this is really serious now, we can't just lose someone like that, even if he was the 'enemy'!

It was Bob, whose voice rose above the rest of us and managed to get us to order. He just said "camera feed, check the cctv log!" We had omitted to properly point a camera at Smyth, as we, obviously, had no expectations of anything like this happening. The only camera that had anything like a view was pointing at the centre of the cube and some of Smyth's back was in view through a layer of polythene and was consequently shadowy. We ran the video, there were only three minutes of it to study, nothing moved until just over a minute had passed, Smyth appeared to stand and move forward, again we all gasped, we could see the shadowy figure of Smyth moving away from the rig, accompanied by two more shadowy figures, one on either side. One of the figures appeared to move back to the rig and seal the slit with tape, we guessed it was that, but obviously nothing was clear.

How could there be anyone in HRT?

As far as I had ascertained from several experiments, immediately outside the rig was where time passed 480 times faster than in the rig during HRT. We should not be able see anyone move away from the rig, appearing as if that area outside the rig was also the same as rig time.

"That should be impossible" was all I could say.

We were all at a loss to explain anything we had seen and experienced this morning, it was difficult to take in, it really felt as if we had murdered Smyth! Both Jane and I felt physically sick with anguish. If nothing else we had lost him to some other time, some other World. Where is he? When is he? Who are those other people? We had no way of seeing any clearer what had happened. This really brought it home to me that despite making lots of observations and developing some understanding, I actually knew very little about what was actually happening, and because of this I had caused everyone to be in danger, even the so called 'enemy'. Although I was, obviously, not in floods of tears, I did feel very distressed and in a state of shock. It was Bob, yet again, who brought us back to the task at hand. Bob wanted to know, are we able to proceed as planned, as this has just taken on a whole new direction? We could not ignore that we have a major casualty, a secret casualty, one we can almost do nothing about, but one we have to take seriously and choose our time to own up to, one where we select very carefully who we inform.

There was still the issue of preparing for the reveal to Bob's academic colleagues. I was extremely nervous about doing this at all now, but as Bob (and Dave) and Gregori are already involved. Come to think of it, is Gregori in the know yet? (Bob said not yet)

I asked for a group discussion, we really needed clarity on our direction and all need to agree the way forward. After yet another long discussion it was agreed we would proceed as planned. Bob had already set up a meeting at his hotel, with his Research Leader, Professor Rachel Williams, his counterpart in Birmingham, Doctor Tim Baker and of course his colleague, Gregori. They are all to meet at 3.00 pm. Bob does not know the whereabouts of his security man, Alexander Alexandrou, obviously an American with Greek origins.

Bob went off to get freshened up at the hotel before his meeting, I would only let him take video clips on his mobile, not all the information or the diary.

Meanwhile, we had to prepare the rig and send it in to HRT to reappear at 6.00 pm. I removed the insects and kept them in a jar with a breathable lid and lots of vegetation. The wood and polythene was tidied up and stacked in a corner of the garage.

As I was doing final checks and programming I decided to find some cards and place them in the tobacco tin, I put in - WHY, WHERE and HOW and five individual letter cards to spell, WHO R U. When I'd done this I could not resist, sending the rig for immediate return, with the message on-board.

The rig is back, no one knows I did it, Jane and Tom are in the house. I quickly looked in the tin. Inside were different cards, all individual letters, E, K, Z, O and U.

It could mean anything, it could be a name, Kezou, Zukoe or Zouke or any number of combinations, none seemed to make any sense. I decided that the letters probably represented words, OK, EZ and U. The message made most sense to me as EZ, U OK. Signifying what they did was easy and am I OK, or it was easy, Smyth OK are you? I replaced the cards with some phonics/picture cards as well as letters to read as follows - Can (a picture of a can), HE, plus the letters R E T U R N.

I sent the rig into HRT to return at 6.00 pm as agreed. I glanced in the corner where I had stacked the wood and polythene that had enclosed Smyth, as expected they were gone.

Day 400 – 5th July 2017 - 5.30 pm

Jane, Tom, Dave and I are in the garage waiting for Bob and the invited guests. I feel utterly exhausted, so much has happened in two days, physically and emotionally. There was a small and polite tap, tap on the garage door, in walked Bob and all the expected guests. Bob introduced me, as the inventor. I introduced Jane, Tom and Dave. As previously agreed, Jane and Tom ushered everyone to their own mark chalked on the garage floor and all were instructed not to move.

The garage was suddenly very full, and very stuffy, I needed air. I went to open the side door, Bob, seemed nervous, asked where I was going. Somewhat taken aback I replied that I needed air, I turned the handle and opened the door to be confronted by Alexander Alexandrou, arms folded blocking my exit, I could see behind him, with their backs towards us, at least five more smartly dressed, obviously very muscular secret service men, with the typical ear-piece that you see in every American movie. I turned to Bob with what must have been a look of shock and betrayal. He said "Don't be surprised, just a precaution, they are only here to protect us". Yet again I had a very sick feeling in the pit of my stomach, I couldn't speak, I didn't know what to feel, apart from a feeling of impending doom (I don't know how else to describe it).

He nodded at the huge security man who pulled the door shut. Bob took my arm and pointed me in the direction of where the rig should be.

We had made sure that no one was in the M space, by standing them on their own chalk marks. At 6.00 pm exactly it returned, as did the wood and polythene, neatly stacked in the corner. There was an immediate cacophony of exclamations from the guests, I got the impression that they had half expected nothing at all. The Professor, Rachel Williams, was the first to come to her senses and in a very authoritative and commanding voice got everyone's attention. Just like Bob, her first words were "Tell me everything". We went through everything, demonstrations, videos and diary, even discussed some of the rules we developed and tried to unravel the mystery of the cards.

It was now 10.30 in the evening, the Professor called a halt and made a pronouncement. Apparently this invention and its effects are super important and the quicker this is removed and a whole study programme set up and started the sooner this all gets under control and everyone will sleep easier in their beds. Each individual aspect and effect needs to be studied in depth by dedicated teams. From today the World has changed forever. Everyone, including me, agreed. The enthusiasm was infectious, there was a lot of backslapping and the new academics present seemed to be congratulating Bob on his great find. I was feeling a bit miffed, a bit left out and if truth be known I had a terrible feeling I was making a huge mistake.

It was almost at that point in time where I was hoping tonight would end and we could shut down, lock up and retire to our respective beds, when there was a sudden commotion outside the garage. It sounded as if lots of people were running about, one or two barked orders and some loudish popping noises, that we immediately recognised as silenced automatic weapons, everyone began to talk at once. All of us demand to know what was going on, no one appeared to know what to do. There was an air of desperation and panic. My heart was pounding, I instinctively looked for Jane and Tom.

Before I could get to them, the door burst open and Alexander jumped in, he immediately shut the door hard. He commanded loudly for us all to shut up, keep still, everything is under control we will be removed as soon as it is safe. There was a sudden burst of unsilenced, automatic fire outside the garage, it silenced us. Everything seemed to be happening in slow motion, it sounded as if the bullets were hitting the wall of the garage, moving from right to left, towards the door, several bullets splintered through the door, at least one went straight through Alexander, throwing him forward in a shower of blood and flesh. Someone screamed, another wailed and began sobbing. Most of us were low to the ground, I began to crawl towards Jane, the only person I could see standing was Gregori. He had a gun!

I thought, what's he doing with a gun. Instead of firing it out of the window or something, he turned, and very quickly, to my totally helpless horror, expertly dispatched a bullet into the heads of the Professor, Bob, Dave and Dr Baker, none of them had time to utter even a single syllable, before they slumped to the ground in unison. He then turned to me (I felt paralysed, I braced myself), he said in heavily accented English, "Not you or your family Mr. Charles, you are required". My heart was beating so fast and loud, I thought it might burst right out of my chest, Tom and Jane managed to scramble across the garage and the bloody corpses, both were wild eyed and sobbing. Jane was giving me an imploring look, that spoke a thousand words.

It fell silent outside the garage, a terrible hush fell on us inside too, the only

ANTIGRAVITY DRIVE - THE DIARY OF AN INVENTION

sounds were Jane and Tom quietly sobbing, the generator idling, the distant sirens of approaching emergency vehicles and my heart beating a tattoo in my ears.

Gregori opened the door and began speaking in Russian, in hushed tones, to someone outside. Gregori turned to us and instructed us to stay put, stay quiet, we will not be harmed if we are sensible. He stepped outside and shut the door.

I sensed this was our only chance to somehow respond to this, I quickly ordered Tom and Jane to get the wooden frame and polythene, they both just looked at me dumbfounded and scared, I whisper-shouted for them to hurry, it's our only chance, we can squeeze in, go to HRT and take our chances there. I quickly programmed the controller to be away for 100 years. (A random huge figure, which meant it would come back when it ran out of fuel) I grabbed a can of petrol and topped up the fuel tank, we all worked in silence. The tension was palpable almost like a presence, he could return at any moment.

I couldn't help but think of Dave, he got a bit more than he bargained for getting involved in this, I felt terrible, mortified. At least he will achieve lasting notoriety, he will be pleased about that, I chuckled out loud, Jane gave me a look that would have frozen an oven-ready chicken.

The frame was clamped to the rig, Tom, then Jane, squeezed inside. I closed the rig doors, grabbed a roll of tape and squeezed in too, it was a very tight fit, but we were in. There was about 30 seconds to go. I could hardly move but managed to seal up the slit with a great amount of difficulty. Five more seconds, it felt like a life time.

Suddenly, I heard the garage door open, there was a lot of shouting, deafening gun shots assaulted my ears. Bullets pierced the polythene, both Jane and Tom jolted and cried out in pain, Jane's head immediately slumped forward. I felt an enormous pain in my left arm and could feel warm blood trickling down and dripping from my fingertips.

Outside of the rig, bright lights, like spot lights, came on with a mechanical/electrical "Thunk", I could hear people talking, the fingers from two hands appeared through the slit and pulled it wide open. Strong hands took a firm hold of me and helped me out of the rig and eased me onto a waiting trolley stretcher. I could feel myself drifting towards unconsciousness, I heard myself say Jane, Tom.... a familiar voice in perfect English said "Don't worry Mr. Charles, you are all in safe hands now".

It was really strange, there were quite a lot of people, mostly in white coats, milling about, I could just manage to see Jane and Tom being carried to stretchers too. There must have been ambulances when I heard those sirens, was my last thought as I drifted into nothingness.

DIARY THREE - DIVERGENCE

Day 402 – 7th July 2017

I had no idea what day it was, what time it was, where I was or even who I was. I had no immediate memory of how I got to be where I was, for the first hour or so of being conscious I was completely confused. I woke up slowly as if waking from a good hard sleep and tried to have a stretch, sudden pains in my left arm, left side and left knee immobilised me, I had no idea I had been injured and the excruciating pain shocked me deeply. As I opened my eyes and eventually focused, I could see I was in a one-bed, hospital room, no windows, plenty of equipment, most of which was connected up to me. There was very little else.

That was two days ago, I am now fully awake and more than aware of who I am and the events that led up to my current situation. I have been given my tablet computer, apparently I was clutching it very tightly when taken from the rig and wouldn't let go until I had passed out. I have spent some time getting the events recorded as I remembered them. I was desperate to know the whereabouts of Jane and Tom. As soon as I had fully found my senses, I recalled everything. My first action was to start shouting until someone came to my assistance, all I wanted to know was what had happened to them and where they were. A doctor, whose name I can't remember, came in and explained that all three of us had suffered gunshot trauma and were being treated in this facility/hospital, both Jane and Tom were considerably worse, consequently, none of us were well enough yet to visit each other. I was totally shocked and scared, I demanded to see them immediately, I was repeatedly assured they were sedated, stable and in good hands. Other than that they were instructed not to give me any other information about my circumstances or the events that led up to my being here.

I kept reliving those final moments, cocooned in the rig with Jane and Tom, before I lost consciousness. All those poor people, killed, mercilessly, because of me, because of my invention, why would anyone go to those lengths, why was there so much aggressive competition between countries and their secretive organisations?

At that moment in time I no longer cared if I ever saw the rig again.

I had absolutely no idea who had lifted me out of the rig, had the Russians got us, or had someone else overcome the Russians and rescued us, could it be the Yanks or the Brits, I really had no idea. All I knew was I wanted to be well enough to see Jane and Tom, nothing else mattered.

Day 404 – 9th July 2017 - 2.00 pm

I am suddenly ravenously hungry and wondered if I could eat, I called for a nurse using the appropriate button on my bed's handset.

Yippee, I can eat, they have gone to get me a cheese sandwich (Oh no not again, I can here you saying!).

The sandwich was so good it was like eating the best meal I could remember. When the nurse brought it, she announced that I would be getting visitors at about 3.00 this afternoon, but not to get too excited, it was some officials or other.

Day 405 – 10th July 2017 - 7.00 am

My nerves are mangled my brain is working overtime, this time I really don't know if this is all a dream or not. At three-o-clock (yesterday) I got my visitor(s). There was a polite knock on the door, it opened and in walked Colonel Smyth, Mr. Pinstripe himself, dressed immaculately as usual. I was struck dumb, I couldn't believe he was here, he was last seen departing into HRT. How did he get back? How did he get here? He had that same perfect accent, "Good afternoon Mr. Charles, let me introduce Colonel Smyth". I thought it was a very strange way to introduce himself and was just about to reply, when, with a flourish, another Colonel Smyth entered the room, this one sported a huge grin. They were identical in every respect, exactly the same features and stature, attired in a pinstripe suit, pale pink shirt and red bow tie.

The way they had planned this obviously had the impact they desired, even with my injuries I was so startled my whole body jumped upwards and backwards up the bed, I cried out in a mixture of pain and shock. My face must have been a picture, both Pinstripes erupted into laughter, turning to each other, one said "What a hoot, Colonel Smyth" the other replied "Well thank you, Colonel Smyth, what a hoot indeed". I was completely shocked, mouth agape, eyes boggling, heart monitor beeping so fast it sound like one note. "Shall we continue Colonel Smyth?" "Yes, Colonel Smyth, let's." They both still had that really annoying habit with names! "Mr. Charles, let me introduce Mr. Charles". In I walked, well at least my doppelganger did. He too was sporting a huge grin.

ANTIGRAVITY DRIVE - THE DIARY OF AN INVENTION

I passed out.

Apparently, the shock of meeting myself and both of the Colonel Smyths sent the monitoring equipment into overdrive resulting in the three of them being ushered away whilst I was stabilised. I was sedated, and spent the whole night in drug induced oblivion.

Day 406 – 11th July 2017 - 10.00 am

Waking up today was almost like the first experience all over again, slowly coming back to full awareness. It was only after being propped up by the automatic bed and having a slice of toast, that I remembered my visitors from the day before yesterday. The memory seemed murky like a half remembered dream, I came to the conclusion that it was just that, a dream, not reality, it is just not possibly real. It must be all this sedation they have been giving me. The drugs must induce hallucinations. It is very scary because it felt so real. I can vividly remember the distinctive laughter of the Pinstripes, the memory sent a shudder down my body. Colonel Smyth is definitely the scariest and most dangerous person I have ever met. Cool, calm, self-assured and obviously completely at home in the realms of subterfuge and the political underworld. The sort of world us ordinary people only experience in books and films. The cold, sharp reality is much, much more dangerous and very scary.

I spent the rest of the day bringing the diary up to date, tidying it up and adding more details throughout as I remembered them. It was a very sobering experience, reading and rereading whole sections, reliving some of the startling revelations and some of the inexplicable happenings, in particular, the card messages. I again noticed how the diary had evolved, by necessity, having greater detail and more descriptive observations. I had this weird feeling that I was reading a novel rather than a detailed journal. If it was not for the fact that I knew I had personally experienced every word, I would believe it to be a work of fiction.

In the early evening, one of the nurses delivered a lap top computer bag, that appeared to be reasonably heavy as she lifted it onto the bed. It came with the instruction that I should look at the enclosed tablet computer, before anything else within the case. It was the same as my own, a Kindle Fire HDX, it even had the same dent on the top right hand corner, I quickly looked for my own on the bedside cabinet, it was there, charging (it suddenly occurred to me that there was a charger to use, where did that come from?).

I touched the power button and it sprang to life, the carousel and icons looked very familiar and, as with my own, the first item in the carousel was a word document, saved as 'antigravity.docx', my diary. I instantly felt queasy and broke out in a cold sweat, trembling slightly, my forefinger selected the Word document. There before me was my diary, on my tablet.

I grabbed my own from the bedside cabinet and switched it on, it was exactly the same, I opened the document, it was mine, updated from my earlier session. I placed it back on the cabinet and concentrated on the new and identical tablet and diary.

I recognised it immediately, it was an earlier less edited version of my own, but definitely mine. I continued reading, everything was reasonably identical (apart from recent editing) until I got to the time when I was first testing the rig, In this version, I had made a different choice, I had immediately used a shorter gradient to achieve max pressure, only 5 minutes. This was followed by the first run, which went into HRT with me observing and was programmed to switch off at maximum pressure. That meant I witnessed the first time the rig went and then returned, the discovery was completely different, it was never reported stolen and I never experienced the abduction and questioning. I did not meet Colonel Smyth at that time.

I stopped reading to catch my breath and think about what I had just read. Then read that part again and again before moving on.

I don't know what is more bizarre, my own sequence of events or sitting here reading an entirely different version of essentially the same sequence. I couldn't figure out why this version existed, am I supposed to approve a different, edited, version, for others to see, perhaps, with my abduction conveniently written out?

I continued reading, compelled to find out what happened next in this alternate version.

Strangely enough some of the early experiments were similar, except that I started them straight after the discovery, in this version I very quickly grasped what was going on and never had to wait six months for it to reappear. Comparing both sequences, timewise, it meant that in the alternate sequence many of the discoveries were made and further investigated while I was feeling paranoid and depressed in my own timeline.

What happened next in the alternate version really shocked me, I had to again read and re-read.

Because I had none of the pressures of secrecy imposed on me along with threats of disappearance, I almost immediately showed the rig to Jane and Tom. The three of us then decided we must involve academia and, after a small amount of research on Tom's behalf, we got in touch with the team at Birmingham. The Professor was exactly the same, as were the others that came with her. They saw demonstrations and almost immediately arrangements were made to dismantle the rig and reassemble in laboratory conditions back at the University. It was there that a very rapid research programme was put in place and my early discoveries were soon built upon enormously. Even more bizarrely, the University held a series of press conferences, the whole thing was announced to the World. I became a bit of a celebrity and made numerous television appearances.

A huge amount of Government funding was obtained and plans were made to build a whole new research centre at the University. They did not announce what was at the heart of the invention, only that it involved squeezing, strong magnets of a particular metallic composition. The veil of secrecy was yet again thrown over the project. That part of the University and the proposed new build, was made into a closed and secret facility, the operation was carried out with minute military precision, the man in charge was, Colonel Smyth!

It began to dawn on me what was happening and where I might be, my heart began to race, I came out in a cold sweat, I think I began having a panic attack or something. A nurse burst into the room, obviously my monitors had set alarms off, she managed to get me under control, by gentle talking and calmly fussing about.

I asked her who had brought the case with the tablet computer, her answer stopped me in my tracks. "It was your other self, Mr. Charles". She said this with an air of complete normality. It was as if two of me, or anyone for that matter, was commonplace.

So I had not been hallucinating yesterday, it was real, two Colonel Smyths and my doppelganger really did visit! I was scared, excited, curious, frustrated, but, most of all desperate to see Jane and Tom. I couldn't carry on reading, my mind was racing and I couldn't concentrate, I needed answers, and I needed them now. I pressed my buzzer to attract the nurse again. She came back, but this time was followed in by my doppelganger, she said nothing but ushered him/me further into the little ward, turned around and exited, carefully closing the door as she left.

He just stood there, grinning at me, shoulders hunched, questioningly, just like I would. We both said "So what next?" Exactly at the same time with the same voice, he was relaxed and confident, I was not! Why is it we behave like idiots when we should be ultra-serious? I asked him/me if we were a paradox and would we annihilate if we touched, he/I (I've got to stop these / pronouns, I will refer to him as me2 from now on in the diary) smiled and laughed, in that 'oh so familiar' way.

Me2 reached out and grabbed my right hand and squeezed, I reciprocated and was very reluctant to let go, it was the strangest and at the same time loveliest, handshake ever! I really cannot describe the feeling of holding your other self's hand and looking your other self in the eye, it is beyond surreal and yet full of warmth and love.

We hung on to each other for a time that far exceeded embarrassing for men, quietly staring, slightly smiling, just getting used to the idea that we knew every intimate detail of each other's experiences, memories and the deepest most secret thoughts. Well almost all, I and me2, knew nothing of each other's memories since the divergence, on the day of the first run of the rig. Divergence is the term me2 used to describe how we got to meet each other. His immersion into the academic world, since, in his World, the rig got relocated to the University, really shows in his understanding of what has happened and why it has happened.

We chatted about silly and almost mundane things for about an hour, before I again made an idiot of myself, I asked him if he was married to Jane and had Tom, he laughed, I felt stupid. "Of course", we both said together. I asked if I could meet them, somehow not being sure what the answer would be. Apparently they were outside the room, waiting. He opened the door and called them over.

Jane and Tom rushed in, came straight to the bed and, as best they could, embraced me. My brain did cartwheels, I passed out.

Day 407 – 12th July 2017

When I came round, the room was devoid of visitors, only two nurses were here, fiddling about with drips and syringes. I was again unsure if my immediate memories were real or hallucinations. I had a sense of loss, of isolation and uncertainty that made me feel very uncomfortable indeed.

A sudden and startling revelation popped into my head. This is my sixth day since first waking in hospital, if I am in HRT, then the rig has gone back without me. It would have run out of fuel after 24 hours or so and gone back to normal time, where approximately 16 months would have elapsed. That means, whoever it was shooting at us, would now have the rig. That must be why I have this empty feeling, this feeling of losing something. I needed to know, I asked the nurses if my other self was still here. The answer was, no, but he said I must continue with his diary, he will be back to see me later today.

I have to admit, I am really baffled, if this is HRT, why is it like a parallel world, and not just the same one slowed down, but only in the region of the rig. I'm sure that was the conclusion I came to, come to think of it, our experiments pointed in that direction too. We saw all sorts of effects that pointed to the rig occupying the same space but with time passing 480 times slower. Maybe the answer is in the me2 diary, I opened the file and found the point at which the rig had returned from its first journey into HRT. I read avidly until lunch time, I found it absolutely fascinating how different it was but, at the same time, how similar, for example the following entries on days 181 and 182 and onwards;

ME2 DIARY

Day 181 - 28th November 2016

.... Yesterday's trials went so well that I have tweaked some parameters, I have found the shortest time to achieve max pressure is 1.7 minutes. This seemed a tad too vicious so have picked 5 minutes for ramp up time and have corresponded with a 10 minute hold time.

Several runs were successful with my solid cube and have consistent data, so will run with that tomorrow with the real cube.

Day 182 29th November 2016

I am as nervous and excited as Hell, hands trembling, I am going through the same procedure, except I have put no limit on pressure, so it will run for 10 minutes at peak pressure or until I stop it. I am again writing in real time, but with difficulty as I have the shakes. One hundred and eighty days of thinking, dreaming, planning and effort, here we go. I have set it going, with full fuel tank, it's running and locked.

Watching pressure readings ramping up along the same gradient as the trials.

Not sure what to expect.

Bloody Hell!

It's gone, disappeared, just vanished, no sound, no fuss just gone. I can't believe it.

It just was there one moment and gone the next, I'm almost lost for words, what on Earth has happened? I don't know where it has gone, but squeezing the cube to higher pressures definitely caused this. It's bloody amazing, something has happened, something remarkable, but what am I to do, what if it never reappears?

Should I rebuild? Shall I tell Jane and Tom?

I've decided to tell Jane when she comes in from work. ....

There we are, there is the difference. Me2 told Jane straight away and never had to lie. Never had to report it stolen, never got abducted and interrogated, he knew whatever had happened he had done it. This is now completely different to my own timeline.

It continues;

.... it should hold for 10 minutes at peak, so it should be back anytime now.

It's not here, an hour has passed and no sign of it. Where has it gone, I've poked a sweeping brush into its vacated space, it is definitely not there, I dare not stand in the space, what if it reappeared? It is still not here, it's 5.00 pm Jane is due home, so I will lock up and go and put the kettle on.

Day 183 – 30th November 2016

Last night was a bit awkward, after lots of apologising and grovelling, Jane (and Tom) forgave me for my white lies, the ratbag (Jane) actually knew all along, she had read my back up diary on the PC, so she had a bit of grovelling to do too. Anyway, we all had a look in the garage, it was still not there. We were all at a loss, what to do next has us completely at a loss. Where has it gone, why can't we see it? Tom is completely fascinated by the whole thing, he has read and re-read the diary. He appears to have lots of theories, but they seem like over imaginative ideas to me. But, I cannot escape the fact that something new, something exciting, something outrageous has happened here, but how do I proceed. I was never expecting this so have not got any evidence now it has gone. I have been popping in and out of the garage all day, no sign of the rig whatsoever.

Day 184 – 1st December 2016

Nothing! I have really mixed emotions, the initial excitement has worn off a bit and now I have a sense of loss, I feel empty, I want to do something, but what, what should I do?

Day 185 – 2nd December 2016

Still nothing, sunny crisp winter days, feel listless and lost.

ANTIGRAVITY DRIVE - THE DIARY OF AN INVENTION

Day 186 – 3rd December 2016

I'm so excited, I'm beside myself, with a huge boiling mass of emotions.

I can't believe it.

This morning, it was beautiful and crisp, almost like a bright sunny summer's day, I unlocked the side garage door to get the lawnmower out for a service, stepped briskly inside and "SMACK!" I walked straight into the rig, I think I might get a black eye, my head is pounding. I have a large red bump on my forehead, just above my right eye. It really hurts.

But it's back!

I went out and came back in, fully expecting it's absence, but the lump on my head cemented the reality, it really is here.

How? Why?

Where has it been? ....

The Diary continued almost identically to my own, except he had no paranoia, and no attempt to keep it secret from anyone, particularly Jane and Tom. Weirdly, he had gone to service the lawnmower not to cut the grass. Me2 had exactly the same experience with the exhaust and window, and quickly came to the same conclusions that I did about time passing differently, and very quickly found the 480 times factor.

Another strange difference, without all the fear of discovery, there was no attempt to hide the rig by holding in rig time. So the term HRT was not coined. Materialising and merging were also quickly discovered as were the fascinating merging effects, strangely the same materials were used for the first merging experiments. All this done on the same day the rig returned.

That same evening Jane and Tom saw the rig disappear and materialise, twice! Also that same evening Tom had researched which University to contact. The next day's entry included the following:

.... the email, with short video clip, sent to the Professor at the University of Birmingham, has had an immediate response, mostly berating me for time wasting. She asked one very searching question regarding merging (I had included the short video of merged objects), She wanted to know about the merged object interface. My response admitted I didn't know, but would look, video it, and send clip...............

Me2 carried out the same experiments that I had done, looking at the merged object interface, videos taken and sent to the team in Birmingham. There was a quick response and a rather rapid visit from Professor Rachel Williams, along with a colleague I had never met. They did multiple runs and the diary was read and re-read. Very quickly Me2 agreed to have the rig moved to the University facilities.

I'm mentally and physically drained, exhausted with a head full of unanswered questions, it's almost lunch time but I need a sleep. I woke later that afternoon, exhausted after a very fitful sleep, aching deeply to see Jane and Tom. I really needed to see for myself how they were. After much pleading, and a few tears, it was agreed that, if I was up to it, that a visit with all my attachments would be arranged for tomorrow morning.

I had a small lunch and drifted off to sleep again.

In the early evening I picked up the Me2 Kindle to read the diary, before I looked at it, I had the presence of mind to check other settings and found that just like mine there was a cloud account. I quickly opened the Me2 diary and immediately saved it to the cloud. I picked up my Kindle and opened the Me2 diary from the cloud and saved to device. I have no idea why I felt I was doing something wrong, but it felt like I was stealing the Crown Jewels, in fact my heart rate increased so much that a nurse came in to see if I was OK.

I now had my own copy of the doppelganger diary, to read and compare, at my own leisure. Just as I was putting the Me2 Kindle in its case, Me2 walked in. The very first thing he said to me was "Have you taken a copy yet, if not hurry up, then I can have it back. I have a copy of yours, you know." I must admit I felt a little stupid. Having admitted I had a copy, Me2 said he would take the case away with the Kindle and other contents, I could have them back later. I asked if he was able to throw some light on what has happened and possibly answer a few questions. We had a long, deep and meaningful conversation trying to cover all my big questions and more.

It is now 11.00 pm, Me2 has gone and is coming back in the morning for my visit to Jane and Tom. I feel a little dazed, a bit awestruck, but somewhat relieved that I now know the answer to some of the burning questions I had in my head, it also feels a bit like an anticlimax, I should be singing and dancing, whooping and screaming with the enormity of it all but I feel strangely deflated, knowing where I am and what else is happening. Just for completeness in this diary here are some of the truly fascinating and amazing things we cleared up.

ANTIGRAVITY DRIVE - THE DIARY OF AN INVENTION

I really needed to know if this is HRT or something else. It turns out I am in a parallel universe!

A universe where both I and Me2 believe each is the original and the other exists because we made a different, but crucial, choice. It is really hard to take in exactly what this means and how it can actually, physically come about, well what follows is the explanation I was given by Me2:

Because, for whatever reason, this has all happened, the two diaries existed together and could be compared by the academics, which meant that hypotheses and theories could be made about many of the strange effects and experiences. Me2 gave explanations given to him by the academics, who are fully involved in his version of existence.

Parallel universes have long been postulated and apparently mathematically proven, but with many sub-theories about how they exist, whether they interact, diverge, converge and all sorts of other possibilities. But most agree they exist, or come into being, when decisions and choices are made, not just by humans but by the interaction of matter anywhere in the universe at any time.

It is also understood, or almost understood, that different sorts of physics are dominant under differing environments and circumstances, in our observable world, Newtonian Physics appear to dominate, but at the atomic scale quantum physics are in charge, this is further complicated by Relativity, a theory introduced by Einstein early in the 20th century (as an aside, proving these things dominated the academic world of physics throughout the 20th century.) It is also further understood that all sorts of weird things happen in the quantum and relativistic universe, that appear beyond strange to us in the Newtonian environment.

This waffling about physics is relevant because the simple act of squeezing the cube of magnets, that I had so carefully constructed, caused the quantum and relativistic world to dominate the Newtonian world in the immediate environment of the rig. Squeezing all those little magnets aligned with opposite poles touching caused, amongst other things, time to pass differently, in fact slower, in fact 480 times slower. Einstein had shown that time is relative and can, and does, pass at different rates depending on the interaction of matter in the Universe due to effects of mass and gravity distorting space, he coined the term space-time, although it is a difficult concept to visualise it is a proven theory, time does pass differently to an observer near objects of differing mass, the larger the mass, the bigger the distortion of space-time. As yet the academics in the Me2 reality (apparently that's what the academics call it, a reality) do not understand why this actually happens, something to do with compressing magnetic fields, aligned in the special way of the cube, simulating very high densities of actual matter. They have a huge dilemma, they now have two working cubes to play with, but there is huge pressure not to interfere with the cube from my particular reality, this is causing a bit of a rift between different academics and some government bodies, but more of this later.

The more astute reader of this diary will remember I took a lot of effort to make a back-up cube, which, when tested on the same rig didn't appear to work. At the time I assumed it was something to do with the attachment issue and that I was lucky not to have caused a serious problem. Me2 has confirmed this, he also made that same back-up, but never tested it himself. The researchers did, and it did not work, they even built it a new rig and it still didn't work.

Further studies found that the two cubes (original and back-up) were not identical in the way the poles are aligned, the trouble is, and this is a very major point, that even though I, and Me2, took great care in forcing like poles to attach, first in a row, or rod, then in 2 dimensions, then in 3 dimensions, contrary to what I actually thought, the cubes (original and back up) were not the same and, in fact, the orientation of spheres in the original cube is only one of a great number of possibilities (again, contrary to what I actually thought, I believed the cube was made with only the one possible orientation of like-poles touching). The academics also postulate that it is possible that the actual orientation is the only one that works and that arriving at the working cube was completely down to luck! Any other orientation would not have the same effects.

This gives the academics that serious problem, mentioned earlier, they have not, as yet, been able to produce another working cube, furthermore they are afraid to analyse the cube in detail, in case they stop it from working. Hence, the problem that is causing great arguments, they now have two working cubes, one could be destructively tested so that more can be built, destroying my cube may close off the connection between the two realities. Destroying their own original, may mean they end up with nothing, as mine could depart to the other reality, never to return, some argue the connection between the two realities depends entirely on the quantum relationship between the two cubes. I found it, and still find it, almost beyond belief that two realities exist and that I/we have crossed over. Me2 is less amazed, maybe because he is more immersed in the academic world, he tried to explain what has actually happened.

Some schools of thought on parallel universes believe that a universe

ANTIGRAVITY DRIVE - THE DIARY OF AN INVENTION

branches when a decision is made, with one universe per decision direction, others think that they do not branch at all but come into existence in a parallel way, but having a shared history, but being physically separate. This means each parallel universe share the origins. This is the case with our experience, we share the same history up to a certain decision when testing the rig. There are also mixed views on whether once a universe has diverged from the other that they could ever converge again. Our experience appears to prove that they can, or have they? If they truly converged we would actually see two histories back in the perspective of one reality. It is believed our experience is not the case, what we have done is forge a bridge, where both realities continue to exist in a parallel way. As an aside there is a whole team immersed in trying to understand the phenomenon now it has been proved by observation.

One of the more interesting aspects is why a history exists in both realities, common sense says that if the realities branched, there would be one shared history, if they are parallel how did the history in one of them be created before the decision point causing not a branch but a parallel universe. I am unable to bend my mind to it, whichever way I think of it, it appears a complete mystery to me.

Diverging, converging and bridging? I wanted to know what has happened in our dual realities, why are we bridged and not converged?

Me2 confirmed that somehow, by luck, we had created a device that simulated a massive space-time distortion and that to begin with, in both realities, time slowed down by a factor of 480 on the rig. Because, as I put it in the diary, we zoomed away in a torrent of time, the rig was not visible in our nondistorted time. Also, to start with, that is all it did (All???!!!!). When they removed the rig in the Me2 reality to the University, the academics have postulated that some sort of quantum/relativistic effect between the two realities allowed the rig from my reality to fill the vacated space left in the Me2 garage, thus existing in both realities at the same time. All the academics are perplexed by this as it has never been predicted in the physics/mathematics of parallel universes. They also cannot understand why the rig chose (if that is the right term) that particular reality to bridge, as they postulate there may be many more!

They surmise that it may not be the case, it could well be bridged to many realities, they use the evidence of the message cards, to support the theory.

One theory says that the connection, or bridge, happened in this way as this was the first parallel reality created after the rig made its first journey into

HRT, making it the shortest path, or path of least resistance. It must also be noted the academics see the Me2 reality as the first reality, meaning mine was a reality created from theirs. As a matter of interest, I perceive it to be the other way around, that my reality is the original.

Me2 had a deja vu moment, sometime after his rig was removed, he again walked into the garage and smacked straight into the rig. Naturally, at first he thought it was his original, somehow returned. When he contacted the University it caused all sorts of confusion and started a wildgoose chase, they were doing a run at the time, when he went to look again it had gone, theirs had also come back to them at the research facility. It took some time before they realised that the comings and goings of the two rigs were not coordinated. It was not until I had started to connect things to my rig that the difference was observed. They had not dared to touch the "new" rig anyway as they thought it was their own and dare not approach in case they might damage it. They set up an array of monitoring equipment and a permanent presence in the garage, which became part of the research facility, including the security aspects. All of which came in really handy once they realised it was not their rig that kept appearing in the garage.

One thing really surprised me, the card messaging was not them, they had not had the experience with their own rig and they were equally intrigued by them and have no explanations, apart from the fact that there are other parallel universes and that the messaging may come from one or more of them.

They had had a large number of theories about where the rig was coming from but had not realised it was a parallel reality. That is, until Colonel Smyth arrived, trussed up inside the makeshift cabin. They couldn't believe their eyeballs, they thought he was their own Colonel Smyth and helped him from the rig, even though he appeared to be merged, he just stood up (with their support) and walked, it was only when he was utterly confused they realised something was going on, he insisted on staying with them. Someone taped up the polythene and the rig returned. Once the two Colonels were seen in a room together and our Colonel swapped stories with their Colonel, the academics began to make sense of it and began working on the parallel universe theory.

Two things really had me foxed. Firstly, the passage of time in both realities, HRT, the bridge, the 480 factor, how can one reality be 480 times slower than the other? Secondly, how did Colonel Smyth become unmerged?

Although I am a little hazy on why it is like it is, the passage of time thing seems obvious to the academics, apparently it's a quantum/relativistic thing, time is completely relative and the way time is perceived is as a result of the observer and not the relationship between the realities, so the observer in my reality sees time is slowed in HRT. The rig being "away" for 24 hours means that about 480 days pass in real time. However, in the parallel reality the relationship with the observers view of time is the same as the original and so 480 days also pass there and it would appear to them that the rig also stays with them for 480 days. So, and this is the hard bit for me, HRT (or the bridge) is equal to both 24 hours and 480 days. This is further validated by the fact that both I and Me2 perceive ours is the original reality and before the second reality came into being the observation of time was the same as we now perceive it to be. I think I can accept that explanation, but really I'm completely and utterly at a loss to be able to really grasp the concepts. It is also this 24 hours equaling 480 days thing that allowed Colonel Smyth to become unmerged, something to do with vibrations, I'm even more unable to grasp that!

I am absolutely exhausted, I need to sleep and be fully rested for my visit to Jane and Tom in the morning. My diary is now completely up to date, as far as I cannot think of anything else to add. It's a big day tomorrow, I am full of expectations and trepidation.

Day 408 – 13th July 2017

One full week since I regained consciousness in this reality.

I have eaten a substantial breakfast which, in itself, was a big achievement due to the excitement of the next few hours producing butterflies the size and ferocity of peregrine falcons, in my stomach.

Two nurses and a doctor are, as I write this, disconnecting tubes and wires and reconnecting them to new, mobile equipment that is attached to my bed, so that the whole thing can be moved, with me propped up, ready for my trip, at last, to be reunited with Jane and Tom.

Me2 has just walked in with his Jane and Tom, they will come with me on my visit. We are also to be accompanied by the doctor, two nurses and both Colonel Smyths.

Our substantial entourage, set off at 09.30, I was expecting quite a journey, but was absolutely shocked to find that we were almost next door to each other and not in a full size hospital at all, but in a rather posh prefabricated building with only four wards/rooms one of which was fully equipped as an operating theatre. The biggest shock of all was being able to see outside, we were in my garden! Or rather, Me2's garden.

I must have shouted out in alarm when I noticed our incredible location, as all the entourage came to a sudden and rapid halt, thinking I was in pain or something. "Ah", said the Colonel Smyths, both at the same time, together, "Perhaps we should have told you". The Colonels very quickly filled me in on where we were. Once the research facility had been set up in the Me2 garage, they expanded with several modular buildings, they compulsorily purchased the immediate neighbours houses and gardens. The same day my Colonel Smyth appeared, they began to build a transit facility adjoined to the garage, just in case there were more unexpected arrivals. "And not a moment too soon" they both said together. Obviously, it was still under construction when we appeared a day or so later, fortunately, they were almost ready for us, they rushed in a trauma team and kept us in this facility, it's only patients.

In a way, it's comforting to think that this hospital unit is dedicated to the care of the three of us. But, at the same time quite unnerving, a 'secret facility', something that gives me goosebumps and twitchy bowels! We stopped at the door next but one to my room, the operating theatre unit was between us. This is the room occupied by Jane, I felt Jane2 take hold of my hand and squeeze gently, the action filled me full of dread. Nothing could have prepared me for the assault on my feelings and senses that I was confronted with once inside the room.

Jane was barely visible. Dressings, tubes, supports, cables and other paraphernalia, that I don't have names for, covered her body, including face and head, a bundle of tubes into her mouth were evidence that she was not capable of breathing unaided.

Jane2 squeezed harder to counteract my sudden and sharp intake of breath and flood of tears. I couldn't speak, the shock of it all made my breathing spasmodic all of it being in the inward direction, when I did breathe out it was accompanied by a wailing sound that felt as if it was not me making it. I could hear Me2's voice, as if he was talking into a tin can, I could hardly hear him, his voice was drowned out by my own, barely, suppressed sobs.

He eventually managed to get me under control, just hearing his voice and feeling his touch was incredibly reassuring, I stopped sobbing and asked to be told the full extent of her injuries, I insisted no one hide the truth.

Jane had received a large number of bullet wounds, the most significant being a bullet that had penetrated her cheek and exited at the back of her head. This wound is an injury she may never recover from. Many of her other wounds are serious but healing, almost all without complication. Unfortunately the head wound means she is paraplegic, and cannot breathe without help, they are not sure when she will regain consciousness, if ever. I was completely devastated, trying ever so hard to be brave, trying ever so hard to accept the reality and enormity of Jane's injuries, but I feel I am only just hanging on to my own sanity. I feel utterly helpless and empty, I had this terrible weight in the pit of my stomach, an overwhelming feeling of guilt and responsibility, I cannot allow myself to become depressed or to wallow in self-pity, Jane needs me to be strong. I needed to see Tom, so that I can fully assess our situation.

Reluctantly I allowed myself to be extricated from Jane's side and to be wheeled to Tom's room, which was conveniently adjacent to Jane's. Again, the sight that greeted me was shocking, but, this time somewhat comical. Tom was laid on his back. Stretched out in bed, all four limbs in plaster and all four strung up in the air, like some poor character in a "Carry On" film. To my great relief, Tom was conscious and grinning from ear to ear. Me2 explained that although Tom had taken hits on all four limbs, shattering bones, he had not taken any bullets elsewhere on his body. He had had multiple surgical, rebuilding procedures and would make a complete recovery in time, with lots of very focused physiotherapy.

Tom was, as I said, really pleased to see me at last. His grin did not wear off for the remainder of the time I was with him. We talked for a good hour, getting each other up to date on all the things we knew or had found out since we had both regained consciousness in this familiar but very strange place. Tom kept interjecting with "I knew it, I knew it" at key points in many of my and Me2's revelations about where we were and how we got here. He said he had suspected this sort of thing when we were investigating card messages. Tom was, obviously, still suffering, mentally and physically from the events of that terrible evening, which felt more than a little under two weeks ago. Although he kept grinning at me, there was a deep look of hurt in his eyes, he seemed older somehow, matured in an instant, an instant of extreme violence and unthinkable consequences. Tom already knew about his Mum, maybe that was the look of hurt and sorrow I could see behind his eyes.

I felt exhausted, it was nearly lunch time, I needed a rest. We said our goodbyes for now and I was wheeled back to my room. As exhausted as I was, I felt determined to make a full recovery, as quickly as possible, so that I could more effectively help and support Jane and Tom in their recoveries and rehabilitation. It is going to be a tough time ahead, I'm not sure how long it will take and, even more scary, not sure how it will all fit in the timescale that is connected with the rig and its presence in this reality.

After lunch and a nap. Me2 called in to sit with me and discuss future options. Now that I had seen Jane and Tom, I felt a new sense of urgency and excitement, although I was very subdued by the seriousness of all our injuries, I began to think about what our future may hold and, strangely, in which reality that might be.

Me2 was worried about something one of the academics was concerned with. They have a hypothesis that, just like attachment on the rig and that strange "always attached" phenomenon, they are concerned that when the rig returns that the three of us will go with it, I immediately countered that with the fact that Colonel Smyth did not return when the rig went backwards and forwards, he agreed but said that what they really mean is if one or two of us go and attempt to leave the remainder here, meaning I or we may return leaving Jane here. In which case they are concerned that Jane may just whizz off from her bed, leaving all the attachments behind, sealing her fate.

None of us, including the academics, have any way of knowing and have not found a way to experiment either. We can only find out by doing, whatever we decide, and trying our best to manage the risks that we think we understand.

There is also no experience of keeping the rig on the realities bridge (I like that, it sounds like Rialto Bridge in Venice, he he) longer than was originally intended, by altering its control programme and or refueling. There has not been a compelling need before.

They also realise someone has to go back with the rig or it may never return.

We tried to work our way through the possible scenarios:

1. Refuel, keep the rig here, but for how long?

2. Face up to the fact Jane can never return, would we (Tom and I) stay too?

3. Would either or both Tom and/or I leave Jane and return?

4. Send someone else entirely to do a reconnaissance

ANTIGRAVITY DRIVE - THE DIARY OF AN INVENTION

5. Send a team to develop a relationship with appropriate people in Reality One.

6. Plan to keep coming back and forth

7. Plan to go and never come back, but would we have to leave Jane?

We quickly realised that it may not be possible to make decisions on most of the possibilities until someone goes back with the rig to do a reconnaissance, someone who will not mind staying if it becomes impossible to return, someone who knows how to operate the rig, someone able to assess the environment, politically, legally and other important aspects. We both said, at the same time, Colonel Smyth and me! Of course Me2 meant himself and I meant me. I knew having said that, that it might be a possibility I may never see Tom and Jane again once I make the return journey with the rig, but also I could not let Me2 take the risk either. We are of course assuming we will be allowed to make such decisions, after all, I'm not sure who is in charge.

It was nearing the time of day when I lose my battle with consciousness and give in to sleep. Me2 said he would be back tomorrow.

Day 409 – 14th July 2017

It is after breakfast. Me2 is here and after sleeping on it, we are progressing our thoughts on the options we came up with last evening. The option that made most sense was the same as before, send a reconnaissance team, Colonel Smyth and me, or Me2. I emphasised that although we need this plan, my prime focus is for me and my family to make the best recovery we can, it looks as if mine are the least serious injuries so it is up to me to get fit as soon as possible so that I am in a position to best support and help Tom and Jane. I am really scared about the future for Jane. Making a return to "normality" looks forever out of reach. Me2 and I absolutely agree, that whichever of us goes with him, it has to be Colonel Smyth that leads the team. He left, promising to progress our ideas with Colonel Smyth and the Director of research. He will report back as soon as there is any progress.

I now wanted to see the doctor, I need to plan my recovery in detail, discuss the severity and prospects of Jane and Tom and to agree a schedule of visits.

Day 410 – 15th July 2017

It has been agreed that in two days, I will have a major review of my injuries and be assessed for my rehabilitation. It has also been agreed that, regardless of my continued improvement and assessments, I will be visiting Jane and Tom every afternoon, at approximately 2.00pm, starting today.

My injuries, I now find, were simple bullet wounds, SIMPLE!!!, the bullets had not pierced any major organs and had not shattered bones, they had merely penetrated through muscle, blood vessels and nerves, all of which required corrective surgery, including skin grafts on the exit wounds. It is not expected that there will be any complications and that my full recovery should be rapid once I begin physio.

I was in buoyant mood when Me2 popped in around 11.00am. After getting him up to speed on my progress, I asked him some niggling questions, the sort of question I always think about asking after he is gone from a visit, the sort that I still never ask when he visits again, frustratingly simple questions that pop into my head and never seem to be answered. Where do he and his family live? To start with they lived, as I expected, in our home (I say 'our' as it feels odd to call it anything else) they found it increasingly difficult, but still convenient, as the research facility began to grow and extend into the adjoining properties. When they realised it was not their own rig appearing, the whole operation stepped up a gear or two, temporary buildings were erected, some rooms were seconded in the house and eventually they moved out. The hospital facility was created in a major hurry, it is connected to the house and has some facilities within. They are developing a guest facility/small hotel utilising some rooms, for visiting academics, in each of the three houses, Me2 occasionally stays overnight in one of those. The family initially moved to a hotel before a suitable and secluded property was found for them, where security can be maintained. I did not realise that because they went 'public' Me2 had celebrity status, and had made a considerable amount of money by capitalising on the situation. I was amazed, all that in such a short time, there seemed to be no expense spared.

Other questions, like do you or Jane work? No, they are wealthy now and are very involved with all sorts of aspects to do with the rig. Tom is an integral member of the academic team and spends most of his time in the Birmingham facility. I wanted to know how different the two realities were, a laugh was just about the only response I got, apart from that they are the same except for the obvious. I remain unconvinced, not sure why but I am. What happened to the neighbours? Was Dave just the same? Was he involved, even? The two immediate neighbours were heavily compensated with cash and a new fully owned home of their choice (within reason).

ANTIGRAVITY DRIVE - THE DIARY OF AN INVENTION

Dave moved to Kent, he was never involved at all in any detail, although he was pleased to meet his 'nephew', when he came to see the facility and rig. Other neighbours, at the now adjoining properties, are also in discussion for purchase relocation and compensation. The feeling is that they will end up with quite a large campus here, a whole new Research establishment is being created, it is being mooted that it will be named, "The Charles Research Institute". Amazing or what?

How well have the research team taken it that their Reality One counterparts were murdered? The response surprised me somewhat, for a start they call it Reality Two! Also, all of them took it really badly, they were shocked, saddened and angered. Gregori2 was immediately arrested, questioned and subsequently deported! No amount of reasoning could dissuade anyone that it was different in this reality. The government has joined in the condemnation and there have been minor diplomatic incidents as a result. There have also been memorial services for those murdered, with their doppelgangers being the chief mourners (Including Dave, of course. Although he now has little contact). Apparently they are genuinely grieving! They say they feel as if a close family member has passed away, they feel the hurt and loss deeply, and mourn the fact that they will never meet their counterpart, unlike me, Me2 and the two Colonel Smyths. They see the magical relationships and feel the loss all the more.

There are probably more of these questions, but as usual they have slipped my mind.

Me2 had news on our thoughts on the future. He has seen both the Colonel Smyths and had a brief discussion with the Director of research. The Colonels are more than up for it and are keen to get planning if it is agreed by all concerned, they also agree that it should be my Colonel Smyth that makes the return journey. There are mixed views from the research team, The director feels that there are issues that need intense scrutiny, she/they are massively concerned that what they have could be lost if any operation is carried out without ultra-experimental control.

We both agree that this idea is probably going to go ahead. I suggested that we begin discussions with the Colonels, develop our approach and then discuss with the academics, after all we both developed this on our own in the first place. Me2 agreed but pointed out that it is very different now, he is no longer in charge and the Director's grip on everything, and he means everything, is to the point of paranoid obsession. Lunch, then visits to Jane and Tom. I am determined that every afternoon, from now on, will be taken up with our joint recovery.

Day 411 – 16th July 2017

Jane and Tom were much the same as my previous visit, Tom seems brighter now that I plan to visit each day. Jane shows no visible change.

Me2 sent a message, that he, Jane and Tom are being whisked away to Australia for some conference or other, said he will be back in three weeks.

He also said that the Smyths are busy hatching plans and may be in touch themselves before he gets back.

Day 415 – 20th July 2017

Major progress since last entries, I am off the machines and drips and have begun physiotherapy, I am mostly pushed around in a wheelchair, but also able to walk a little with two sticks.

Jane still shows no sign of waking, in fact no change, it's very worrying, I am beginning to come to terms with the fact that there will be no recovery for her and that I should start planning for a future based around her care.

Tom, on the other hand, is improving every day. He was no longer in traction, but still immobile.

Day 421 – 26th July 2017

Tom and I continue to improve, we are both on a physio programme now, I have graduated to one stick and no wheelchair, Tom is doing physio in his bed twice a day.

There is no change with Jane. No news from Me2 or the Smyths.

Today I asked if I could leave the facility, go outside and possibly see the rig. "Soon", was the answer.

Day 426 – 31st July 2017

There is, still, no news from Me2, no contact with the Smyths or anyone from the research teams. I am beginning to be a little anxious about what may or may not be happening with our proposals. I am not dwelling on it too much as most of my time is being taken up with visiting Jane and Tom, interspersed with sessions of physio and exercise, there is now an adjoining modular building equipped as a gym, with a range of equipment, steam room, showers and a small consulting/massage room. (There cannot be much lawn left, if at all in what was Me2's garden)

Jane has shown no sign of improvement, except that some of her wounds have healed, she remains in a coma, paraplegic and having her breathing managed by machines. I am wracked with guilt and trying hard to push this to the back of my mind, I need to be strong.

Tom is completely out of traction and has less rigid support on his limbs, he is able to be moved around in a wheelchair, which I take great pleasure in pushing around on our visits to Jane and our physio sessions. Tom is amazing, he brightens every day in what could be a depressing time, he appears realistic and very grown-up with respect to the injuries and potential outcomes for his Mum, but at the same time very sad and sometimes vulnerable.

Day 431 – 5th August 2017

It's about a month since we arrived in this facility, both Tom and I are making good progress, I can hobble without a stick, but use one anyway. Tom is able to use crutches for short periods, apparently he has issues with his arms not his legs when using them. Jane is the same as every day that I have seen her, I am repeatedly reminded that this is probably the best we can hope for.

Me2 has finally sent a message, they have returned to the UK and he will be in to see me tomorrow. I have not given our proposals much thought since he left for his conference, I have been focused on recovery for both Tom and myself. Now we have daily contact, life is much easier and it's all too easy to forget where we are.

Day 432 – 6th August 2017

After my first physio session of the day, about 11.00 am, Me2 arrived with both the Colonels in tow. They said we should go off to meeting room alpha, apart from being curious about where that could be, I was, in a weird, brotherly kind of way, very relieved to see Me2 again. I hobbled after them, through a door and along a well-lit, windowless corridor. I felt a bit disoriented, the corridor sloped downwards, I was sure we were heading towards the house, but the corridor ought to have sloped upwards. We came to an open space, about 3 metres square, there were three more doors, one marked "Stairs", the others each had a Greek letter, alpha, beta and gamma. Obviously three different meeting rooms, in the cellar level of the house. We entered the alpha meeting room, no one else was in the room, it was a well-equipped facility, with lots of interesting looking technology, including smart boards/screens filling all four walls.

One of the Colonel's indicated we should sit, at one end of a large glass topped table, that could seat about twenty! That particular Colonel remained standing and proceeded to activate screens and other bits of technology. An image of the research director (Professor Rachel Williams) appeared on one of the screens at the business end of the rectangular room. she greeted us with "Good morning gentlemen, particularly you Richard 2", I hadn't realised that Me2 and I were both given a number designation by other people, but then what else could they call us? It took a while, and a bit of nudging from Me2, to realise she meant me, I just assumed the 2 designation was Me2. Of course in their reality they are all without numbers, or at least number one, and us, the visitors from Reality2, are designated 2. This may take some getting used to, particularly in trying to document proceedings in this diary.

The purpose of the meeting was to begin discussing options, for the inevitable return of the rig to its original reality. This, it was assumed, would take place after it has run out of fuel, approximately 24 hours on the Reality Bridge. This, they also assume, gives approximately 480 days of existence in Reality One. As we have already had about one month of that, we have approximately 14 months left to decide what to do and prepare in thorough detail. After a long and protracted argument, sometimes quite heated, it was agreed that a reconnaissance exercise was the only sensible option and that the team can only be a maximum of three, that is, if they were the same size as me, Jane and Tom. Two is a better option, due to space in the makeshift cabin. Two would be the best option. It was also, reluctantly, agreed by the director that there should one of each of either of the two Colonels and the two Richards. None of us could agree which combination would be best, if I was fully fit. But, given that I am not yet fully mobile, Me2 was the favoured option, this could only be changed if I had a full recovery to fitness. However, it was agreed that the original Colonel Smyth was the logical choice, as he would be more likely to quickly assess and understand the situation on the ground in his own Reality.

After a few pleasantries, it was decided to close the meeting and, unless events demanded a change, we would meet one week from today. Meanwhile, each of us had to prepare a document detailing the key objectives from their perspective. It was expected that the four of us would work as two doppelganger pairs. This would ensure that we each think through in detail who should actually go on the mission, as well as what we expect to achieve.

ANTIGRAVITY DRIVE - THE DIARY OF AN INVENTION

Day 433 – 7th August 2017

From today, 80% of each waking day is fully mapped out, made up of visits to Jane, meetings with Me2, physio and fitness in the gym, eating and relaxing, much of all of that is together with Tom. We both want to recover as soon as possible and become fit enough to get back to a 'normal' life.

Day 436 – 10th August 2017

Tom2 is spending quite a lot of time with us and even more time just with Tom. Tom has told me that he is becoming increasingly fascinated by the physics and the research surrounding the rig. He has an individual goal to get fit and visit the research facility in Birmingham, before he may have to depart back to his own Reality. He is aware of the proposal for a reconnaissance mission and that it will not include him.

Me2 and I have had long discussions about what we should do on the return of the rig after its 24 hours on the Reality Bridge. We both agree our main role is as pilot, to get the rig back safely, refuel, carry out any experimental activities given to us, allow the Colonel to carry out the planned reconnaissance and return to this Reality as soon as possible.

For the foreseeable future this is my new home, with Jane, there is still no change with her prognosis. They believe that she will never regain any control of her body and that she will remain in a coma for the rest of her life. This is almost too much to bear, it makes any decision on ultimately returning to our own Reality very difficult, if not impossible. How could I even think of leaving her permanently in Reality2, while I return to a life in Reality1? No, this is our new home.

Day 437 – 11th August 2017

Today I got to see the rig! Immediately after a fitness session with Me2, Tom and Tom2, Me2 calmly announced we should all go and see the rig, right now, no time to change, let's pop in. What I saw blew me away. We left the hospital complex through a door opposite my room, that had said "NO ENTRY" on the door in big red letters. All this time I'd never questioned it! There was a small adjoining corridor which widened to encompass both the up-and-over doors of the garage, they were open. Inside was brightly lit, it looked more like what I would expect in a film studio, lots of expensive looking cameras on tripods and trolleys, more lights and lots of other electronic gadgetry. Almost hidden in the middle was the rig with its wood and polythene 'cabin' intact, the generator gently throbbing away. Nothing looked different, in fact, I was told, it had essentially not been touched, no one dare, not even the academics. Theories about everything abounded, nothing was proven, therefore, leave well alone.

It is hard enough to believe 24 hours is also 480 days as I look at the rig, but it is even more difficult to understand how the fuel lasts for 480 days, the generator had not slowed, but the fact is that it will run for 480 days, whilst on the Reality Bridge. The strange thing is, that it really is 24 hours, but the perception here is not the same, proving, as the academics repeatedly point out, that time is relative. It's OK for them, but my senses, cannot adjust to the reality of my acquired knowledge, it does not make it any less weird! Apparently, camera/video technology had advanced because of the rig's existence. They had developed a continuous high speed camera, not one that ran in short bursts, but one that ran continuously. There had been a need to see an appearance in ultra-slow, high definition, slow motion. Not knowing when it will happen, means constant vigilance, they want to observe the transition, because, to the naked eye, it is there in an instant, as I have said before no fuss, not anything it's just there. So far my rig has not 'appeared' since the new camera was developed and the inventors are keen for us to go and come back again. They have the same technology with their own rig, so I don't understand why this is different. Anyway, the whole thing, in the garage is astounding!

I asked if there was a reason he had brought us today? Not really, just seemed like the right time, was the reply. Up close the rig looked as it always had to me, even the curious effect of no bullet holes in the polythene, it's that once attached always attached phenomenon. The academics have created a portable, glass screen that has the predicted bullet hole locations in place, so that it can be lined up and those areas of polythene examined, nondestructively.

We had a good look around for about 20 minutes, before Me2 suggested we return to the hospital wing. Tom asked if he and Tom2 could stay a little longer, there were a few more questions he wanted to ask and he was sure Tom2 would be able to adequately provide answers.

Day 439 – 13th August 2017

We are to attend the second meeting later this morning, Me2 and I have prepared a short presentation based on our thoughts, quite simply being a pilot, nothing adventurous, simply to get the Colonel back to do the recce and to carry out any experimental work directed by the research team.

ANTIGRAVITY DRIVE - THE DIARY OF AN INVENTION

Me2 and Tom2 came to collect me, they asked if I would like Tom to attend, which both Tom and I readily agreed to. We were both reasonably mobile now, although we carried sticks, we could get about without them.

After a quick visit to see Jane to get her up to speed, I always did this in the hope that she could hear, even if she was not able to reply. We collected Tom and went to the meeting, which was in room alpha again.

This time the Research director and two other academics were there in person, we were introduced, but now I'm writing this I can't remember their names fully, I know they were both doctor something, one was Ali, I think, but really cannot remember the other. Also at the meeting were, the research director's PA, the Smyths and, astonishingly and scarily, the American drawl guy I met when I first met my Colonel Smyth, it is Reality2's American drawl guy, and so appears to have a completely different attitude. It really brings it home to me that there is a Reality2 equivalent for everyone. It's a bit unnerving actually, thought I'd got used to it, but I haven't. Apparently he is a military attaché, from the American Embassy, they all referred to him as agent Hendricks, no first name, very peculiar.

Everyone readily agreed to our 'Pilot' proposal, Colonel Smyth adding that I and/or Me2 would need some extra training in combat and firearms usage. After some discussion it was agreed that it was a sensible option, as there was no way of knowing what we might meet when we got there. Agent Hendricks argued for some time that one of his agents should also accompany us, but this was persistently and adamantly refused by everyone else. In the end it was agreed, two to return on a reconnaissance mission, the original Colonel Smyth, and either me or Me2 as pilot. Planning will commence immediately, daily meetings if necessary, regardless of any other meeting, there will be a full meeting once a week in the alpha room.

Both Colonel Smyths, collared me and Me2 as soon as the meeting finished, they wanted to schedule daily sessions, starting today, to begin our rapid combat training.

We both agreed, we were apprehensive, but could see the sense in being able to protect ourselves under the circumstances. They laughed in unison, a loud coughing laugh, "You", they said, "it's not you I want you to protect, it's him, me! We need you to watch my back, I don't want some amateur, crackpot inventor getting me killed!" Both of us just stood there, mouths agape, quite a bit taken aback, but then, I'm sure they have got a point, they're right, because of me, people are already dead!

After lunch, we both met the Colonel Smyths in the gym module. He had another man with him, he was introduced as Jerry, our personal trainer. It was decided, both of us and my Colonel would be put through our paces, twice a day, one session on close combat, the other on small arms weaponry. The latter, was to be in a facility, currently under construction in, what was, Dave's garden.

Jerry, appeared to be of medium build, about five nine/ten tall, I say appeared, as he was wearing a sloppy, very old fashioned tracksuit. He had a lightly tanned look, mousey hair, blue eyes that had a very definite sparkle, they seemed to be old eyes in a young face, they conveyed a lifetime of experience, difficult to describe but he had an aura of a depth of knowledge and experience way beyond his fairly youthful exterior.

He started us off with 'exercise by standing still'. I was extremely skeptical, at first, then became respectful, then was in awe. An amazing concept, he linked this exercise with Tai Chi. I actually thought he had gone mad. One hour later, as I write this, I already feel different. Truly amazing. This is what we did:

We had to be attired in loosely fitted gym wear, bare feet and no attitude. After a few stretch and loosening moves, we had to stand in line, all facing him, so that we could observe. Feet, parallel, facing forward, shoulder-width apart. Knees slightly bent, pelvis tucked under, tummy pulled in, shoulders loose, arms dangling by sides, fingers loose, pointing at the floor. Chin up, but not too far. Slightly shift weight forward so no weight on heels, it should feel shifted to balls of feet. It will then feel like you are standing in a semi-sitting position, weight on balls of feet with heels still touching the ground. We could keep eyes open or closed, but now do not move anything. When you feel you have to move, quietly sit, lotus preferred. No noise, wait until everyone has finished, then wait until asked to move.

I tried with eyes closed, but felt as though I would topple, so opened them. I lasted less than a minute standing, everything began to shake, I sat, as cross legged as I could and waited. I was very quickly followed by Me2. The Colonels lasted at least another minute. We were sat in line watching Jerry, he continued for 15 minutes, he slowly opened his eyes and returned to normal standing. We then did some stretching to finish and were dismissed with the instruction to attempt this first thing in the morning and last thing at night, do no other exercising!

Jerry's performance was very convincing, when asked how long he could hold? His reply, one word, indefinitely. I tried later before bed, could not last any longer, without having to move. I still am unconvinced how this

ANTIGRAVITY DRIVE - THE DIARY OF AN INVENTION

helps, but I will persevere. Already several muscles ache as if been through a good workout.

Day 446 – 20th August 2017

One week later, after three sessions of standing still per day, I can manage up to 2 minutes before I begin to shake, try as I might I cannot control the shaking. Me2 manages nearly 4 minutes, the Colonels are up to 10.

Tom and Tom2 have joined in, curious about the technique. They thought youth and fitness would enable them to far exceed what we do, it didn't, they can't. We have also begun Tai Chi, again I thought all this gentle and repetitive movement was a bit pointless, stand in fight pose, one foot forward, hips square, push the imaginary beach ball, pull it back, slow, flowing movements, repeat 20 times, change legs, repeat 20 times. Change pose, push the imaginary ball on different ways.

We began to learn different little moves, cat pose, dragon, praying mantis and a few others, we began to link them, it became apparent they were slow motion, attack and defence moves, repeat, repeat, repeat over and over. stand still, shake stretch. 3 times a day.

We started small arms training yesterday, the facility in Dave's garden is finished, again linked with corridors. They seem to have an aversion to going outside. Just showing us different weapons, letting us have a feel, no shooting, not yet. Apparently plenty of time for that, we need to know the weapons inside out first.

The 11.00 am meeting came and went, just a quick progress check, nothing much to report.

Both Tom and I are making really good progress with our recovery, I don't even bother with a stick now, but still have a slight limp. Tom is making great progress, he works much harder than I do in the gym (Unrestricted by Jerry). He is looking fitter than I have ever seen him, a bit 'ripped'. He actually had quite good muscle definition last time I saw him on the exercise machinery.

Jane is exactly the same as every day we see her. Her prognosis has not changed. Every day I sit and have a one-way conversation, bringing her up to date on progress. It makes me feel better to think she might be able to hear me. I live in hope that one day she will respond in some way.

Day 453 – 27th August 201

Training continues, we are making steady progress, increasing our time to stand still. The Tai Chi moves are coming naturally now, it's easy to remember each move, repeat and repeat, not really thinking, just doing. Jerry keeps adding more moves to our repertoire, he also keeps linking more and more of them together in little choreographed sequences. It's like watching a graceful ballet, all of us in unison, dancing to a private tune. We are also adding to our standing still exercise, he has introduced standing still in one or two of our Tai Chi poses. This is harder than ever, feels impossible, but Jerry, clearly demonstrates that it is not, his 'indefinite' also applies to this. I was in awe of his abilities before, I am doubly so now.

The 11-o-clock meeting was much more interesting today. Colonel Smyth2, gave a detailed presentation on their planning and the Prof gave a brief overview of the experimentation they are hoping to achieve.

The Colonel believes his mission revolves around who won the shoot out and who now owns the ground. Because of prior knowledge, all those assaulting or defending the rig on that fateful evening, know something of the rig's capabilities. Therefore it may be a possibility that someone or something is waiting for the return. It is also possible they could have given up after more than a year, when we plan to return, and it could be unobserved. The risk is, that the garage looks like it does now in this reality, all cameras and lights. He laid out all the possibilities that he could envisage, the risks and contingencies. To me, most of them boiled down to two basic scenarios, observed or deserted. However, he went through all the possibilities in great detail and gave a description of what we would do in each of them, the equipment and skills that we would need too. His presentation, with questions and answers, took three hours! The academics presented lots of issues they would like covered and the way in which they would collect data. Most of the work they want to do really is dependent on repeated return journeys, not the first one. All they really want is for us to carry recording data loggers video and audio equipment. They dare not risk attaching anything important to the rig, for lots of reasons, but, mainly because that whatever they put on the rig may stay behind and not travel if not attached, and if attached, well they just don't know.

Day 481 – 24th September 2017

Four weeks have passed since my last diary update, We have continued our intense, physio, exercise and training, including small arms and knives! I feel we are becoming very proficient at the Tai Chi that we have been taught

ANTIGRAVITY DRIVE - THE DIARY OF AN INVENTION

and can now achieve in excess of 15 minutes standing still in any of the poses which Jerry chooses. I am amazed by myself and the others.

I have broken my diary silence (There has been little to write other than daily routine) to report an amazing event/revelation. In our session with Jerry today he brought in a colleague, no name, he never spoke. Jerry announced that it is time to demonstrate why we had been training this way all these weeks. Jerry and his colleague faced each other across the gym, about 10 metres apart, both bowed their heads in unison, slipped into a fight pose, both different, then, with barely a sound, they rushed at each other in a blur of movement, arms, legs fists, heads, everything moving so fast it was impossible to see, a flurry of attack and defence, over in seconds. They stepped apart, the colleague left the room, Jerry asked us what we thought we had just witnessed. Neither me nor Me2 could speak, Tom asked if it was Kung Fu? Would we be doing that next? Jerry's reply is the revelation. He asked us to sit, he activated a screen on the wall, and showed us a video of what we had just seen (I hadn't realised everything we did in there was filmed, I suddenly became a little self-conscious). Again the very short blur of action, he played it back, in slow motion. He asked again what we saw, all of us began to speak at once, each move was, obviously, a move, we had learned in our Tai Chi sessions. Jerry then proceeded to inform us that we were proficient enough with repetitive muscle memory training to begin to use what we knew, at full speed. The repeated movements, combined with standing still, had trained and strengthened our muscles sufficiently that we can now use the full potential of Tai Chi. Apparently that is the whole point of Tai Chi. He agreed some call it Kung Fu, but that is not its true name, he instructed us to continue to refer to our sessions and newly acquired skills as Tai Chi.

He announced that from now on we would be building up to full speed and use it in combat. I had no idea this was where we were heading, I naively thought that we were just building up strength and fitness. He also introduced a new instructor who would concentrate on suppleness using Yoga techniques. We are to do yoga, first thing every morning, before breakfast.

Tom and I feel as if we are up to some sort of full fitness, neither of us really notice our injuries now, although, occasionally we both get a twinge when making twisting moves or when we take a hit on a scar. Jane, however, shows no change and no sign of improvement.

Day 488 – 1st October 2017

Today we had another full meeting, with a long and interesting agenda. First on the proceedings was a discussion as to where Tom and I will live. It was agreed we would move into the apartment at our (Me2's) house. The full house is no longer available. Jane is to stay in her room in the hospital wing. We will begin the move tomorrow. It all seems OK to us. We are not allowed to leave the campus unless on an agreed and accompanied outing. The second item, was just headed Tom2 (This means my Tom, of course). This, amazingly, was an offer for Tom to work with Tom2 in the research team based in Birmingham. They would also have occasional business here on the Mill Street, campus (Just realised that's the first time I have mentioned the street where our house is). The appointment is salaried, starting at £25k pa, and he will be studying for a doctorate alongside Tom2. I was overjoyed, as was Tom. He, we, readily agreed. He is to start immediately. The long term ramifications did not seem important at the time, the excitement of the moment clouded all negative thoughts. So, I sadly realized, it's just me moving into the apartment. Tom has a room but, I fear, I will not see much of him. I was/am too pleased for Tom for me even to mention it.

The rest of the agenda was taken up, yet again, with more detailed discussion from the Colonels on the depth and intricacies of their plan for the eventual return, in just under 400 days. It was reported that we are all making excellent progress in fitness, combat and weapons training. His level of confidence in either me or Me2 accompanying him on the return, was increasing week by week.

Day 489 – 2nd October 2017

Began the move to the new apartment, quite easy really, I have nothing, other than a few clothes and my Kindle.

Had a long discussion about the move, and Tom's new job, with Jane. As usual the conversation was one way, but I was happy to be able to deliver the news in any case.

My apartment is a complete surprise, it is nothing like the house as I remember it. Bedrooms, sitting room, kitchen, bathroom all on the first floor, the main sitting room used to be next door's front bedroom, amazing! Tom has gone immediately to Birmingham to meet the team, see the facilities and see his own accommodation on the campus, he has promised that once he gets settled in, he will get me an invite to also meet the team and see the facilities.

Training seemed quiet today without both the Toms. Me2 was also absent, he wanted to be present in Birmingham, he is an integral member of the team there, although he knows it is paying lip-service to him, he cannot leave them to it. I have every sympathy, I would rather be there too, in fact, I feel resentful, everyone but me, and I am the one who invented it, accidentally invented, but I am the only one not there.

I feel terrible now, I almost deleted the previous entry in shame, but thought it ought to stay as a testament to my selfish, self-pitying, attitude. I should be and am thoroughly ashamed of my mental trip of resentfulness and self-pity. I am not the only one. Jane is here too, she has no choice, she is here as a direct consequence of my action, how I even dare think I was hard done to, is beyond reproach. I leave this here as a reminder never to forget my true place in all of this and never to place my situation ahead of Jane's.

Day 503 – 16th October 2017

Tom is back for today's meeting, he has settled in to his new role in Birmingham, he was full of excitement as we talked long into the night in the new apartment. We both chatted eagerly, swapping news and progress. There was little to report on my behalf, his mum was the same as when he'd left, no change in prognosis. I continued to develop my skills in combat, ready for the big day. Tom pointed out to me how amazing it was that I had become so fit and reasonably proficient at this martial art, whatever it is called, and that I was now very useful with a gun. I was so wrapped up in the daily intensive training I almost had forgot to notice. He couldn't imagine how good I would be by the time our departure back to Reality1.

Tom, on the other hand, had lots of news. He was a member of the team directly involved with Me2's version of the rig. He was not allowed to take photographs (Secrecy rules) but, described some of the differences and experiments they were working on. They would not be on the agenda for today as this is not the meeting for discussing anything other than the return.

Tom, described the rig in Birmingham, it has been extensively enlarged to be three or even four times the size of our own. The attachment principles meant they now had a structure with the original rig in the centre. They almost have it looking like a real vehicle of sorts, with a chassis and six steerable wheels, it is like a mobile laboratory, it is capable of movement, but as yet they have not done so. Their larger construction can carry up to five researchers and lots of experimental equipment. The structure is completely sealed, with six observation windows and two doors. So far they have had 10 runs with people onboard. Amazingly, the rig does not travel to another reality, it does exactly what we discovered, it stays in the same place with time slowed by exactly the same factor as our own. He described some of the video taken from within the rig looking out. Everything speeded up to a blur of motion, only visible when played back at slow speeds. What they see is only the immediate environment of the rig in its new hangar sized building. They have confirmed it is their own Reality by placing clocks and other devices to be filmed from within.

Tom confided in me that he is involved in developing concepts to make the rig do the same as ours, travel to another reality. He is really not allowed to discuss it, not even with me, but thinks it would be outrageous not to do so. He went on to describe other rig developments, such as a new power source, which is a small nuclear driven power plant similar to those used in space programmes. Completely upgraded electronics and computer systems. Bizarrely, the old equipment is left on board, what is attached stays attached phenomenon. There is no point removing it. There are lots of other sensors and recording equipment. They even have equipment that can detect some elemental particles, he is not involved with that so does not know which. They are also working on communication devices and studying what happens to radio (and other waves) transmitted to and from the rig. Again, he is not involved so does not know detail. He pointed out that there are numerous other programmes and areas of research which he, as yet, has no knowledge whatsoever, but will update me as and when. All he does know is that it is a large facility with more than a hundred people involved, many teams and new professorial chairs. A massive new area of research that, in knowledge terms, is only just beginning. Excitement levels are high, not only in the academic world, but in the media and with the public too. There are regular press conferences and several documentary companies filming.

I asked if they had tried what happened to us. It took a while for him to get what I meant, then the penny dropped. Move it to a new location, see what happens to its vacated space. We had to get off to the meeting, so no further discussion.

The meeting was, as usual, dominated by the Colonels. They are continually refining their plans, working on a seemingly endless list of risks and contingencies, to the point, on my behalf, of utter boredom. I know it's a bit rude, amongst other things, but I really don't listen very intently at all, so cannot relate any detail here of the discussion. Needless to say the academics appear to love the attention to detail and dive in to the discussions with an enthusiasm that completely mystifies me. Afterwards I had chance to ask Tom another question, before he set off to Birmingham, I wanted to know if the media knew about here and the events that led to us being here. As far as he knew they did, both he and the Colonel have been seen and interviewed, questions have been asked but they are so excited by their own rig, this is being kept in the background, he also said, to my increased shame, that I was not invited to his first day introduction to protect me and his mum from media attention. It had never crossed my mind this had been so carefully thought out, but in future I will be less quick to doubt how things are organised.

Day 538 – 20th November 2017

This is only the second time Tom has been back since he moved to be with the research team in Birmingham, just as last time we talked long into the night before today's meeting.

There was lots to hear from Tom, but, very little from me. I am completely engrossed in all areas of my training, in fact I am somewhat obsessed and very competitive. When not training, eating or sleeping I spend my time with Jane, keeping her up to date on progress from all the information I am given. Me2 does not train here as often as he used to, Tom2 is hardly ever here, he is with the research team in Birmingham too.

Jane2 spends quite a lot of time in the facility, mostly with Jane. Frequently, when I visit Jane, Jane2 is there too, holding hands and chatting, a one directional chat. Usually, when I arrive we exchange a peck on the cheek and, more often than not, she makes her excuses and leaves me to chat in private. On a few occasions she stays and the three of us have a heart to heart, sometimes we get tearful and have to hug. It is so surreal hugging your wife, not wife, having the same feelings but keeping them suppressed. It's a bit awkward actually, but I don't discuss that with anyone.

Tom had heard, via the Me2 - Tom2 grapevine about my progress and the developing competitiveness, he said he was looking forward to training with us and seeing me in action in hand to hand combat and my prowess with the various handguns that we have selected. Most of Tom's news was, I am sorry to say, a bit tedious, lots of physics and maths. It brought it home to me that I was more interested in doing than understanding, it probably was always the case and may well be why we have ended up like this.

One area of news interested me greatly, Tom had taken on-board the thought I had left him with last time, he proposed a move of the vehicle to the team and after long discussions they agreed. In fact they are building a new hangar to move the, now mobile, rig. They are taking the opportunity to build the new facility with lots of enhancements that could not be accommodated in its current location (This is due to the rapid development they are undergoing, new ideas blossom almost every day). The move is scheduled for four weeks' time. The even better news is that I am to be invited to witness the event. Tom has been there quite a long time now and I was beginning to think he had forgot his earlier promise.

Today's meeting was one of the most interesting that there had been for some weeks. The Colonels have drastically condensed and reduced their long lists of risks and worked out all the contingencies, they finally have a detailed plan of who does what and when. The academics loved it and are to mesh their own plan with the Colonel's plan. The new plan is to be presented at next week's meeting. Plans, plans, plans, risks, contingencies and other bollocks, if it was not for the fact that I am to be pilot, I would not bother to attend the meeting. It's a wonder anyone gets anything done at all. Tom has gone back to Birmingham, full of enthusiasm for the preparation for the move of their rig. Me2 and Jane2 have joined me in the apartment, they are staying the night before they leave for a trip to the USA tomorrow.

Day 539 – 21st November 2017

I am both angry and frustrated with myself, last night was an absolute nightmare. After enjoying a lovely meal, prepared by Jane2, a few glasses of wine and some interesting chat, we said our goodnights and went off to bed. Their room is across the hall to mine. I could hear them, as clear as day, making love, the same noises emanating from the room as there would be if it was Jane and I, naturally it's the same noises, the same actions, the same little foibles we have, I could picture everything, I could almost feel it, almost experience it. It was excruciating, I couldn't turn off, couldn't not listen, it was the most frustrating few hours of my life, I tried headphones with Pink Floyd on full blast, I could no longer hear them cavorting, but I could imagine what they were doing it was unbelievably horrible! I thought of banging on the door and letting them know I could hear them, but that would have been ridiculous. After an hour or so I got up and went down to the gym, I ran myself to exhaustion on the treadmill and collapsed in heap on the floor sleeping fitfully until about 6.00 am. I woke with aches in every muscle possible and sneaked back up to my room to be awakened an hour later for my early morning yoga session. We were joined, on what was left of the lawn, in the developing dawn light, by Me2 and Jane2. It was the most difficult and painful yoga session I had had for weeks, aches, pains and tension. After freshening up and a light breakfast, they set off on their planned trip to LA for a week at some conference or other.

I took out my frustration during Tai Chi, fighting with a fury I did not know I possessed.

Day 552 – 4th December 2017

Quick note in the diary, before I leave for Birmingham, this is not only a red letter day because I am to witness the rig moving from one hangar to the other, but it is also the first time I have been allowed to venture away from Mill Street. I do not feel as though I have been kept against my will, as I have had purpose and direction, as well as Jane to see every day. I have not seen Tom, Me2, Jane2 or Tom2 since that awful day when Me2 and his wife left for LA. They are complete innocents in that awfulness, it was my own mental torture, but there was nothing I could do about that.

I am in Tom's apartment after a very eventful day, I feel mentally exhausted, I have been on an adrenalin trip all day and am now suffering the after effects, complete and utter knackeredness. Earlier we arrived at the campus, it was like getting into a high security prison, fences, doors, guards, cctv and strict checks on people and baggage, similar to airport security. Once inside it was like any other modern university campus, a variety of architecturally interesting looking buildings with lots of students and academics milling about or standing in groups.

I was astounded to be greeted by a reception committee led by the Director of Research and other University dignitaries. There were press and TV cameras lined up to bathe us in an explosion of flickering white light. The Director had me pose for an uncomfortable amount of time, shaking hands, first with her, then with a succession of the University Dignitaries. I was almost blinded by the time we finished and was led off in the direction of, what appeared to be, two large aircraft hangars. One was the original, and nearly new, facility for the rig when it was moved from Mill Street, the second is the much larger version where the rig will move to, under its own 'steam', today. First, I was informed, I had to perform the opening ceremony for the new building. I was both shocked and flattered in equal measures. I never expected it. Most of all I never expected the name of the new building "The Richard Charles(2) Workshops and Laboratories". It was explained the (2) was a device for the reader of the plaque, it could mean both or either! Quite clever, but what else do you expect in a university.

After all the razzmatazz of the opening the press were ushered away and we were left with those directly involved and only one or two from in the university at large. I was shown into the facility housing their rig, I was completely blown away by what was laid out before me.

The space appeared huge, big enough for a small airliner, parked in the centre was, what appeared to be, a large metallic caravan (surrounded on three sides by a vast number of electronic gadgetry, cameras and detectors) it had three axles, each with two rubber tyred wheels having a diameter of at least a metre. There was a tow bar at both front and back, two large double doors, one on each side. There was a large window in what I assumed was the front and slightly smaller windows on the other three sides. The roof was bristling with antennae of all sorts of shapes and sizes. The height appeared to be about 8 metres, width about 6 metres and length about 10 metres. A huge vehicle, by any standards, all metallic and shiny, an amazing space-age transport.

We had to don overshoes and disposable white overalls to enter the vehicle. Once inside the sight was again breathtaking. The rig was, as expected, in the centre, and just like in Mill Street the rig was surrounded by cameras and detectors. There were a variety of workbenches, seats, electronics in cabinets, computers. At the front, or end with the biggest window was an array of screens and controls, with seating giving an appearance of a bridge on a ship. I was shown to a seat at the front and strapped in with an airline type seat belt. There were no standing spaces available, so quite a few people had to leave. The door was sealed, the engine started (although I couldn't hear it) and with the 'drivers' in communication with an outside control room, we started to move, slowly (top speed is only 5 miles an hour). We were heading towards the wall adjacent to the new building. When we were within 10 metres, huge doors began to slide open revealing a large connecting corridor/tunnel between the two buildings. After we had moved half way along the tunnel, the door behind us closed and the door in front of us opened, revealing the interior of the new building. As we moved through the door the new interior was revealed to be even more huge than the one we had left, there was a marked-out space in the middle of the shiny new floor, again with equipment surrounding it on three sides. There was also an array of instruments on a low trolley, ready to move into position at the open end of the bay, once we were parked.

I was informed that there was not an enormous amount of difference at this time between the two buildings and its instrumentation, but the new facility had more potential for development. Other mobile facilities were to be brought in at a later date.

The whole party decamped and disrobed and were led to a lecture theatre within the new facility. I sat through welcome speeches, short presentations on key areas of research, all of which have set my mind racing, my mind is boggled by the breadth and depth of research they have already achieved and the directions they intend to go. We were then led off to dine with the Chancellor, the Vice Chancellor, the team of Pro Vice Chancellors and the directors of the University. I was sat with the Chancellor on my left and the Director of Research on my right. I was extremely touched that the very first thing the Chancellor said was how sorry they and everyone were for the situation Jane is in and for the events and loss that led to us being here, I had to fight back tears and take a few deep breaths not to begin sobbing. Conversation after this was filled with discussion about Mill Street, accommodation, training and so on and so on. A really wonderful experience. I realised that this is similar to the life Me2 had been living, without all my trauma, until we got here. Although nothing much has changed for him, research at the University has accelerated beyond belief. He, and his family, are still very much at the centre of it all. I am totally blown away for the umpteenth time as to how different, yet how similar the two Realities were.

After a long and full day, I find myself, sat on the edge of a bed in Tom's apartment, completely exhausted updating the diary and feeling very contented with life, even though I have very serious personal issues to deal with, not least Jane, it feels so good to be part of all of this, especially when thinking back to my initial very strange dream. It is beyond any expectation for that dream to have led to this.

Before I forget to record details of any conversations/presentations about the research, one thing needs noting here now. I think I may have mentioned it before, but, there is quite a large team focused on the core of the rig, the array of spherical magnets. They have consistently failed to reproduce the cube! Their areas of research include trying to decipher the orientation, trying a host of alternative materials and squeezing mechanisms. They have not had even a hint of any effect in anything they have done. They are contemplating dismantling the backup cube and remaking it with one sphere at a time changing orientation. I pointed out that they should do that in reverse, fix one and move the rest. Now I think about it that doesn't make sense either, the upshot is they are working on a computer programme to work out all possible orientations and begin filtering for most likely possibilities. It may take tens of years but they feel it may be the only way. There is a small but weak movement to dismantle the working cube and reconstruct, once they know the exact orientation. It goes without saying, that this is not looked on favourably, they dare not take the risk. On the plus side, the body of knowledge on magnets and magnetism is growing at an exponential rate.

Day 566 – 18th December 2017

Two weeks after Birmingham, today's meeting had the usual agenda, apart from one item - Rehearsal. I was curious but could hardly imagine what the set up would be. The agenda item was the announcement that they had the mock-ups ready in studio and will require the potential pilots and reconnaissance experts to attend weekly rehearsal, the day before the weekly meeting. Reconnaissance expert? He was talking about himself, what a farce!!

Our first introductory session is scheduled for the day after tomorrow. I am curious but very skeptical. I had a bit of a telling off at the meeting by Colonel Smyth, he thought I should know all about the rehearsals seeing as though it had been discussed at the last four meetings and fully documented in the minutes. Whoops. Should have listened and possibly read minutes.

Jane, I imagined, had a chuckle about my faux pas at the meeting, when I had my chat this afternoon. She shows little change, apart from the fact her body is slowly wasting from lack of movement, it is also becoming more rigid and fixed. The nurses turn her frequently and move her limbs, but this cannot make up for proper motion. As yet, she has not developed bed sores. The bed she is in has an intelligent mattress, constantly moving with programmed rippling and churning.

Day 567 – 19th December 2017

Today we (me, Me2 and the two Colonels) were helicoptered to Pinewood Studios, the Colonels informed us they have several installations prepared where our arrival in Reality2 can be rehearsed. (They mean Reality1, it's getting a bit tedious, 1 or 2!!!)

Pinewood Studios! Helicopter! I had to pinch myself, I couldn't even begin to think about how many famous and iconic films have been made there, not least all the 'Bond' movies. Getting there in style, amazing, first time ever in a helicopter, wow!

I am still a little in shock, the attention to detail was fascinating but very, very realistic, so realistic I am still not sure what happened. We were taken inside what they called a sound stage.

A very large indoor space, not unlike the research facilities in Birmingham. In the centre was an exact replica of my house, garden and garage, which,

ANTIGRAVITY DRIVE - THE DIARY OF AN INVENTION

once we entered, contained a duplicate of the original rig, the interior of the garage being uncannily filled with all the paraphernalia all in the right places.

Inside the house was a control room where activity in the garden and garage could be monitored. We were told we would practice in pairs, me and my Colonel, Me2 and his, occasionally, the teams would be mixed up. We were introduced to a number of people. It was all a bit of a blur, I can't remember all their names. There were a couple of academics, two colleagues of the Colonel's and an action director, all of whom would be in the control room directing and observing, along with the pair not practicing.

Today it was me and my Colonel, we were given the simplest of briefs, nothing on possible scenarios, suitably 'suited and booted' and each equipped with a belt full of pouches for compact instruments and four holsters for two automatic weapons and two knives. We were wired up with earpieces and mikes, we could communicate with each other and the control room.

At the time I felt a bit dazed, as though it was not me doing all this, being helped into clothes, belted up, wired up, stood in front of the rig waiting for orders. I had to check the rig for its imminent return, climb into the makeshift cabin with the Colonel, a very tight squeeze, it was a very awkward moment. The polythene was sealed, the garage went dark, we were instructed to wait, no other brief. I could hear movement in the garage, the odd shuffle and clunk of equipment. Then a countdown, three, two, one, action. Lights blazed, the polythene ripped open, there was a gunshot, the Colonel slumped, I was hauled up and out, face down on the ground, ankles and wrists bound tightly. I was lifted to a chair, dazed, shocked, confused, I was slapped hard on the right cheek (It is still sore as I write this). I heard a voice shout CUT. Lights dimmed, I was released, the Colonel climbed out of the rig. That went well, I heard him say. I didn't think so. All that training, useless!

We wandered up to the control room to join the others, the director asked us to sit, he started the video playback, I tried to speak, but was shushed, wait, watch first. I sat there, glumly, rubbing my sore cheek. When it had finished, the director asked all of us in the control room to think about what went wrong? He asked for my thoughts first, I protested I, we, were not ready, not prepared, not briefed. Hmm? He said, let's go again then. Everyone in position please he barked.

Again, the Colonel and I were squeezed and sealed into the polythene cabin, we gave each other a knowing look as we held our automatic pistols, safety off, it went dark. As last time I could hear similar movements. Three, two, one, action, as the lights came on we let rip with the guns firing through the polythene in opposing arcs, raking, the garage before us. We stopped after 2 or 3 seconds, there was no movement, we grinned at each other and undid the polythene ready to climb out. We stopped in our tracks, before us was carnage, six or seven technicians were sprawled on the floor, white lab coats soaked in blood, a look of horror on their lifeless faces. CUT.

Back in the control room, the same question, what went wrong? You are not giving us a chance, I protested, how can we practice if we don't know what's coming? As the words left my lips I felt stupid. Of course, how can we know, we have no way of knowing what we will be presented with, we just have to be prepared.

At that moment I had no idea at all what we should do. We were cleaned up, fed and watered, no one spoke much, shock I suppose. Back on the helicopter, into my room, sat here, weary, dazed completely at a loss. (By the way, the technicians were not dead, blanks in the guns, fake blood etc.)

Day 572 – 24th December 2017

No respite for the Christmas period, we seem to be ignoring festivities completely, which, frankly, suits me down to the ground. Celebrating is not on my agenda!

Today's meeting was quite a fiery one, lots of heated discussion concerning the rehearsals in Pinewood Studios. I thought it was a disaster and argued long and hard that we should have known what was going to happen and then developed a coping strategy, a strategy to give us an edge. The Colonel was vehement in his response, making the two of us completely skilled in dealing with the unexpected was the objective. Each scenario, including those not yet used, have been developed, based on his brief, but without his input. He, himself, is just as in the dark about what we would face once transported back to our own Reality. After two hours, of a very passionate debate, I had to concede to the majority that his approach was the right one, we will proceed on that basis, with an addition from my part to have a detailed debrief and discussion at the end of each rehearsal day. One or two rehearsal days per week are now planned. Every day of every week is fully mapped out for me now, until the day we depart. The daily session with Jane is sacrosanct, regardless of the time of day, I will not be moved on that.

ANTIGRAVITY DRIVE - THE DIARY OF AN INVENTION

Day 601 – 22nd January 2018

I hardly noticed the end of 2017 and the start of 2018, as I said before no time for festivities or frivolity, training and the daily schedule is intense and very focused.

We have given up on our weekly meetings, they became repetitive and meaningless, they only served for those involved to update each other face to face and once key people began to make excuses because they were busy doing something urgent, when really, there was nothing in it for them, the meeting became useless.

I'll say one thing for the director, if nothing else, she is very decisive. If something is not working, stop, change to something useful. The weekly meeting has become weekly sub-team video conference calls, an excellent idea, although I am involved with three (Rehearsals, Personal training and Jane), they are short and sharp, not intrusive to daily routine and can be done from anywhere within University facilities. The downside to this is that it is difficult to get an update on what is happening in other sub-teams, although I am too occupied to feel left out, I occasionally get curious. There has been a proposal for one large meeting every two months, as yet this has not happened.

Jane has never shown any sign of recovery and the deterioration of her body through lack of movement is becoming more evident, week by week. I am increasingly concerned for the future, as her condition worsens. Jane2 seems to be spending even more time with Jane and has more or less moved in to an apartment adjacent to my own.

Rehearsals are, at last, becoming meaningful. I have not put much detail here about every rehearsal, suffice to say they were similarly different! Almost all were variations on the first two, in some instances they were exact repeats of earlier scenarios, occasionally we used different sound stages. Sometimes we were taken blindfold to the rehearsal, you would expect that would make it predictably different around the rig. Not so, they cleverly took us to the first set up, blindfolded on a number of occasions, to eliminate as much as possible any predictability of that nature. Because we were mentally becoming accustomed to the unexpected, we were more and more able to get past that very first few seconds, make it out of the rig, and have, either close combat with aggressors or initial friendly help and support from waiting 'friends' or academics. Once or twice we were presented with scenarios where there was complete darkness, arriving in the night, with no welcoming parties of any description, only to meet them outside the garage, or in the immediate environs of the house. Once we even waited for daylight to appear before we made progress after arrival, only to be met by guards outside the garden manning a perimeter fence. The upshot is that, although we progress further into each rehearsal, some of which are a rerun for the first, second or even third time thrown in unpredictably, we have not yet reached an endpoint where a scenario feels completed, even those that appear completely friendly, because in that reality they were never completely friendly in the first place. The Colonel, in that scenario has never got past the point where he is treated as an imposter or a traitor. All of us have to realise, at last says the Colonel, that it is not the scenario we are rehearsing but the unexpected, how we deal with unpredictability. The Colonel believes that when we do make the return the actual situation we find will have elements from every scenario we have rehearsed, and just like Tai Chi, if we do it often enough the repetitive nature of the exercises will become embedded in our ultimate actions. As time goes on I am becoming converted to his point of view.

I have, on a number of occasions, tried to get out of the Colonel why they behaved the way they did with me and the rig back in our reality, his response is always the same. I should not have lied, beyond that he will not discuss, except that he now says he feels it was regrettable and that he will attempt to make amends as, clearly, Reality2 is a better place to be, more control, more direction, more freedom and developing science for the good of the Nation.

Day 641 – 3rd March 2018

Halfway!

Today I sat with Jane and had a long reflective discussion about the 'state of the nation' and what has happened to us since the fateful day I had that dream and got working on the Antigravity Drive, how it started as idle curiosity more than real intent. I chatted about how fantastic it was, here, in Reality2 and what a future Tom was making for himself here. It struck me that if he came back with me he could not continue with his PhD, it really hit me that he would probably choose to stay here and come back at a later date, a bit like emigrating to Australia in a normal reality. It also struck me that it was probably impossible for Jane to return too. It further struck me like a thunderbolt that because of Jane and Tom, I am also likely to choose to stay here in the long term. I wondered how Me2 would take to that and even if I would be allowed to stay.

There was no event or meeting to mark the halfway point, it was just like any other day, yoga, work hard in the gym, weapons training and seeing

Jane. The only thing that was different was that Jane2 knocked on my apartment door at about 8.30 pm with a bottle of wine, my favourite Burgundy, for a split second I thought "how did she know?" Then quickly and stupidly I realised why. She thought we ought to celebrate the halfway mark. We sipped our way through the bottle chatting about all sorts of things in both Realities. She was really curious about my abduction and appeared genuinely concerned if I was now OK about it. Just before midnight, she got up to leave for her own apartment, we had a goodnight hug at the front door, the sort of hug you reserve for a close friend or relative. We pecked on cheeks, then a quick peck on lips, I had sudden and very normal urges and I think she did too. We locked eyes for a split second then suddenly let go of each other and jumped back a pace in alarm, we both blushed, she said sorry, turned and ran to her own door. I was sorry too, mortified even. It was both natural and at the same time very wrong. I went in, shut the door and went off to bed. It took a long time to get to sleep.

Day 642 – 4th March 2018

Earlier than usual today I got up, showered and left the apartment to go for my yoga session, I intended to spend extra time in meditation. Jane2 was standing immediately outside my door, she was building up the courage to knock. She was startled when the door opened, just before her knuckles hit the wood. She asked if we could go back in and have coffee, which, semi-reluctantly, I agreed to.

Once inside she began to sob slightly and repeatedly said that she was sorry, sorry for putting me in that compromising situation, I protested saying it was just as much my fault. We hugged again, both with teary eyes, I said, "look, me and your Richard are the same person, you and my Jane are the same person, we all have the same feelings for each other, we can't help it, we can't stop it. We just have to understand that you and I, although we love each other and know each other in every single detail, we have to show restraint and respect for each other's situation. It's very difficult, I can't stop my feelings but I, we, have to control our feelings, for everyone's sake."

 We continued to hug, not speaking, not moving for at least five minutes, both still teary, both sobbing ever so slightly. A hug that was warm, natural and very comforting. We stood back, looked at each other, smiled and said at the same time, "Right, that's it then, good" We agreed to continue as normal. I went off to yoga, she went to have breakfast and then to see Jane.

Day 661 – 23rd March 2018

Train and rehearse, train and rehearse, train and rehearse, it is such hard, work, but, it is never tedious or boring. The rehearsals are showing real promise, we seem to have developed a sixth sense about what will confront us once the simulated arrival confronts us with the unexpected. If it is aggression we disarm and take control very quickly, if it is initially friendly, we cooperate and continue our mission. If it is seemingly deserted we do our stealthy recce and simulate a return. In most cases we manage to carry out our scientific work for the researchers (mostly video and secreting equipment to be left behind). More often than not we gather information and simulate a return. Both teams and both mixed up teams perform equally well, meaning any choice of pilot and recce expert could make the first trip.

One thing we discovered, very recently, even though it was quite obvious, no one had thought of it. When the rig returns it means it has run out of fuel, so how would we get back to Reality2 if there was no fuel, or no opportunity to get fuel? The answer was obvious, take some in the makeshift cabin or, alternatively, force a return early, leaving enough fuel in the tank. The first option was favoured by the academics, the second by me and the Colonel. Non-interference influenced the academics' choice. Speed, control and less complication directed our choice. In my favour is the fact that the exact amount of fuel is not known, therefore, the exact moment of return as it runs out of fuel is also not known.

Jane shows no sign of recovery and her muscle wastage continues to get progressively worse. Jane2 spends at least 2 hours of almost every day, with Jane. I often overlap with her, we sometimes sit and hold hands, hug and peck kiss, all in a very grown up way, no complications. I know we do these things for comfort and that the real feelings are suppressed just under the surface, it continues to be difficult, but as I said, we have to be grown up about it.

Me2 has not been on the Mill Street campus for weeks, I see him every time at rehearsals and we discuss projects on the video conferences, but he spends the remainder of his time in Birmingham, some of the projects are, apparently, hitting exciting phases. I have news from Tom, his project is not showing much in the way of results, in that no other rig has yet appeared in the vacated space, but he is immersed in the maths/physics of parallel universes and, he says, his understanding of the theories has come to a point where he, and his colleagues, are describing our situation mathematically. He completely lost me when trying to explain it.

ANTIGRAVITY DRIVE - THE DIARY OF AN INVENTION

Day 666 – 28th March 2018

I went to see my rig today, just for curiosity's sake. I did a simple standing still exercise, staring at the rig, not moving for 20 minutes or so, just staring, not thinking over much, almost meditative. I began to visualise our return, I could easily imagine this garage without the rig, waiting, never really knowing if it would return. Then, a thought surprised me, we would, after the return, be doing this journey on purpose, I wondered if that would make a difference in any way, given that a lot of what has happened has been governed by chance, not purposeful choices. I made a mental note to discuss with Tom.

Day 667 – 29th March 2018

I stewed overnight on my thoughts and contacted Tom first thing, over breakfast. I explained my little revelation, he said it was curious and would discuss with the team. Another thought had crossed my mind in the night about choices and in particular purposeful choice. I asked him if we had not all missed an opportunity when moving their rig from one location to another. I said they should have built two destinations and chosen one at the last minute on the journey. This being a purposeful choice may have forced a parallel universe into existence, one which they could know with certainty existed, when it came into being and it may have been available, somehow. After a fairly lengthy silence, Tom blurted out, "Brilliant dad", he rapidly said his goodbye and ended the call.

He called back at lunch, the team were very impressed and have decided to build two new bays in the newest of the two hangars. They will be identical, side by side, only in the last seconds of relocating their rig will they decide which bay to park in by tossing a coin leaving it to a chance that hadn't been predetermined. Tom was quite excited about all this and said the relocation was scheduled for the day after tomorrow. He will call when finished, or if there is anything significant to report.

Day 670 – 1st April 2018

Big news, a full meeting has been called in meeting room alpha. Not sure why it has been arranged so urgently. I am writing in real time at the meeting. Lots of people turning up, some I recognize immediately, the Colonels, the director, Me2, some academics. There are a few people I have never met before. Introductions have been made, the new people are all from the government, people senior to the Colonels.

The director, Prof Rachel Williams, is chairing the meeting, there are only two items on the agenda.

Sodding Hell!

1 Parallel Universe Research.

2 Early Return Proposal.

Early Return? Can't wait to see what that is, I have had no real discussion with anyone about it, apart from wanting to go a day or two early to keep fuel in the tank. What? I can't believe what I am seeing! To begin item 1, they have put a live stream from Birmingham on the big screen. There in the hangar, <u>two</u> rig vehicles, their own in its new bay, next to an empty bay and another version of their own in the recently vacated bay. The Prof has just thanked me for my inspiration, she said that only two hours after they vacated the bay, the second rig appeared. There was no one onboard, it has just sat there, all systems running, doing nothing. They have not yet ventured inside. Today's triumphal meeting has been arranged in order to watch the live stream as they enter, to have a discussion and gather ideas and opinions on what to do next. There were four researchers, kitted up ready to enter the recently arrived rig vehicle, much to my surprise and amazement, the first two are Tom1 and Tom2. Because of their key input and obvious link to me and Me2, they have the honour of entering first. All four have head cams, we can see those on separate screens on the adjacent wall in the meeting room. All four are now inside, each looking in different directions, to me it looks identical, but commentary from them indicates that there are differences, some gadgets missing and some they cannot identify.

Five minutes have elapsed since they entered. There is a tangible buzz of excitement in the meeting, there are a few whispered oohs and aahs. They are now making an itinerary of equipment they can identify and are numbering those they cannot. Tom sat in the driver's seat, his head cam feed went black, the others quickly followed suit, we turned to look at the big screen, the rig was gone! There was a collective gasp, in the meeting room, one or two stifled screams, then everyone began to speak at once. The noise was deafening. I'm sat here in shock, both Toms, gone! Where? When? Oh my God!

The Prof banged hard on the table, shouting for everyone to be quiet, look, she said, pointing at the screen, the rig was back. Someone in the hangar raced to the vehicle door and opened it. They turned to the camera with a shake of the head. No researchers on board. Whoever it was at the vehicle,

ANTIGRAVITY DRIVE - THE DIARY OF AN INVENTION

reached in and retrieved a large white envelope and held it up to the camera. The Prof shouted, meeting adjourned, reconvene in Birmingham as soon as we are all there. Colonel Smyth2 bellowed above the noise, he wanted everyone to wait, they will organise helicopters, we should all be there together. He also instructed the team in Birmingham, over the video link, to do nothing else, do not open the envelope, wait until we are there.

One or two of us that were based here had a few minutes to grab an overnight bag, Me2 collected his Jane, she had to come with us on the short flight. We were in the first helicopter to leave the campus, there were six of us squashed into two rows. On our row, Jane2 sat in the middle between me and Me2, my right hand clasped in her left, Me2's left clasped in her right. Apart from Me2 telling her exactly what we had witnessed, there was no conversation. All six of us travelled in silence, each lost in their own private thoughts. It was like a very bad April the first joke, a stupid deception. It was all too real for that.

Once we touched down we were whisked away in a fleet of black limos, to be dropped in front of the entrance to the new hangar. Everyone rushed, almost mob-like, into the large hangar space, there in the middle were the rig vehicles, just as we had seen them on screen, nearby there was, what appeared to be a meeting room with no walls, large table, chairs, mobile screens circling the table. There were cameras too, including an overhead camera at the head of the table, under which was the envelope.

We all took our places, although it was difficult to tear my eyes away from both of the rig vehicles, I looked at the main screen that was projecting the live stream from the camera focused on the envelope. Rachel, reached forward and picked it up, there was complete silence, no one was even breathing, the envelope was, astoundingly, addressed, 'For the attention of Professor Rachel Williams'. She opened it and removed one sheet of A4, folded in three and placed it under the camera, so that anyone viewing the live stream could read it for themselves. (As an aside, I did wonder who else was watching) This is what we saw, and heard, as she read it out loud.

29th March 2020,

Dear Rachel,

I know this will be a major shock to you and everyone at the assembled meeting. We have your researchers, they are safe and well. Richard and Jane will care for them during their stay here with us. Rest assured both Toms will be encouraged to continue with their studies here, with our two Toms, except they only have the original rig to work on.

We have taken an enormous risk in this undertaking, but we feel that the action we are taking is one that is worth the sacrifice. Also, like you, we have completely failed to unravel the structure of the cube at the centre of the rig. After many failed attempts to build a new cube, we have concluded that we may never build one unless a cube is taken to pieces, one sphere at a time, and then reconstructed and copied. We are not allowed nor even dare not do this ourselves, so here is the crux of this situation you find yourselves in. We want you to deconstruct the cube on our rig, rebuild and copy. When you have successfully done this and returned this rig to us you will have your researchers returned to you.

I know this will present you with serious issues both scientific and moral, but it has been decided that there is no alternative open to us. We know you cannot communicate with us, other than returning the rig and/or sending a crack team to rescue them, via our rig. We are able to block and control the return, it is quite simple really. You cannot send the rig back until we know there is a working copy. We have also solved some of the communication issues, there is a live link viewing into the cabin. It is not possible, at this stage, to have two way communication. Once we see evidence of a working copy we will unblock it's return. We will also share all of this knowledge with you once you have successfully completed what we ask.

Please direct extra resource and effort into making this a success for all our sakes.

Kind Regards

Professor Rachel Williams (Director of Research)

There was a moment of silence as we attempted to take in what we had just read/heard, the silence did not last long, there was a sudden cacophony of voices, all talking at once. I, Me2 and Jane2, were completely stunned, not speaking or moving. I was really worried, Tom, both Toms, will we ever see them again? I was not even thinking about what had been asked, just that it was so difficult to take it in.

2020? What is that about?

The Professor and the Colonels, went off to a press conference, the three of us, numb with shock, were ushered away to a hotel, protected from the media. There was no attempt at conversation on the journey.

Day 671 – 2nd April 2018

A meeting has been called, a closed meeting, only the Professor, the Colonels and the three of us are to attend. It is scheduled for 1.00 pm here in the hotel.

ANTIGRAVITY DRIVE - THE DIARY OF AN INVENTION

The meeting is over, I am back in my room updating my diary before meeting Me2 and Jane2 for dinner at the hotel.

Briefly, the meeting was called with just the 6 attendees because it was felt that we needed to be able to understand which options are available and what choices we make without undue pressure from others who have different interests to our own.

Rachel was clear that they will not rush into any work of any description with the newly arrived rig, regardless of the situation and emotional pressure. They are not convinced about the assurances given in the letter and, just like me and Me2, cannot envisage any way the rig can stay here if they stop squeezing it's core, as surely that is what will cause it to return to it's own Reality. They feel it could be some considerable time before they even set foot in the new rig, let alone begin to interfere with it. We all knew it would be fruitless to argue further for any other course of action. As for the date, 2020, all they said was "Time is relative, it's to be expected".

Rachel and the Colonels, referred to what would have been item 2 in yesterday's meeting - Early Return Proposal. Rachel, it seems, had been open to a discussion on an early return, e.g. ~ 300 days, which had been proposed by our Colonel Smyth. He was convinced that the four of us were as ready as we will ever be and that continuing to train and rehearse will not add value to our readiness. Furthermore he was convinced that if in Reality1 there is a hostile environment, regardless of who is in control, it is likely they will know a full tank is 24 hours and a return of 480 days and will be extra vigilant around that time window. Returning early will, he believes, give us an element of surprise and therefore an upper hand. Me2 and I both agreed that if all had gone to plan and the current situation had not arisen, that we would have wholeheartedly agreed with the Colonel and opted for an early return.

We both, also, agree that the situation with our Toms, and the other two researchers, throws a different light on the situation and at this time are reluctant to leave this Reality. We asked if it is possible to join the investigative team on the new rig? Rachel point blank refused. Too near, too emotional. We will be allowed to join a steering group. That is as near as we will be allowed.

After some reflection I proposed that we continue with the early return. Much to the surprise of the others, I argued that it will not be the two of us going, just me, and it is our intention to return almost immediately once the reconnaissance is complete. Only then will we be in a position to really understand the options. I pointed out that I need to return for Jane in any case, and that in all likelihood Tom would have elected to stay to complete his doctorate. After further discussion it was agreed that 'Early Return' was back on the agenda but not yet approved.

We were just about to finish the meeting when Jane said to hold on, we were missing an opportunity with negotiating and with cutting short the return of the boys. She pointed out that, although a two way live conversation was not possible, surely a one way one was. None of us could see what she meant. Somewhat exasperated, she continued to point out that we need a volunteer to stand in the rig and say something like "We agree to your proposal, but first we need proof and reassurance, I (the volunteer) am willing to travel in this rig, right now, back to your Reality, to witness that everyone is safe and well and to gain assurance that when, ultimately, we stop squeezing that the rig will not return. If you agree to this, when you return me to my own Reality, we can work together on a much shorter timescale" We all agreed that the logic seemed sound, Rachel agreed that it was a pretty good way forward, but first we need a volunteer, not one of you, she added very quickly.

That concluded the meeting, I feel a little better about the situation and hope the early return is agreed.

Day 680 – 11th April 2018

I just heard from a conference call with Rachel, that an early return has been provisionally agreed. Also, they are going to progress Jane2's idea, they have a volunteer, Dr Graham Holding, he is the leader of the parallel universe team, Tom's supervisor and boss. He obviously feels he is well placed to take on the challenge.

The early return date is proposed for 3 weeks from today, ample time apparently.

The negotiation is to take place next week.

I have had long discussions with Jane, getting her up to date on everything, particularly with Tom. I am almost sick with worry about him and Tom2, as is Jane2. Me2 seems to be taking it all in his stride, he is preparing for the return, he believes it will be him not me that will be going.

Day 685 – 16th April 2018

Today, Graham Holding is to enter the rig from the alternate Reality in

ANTIGRAVITY DRIVE - THE DIARY OF AN INVENTION

Birmingham. He is to sit in the seat which Tom sat in, that appeared to trigger the abduction of the four researchers. I am booked to watch on live video link, at 2.00 pm, in the alpha meeting room, along with Jane2. Me2 is in the hanger to see it live. Almost as predicted by Jane2, as soon as Graham had delivered his negotiation speech, the rig vanished. It has not yet returned. It is now 4.00 pm, we have abandoned the meeting room to get on with other daily routines. They will contact us if there is any news.

Day 688 – 19th April 2018

The rig has not yet returned, there is a general concern setting in that it will not come back and that if it does Graham will not be onboard.

Jane's temperature is up a degree, they say not to worry, this type of thing is normal, she will be given intravenous antibiotics if it continues to rise.

Day 689 – 20th April 2018

Jane has been on antibiotics for almost a day, her temperature continues to rise, if she does not improve by the end of today they will give her different and stronger antibiotics.

The rig, with Graham onboard, has still not returned. There is almost alarm now, the media are whipping up a storm and some are demanding an enquiry.

Day 693 – 24th April 2018

Jane is really deteriorating, her temperature has not been controlled and is holding steady at 39. I spend most of my waking hours by her side, holding her hand and trying to reassure her that everything will be OK. Jane2 spends much of her time here too, we mostly take it in turns to sit with Jane so that she is never alone.

I am so focused on being with Jane I have not attended training or briefings on the early return, today they informed me that Me2 will be the pilot. Although it is a bit hurtful, I just shrugged it off, being with Jane is more important right now, in any case the return is a formality, nip back to Reality1, quick recce, return to Reality2.

Day 699 – 30th April 2018

Today is the day of the return, Jane is hanging on, her temperature continues to be high, holding steady at 38.5, they now have a continuous fluid drain on her lungs, the doctors have told me she has pneumonia, I feel sick with worry.

Jane2 is to sit with Jane while I observe the departure of the rig back to Reality1.

Big news, we just heard that today is a double return day, the rig with Graham onboard has also reappeared. He is, apparently, ebullient about his trip. There is even more and greater news, two of the researchers have also returned, with Graham, to show the good faith of those in the alternate reality. None of the them are either of the Toms, they both elected to stay as they are having a great time with four Toms working together. It sounds a bit nightmarish actually, I also feel a little concerned about mix ups between them all. I mean, how will anyone know, how will I know if it is my Tom when he returns and which Tom belongs in which Reality, no one except the Toms themselves, unless there are obvious age differences with associated changes in appearance. If they choose to play around with identity mischief, no one would know.

We are all assembled in the garage, me, Me2, both Colonels, Rachel and other essential personnel. There is a real air of excitement, particularly on top of the news from Birmingham. Me2 and the original Colonel are suitably attired in army combat gear, belts, equipment and weapons all in place. I am to operate the controls, rather than Me2. At 10.00 am precisely, they climbed into the makeshift cabin, I set the control programme to reduce squeezing in one minute. The rig door was dropped and locked. We all stood back, someone started a countdown -

10, 9, 8, 7, 6, 5, 4, 3, 2, 1 -

We saw a sudden blur of movement, behind the semi-opaque polythene, accompanied by the beginning of a yell of alarm, then it was gone, we had no time to stop it and no knowledge of what had happened.

We stood there, shocked into silence, for what seemed like ages, but it was actually only just under two minutes. Without any warning, with a sudden and very loud wailing sound, the rig returned. Someone whipped open the polythene, the Colonel was there, wailing, merged, in exactly the same position as he first arrived here. He was, again, helped to his feet. He looked extremely shocked and flustered. There was no evidence of Me2.

The Colonel immediately started to bark orders, Colonel2 and Jerry (I was amazed to see he was already suited and prepared identically to the

ANTIGRAVITY DRIVE - THE DIARY OF AN INVENTION

Colonels) were squeezed into the little cabin, 3 pre-prepared rucksacks were also crammed in, as was a container, that looked like a suit carrier, full of water and a 10 litre container of petrol. The control programme was quickly adjusted and before I could utter a word or even take a breath, the rig was gone.

The Colonel urged everyone to join him in meeting room alpha. He ran out, we all followed, sounding like a troupe of jabbering chimpanzees. As we rushed into the meeting room and began taking seats, the Colonel was already inserting a memory card into a reader on the computer. Images flickered onto the screen, there was an instant and stunned silence.

Colonel Smyth gave us explanations for his sudden return and subsequent actions. He had secretly thought that it would be a distinct possibility that he was trapped in this reality for good, hence the preparations, he explained that the instant the rig left this reality he was literally sucked into the rig, back to his merged position, when they got back to Reality1, Me2 disassembled the cabin and sent the rig back, in a bid to unmerge him, unfortunately, the once attached rule came in to play, in the instant the rig returned, the cabin was also back in place and he could not be left behind unmerged. We hardly heard his explanation we were all goggling at the screen, open-mouthed. What we saw, had me gasping for breath, I had to keep wiping away tears. I saw Me2 had hurriedly placed a camera about 4 metres from the rig before trying to effect the Colonel's release, but that is not the upsetting part. There was no garage. No house. No row of houses. Nothing but brown/black desolation, I could vaguely make out scraps of ruins in the distance. Before he sent the rig back, Me2 picked up the video cam, did a 360 degree pan, walked back to the rig, removed the memory card and gave it to the Colonel.

The short video was playing on an endless repeat cycle as the Colonel spoke. He explained that what we could see was consistent with the aftermath of a thermonuclear detonation. He estimated that the event had taken place at least 6 months hence and based on the evidence he had seen he believed our location was less than one mile from ground zero, the detonation centre, it was possible there were high levels of radiation, hence the rush to get the packs, containing radiation suits and other equipment, sent back with Jerry and the other Colonel. In the video clip we could see one wreck of a building that was estimated to be about 3 miles from their location. The Colonel gave me a knowing look, he thinks he knows what that building was. Their first mission was to get to it and check for survivors and/or find out what the larger scale of the event was. This was one scenario we had not foreseen, one we never planned for, or rehearsed.

Meanwhile, he added, the rig should be back here now for 24 hours, to protect it for the duration of the mission. No one is to enter the garage until it is certain we do not have a radiation problem. He also added that, for the time being, there is a complete press and media blackout, there is to be no disclosure to anyone outside of the University research teams. I am too stunned and shocked to write any more today.

Day 700 – 1st May 2018

Jane2 was brought up to date on all the news last night, she joined me at Jane's bedside.

Jane's temperature was almost 40, the breathing machine and drain were making terrible gurgling noises. There was a doctor and two nurses fussing about with equipment and intravenous drips and things. Fortunately I had had some quiet time with her last night and I let her know the news about Tom. I didn't mention that her home had been nuked.

Jane2 was very quiet, I knew when she was quiet and looking serious, it meant that she was brooding or worrying deeply about something, I guess it must be that Me2 is in such apparent danger and her Tom is also missing (although we hear he is OK and enjoying his experience). I tried to reassure her that everything, although it appears complicated and dangerous, will actually turn out OK, everything is under control. She shook her head, tears welled up, it's not that it's something else was her whispered response. She said we needed to talk, not here with Jane, outside, over a coffee.

We went to the cafeteria in the house complex, got two strong black coffees and selected the most secluded table that we could. I was full of trepidation, I hoped this wouldn't be embarrassing. Jane2 appeared to be having great difficulty in speaking and wouldn't really look up from her coffee. She eventually looked up and, with eyes full of tears, blurted out "Richard, I'm so, so sorry, Jane has gone, she passed away in the night, the doctors have done all the tests three times, there is no doubt, only the machines are keeping her body going." I was completely and utterly floored, I couldn't believe it, wouldn't believe it, it can't be true, she's breathing, was all I could think.

I leapt up ready to run back to Jane's side. Jane2 grabbed my wrist and wouldn't let go, I tried to shake her off but couldn't. She had more strength than I remembered, she pulled me to her and fully embraced me, her chest heaved with each huge sob, I stopped fighting, and clung on, I cried like a baby for a full 30 minutes.

Finally she whispered, "They need your permission to turn the machines off". I could only manage a nod, too weak to speak, exhausted by my outpouring of emotion. OK, was all I could mumble. Let's go.

All I could think about was that Tom was not here to say goodbye to his Mum. I felt some resentment to those in the alternate reality for taking Tom, he might feel like that too when he eventually returns. Every step back to Jane's room was like wading through treacle in lead boots, my legs and feet just didn't want to take me there, by the time we reached the door Jane2 was having to support me as if I was a drunk, incapable of walking. As soon as we entered the room the doctor stopped what he was doing and gave Jane2 an enquiring look, I perceived she gave the briefest of nods. The doctor then said "Mr. Charles?". I too gave an almost imperceptible nod. Jane2 sat me down at the bedside and put my hand in Jane's, again she nodded, I can vaguely remember the doctor dictating the date and time and other facts at the same time as flicking a number of switches, then checking vital signs on Jane, none of it really registered, it was all shrouded in a mist of tears and grief. I was sobbing relentlessly, it felt as if I would never stop until my heart broke completely and I would be pronounced dead too.

Jane2 was holding my other hand, the nurse slipped a chair under her and we both sat, crying for almost an hour. Eventually a nurse came and coaxed us into standing, and managed, with a not a small amount of physical guidance, to get us to the door. Once we were through several nurses went in to the room behind us.

Day 703 – 4th May 2018

It's been three days since Jane, my soul mate, my only real love passed away. I have managed to get something in the diary about that terrible day, but it is only an approximation of what happened, how I felt and how I continue to feel. The weight of it all, everything, has brought a cloud of blackness in my head and a heavy weight on my chest, so heavy I can hardly breathe, I've eaten almost nothing, when I do it's like eating sawdust and wood shavings. I am lost, lost in a pit of despair, nothing matters, nothing makes sense, just blackness and heaviness.

I hear someone knocking, I'm not answering, nothing, no one is important, no one can help, I don't know why I bother to continue, I only bring death and destruction, no one will want to know me once they realise it's me that's the problem.

Jane, Tom, all those people in my garage and possibly millions more all gone, gone because of me. I don't feel I can live with myself, I can't bear the weight of responsibility. I don't deserve to live. I deserve to be nothing.

Day 705 – 6th May 2018

Today we knocked down Richard's front door, he was collapsed in the kitchen, curled up like a baby in a corner. He was delirious and barely conscious, he looks as if he had not washed, shaved, changed his clothes, eaten or had anything to drink since Jane died.

This is Jane, from this reality, bringing the stupid idiot's diary up to date.

He is so annoying, no different from my own Richard, stubborn and more self centred than he ought to be. Why does he think it's all about him? All those people have suffered, not him. I'm so cross with him I'm writing this so he can read it later, when he's recovered and stopped feeling sorry for himself. No one has any sympathy for him now. The self centred, arrogant idiot. But I still love him. Did you read that Richard? I love you! Of course I love you, you are my husband, even if you are from a different reality you are still my husband!!!!! Angry does not describe how I feel right now writing this. Euarghhhhhh!!!!!!!! I don't want to lose both of you, one in another reality, your Reality, and you trying to die in a heap of self-pity. He is back in the hospital wing, on a drip (he's a drip!), on suicide watch. The sooner he gets over this the better, they are waiting for him to make decisions about Jane's funeral.

Day 712 – 13th May 2018

I have never felt so ashamed and humbled as when I awoke this morning, the morning after I was discovered in a state of complete self-pity. Of course I have read Jane2's entry from one week ago. I am so ashamed I dare not leave the apartment I cannot face anyone. Jane2 texts or rings every hour or so. No one else seems to be interested.

I have insisted that Jane be kept in the mortuary, no funeral until Tom returns. Several people, Jane2 included, have pleaded with me to reconsider. I will not, I am certain that both Tom and Jane would want this. I have been informed that the rig went back to my Reality after 24 hours, it came back, unoccupied, an hour later, it is still here. They have not detected any residual radiation. Investigating the control programme showed it has been sent back for 3 weeks. Other than that there is no news, no video, no messages.

ANTIGRAVITY DRIVE - THE DIARY OF AN INVENTION

There is no news of any real consequence from the team in Birmingham, there is still an upbeat mood after the return of the researchers. The only news is that they are to begin planning the programme of work as soon as there is a full debrief, documentation and conference to discuss all the new information from their alternate reality.

One curious bit of news from Birmingham is that they are mapping Realities. Briefly, this reality has a bridge to my own, it has some unknown bridge, or possibly the same bridge, (the cards), there is the alternate reality from Birmingham, which we know, also, have the link back to my own or another version of my own (there are two Tom's), it possibly also has a bridge to the other reality with the cards. The alternate reality, may have other bridges, this was hinted to Graham. The whole parallel Realities thing is getting very complicated, especially with time differentials and with multiple versions of "known" people, is it a circular relationship or are they all different, hence the mapping. The whole thing is deliciously intriguing, imaginations are running wild, particularly in the media. Speculation is rife about what the future may eventually hold if they find a way to make permanent bridges that come into common use. Each Reality may have the opportunity to learn from the others, but I can't help thinking of the unknown Reality, the one with cards and messages. It may be that instead of friendship and cooperation between Realities the opposite may be true, what if there is a reality where the whole World is governed by extreme right wing politics, it's possible they should be avoided somehow. I wonder if there is a reality where my Jane was never wounded so badly and survived to share these experiences?

Day 713 – 14th May 2018

Jane2 has coerced me into leaving the apartment, there is something I should see. She led me to the little bit of garden that remains, it's a little corner that has the benefit of the Sun from mid-morning to early afternoon. Jane's favourite corner, she had all the bird feeders there. As we walked up, from behind one of the sectional buildings, I could see the garden now had a low, wicker fence, with a narrow wrought iron gate. The gate bore a plaque - Garden of Remembrance - Dedicated to all those who lost their life in the 'Mill Street Massacre' - We walked through in silence, the garden itself was largely unchanged, in one corner was a solid looking wooden bench, also with a plaque - This bench is dedicated to Jane Charles from Reality2, loving wife and mother. I was again overcome with grief and collapsed onto the bench, Jane2 sat beside me, put her arms around me, cradling me into her bosom. We stayed like this for almost an hour until my tears subsided.

I asked who had been behind all this, apparently it's everyone, particularly Jane2 and her Richard. I was lost for words really, but knew that this would be a place I could once again talk to Jane. She said there are plans for a memorial stone of some kind with everyone's name on.

Day 717 – 18th May 2018

There is no news from Birmingham, they are still documenting, planning and mapping. No one is in a hurry, since Graham's return they know both Toms are OK, they are quite happy continuing their research in the alternate reality.

There has been some debate and not inconsiderable pressure to send people (Jerry equivalents) a few at a time back to Reality1 instead of waiting 3 weeks for the rig to go back as programmed by Colonel2 and his team. So far it has been resisted, the team are there for reconnaissance, there is no point putting more people at risk.

I have been to Jane's seat every day for a little chat, it is very therapeutic, I feel more myself day by day. Tonight Jane2 and I are having a meal in her apartment, I am confident we are now very 'grown up' about our relationship and we both manage to keep our, quite natural feelings, under the surface.

Day 718 – 19th May 2018

As I predicted, the meal was excellent, the wine superb (my favourites again) and our behaviour exemplary. I am almost certain it is the same for Jane2 as it is for me, I do not find it easy to behave as friends or relatives, it would be far easier to fall into each other's arms and behave as husband and wife. I left for my own apartment a little after midnight.

Today I have an appointment with the Professor of Psychology from Birmingham, I was a little uneasy agreeing to do this, I felt some resentment, no it's fear. I fear it's like an intrusion into my private world.

However, I agreed because my behaviour has not been good and has been really obvious to the people on campus, I feel I would be letting them down if I fought against it.

How wrong can you be, here I go again, self centred, all about me. I made the classic mistake of mixing up psychology and psychiatry. Well it was not really about me at all, not in the way I thought it would be. The Professor, Clint McDonnell, was beginning a study and would like me to be part of it.

He feels there is a unique opportunity to study the human mind and behaviour by comparing individuals from the two realities, because, as he pointed out that before the point of divergence, each was one individual, the same person, now they have travelled a slightly different path, are they still the same or different. If they are different, why and how did it happen. He was also interested in the relationships that develop, particularly between the same individuals, such as me and Me2. I wholeheartedly agreed with him that it was a superb opportunity and one which had not occurred to me at all. As he described his approach and reasons for doing the study I was absolutely fascinated and felt enthusiastic for him and his team, he has really got something here and I look forward to taking part and seeing the results.

I picked up my training regime today, it was really hard, I feel exhausted, a break in very hard fitness work, really shows when you take it up again, the longer the gap, the harder it gets. We are not rehearsing, most of that team are in Reality1.

Day 721 – 22nd May 2018

The rig is due to return to Reality1 today, the time in the control programme is 10.00 am. All the relevant individuals are assembled outside the garage, the Colonel and his team will not let us any closer. He rattled off a list of reasons for doing this, to be honest most of it makes sense.

At 10.00 am, precisely, the rig vanished. As usual no fuss, no theatrics, nothing, just vanished. We waited for an hour, nothing happened. We all agreed it makes perfect sense to go about our business, we will be called if needed. Jane2 and I went off for coffee in the little cafeteria. Halfway through our second coffee, one of the Colonel's men rushed in and asked us to go to room alpha as soon as possible, it was 11.40, we left our coffee and half eaten biscuit and dashed to the meeting room as quickly as our legs could carry us.

Standing at the business end of the table were Jerry and Colonel Smyth. Jerry had the appearance of someone who had been sleeping rough for days, grubby, weather beaten and in desperate need of a change of clothes, we could smell him from where we were at the other end of the table. He still had that youthful, peaceful, sagacious look about him. Even in the state he was, he looked as if he was ready to start the mission not be at the end of it.

Colonel Smyth gave his distinctive cough, the signal for us all to shut up and pay attention. He addressed us all, in a very subdued tone, - Its very mixed news I'm afraid. It has been confirmed there has been a thermonuclear, or similar, skirmish, not one that has obliterated the World or indeed whole countries but one where major cities have been reduced to dust in many of the larger countries, probably, on all continents. The team did reach that ruin we observed in the earlier video clip. The building was, as I suspected, one which I knew very well. It is the same building that Richard was taken to, early in his own personal adventure. Let's call it a Government building. Below street level there was a substantial complex, designed to withstand the sort of conflict we now know has taken place. However, it did not fully withstand the conflict, there were very few survivors, as far as we can ascertain they were rescued and taken to a safer area at some point after the dust settled. What remained did contain a variety of equipment that has some record of the event, some of which has been brought back by Jerry for us to clean up and analyse. They, Richard, the Colonel and Jerry managed to view and listen to recordings from just before the conflict and know with certainty that substantial areas of London, Birmingham, Manchester, Liverpool and some other larger towns and surrounding areas have gone. It is known that a government of some sort has survived and Martial law is in operation. They do not yet know the extent of the overall impact on the entirety of the UK. They also know that some of the Capitals or major cities of Europe, Russia, The Far East and North America have also suffered the same fate. The timing of the conflict was 11 weeks and 1 day after the "Mill Street Massacre" and is a direct consequence of failed diplomatic efforts to resolve that situation. It appears that 80% of weapons were launched within the first 10 minutes the duration of the entire event was 5.5 hours from the first impact to the last. Jerry has further news that, I'm afraid, is rather worrying.

Jerry gave us a fairly detailed description of the events after he and the Colonel arrived in Reality1. They followed Me2 to the ruin and caught up with him there, they saw no other surviving buildings or signs of life or any remains of life. After a detailed search they found the records discussed earlier. One room, largely intact, was a communications centre. They managed to tune-in to several broadcasts around the world and came to the conclusion that the event was a Global Disaster and that it may not yet be over. They got a hint of land battles in different countries in Europe. The Colonel then made, with hindsight, a huge mistake, he attempted to contact his own organisation in order to establish a link and begin to negotiate a relationship. They were told to get off air, maintain radio silence, stay where they were and wait to be contacted. It was decided that Jerry should conceal himself, if anyone arrived, as his presence would be more difficult to explain. Indeed what took place confirmed that to be a good decision.

ANTIGRAVITY DRIVE - THE DIARY OF AN INVENTION

A single helicopter appeared 15 minutes after establishing contact, Jerry disappeared himself, but was able to discreetly observe. The helicopter landed, a crack team emerged, overpowered Richard and the Colonel, drugged them, trussed them up, heaved them into the helicopter and were gone in, literally, seconds. Jerry waited around for days but there was no further activity. He gathered what he could, took plenty of video footage, including the abduction. He then made his way back to where the rig would appear and waited.

He believes the best course of action is to expand the rig if possible and send him and a team back to Reality1 to retrieve Richard and the Colonel or to be able to further develop the relationship that they may, against odds, be developing right now.

We were all stunned into silence throughout both of their presentations. As soon as they finished everyone began talking at once. Jane2 looked visibly shaken, Richard was taken, he may never come back, she was on the verge of tears. I took hold of her hand and squeezed.

Eventually the room was brought under control and it was agreed we would disperse and await further communication, meanwhile we had to maintain complete secrecy and media blackout.

There were lots of questions and discussion, most of which went in one ear and out the other, I couldn't focus on what was going on, I was, Jane was, deeply shocked. One stream of thought did stick in my mind – How are they dealing with radiation and its catastrophic effects, are Richard and the Colonel sick with it now? Come to think of it, is Jerry OK, he didn't look as if he had gone through any decontamination procedures.

Jane and I went back to the cafe, more coffee. We mostly sat in silence, neither of us knew what to say, it's not just Richard, it's the whole thing, nuclear war, bloody Hell, nuclear war. From my stupid little dream all the way to nuclear war! All those millions of people, gone, all that history, culture, architecture, the future. I felt so helpless, it was really difficult not to slip really quickly into the depths of self-pity and despair. I couldn't let that happen, Jane needs me to be strong.

Day 722 – 23rd May 2018

It took all my inner strength, as fragile as it is, to both remain sober and not to take advantage of the relationship Jane and I have. It is very, very difficult not to be completely normal with Jane, she is exactly the same as my own Jane, she is Jane. If ever we are again tempted, by each other's actions, it will be difficult to resist.

Nothing happened all day, there was very little activity wherever we looked. Just little knots of people talking in hushed tones. I don't think anyone could take it in, let alone really know what to do next. Jane and I sat about in the cafe, hardly talking, holding hands occasionally, there seemed little point in discussing it. We waited to be summoned.

Day 723 – 24th May 2018

It felt as if days had passed, we were sick of tea, coffee, fizzy drinks, water and snacks. The cafe was permanently full, the counter staff appeared to be the only busy people on the campus.

At 2.30 in the afternoon we got the call, meeting room beta. It was the first time I had been in there, it was more of a lecture theatre than a meeting room, it could have easily seated a hundred in curved, tiered rows. Entering, from the shared lobby with alpha, took us to the highest tier. We sat near the front on the lowest level. The whole place filled rapidly, probably everyone on the campus.

As Rachel and Colonel Smyth walked out at the ground level, there was an immediate and hushed silence. The anticipation was painful. I'm not sure anyone was even breathing.

Neither of them said a word, the lights dimmed and the large screen behind them shot to life. The video, I surmised, was a compilation from a variety of cameras held, or worn, by the three of them in Reality1, as they journeyed from Mill Street to the ruined building, the only ruin visible. They appeared to be in an alien landscape, there was no commentary, but we could hear sounds, like the crunch of their feet as they walked through dust and gravel, occasionally one of them would speak to describe what they could see or to ask a question of the others. There was no background noise, nothing, no birdsong, no distant hum of traffic, no wind noise, total silence. If they stopped walking, talking, breathing, there was an absolute, ear aching silence. It was total destruction, there appeared to be very little evidence they were walking through what once were roads, buildings, houses, there were no wrecks of the buildings, no burnt-out cars or lorries, no bent or distorted lampposts, no stumps of trees, just the mind numbing crunching of gravel, vague outlines of roads and occasional low mounds, these were, I assumed, the actual remains of buildings, covered in gravel and dust.

ANTIGRAVITY DRIVE - THE DIARY OF AN INVENTION

It was almost a relief when they arrived at the ruin. There was very little that was recognizable above ground, just a burnt and blackened shell of one corner, protruding approximately forty feet into the air. It took quite a lot of searching and scrabbling about to find an entrance into the lower levels, they located a staircase, strewn with rubble and had to clear lots of it by hand, they were still hopeful they would find survivors at the lowest levels.

We watched them searching deserted corridors and rooms, lit only by their torches, descending to lower levels, deeper and deeper underground. They eventually reached levels that appeared not to have suffered damage and had a low level of emergency lighting. Everywhere they searched they found evidence that they had recently been occupied and abandoned in a hurry. Eventually they stumbled upon the communications centre, we saw some of the recordings from there but the edited video jumped forward to a view from Jerry's headcam when he was discreetly observing the abstraction of Richard and the Colonel. There were eight of them, in completely black uniforms, faces and heads masked, carrying a variety of weapons, looking extremely, stomach churningly, spine tinglingly effective. Totally awesome, scary and very, very capable. The video stopped, the lights came up, there was a collective intake of breath, at last, we could all breathe again. A faint hum of conversation almost began, the Colonel held up his hand for silence.

The Colonel informed us that decisions at governmental levels had been made, we are to construct an extension to the rig, modify the rig (power supply, equipment and controls) and effect a mission to establish peaceful relations and to secure the release of Richard and the Colonel, both of whom are citizens of this Reality.

Firstly we will send Jerry and two others to gather more intelligence and to establish a base from which we can work.

I had absolutely no idea how or where they would do that, but, knowing Jerry's abilities, I'm sure they will be successful.

We are all to maintain media and off-campus silence. We will be called again when there is anything to report.

The room emptied almost as quickly as it filled, the Colonel motioned for us to stay behind, they had a proposition for us.

The Colonel and Rachel came straight to the point, would I like to join the rig refurbishment team? The team will, after all, be modifying my rig, the rig I built that started this whole thing. I snapped their arm off, of course I would, I had been scared I was being sidelined, this is just what I needed. A purpose, a reason for being. I can do this and wait for Tom to return. Not only that, it looks as if there is no future at all back in Reality1.

Jane was asked if she too would like to join the team, with a focus on planning. She also wasted no time in agreeing.

When do we begin, we both said in unison.

DIARY FOUR - BUILDING BRIDGES

Day 724 – 25th May 2018

Today I began, what feels like, a permanent beginning, here, in Reality2. A new phase in my life, without Jane and separated from Tom. The only physical connections remaining with my own reality are the rig, Colonel Smyth and my tablet computer containing my diary. I try not to think about what has been lost, obliterated, back there, back then. Time really is relative, I feel as if I have completely lost track of it, when I try to think about how much time has passed since my dream or the Mill Street Massacre, I have real trouble getting an accurate or consistent figure. Time and dates almost seem unimportant compared with the scale of day to day events.

At 10.30 am we are scheduled to hold the first meeting of the refurbishment team, in the garage, around the rig (Its strange to think, that after all the things that have happened it's my rig in my garage, well Me2's garage but they are identical). Rachel and Colonel Smyth will be there to start the process off and give us our objective - what we have to achieve, when we have to have it done by and the budget. That will take some getting used to, I never had that sort of discipline when first developing the rig. When I look back now it was a very hotchpotch effort of amateurish trial and error. No wonder Reality2 is so different. The University took control, in a very professional way, and systematically controlled its development, understanding, knowledge and the wider sharing of information including the impact on society at large.

Jane2 met me in the cafe half an hour before the meeting, it is just two days since the return of Jerry and the rig. The mood in the cafe, indeed on the whole campus, is downbeat and sombre, people are still gathered in knots, talking in hushed and shocked tones, seeking out each other's company, not wanting to be alone with their thoughts. There is a genuine feeling of loss, it's as if it has happened to them and their relatives, reminiscent of the feelings of those who lost counterparts in the Mill Street Massacre.

Putting everything into perspective, although we were a little deflated, we both agreed it was exciting to be involved, good to be taken seriously and definitely good to be working together. Our team, including Jane2 and I, included; Team leader - Dr Ged Green, a research physicist, specialising in off-Earth construction, Engineers - Dr Phil Thomas and Dr Avril Lennox,

Engineering Technicians - Baz Goodall, Xavvy St Just and Ed Morton, Software and Control Systems Specialist - Dr Esther Jacobs. We were also able to draft in any additional personnel as required, as long as we could justify them.

We are set up to work closely with the return team, modifying the rig to facilitate their objectives, incidentally I am no longer included in that team. Money is no object, we have been given an open budget from both the British and American governments, via the University. Time is of essence, they want results quickly but not at the cost of safety. Our overall objective is to modify the rig, in line with developments in Birmingham, so that passengers are easier to carry, along with equipment for experimental and intelligence purposes.

We kicked off immediately. Jerry and a colleague are planning to return to Reality1 at 6.00 pm. They are going to begin the establishment of a base. I've no idea how, but there is no time being wasted for the retrieval of Me2 and Colonel2.

We left the garage and assembled in the alpha meeting room. Ged began by showing plans and pics of the finished and extended rig in Birmingham. The biggest issue he could see was size, the garage will have to be demolished along with some relocation of sectional buildings, it would also mean, the memorial garden would have to be moved. The design, it's construction process and technology are already developed, we merely have to plan the two projects (the rig and its building) and get on with them.

I objected, I felt he was jumping the gun by a mile. I pointed out that the rig is completely different, for a start it's not from this Reality, also it is in the garage sat on a 'bridge', it is there by some quantum effect we do not yet understand. Don't forget the bridge is both 24 hours and 480 days, if we destroy the garage it may not come back again from Reality1.

I had started quite a heated discussion, but I was adamant we needed to carry out tests first. I also suggested we need to co-opt one or more theoretical physicists to get us past this point and to assist in experimental design. I was certain this was more than a construction project. I held my ground and the construction advocates conceded, we opened a video link to Birmingham and connected with Graham, he ought to be best placed to give a quick response and maybe suggest a new team member or two. It was a relief when he agreed with me and added that we should capitalize on opportunities when the rig is scheduled to travel between realities, try things, but in a considered way, bearing in mind the potential fragility of the situation.

ANTIGRAVITY DRIVE - THE DIARY OF AN INVENTION

It was Jane2, yet again, who saved the day. She pointed out that there is an immediate opportunity, the rig departs in exactly 1 hour and 15 minutes, it was short notice, but why not just clamp something to the rig or even drill a little hole and attach a small object of some sort?

The team quickly agreed and headed for the garage, we had to be there to control the departure in any case. Once at the rig, suitably recorded on video, Baz and Xavvy, using a small G clamp, attached a 2.5 cm square of thin metal plate to an unused door strut. They also drilled a small hole through the metal and strut and inserted a nut and bolt. They collected the small amount of metal expelled from drilling and studiously weighed it.

At 5.30, Jerry and an anonymous colleague arrived with supporting team, the two of them were squeezed into the cabin, along with a huge array of equipment which was shoe-horned in too. I could see, spades, a pickaxe, lump hammers, bundles of metal rods, tool boxes and other unidentifiable packages and rucksacks. There was not an inch of spare space in the little wood and polythene structure, it's a wonder it didn't burst open when taped up. It was obvious they had used a mock up and planned in detail the location of every object to make optimum use of the space available.

They had another two loads of equipment and provisions to send to Reality1 in repeated return journeys. Neither Jerry nor his colleague uttered a word throughout the loading exercise, his support team appeared to be communicating in numbers, obviously a sequence, well rehearsed and well operated.

They were gone at 6.01 precisely.

The moment the rig disappeared, the small metal plate, the clamp and the fixed together nut and bolt, fell, with a little clatter, to the concrete of the garage base, all caught on slow-mo video. We made no attempt to retrieve them as we knew the rig would return almost without delay. The collected metal scraps from the drilled hole had disappeared too, but not the tiny amount of metal from the metal plate.

The rig reappeared and was reloaded in a similar way twice in succession, the whole operation was over and the enigmatic support team were gone by 7.00 pm. Each time we observed that the clamp, metal and bolt repeated their rejection and restoration, as did the collected metal scraps.

We sent the rig back for a duration of one minute, in order to retrieve the clamp, metal and bolt. We assumed Jerry would know to keep the rig space clear and as we had no instructions from them not to send the rig back to

Reality1 we also assumed it was OK to do this whenever we deemed it necessary. We were not at all sure if the metal it's clamp and bolt would always attach when the rig was here in Reality2. We would have to wait and see. I suspect it will, it's like a reverse of attaching things back in Reality1.

The rig returned, the metal, clamp and bolt reattached themselves. This time we purposefully removed them from the rig, we sent it back again. The filings disappeared. When it returned, the metal, clamp and bolt did not attach, but the metal filings appeared in their receptacle.

Not quite as I predicted, but, it is like the reverse of the attachment principle, except the objects do not have to be always attached, very strange. So, we can't attach an extension to the rig here in Reality2. Whatever is constructed has to be attached in Reality1.

Day 725 – 26th May 2018

We learned this morning that there will be a repeat of yesterday's efforts for the return team. Two more of Jerry's colleagues and a pallet of equipment and materials to be delivered in three runs. Apparently, this is to be repeated for the next three days. That will be a team of ten and more than five pallets of equipment and materials. I can't wait to see what they build. More intriguing is how it will be concealed and not be obvious in that bleak landscape, surely they want to remain covert, only to be discovered if they wish to be.

At 2.00 pm we convened in the alpha meeting room to discuss our findings and develop a way forward, whilst still attempting to meet our objective.

I started the whole thing off by pointing out that we cannot construct modifications and extensions to the rig here, but we can follow Jerry's example, design them here, prefabricate them here, send them to Reality1 to be added to the rig. Ged was excited about this approach, as it had parallels with constructing a space station in orbit, his own area of expertise.

In fact, if we design and build a new cabin, prefabricate, and send to Reality1 for construction, we can send more people and bigger sized modifications as the rig gets progressively bigger.

There was general agreement that was the way forward, but the garage will still be too small. Again, I argued that the garage must remain the same as it always had, we cannot risk damaging the Reality Bridge. In my view the garage has the space, we just have to modify the rig to fit. May be we could make it long and thin, have retractable wheels like on aircraft, make it a

ANTIGRAVITY DRIVE - THE DIARY OF AN INVENTION

hovercraft, anything. The thing is it cannot be the same as Birmingham, it has to be one that will fit it's circumstance. We need to be creative, once we have a bigger cabin we can do lots more things, it may change design as we progress, but let's get designing.

At last I had full agreement, all the team members became enthusiastic with the idea. Ged called us to order and got us into two smaller groups to come up with ideas that we can share later in the day.

My sub-team stayed in alpha, the other went off to another meeting room. With me were, Esther, Avril, Xavvy and Ed. We initially threw lots of ideas in about all sorts of mods. Avril, who appeared to be getting quite frustrated by this approach, shouted loudly for us to stop, slow down. She said let's learn to walk before we run, focus on the extension not the mods, let's just see how we can expand the space available. She was right of course and she had an idea. We shut up and listened. She explained that it's quite simple, staring us in the face, the rig fits in the garage with all its sides/doors raised, they lock in position like a cross-shaped roof, if we use that to start construction, fill in the four corners, we have a roof that is 6 metres by 6 metres. That will give us a rig that is 6 x 6 x 2 metres, surely that's big enough to get us going? It will give us 8 extra rig cube spaces, either as separate cubes or linked. It will have the original rig in the centre.

We were all stunned into momentary silence, then all began nodding and agreeing with Avril this was the obvious way to develop the rig extension. I suggested we build one at a time, a cube on one side using the current door as its roof, but two sides will then open to fill the corners, just like the existing doors. In fact if we made two new cubes on opposite sides, their sides would lift to fill all four corners, with at least one of the cubes carrying the parts to fill in the remaining sides and floors.

We all agreed, we felt that was the way forward, it made perfect sense, use what we already have as the basis for expansion, but first we have to get the others to agree and, secondly, if they do agree, to take it steady, run trials, make sure it will travel with door-flaps open and attachments that are sent back from this Reality and added in Reality1, behave as expected.

The other team came back to join us, they presented first, they had a large number of interesting mods and add-ons, quite a few of them made real sense too. The add-ons were, in some cases, very elegant, but all were overly complicated.

We presented just the one idea, but in some detail, we had sketches and an outline of the programme of work, including the first steps to test the theory of the design. Everyone loved it, the idea was very quickly adopted .

I volunteered to travel back to Reality1, to open a door and also to fix a small bracket on the rig that would be taken to Reality1 from Reality2.

It was agreed, we would use the rest of today to prepare and carry out that quick trip back to Reality1 first thing after breakfast.

Day 726 – 27th May 2018

Jane and I ate yet another hearty breakfast in the cafe, I was to return to Reality1 after all, albeit briefly. I should have been looking forward to it, but, I was full of trepidation, I know the sight that would greet me and I'm not looking forward to it.

Colonel Smyth and Rachel were waiting for us in the garage when we got there. The Colonel was adamant that I should not go back, we cannot afford to be without both Richards, was his argument. I'm afraid to say we had a blazing argument. I lost! I feel like sulking, taking my bat and ball home. I won't, can't, what we are doing is too important. One of his men, was briefed, I set up the control programme, he took the bracket and some tools and was gone. He will not be coming back today, he will join. Jerry's team. The obstinate, self centred part of me has now become determined to travel back to Reality1, it's now a personal and secret goal, one that I will make every effort to achieve.

The rig materialised an hour later, one of the doors was open and the bracket firmly attached as planned. We were so pleased with that positive result we didn't realise that the cabin was occupied and minutes later there was an almost imperceptible moan. When the polythene was pulled back we saw our first casualty, a horrific sight, a young man, features barely recognisable, with partly healed and very infected burns to at least 50% of his body, someone pointed out, as we were calling for help from the medical team next door, that he must have been like this for months, how on Earth has he survived? We dare not move him, we waited for the medics. The trauma team arrived, the very same people that had helped the three of us.

It brought it all back, it took an enormous amount of self-control not to lose it. We cleaned up the little cabin, lots of disinfectant, and got ourselves back on track. We now know we can proceed with our idea of design, build and prefabricate here and assemble in Reality1.

ANTIGRAVITY DRIVE - THE DIARY OF AN INVENTION

Most of the team went off to the laboratory and workshop to work up the design and the overall build plan. Once they have a fully documented design and plan, the full team will meet again, with Rachel and Colonel Smyth in attendance. It is hoped they will approve and we can then get on and build. The team are aiming for that meeting to be 5 days from today. Meanwhile Jane and I were free to do anything we wished.

The very first thing we did was attempt to visit the casualty. There was tight security, no visitors, not even us. The doctor curtly informed us that they were under control but was not allowed to discuss detail. We made our way to the garden for a bit of down-time.

Day 728 – 29th May 2018

Jane and I, with appropriate permissions and accompanying close protection guard, made a visit to Birmingham. We set off yesterday, stayed overnight and got back this evening.

We had asked if we could meet the team working on the rigs, in the interests of research for our own project. The real reason we were there was that we were extremely curious about progress with the core's deconstruction and the developments based on the new ideas from the alternate reality.

We were not disappointed. When Graham visited the alternate reality, they gave him many ideas on how the deconstruction may be approached, which he and his team later developed into possible methods and had subsequently done trials on the non-working backup cube to test them. They now have a working process and are currently working on that backup to validate the overall deconstruct, reconstruct methodology. The biggest issue was removing the plastic resin and then not allowing the individual spheres to rotate, or flip, their magnetic orientation. It is all done with lasers, microfine, cutting and etching lasers. The marvel to me were the compression plates touching the surfaces of the cube, six instead of three, each made of a matrix of removable plates, corresponding to the number of spheres, each with their own micro rams. The micro rams were retractable to be replaced with laser components. All is automated, roboticised and environmentally clean, overseen from a control room next door. They never actually remove the resin, just separate each little cube/sphere by micro laser cutting. They are able to etch each sphere with its own serial number and orientation marks, remove, test and replace at will, they can also remove smaller arrays of spheres, 2 or 4 at a time, and replace them. They "re-glue" with a very accurate spray of a molecules-thick layer of molten resin, which they can apply, laser cut and reapply as many times as they wish.

They were about halfway towards the full orientation elucidation of the backup cube. It was scheduled to be completed in four days' time.

Another exciting development is that they will use this equipment to construct new cubes. The enthusiasm and excitement levels are very high in the team. They are certain we will have a new working cube inside four weeks.

Graham also hinted that with knowledge he gained from their counterparts, who were 2 years in advance of us, in the alternate reality that they believe they will be able to build a permanent bridge between the realities, with, at the very least, a two way communication pathway.

Day 729 – 30th May 2018

No news from our project team, they are working day and night on the designs and plans. They do not wish to reveal anything early, suffice to say everything is on track.

Jane and I are almost inseparable, we go everywhere together, it feels natural, we feel natural together, no one appears to notice that we are not a "proper" couple, no one except our psychologist friend.

Quite often, when we are not expecting it, the Professor (Clint McDonnell) or one of his team, would just seem to appear, or request a meeting. Apparently they are like it with everyone on the project, not just us.

Right on cue, there was Clint, waiting for us in the cafe, he beckoned us over to sit with him. After the semi-formal niceties of meeting, he launched in, went for the jugular, he wanted to know if we had slept together yet, made love, had sex, how far had we gone. We both must have blushed, said nothing, looked embarrassed. Ah, just tempted, not followed through just yet. Why not, he added?

He was amazed at our response, we said it would be being unfaithful, cheating, having an affair and all the ugly things that go with it. What would people think, Jane only recently passed away, the other Richard, lost in Reality1, it would look crass, uncaring and unfeeling.

He could see our point, but at the same time he could not. Think about the logic of the situation, before a certain point in your joint time-line, there was only one of each of you, you knew each other in every intimate detail, this is not a different person you see in front of you now, it's that same person, you became two people, but the same person with the same memories, same feelings, it is not only natural to have feelings for each other it is inescapable, impossible to resist, no one in your situation should be denied a normal relationship, you are man and wife, you looked each other in the eye and said your vows at your wedding, it is not right that you have to suppress your feelings. In the long run, it will do more harm to resist than to give in to your desires. We found it difficult to respond, we both just looked at him, saying nothing. He smiled and added, as he got up to leave, "It's up to you, I've said my piece". We ordered coffee, hardly spoke, hardly looked each other in the eye. After a long awkward silence, I said I was popping back to the apartment I'd forgot some papers. Jane came too, she was going to freshen up back in her own apartment. We walked together, no contact. I broke the silence saying I thought it still felt as if there would be something very wrong about it, she just mumbled something I couldn't catch. Oh, oh, I thought, that's a sign something is wrong, she always does that when bottling up something for later.

We arrived at my door, hers was opposite, I moved away, unlocked and opened it, I turned my head to say that I would see her later, the words never left my mouth. Jane rushed towards me, pushed me through the open door and followed me in, she deftly kicked the door shut with a slam, at the same time she was removing her jacket, kicking off her shoes and scrabbling at the buttons of my shirt. Our lips met with a jaw jarring thud. I fell over backwards onto the hall carpet, Jane on top, we grabbed and ripped at each other's clothes, she was on top, then I was on top, we rolled and twisted, our hands were everywhere, frantically removing stubborn obstacles of clothing, taking time for rough caresses of whatever our hands had chanced upon, from that first jaw jarring, face coupling our lips had not parted, breathing was difficult, our mouths, through desperate necessity, separated with a pop, we sucked in air and dived in for more, lips grinding, tongues dipping, searching, caressing trying to tie a lover's knot. I entered her with eye popping force, we both let out a groan, the relief, the weight taken from my, her, shoulders, I'm where I should be. It was about to be over in seconds, I was ready to climax, Jane kept going, she writhed and gyrated her hips frantically, we continued to kiss, our tongues making renewed efforts to get tied in knots, I kept on pumping, thrusting, heaving, any thoughts that I might stop were gone, we moved in mad-abandoned unison, thrusting faster and harder, our bodies making clapping noises on contact no longer kissing, breathing heavily, rasping unrecognizable words of emotion, then it was over in a crescendo of all things carnal, we collapsed in a sweaty and exhausted heap. We continued little kisses, both crying, laugh crying, kissing lips, cheeks, neck. I withdrew, collapsed onto my side against the wall, she turned towards me, caressing my face, she just smiled and said "At last".

An hour later we woke, sweaty and exhausted, where we had collapsed on the hall floor, every bone and muscle in my body ached, it was a real effort to stand. We helped each other get to our feet, we stood, facing, holding hands and burst into laughter. What a sight, hair stuck up like we'd seen ghosts, clothes half on, half off. I still had one sleeve of my shirt on, she had her panties on one thigh, I had one sock on, she had her bra dangling with one strap clinging to her watch. A comical but wonderful sight. We made it through to the bathroom, took off the remainder of our clothes and showered together, washing and rinsing each other, tenderly caressing, occasionally kissing.

I got dry and was about to get dressed, when, uncharacteristically, Jane took my hand and led me to the bedroom, we climbed under the duvet, cuddling, kissing, caressing we had the most tender and loving intimate adventure for the rest of the day, exploring each other's body like it was our first encounter, I fell in love with her nipples, could hardly leave them alone, tweaking, kissing, licking, sucking. We made love over and over, intermittently falling asleep, waking, making love again and again. We eventually fell into a deep sleep well into the night, cradled in each other's arms, we couldn't have been closer if we had tried.

Day 730 – 31st May 2018

At breakfast, Jane announced she was moving in with me, no arguments, she had decided, I couldn't, didn't, want to, argue. We just grinned at each other over muesli and coffee. From today we are back where we should be, husband and wife. I didn't even feel guilty, I wasn't even thinking of consequences. All that was important was that we were together, not suppressing feelings, accepting them. Maybe Clint was right, there is a way of 'being' for people caught up in the joining of parallel universes, something we had never known before, but it appears we had better get used to it. Yet again I'm a pioneer!

Later we went off to the hospital to see if we could gather any more news, again we were ushered away, nothing we can do was all that was said, everything under control. We made our way to the workshops, again we were given a cold shoulder, we were told to come back tomorrow. So, like love-struck newlyweds, we went back to bed. There was no better place at this point in time.

ANTIGRAVITY DRIVE - THE DIARY OF AN INVENTION

Day 731 – 1st June 2018

Alpha meeting room, 10.00 am. Designs and drawings on screen, on paper, sketches, detailed plans and sequences, everything was laid out. The team looked as if they had not slept, changed clothes or washed for days. Everyone pored over it. It looks great. The basic idea had been developed to a really high level. The overall design and sequential plan of journeys to and from Reality1 to do the construction were agreed. Rachel and Colonel Smyth complimented everyone for a fantastic job. The go ahead was given, prefabricated build would begin tomorrow, with the first trips beginning in 5 days' time.

Yet again it was two of Jerry's men to be drafted in to do the first stages of construction. I never argued, my time would come.

The design and sequence were very similar to our first suggestions, initially not a lot can be packed in to the small polythene cabin so several journeys supplying parts before construction begins in earnest. Once the first two sealed additional cubes are constructed, the construction accelerates with the additional space. Nothing is removed from the rig, it would reattach itself in any case.

The four filled-in corners each have a slightly different roof, all raised by 25 cm, to better accommodate passengers, whilst still fitting in the headspace of the garage, the walls of each corner cube are mainly clear polycarbonate.

Once the enlarged rig is finished, modifications will begin, starting with a new nuclear power source, upgrade of rams and control systems. I found that fascinating, because as mentioned earlier, things cannot be removed. The way they achieved all these was truly marvellous. Seating was to be added, ultimately it could carry a maximum of 10, leaving room to carry equipment and other objects, including provisions. The whole build was to have a duration of 25 days. With final completion 27 days from today.

Once the meeting was over, Jane and I sneaked off, back to the apartment, back to bed. We really do feel like newlyweds, the initial excitement has not worn off, we are finding new ways to bring pleasures unforeseen, experimenting with gusto, inhibitions completely overridden. Sex has never been this good, this exciting. We are enjoying the experience too much to bother finding out why.

Day 732 – 2nd June 2018

Today, two of Jerry's team arrived at the garage, apparently it's a scheduled change-over day. They announced that there would be a further two this afternoon.

We duly sent them back at 10.00 am precisely. The rig returned, 15 minutes later with two, very dirty, very smelly soldiers (I assume Jerry and his team are soldiers or armed forces of some sort, but really not sure). They emerged from the rig, not speaking, no emotion showing on their faces, not even looking fatigued, just dirty and smelly. We tried to engage them in conversation, tried to glean some information about Reality1. There was no response. As they were about to exit the garage, I asked one of them if they knew who the casualty was that they sent back. He stopped in his tracks, asked me to repeat my question. He then said there had been no casualties and no returnees. That I ought to think twice before making jokes, this was a very serious business after all. He then left after he felt I was suitably admonished for my flippant remark.

There had been four of us in the garage at the time, Me, Jane, Ed and Xavvy. We were a bit taken aback by the fact that they didn't appear to know about the casualty. We agreed we would wait until this afternoon's shift change to ask again before alerting anyone.

At 2.00 pm the new pair arrived, again no conversation, they climbed in, we sent them off, 15 minutes later a smelly pair returned. Again we attempted conversation, nothing. This time Jane asked the question with almost the same response, they appeared to be genuinely unaware of a returning casualty.

We subsequently contacted Rachel with our news, she too was surprised and said to leave it with her.

The four of us retired to the cafe for refreshments. The conversation was all speculation about what had happened, was the returned casualty a stowaway or were they just being mysterious and secretive. Maybe they are not allowed to talk about it. If that was the case they were strange responses they would have just remained silent.

The Colonel strode into the cafe, asked us to join him in alpha. We scuttled after him. Waiting for us in the meeting room were Rachel, the doctor and Hendricks.

The four of us were asked to sit. Colonel Smyth started the meeting by announcing that it appears we have a situation. He briefly restated the little bit of background that we all knew, the appearance of the casualty and the apparent lack of knowledge of his existence from the returning team members.

He, himself, had debriefed the four returnees, he was sure it was genuine. Jerry and his team had not found any casualties and in fact they had not even found bodies. They had not put the casualty into the cabin.

The doctor gave a quick summary of the casualty's condition. He had just over 50% burns to his body, mostly on the left side, approximately half of the burns were full thickness wounds. In his professional opinion, he estimated that the burns were no more than 4 days old when he entered the cabin. Also, the burns were caused by combustion heat, not explosion and definitely not from a nuclear detonation, the wounds are entirely inconsistent with that. He is currently sedated in a temporary coma to assist with the healing process. Furthermore, his blood and plasma were tested for contaminants, there were none. His DNA was profiled, we have a match.

Rachel, the Colonel and Hendricks all said in unison, "Well, who the hell is it, who is he matched with?"

"Tom Charles"

Everyone in the room gasped, Jane almost fainted, I manage to stop her falling off her chair.

There must be some mistake, do the tests again. Was all I could muster.

"We have, three times, we are sure."

Hendricks broke the stunned silence, he wanted to know which one of the four Toms that we know about is he.

No one could answer with any certainty, as far as all of us knew, all four were currently in the Birmingham Rig's alternate reality. The Doctor then delivered his final revelation, this Tom Charles is at least 5 years older than the Tom Charles from our Reality! Several forensic medical tests confirm it. The only possible conclusion we can come to is that he is a fifth Tom, but where from, how did he get in the cabin and how was he injured?

A thought suddenly struck me. I said "The cards, the messages. Could it be?

A video conference call was made to Graham in Birmingham, he was brought up to date, we needed to know, could this be one of the four Toms? He was as certain as he could be that it wasn't, they had no plans, when he was there to allow any of them to travel on a rig, in fact they don't have one, we have theirs. I asked about the rig from their other reality, Graham could not answer that, they could be doing anything, but, he thought it was unlikely. He also suggested the cards and messages, but had no idea how that could happen.

Day 733 – 3rd June 2018

No news from the doctors, none from the project teams in Birmingham and only everything proceeding to plan here on the Mill Street Campus.

Jane and I spent the whole day in the apartment, we are discovering new and exciting intimate details about each other we had never known before. It really is like being newlyweds. I cannot understand why I didn't know that Jane loves to be on top, loves to be in control, she takes making love into a whole new direction for me, it's like role reversal. Having said that, I'm not complaining it's marvellous.

Day 737 – 7th June 2018

The project team are ready one full day ahead of schedule, they plan to send the first two loads today with one of the Colonel's men on each trip, they have been suitably briefed and trained. They will begin the rig refurbishment and once the two extra 'cubes' are attached, more equipment can be sent with engineers and technicians from the project team, their security in Reality1 will be taken care of by those first two travelers. All the team are in the garage to witness the first departure, full of eagerness and anticipation.

Incidentally, there is no news from the doctor.

Both departed without incident. I am reliably informed that if all goes to plan the rig will return in 4 hours. New marks were painted on the garage floor for the new size rig space. It has to be kept clear at all times. The rig is back with two opposite faces of the original rig having a new cube made of tubular steel and 20 mm plastic sheets, two sides of which will swing up to form the roof of the corners of the extended structure. One of each was swung up in here in Reality2 to allow entry for more frame and plastic sheets and other items needed to finalise the shell of the extended rig. It was duly sent back for construction. The rig will be back tomorrow morning.

ANTIGRAVITY DRIVE - THE DIARY OF AN INVENTION

Day 738 – 8th June 2018

The rig is back, it looks amazing, the original rig barely visible, all of its sides are permanently fixed open, forming five of the nine new roof panels, those existing panels have also been faced with polycarbonate sheet. In fact the whole of the new structure is encased in polycarbonate sheet. There are new doors, this time on hinges to open in a more conventional way, the whole structure is perfectly sealed and is, therefore capable of carrying passengers and equipment in all parts of its interior. The tatty polythene cabin is still in place and always will be.

The serious upgrades are now planned, nuclear power supply, upgraded electronics and computer systems. A new control panel, to make it easier for the pilot, switches and dials instead of having to get into the code of my original control programme. There will also be lots of sensors, cameras, data loggers and lighting.

The equipment is all loaded along with five passengers; two engineers (Phil and Avril), two technicians (Baz and Ed) and our systems specialist (Esther). I am not allowed to travel with them, strict orders from the Colonel are not to be taken lightly.

The rig is planned to return the day after tomorrow. The whole rebuild project is almost two weeks ahead of schedule, but it does not appear rushed.

Day 739 – 9th June 2018

News from Birmingham, they have concluded the analysis of the backup cube, it has been deconstructed, tested and rebuilt. It still does not work.

Today they are removing the working cube from the alternate reality's rig. There is a huge amount of fear that as soon as squeezing is stopped that the rig will depart back to its own Reality.

I am in the cafe waiting for news from every direction, the anticipation is killing me.

No more news from anywhere. We are in bed I have to put this tablet down, Jane is going to take my mind off things.

Day 740 – 10th June 2018

They have removed the cube from the Birmingham rig, it did not return to the alternate reality. I am unable to conceive of a way that the scientists in the alternate reality can do that.

The process to deconstruct, test and rebuild has begun, it is estimated that this will only take two days, the robotic system can work very quickly, following the same pathways developed from the backup cube, to finally resolve the orientation enigma.

Once completed a new cube can be built and tested, this will be only a matter of hours if they are able to modify the backup cube and squeeze in a rig that has been constructed in readiness. Jane and I are really excited at the news, as this means both of our Toms could be home in a matter of days. The excitement is dampened somewhat at the prospect of giving Tom the horrible news about Jane and on top of that the nuclear devastation back home.

Day 741 – 11th June 2018

Lots of hanging about waiting, lots of rough sex.

Day 742 – 12th June 2018

Lots of rough sex and lots of hanging about waiting.

Day 743 – 13th June 2018

Jane and I are in Birmingham, in the older of the large hangars where the cube testing machine was built and where a new rig, with a newly made (remade backup) cube, is ready to be tested. If this works, the rig from the alternate reality will be recommissioned, squeezed and hopefully returned to its reality.

The rig vehicle almost looks identical to the other working rig that was relocated to the bigger of the two hangars.

A countdown was started at 2 minutes and counting. I don't know about anyone else, but I was hardly breathing.

It went, it worked, they had made a working cube, they know the cube orientation and can make as many as they wish now. It was a massive moment. Everyone was cheering and clapping. Someone grabbed my arm and got me to stand up, it was Graham, he lead me to the open area near the rig space, stood back looked at me, looked at the rest of the assembled audience, sat in the makeshift tiered seating, he started clapping, aimed at me, the audience stood, clapped and cheered louder. I felt extremely humbled and honoured. I retook my seat and witnessed the return of the new rig. Again there was sustained applause, albeit more restrained than the last time, but no less enthusiastic.

We relocated to another set of tiered seating in the newer hangar, to witness the squeezing of the rig from the alternate reality, it had to return to the squeezed state to be unblocked, before pressure reduction to return the rig. This time Graham was onboard to communicate, if necessary. Maximum pressure was achieved, the rig remained, almost a minute went by, the rig was still here. There was a lot of shuffling in seats, whispered conversations started, then, without warning the rig was gone.

We sat in our seats, full of anticipation, half an hour went by, it seemed like an eternity. Rachel made an announcement, we would wait a further 30 minutes, if it had not returned we would adjourn for lunch, which would be a buffet, to be set up near the stand, to enable us to be nearby, just in case. I'm glad that was the plan, there was no way I was moving for hours yet.

We didn't have to wait for long, 14 minutes later the rig, from the alternate reality, reappeared, no warning, no fuss, it was just there. Again the assembled crowd broke into applause. The door opened, a collective sharp intake of breath, Graham appeared. Mobile steps were hastily moved to the rig door. He emerged, there was a splatter of applause, he stopped and extended his hand to the open door, we held our breath again, both Toms jumped out waving their arms. There were loud cheers, Jane and I were in tears, the three of them began to descend the steps and stopped half way, they extended their left arms to the door, out jumped two more Toms, there was an initial gasp from the audience followed by a tremendous roar and sustained clapping. Four Toms! All of this drama was viewed around the World on live camera feed. The media room on the campus must be glowing red hot.

We thought that the dramatics were over, we were wrong, as the cheering died down, a second Graham emerged, waving his arms madly, smiling from ear to ear. I thought it was not possible for us to clap and cheer any louder, I was wrong there too.

The six of them descended the stairs, to be greeted by Rachel and other University dignitaries. Jane and I were ushered to meet them too. The four Toms were identically dressed, my earlier fears were staring me in the face, who is who?

The little buggers all said "Dad, Mum" at the same time! That was not funny, they thought it was!

Each of them, in turn, gave me then Jane a huge hug. It was very strange, I felt restrained, not knowing who was mine, who was Tom2 and who were the other two. Would we ever know for certain? The first Tom that gave me a hug, came back and took hold of my hand, I must have looked overwhelmed, he said "It's me, Dad, your Tom" I scooped him up in a huge bear-hug, tears streaming down my cheeks. I couldn't speak, any thoughts of letting him know about his Mum were put aside for later, when we were out of public view. Buffet lunch was brought out, everyone milled around, talking in groups, lots of the academics surrounded the two Grahams, trying to get a chance to talk to them.

Eventually, when most people had gone, a select group convened in the nearest meeting room. All four Toms, both Grahams, Rachel, Colonel Smyth, three more academics, Jane and me. We sat in expectant silence, waiting for Rachel to get the meeting going. Rachel opened the meeting with an impassioned speech, the meeting was being relayed to other meeting rooms on this and other campuses. There was also a feed to the Colonel's organisation. Here it is in full:

Colleagues and friends I stand before you on this momentous day, a day that will live forever in history, a day that marks the beginning of a new era in science, a new era in physics and a new era in the development of humankind.

We are blessed by the discovery of more than one new science, Magnetic Field Manipulation (MFM - The study of the effects of magnetic field generation, orientation and engineering), Parallel Universology (PU - The study of parallel universes, manipulation, communication, interaction and mapping), Parallel Psychology (PP - The study of the effects of parallel universe-human interaction on human psychology) and MFM Engineering (MFME - The development of engineering solutions as a result of discoveries in MFM). Each of which have their own school and their own Chair, all within the faculty of New Physics. All of these new sciences are as a direct result of the "Rig" built by Richard Charles who was following a dream, a dream where technology enabled advances in society, a dream where humanity's place in the Universe could be improved. How true that dream has turned out to be in this reality.

We are, as a University, going from strength to strength, we have further developed our relationship with our American friends, we are in the process of merging to become one, multi-national University with campuses on four continents. It has been proposed that the name of that combined academic giant will be The Richard Charles University.

Richard is not with us today, he is, unfortunately and worryingly, presumed missing in

ANTIGRAVITY DRIVE - THE DIARY OF AN INVENTION

Reality2, but his counterpart is here. I am, reliably, informed by the Professor of PP, Clint McDonnell, that we should regard all counterparts from different realities as the same entity, i.e. the same person. He did not realise this was about to happen, but, if you could make your way to the front Richard. I hereby award you and all your counterpart entities with an honorary doctorate in physics, I further request that you, in return, honour us with the consent to the use of your name and title as your eponymous university.

I gratefully received an elaborate scroll and was helped into a gown and a large cloth cap with tassels, I gave consent to the use of my (our) name with the proviso that the 'Dr' was added, becoming The Dr Richard Charles University. It was agreed. There was loud applause from the small group in the room. We took to our seats, I removed cap and gown, they were taken away to be only used for ceremonial purposes. I was in total awe of the proceedings, I really am living a dream. Rachel took control of the meeting with the announcement that we were to view a presentation developed since the correct elucidation of the magnetic cube. Both Grahams took to the floor and began talking over a video playing soundlessly on the big screen. They talked in detail about the machinery, technology and the overall process of elucidation, on the screen was the machine hard at work, labelling, cutting, removing, measuring and replacing magnets. It was fascinating to watch, especially with the commentary from the Grahams. Next they showed, and talked through making a new cube, in a new rig with rams capable of up to thousands of tons pressure. They also announced that a new rig had also been built in the alternate reality. They presented a graphical simulation/animation video of how the cube works, with magnetic fields appearing like liquid bubbles surrounding each spherical magnet, with north and south poles coloured in pink and green respectively, squashed, squeezed and distorted by their close proximity to each other. First they showed how the fields interacted if the magnetic spheres were fitted together in a cube of their own choosing (Norths and Souths connected). It appeared as if all the fields merged to make one larger magnet, even with simulated compression, not a lot changed. They then showed the cube made how I had intended, all like poles touching, this time it just looked like a confused and squashed up array of magnetic fields, no merging. Even with simulated squeezing nothing remarkable happened.

Next it was the actual cube I had made. Somehow, and I really have no idea how, I had managed to sort of flip every other plane of four sphere rods (depending upon which way you looked at the cube), incidentally every rod, all sixteen of them, had like poles touching but, not always in the same order (this was obvious really, I never checked, in fact didn't know how to check, I assumed that being as careful as I was that I had it right). There appeared to be a plane of mirror symmetry between two plates on the left and two on the right of a central planar mirror, such that the very top poles were, NSSN, instead of NNNN. From left to right each plane had the same pole at the top, front to back (all Norths or all Souths). Consequently, with each rod in each plane being as I intended (all like poles touching) it produced a very central point of the cube surrounded by four South Poles. The resulting array of magnetic fields appeared to merge into a moving interlacing pattern of shells, surrounding the central core of four souths, once compressed the central point appeared to glow, surrounded by tight, static, shells of alternate Norths and Souths. They admitted that as yet they have no explanation, theoretically or mathematically, but it appears that the central point behaves as a pseudo-singularity having many of the characteristics of a real singularity but with no mass. There was a deathly silence as everyone tried to take it in. Very quickly they showed the structure of the backup cube. It was very similar to how I intended really. The top poles, left to right were SNNS, front to back were alternate, the first being SNSN, the second NSNS and so on, the four central poles were two Norths and two Souths. The overall magnetic field interaction was interestingly complex but nothing like the working cube, when compressed it did not change. It appears that the software creating these animations has checked a significant proportion of possible orientations, as yet none show the same effect as the working cube, even if they happen to have the four central poles as Souths or Norths, it's the combination of all the magnetic fields with the central Souths that work. There are three diagrams at the end of the diary, Appendices III, IV and V that represent the cubes.

If that was not interesting enough they switched the talk to communication and the 'blocking' they were able to do from the alternate reality. They said it was quite simple really (who are they trying to kid), because, as we all know, the rig never actually moves, it always occupies the same space in its own reality, in a parallel reality or on a bridge between realities. An open end of an optic cable is inserted at the interface between the compression plates and the magnetic cube, which is connected to systems within the Rig, once the rig has departed to another reality another optic cable is introduced into the now apparently vacant space in a way that the open ends of the cable would meet, if both cables existed in the same time and space, this cable is connected to systems in the hangar. The blocking is also simple (groan) and is achieved by focusing a strong magnetic field into the centre of the space that would be occupied by the compressed magnetic cube. They then described this by a series of equations and principles that completely lost me. Obviously it works, they proved that when their rig was dismantled in this Reality.

ANTIGRAVITY DRIVE - THE DIARY OF AN INVENTION

There was a bout of sustained clapping, with both Grahams, comically, taking bows. One of them held up a hand for us to stop. After a short moment of silence, they announced that further to this they believe they can introduce a permanent bridge, not just a communication bridge but a permanent physical bridge between realities. A bridge where people can cross at will between the two universes. There was again sustained applause, everyone stood and continued clapping.

Once we had regained our seats, they showed a Gantt chart summary of the project to build, the physical bridge, the first test run is planned to take place in 18 weeks. Rachel thanked the Grahams, then thanked everyone for attending, the meeting was closed, but, we are invited to wave goodbye to Graham and two Toms as they depart back to the Alternate Reality.

Left to our own devices, the four of us, me, Jane and both our Toms, went, with our minder, to the staff restaurant on campus. This was our first chance to catch up and for us both to let them know about Jane and Me2 and, of course, us. I wasted no time, before he could ask me how she was, I let Tom know his mum had passed away. He did not appear overly shocked, although he was visibly upset, we had a hug, Jane gave him a hug. He said he knew, or at least suspected it, the alternate Reality was the same, plus 2 years, as this and the fourth Tom was equivalent to him from our own, but slightly different Reality. Jane, his mum had died in the alternate Reality. He asked if the other Richard, Me2, was lost in our Reality and were we a couple? We both nodded meekly, taken aback somewhat. So it all happened, just the same in the alternate Reality. It had, but not quite the same, hence the uncertainty. Tom announced that the time differentials and dilation factors were key to his interests in his research and felt on the brink of a breakthrough, but could not yet tell us more.

I should have suspected that scenario, but it had not entered my head. It was all a bit overwhelming, the four of us ate a light afternoon tea almost in silence. Tom asked, "Are you happy, the two of you? You were where we just came from." All I could do was nod and grin. Jane answered, "Very."

We all talked about the circumstance of his mum's last days and the fact I would not let them have a funeral until he was here. Of course that had not happened in the alternate version because they were all there. She was cremated, half her ashes were scattered in the garden and they too made a small garden of remembrance. The remaining half were sent back to Reality1. Not the same as our Reality1. Their version of Me2 and Colonel2 were not missing in their version of Reality1, there had been no nuclear war!

Their version of me and Jane2 were also a couple. He, they, both Toms were fully understanding and really grasped the concept of one entity. The four of them had spent a lot of time together and had the realisation they were one person themselves, even with some age differences. They too had the same professor of PP. There were also other people who were crossed over between realities and some had made foursomes, being completely interchangeable with each other. It was all a bit complicated and a bit too much to take in.

We agreed, his mum's funeral would be arranged as soon as possible, we would do the same with her ashes.

Day 744 – 14th June 2018

Back on the Mill Street Campus, the Toms had remained in Birmingham, we made arrangement for Jane's funeral, there were a lot of relieved people who were glad I had made a decision.

It was to be in two weeks, allowing time to make the detailed arrangements and for key people to be available. She will be cremated, and as agreed with Tom, half her ashes will be scattered in the garden of remembrance, the other half will be saved, waiting for an appropriate time to return them to Reality1.

Jane accompanied me and helped with the arrangements, we both found it very strange, because if you accept our counterparts are one entity, then Jane was arranging her own cremation, a bit spooky, but also it seemed to me that the one entity theory is a little flawed as patently Jane, Jane2 that is, is very much alive and not needing cremation.

Later in the day we retired to our bed for more adventures in our latest obsession, a quest for Jane to achieve multiple orgasm, whatever that means. We don't really care, it was fun trying.

Day 745 – 15th June 2018

We spent the whole day on our secret quest, more fun.

Day 746 – 16th June 2018

Had a quiet breakfast and prepared for a project meeting in the garage. We were both looking forward to being brought up to date on progress and finding out if there is any more news from Reality1 and the Tom5 enigma. The plan, in theory, had another eleven days or so to go before completion, but, in real terms, because everyone had worked relentlessly hard and there had been no setbacks, the build was almost complete. The projection was that it would be fully rebuilt and commissioned in two days. From that point it would be available for the use of the Return Team and researchers (with supervision and protection) to use as they wish.

When we saw the modified rig it looked finished to me, barely recognisable as my own rig, it had the appearance of a large glass vehicle, but was in fact polycarbonate sheets, with large tyred wheels retracted on the sides of the external frame, it appeared to me that once the wheels were engaged the whole structure would be elevated by half a metre or more. There were drawbridge type doors at each end. Internally there were 10 folding passenger seats, lots of equipment bays, storage compartments and a 'bridge' similar to the Birmingham rig. The original cube in its original condition was at the centre. It too had been internally modified, it had nuclear powered systems and new, more powerful and controllable rams. The way they had introduced all of this was fascinating to see. They assured me everything works. All that is left to do is some more instrument and data collection installation, plus overall commissioning. It looked amazing, massively different to my own cobbled together rig. We are to return in two days for final commissioning runs. There was no further news on Tom5, he was still in an induced coma, his infection was under control but there was a lot of healing to do yet, consciousness would not help him. Today I contacted Professor Clint McDonnell, I wanted to discuss the single entity theory with him.

Day 747 – 17th June 2018

I feel caught between the devil and the deep blue sea, I love Jane deeply with all my heart but I cannot escape this feeling of guilt, a feeling that I am not doing the decent thing by Me2 and Jane2. I cannot get over the feeling that Jane and I are like young lovers having an affair, full of excitement and exploration. It would not be like that if Jane was alive and well, which makes me think Jane2 is not really the same person as Jane. To further support my view, only one of the four Toms thought of me as their dad.

I explained my feelings to Clint, he just dismissed them, he maintained that the logic dictates that all counterparts originated from the same person, they share experiences from before any formation of parallel universes. Biologically they are the same, their DNA is the same. I argued that I cannot imagine what Me2 will think when he finds out I have been shagging his wife in his absence. I know how I would feel, I would not want to share.

After more, increasingly heated, argument on logic and feelings versus new ways of being, I began to suspect that Clint had different motives. I challenged him with that thought. I felt he was conducting an experiment, playing with the lives of counterpart people, giving tacit approval of inter-counterpart relationships, so that he could observe behaviours, write and publish academic papers, just to satisfy his own career interests and aspirations. His challenge was the typical response I would expect from a psychologist, paraphrasing, repeating what I said as a question, it's so bloody annoying, it gets them off the hook, it's so sodding frustrating I just had to end the session and go.

I met up with Jane in the cafe. I gave her a full account of my meeting, after thinking about it for all of a millisecond, she decided Clint was right and that we had all better get used to it.

I acceded, we sloped off to the apartment to test out more of the theories.

Day 748 – 18th June 2018

Big project meeting in the garage, the official acceptance of the fully commissioned refurbished rig, my rig, from my Reality.

It looked amazing, beautiful in some ways, all gleaming panels of crystal clear polycarbonate, and polished steel. Drawbridge doors lowered, it appeared to be like an extra-terrestrial craft straight from a Sci-fi movie. We entered the garage through the up and over doors, with the rig's increased size, there was not much space left. They have said they are working on a plan to convert all the garage walls into doors, enabling the opening up of the space but keeping its integrity. Meanwhile, it was a tight squeeze. We entered the refurbished rig and took to the seats. The doors closed. The Colonel remained standing, he announced that we were to travel to Reality1, the entire team, and yes he knew the consequence of staying on board, he said he was quite getting used to it.

Ged pressed a button on the console near him and with no sound or apparent movement the Colonel instantaneously travelled 2 metres to his merged position, he gave a cough, his instantly recognisable cough, to catch our attention, he explained that he could not bear the thought of not sharing this moment with us, even though it was a tad inconvenient.

At last I had made the journey.

We were in a very dark place, I could see nothing through the clear walls, the doors lowered, lights came on from the rig and we could see we were

ANTIGRAVITY DRIVE - THE DIARY OF AN INVENTION

inside an enormous marquee, pitch black dark, if not for our lights. From out of the gloom at the edges of the tent, Jerry and some of his team emerged. Jerry welcomed us to Reality1 and asked that we descend quietly one by one into Mill Street Base Camp, the ground was also covered in a fabric of some sort, it felt as if it was sand underneath that. Once we were all assembled next to the rig he handed each a pair of sunglasses, he asked that we put them on as we were to venture outside. Jerry explained that we were in a camouflaged, blackout, modular aircraft hangar, designed for covert field exercises. But it suited this purpose very well. It was apparently stealth coated on the exterior, making it almost impossible to detect from a distance. One end of the hangar, joined to the cellars of the house that originally stood here. They too had been cleared out and adapted to be his HQ base.

Because we were inside a blackout tent it did not feel as if I was back home or anything like home. I asked to be shown the exit. We were all taken to it and were instructed to form an orderly queue and keep physical contact with the person in front. The exit was both an air and light lock, two at a time, once inside it was completely dark. The external door opened to bright sunlight, I put on my sunglasses and stepped out.

I thought I was prepared for the view that assaulted my eyes, in retrospect no one could have been, I was not. It was like a grey/black desert, no features, no sounds, nothing, no wind, fierce sunlight, silence. I was completely and utterly shocked, I was stood in what used to be my garden, there was nothing in any direction, just greyness and dust, except for that sticky, stump of a ruin almost on the horizon.

I felt my emotions rising, my chest heaved, I sobbed silently, my eyes filled with tears, flowing over my cheeks and wetting my shirt. Jane embraced me tightly, both of us were in floods of tears. We were not interrupted, no one stopped us, my emotions ran their course. When I eventually lifted my head from Jane's shoulder, no one was watching, no one was looking at me or us, everyone was stood or comforting each other, silently gazing towards the horizon. I turned to look at the hangar, to my amazement, even from just a few metres away, it was difficult to see, difficult to focus on, it had blurred edges (or seemed to). I really could not see the bulk of it, it was almost perfectly camouflaged. I'm sure it was completely invisible from any greater distance. We were guided and ushered back inside, two by two.

All of us were waiting in stunned silence, most wanted to go home, you could see it in their faces. They looked lost and bewildered, even Rachel had that distant look in her eyes. We were in a state of shock, no one could have prepared us for what we experienced outside the tent. The excitement and honour of being on the refurbished Rig's, first official journey was completely wiped out. I felt a tap on my shoulder, it was Jerry, he asked if Jane and I would go with him to see the Colonel.

There he was, magnificently merged in the corner of the original rig. Instead of being angry with me for being condemned to remain in Reality2 he actually admitted he deserved no less than what he got because of his, now regrettable, behaviour. That aside, he had asked us back in to the rig before the others to bring us up to date on other matters. Jerry had briefed him on the latest intelligence from here in Reality1, they had located both our other selves, they were being held in a massive underground bunker complex near to Middlesbrough, obviously they had found it easily and know it's complete layout due to its parallel existence in Reality2. They have one or two agents inside and know exactly the situation. Our counterparts are suspected of being spies and their story is entirely refuted.

Totally unbelievably and astoundingly, the nuclear conflict was more than two years ago, as their best estimate, hence the almost lack of detectable radiation and immediate obvious conditions had it been sooner. I am totally confused, it should be less than a year. This relativity/time thing completely does my head in. It's hard enough to accept concepts that I have grown used to, now this, it has really blown my mind.

The complex is now the main seat, of government in the UK, there is an ongoing attempt at Martial law, but even now there are no-go areas, areas of local gang type of control, very little communication, almost no transport and almost no proper infrastructure or supply chain. In fact it is as near to 'No-Control' as you could get. They have very few options to retrieve the Colonel and Richard, three in fact, at least what they mean is three that stand any chance of success. They were:

1. Send in an elite team to snatch them, with the risk of casualties on both sides.
2. Send an elite team to snatch one or more key figures, transport them back to Reality2 and convince them that the story is true, let them return as our agents of change.
3. Send me in with as much evidence as possible, to convince them that there really is at least one parallel universe.

Each of these options has major risks, the third they feel has most chance of success and has least possibility of casualties.

Why not combine two and three was my response, I am willing to return, but having a key ally from the start should give more chance of getting the right result. Jerry agreed, he will leave it to us to plan the approach. I further added that the counterpart for an appropriate key figure must also exist, why not enlist their help instead? No need to kidnap a key figure, send me plus the counterpart in, to convince them. Who would it be?

The others were making their way back to their places in the rig, Colonel Smyth said he would continue our conversation tomorrow. We returned to Reality2 in silence. This project is now completed and there is to be an end of project dinner tonight. I've a feeling it will be a very subdued affair.

It was, we were finished by 9.30, no one adjourned to the bar, Jane and I drifted away to discuss the events of today in private.

Day 749 – 19th June 2018

I expected to hear from the Colonel today, but we only got the briefest of messages, he will be in touch soon, do nothing until we hear from him. So we did, we stayed in bed all day.

Day 750 – 20th June 2018

More notes, more bed. You would think we would be getting tired of all this sex and cuddling, but our appetites, particularly Jane's, are insatiable.

Day 753 – 23rd June 2018

Nothing from the Colonel, I might get in touch with Rachel tomorrow to see what we might get involved with next. I wondered what progress there is on the permanent bridge project. I have developed a hypothesis in my head about differing personalities of counterparts. For example why has Jane2 got different sexual preferences to Jane1, why has Jane2 got an insatiable sexual appetite, whereas Jane1 did not. I am not ready to share this yet but think I am onto something.

Day 755 – 25th June 2018

Sad news, we are devastated, Tom5 is dead, he never came out of his induced coma. Apparently he passed away peacefully in the early hours of this morning. His burns were just too severe and too much of a trauma for him to overcome. So now the mystery deepens, how did he get into the rig and which particular Reality did he come from? Perhaps we will never know.

The Colonel gave us the news about Tom5, when he contacted us to arrange a meeting in Alpha this afternoon at 1.00 pm. He said he would try and answer any questions we had then.

At the meeting were; the Colonel, Jerry (when did he get back?), Rachel, me, Jane, Hendricks and four other men we had never met before. Strangely enough, and very enigmatically, three of the four were named Smith, John, David and Alan. The fourth was introduced as Sir Gordon Sykes, a minister of state from the Home office. He had direct responsibility for the facility (amongst other things) in Middlesbrough. In brief, they have detailed plans, policies, procedures, staff lists, everything for the facility. They know who the team will be in the current state of emergency back in Reality1. The key thing is Sir Gordon will be in total charge and, in fact, it has been observed that he is. Our plan is for Me, Sir Gordon and two of the Smiths to appear unannounced at the facility and to persuade them of the existence of Reality2, to ultimately gain the release of Me2 and Colonel2. Sir Gordon knows things, that he has not disclosed, that only he knows, so the Reality1 Sir Gordon cannot fail to be convinced, assuming we get to meet him.

The meeting rambled on for two hours, lots of detail of timings, who had what role, what we would do in differing scenarios. Actually I'm hugely excited to be going back, but full of trepidation for the reality of it all and the danger that we will be exposed to. The expectation is that we will be successful and that a relationship can be made that will ultimately lead to peace throughout the World (A bloody big ask, if you ask me). Reality2 (and other Realities, where possible) will help Reality1 to get back on its feet. Except that, here they refer to themselves as Reality1 and my Reality is Reality2. It's confusing and difficult to keep track sometimes.

My purpose will be to share the diary once we have friendly relations. To explain to everyone, as best I can, what happened at the Mill Street Massacre and that my blundering about was the direct cause of all the problems. (I'm not absolutely sure I agree with that but, in the interests of peace.....)

The four of us will be accompanied by Jerry and a number of his team. They will escort us to the facility and remain covert until it is safe for them to be in the open. We are to leave in three days' time. Meanwhile we will work together to discuss the scenarios and roles in more detail. Not sure why one of the Smiths is not coming with us to the facility, he is to join Jerry's team. Jane asked if she were allowed to go too, there was a resounding, No. The planned funeral and memorial service for Jane has been postponed until such time we are all available again. I feel doubly guilty about my relationship with Jane2, when Jane is being stored away waiting to be significant, being an inconvenient burden on our schedules.

Day 756 – 26th June 2018

All those that met yesterday reconvened in the garage with the rig, we discussed and demonstrated the workings of the rig, where we would sit and who does what. A major shock to me, and why I didn't know is beyond me, was that the wheels visible on two of the sides are not for the rig at all, they are the wheels of the extra-rig vehicle (ERV), a vehicle that is modular and made from other, ostensibly, rig components, these components are dual purpose, forming walls, cupboards, on board systems etc. It was not pulled out and put together as they could not be reached when it is in the garage. It is a vehicle that can carry four personnel. We are to go to Pinewood tomorrow to practice with another version. Amazing or what? An important point with the ERV is that if the rig travels to Reality2 it will immediately reattach, wherever it happens to be. (When I think about it, it's obvious the rig should not be moved, the new communication systems would cease to work.) The ERV is stealthed and apparently invisible to radar, it is exceptionally silent, having four independent electric drives to each wheel, powered by two separate nuclear power supplies. It is extremely quick, capable of 0-60 mph in less than 4 seconds and has a top speed in excess of 100 mph. It is also an all-terrain vehicle, having the four-wheel drive and intelligent breaking and suspension systems. The driver and co-driver will be the two Smiths. I am looking forward to tomorrow at Pinewood, not only am I curious about the ERV, but also about stealthing and something they call dustless driving. Jane is extremely miffed and just a little sulky, tonight's meal and pre bed foreplay was just a titchy bit awkward.

Day 757 – 27th June 2018

The day at Pinewood was fantastic, if it was not for the circumstances it would have been an experience of a lifetime. The ERV was a superb piece of engineering, an absolute marvel, fun and exhilarating to drive. Handled like a dream on and off road. The dustless driving really was true, something to do with airflow and aerodynamics. We had to practice assembling the ERV, but not replacing on the rig as that was automatic. It was amazingly simple, releasing clamps inside the rig freed up all the modules, fitting them together by more interlocking clamps, covering the whole thing in stealth fabric all took no more than 5 minutes, the fastest we did it was 3.5 minutes.

The excitement, for me, was building as the day progressed. It was interesting getting to know Sir Gordon, however, the two Smiths kept mostly to themselves even though they were very friendly and supportive they revealed nothing about their backgrounds or anything else for that matter. Sir Gordon (he did actually insist on the Sir bit to be used at all times) was a very interesting character, a career civil servant with a military background having come from a titled and landed family, his elder brother being the principal heir to the family title and fortune. Educated at Eton and Oxford and extremely well read. He was not dissimilar in appearance and build to Colonel Smyth and had the air of confidence that comes from experience and the natural ability to be in charge, coupled with the capability to carry it off. Sir Gordon filled me with the confidence of success, I had no doubt in my mind by the end of the day, that we will easily reach the planned conclusion of our mission.

Day 758 – 28th June 2018

We had today free from meetings, rehearsals and training. A day to charge our batteries, that is unless you have to cope with Jane's sexual appetite. By 8.00 in the evening I was exhausted and pleaded to be allowed to sleep.

Day 759 – 29th June 2018

08.30 - We are sat in the rig waiting to go, all seats are full, the four of us plus Jerry and more of his men. All remaining space is filled with equipment and supplies. My heart is pounding, the anticipation is almost stifling.

08.35 - Back in Reality1. Silence.

08.50 - All personnel and equipment offloaded.

09.00 - The adventure begins, Sir Gordon and I are watching the Smiths remove and assemble the ERV. All this so far inside the hangar, none of us, as yet, have ventured out. What an amazing machine, we gave a hand to put on the stealth fabric, all supplies loaded. All aboard, hangar doors opened to bright sunlight and we were off.

I'm typing as we go, we are travelling as silently as possible, I have no idea where Jerry and his team are, no sight or sound of them, but I am assured they are there somewhere.

We are travelling in silence, radio and otherwise. Silence is the norm, nothing can be heard, no birdsong, no wind, no other background noise, just a faint crackling of our tyres as we made dustless progress. We were cracking along at 60 mph, very bumpy but the intelligent suspension evened it out.

The sky was cloudless, the heat from the sun relentless, it was 39 degrees and we were in mid England! We were baking in the non-air-conditioned ERV, apparently too noisy, too heavy and an unnecessary drain on the systems. I could do with it right now, hot was an understatement.

There was black dust devastation as far as the eye could see, we were travelling on compass, no GPS, no visible landmarks, only the occasional rolling of hills, nothing to base any visual idea of our whereabouts.

It came almost as a surprise to see the charred stumps of fire consumed trees and the occasional pile of rubble, the further we travelled the more distinct the rubble became, discernible as buildings and flattened, leafless, charred trees and other vegetation.

We had made just over a 100 miles before we saw complete houses, complete villages. We still had seen no sign of people, animals or birds. After three hours we stopped for a short break on a track in a small wooded glade. In this little corner of England it was easy to get the impression everything was normal, Sun leaking through the canopy, bird song delighting the ears and an amazing variety of wild flowers giving little patches of colour in the semi-gloom.

I heard the smallest crack of a twig underfoot behind me, I spun round, heart in mouth, to witness Jerry and two of his men emerging from the undergrowth, all three camouflaged to buggery, all looking as fresh as the daisies on the woodland track.

Jerry put a finger to his lips, indicating for us to remain silent. He produced a small touch screen tablet from one of his enormous number of pockets, he typed - *behave normally, finish your break, proceed as planned, you are being followed, do not panic, do not take evasive action, they are an observer team only. We will see you next at the facility.*

After delivering his message he replaced the tablet into the same pocket, held up his hand in a muted wave, turned with his men and blended back into the woods. The four of us shrugged, asking unanswerable questions with our eyes and grinned at each other. We returned to the ERV and resumed our journey. If we continued with this progress we will be near the facility by late afternoon or early evening.

The ERV emerged from the small wooded valley into open heath, mostly grass with occasional yellow flowering gorse. We picked up a B road and continued on our heading of North East.

Approximately two miles later we came to the edge of the heathland. Finding ourselves in an elevated location, we could see a huge expanse of the countryside before us. We halted to take in the vista. It was jaw dropping, not a tree was standing anywhere, those we could see were leafless and flattened to the ground, all pointing in the same direction, towards us. In the near distance the green gave way to more blackness, no features at all. In the far distance, the featureless blackness gave way to ruins, lots of them. That smashed and ruined city was what remained of Sheffield.

The strange thing was that we had not seen any sign of life, no sign of this anarchy we had been led to believe was rife. Where are all the people, where are the farm animals, cattle, sheep, anything?

Jerry had said we were being observed, we could not see them either. We decided to take a route avoiding the city as best we could and avoiding what was left of major roads and motorways. The ERV made excellent progress, our speed averaged over 60 mph only slowing down for difficult terrain or ruined deserted remnants of buildings.

We saw many, seemingly intact, villages and isolated houses, but still no sign of life. Our main driver, Dave, indicated we should look to the horizon on our left, I could see nothing but featureless black landscape, I looked at him questioningly, Leeds, he whispered. We managed to skirt around York which, with huge relief, looked completely untouched and intact, but there was still an absence of any sign of life. We began to get cocky and used some of the A roads that we came across, even the A1 at one stage. By mid-afternoon we approached Thirsk, which was also intact, lifeless and deserted.

Our instruction was to not investigate anything, under no circumstances get side-tracked. Not avoiding deserted places like York and Thirsk was almost irresistible, it was extremely disciplined of us not to stop and look around. Even some of the isolated villages and houses were very tempting, everywhere was the same, lifeless and deserted. The further north we went the more normal things appeared, no devastation, no blackened countryside, but, eerily, no sign of life, no movement, nothing. The beginning of our journey was unsettling, now it is downright unnerving and, to be honest, scary.

After a very brief, whispered conversation we decided to use A roads from now on, we made an assumption that we were being allowed to make progress, we know we are being observed. They are not showing themselves or making any attempt to stop us, we assume, therefore, that they are interested in our destination and intentions, rather than just capture.

We continued on our heading, north, north east, then east along the A19, to the A172, via Stokesley, to skirt the North York Moors, everything looks normal, green and overgrown hedgerows, green fields, trees, intact villages but still no sign of inhabitants, not even abandoned pet dogs or cats.

At last, birds and some small mammals are now in evidence. Magpies, kestrels, crows everywhere, rabbits, occasional fresh, molehills and one or two scurrying stoats (or something similar). We made fast progress along the A171 to Guisborough then on to A173 to Skelton towards our ultimate destination of Staithes, the town nearest to the massive underground facility at Boulby, which really was a working potash and salt mine along with underground scientific research laboratories.

As we bypassed Skelton to join the A174 we could see, in the distance on the edge of the moors, line after line of tents, white, blue, grey and orange, they disappeared over the visible horizon. Dave did not seem at all surprised, he whispered again, transit and refugee camps. I don't know about Sir Gordon, but I was more miffed than surprised, why had he not told me, why leave me wondering where everyone was, the prat. But, transit to where?

We rejoined the road (A174) just to the east of Skelton and almost immediately blundered into a road block, manned by armed soldiers. None of the guards looked surprised, it seems our approach was expected, if not normal. One soldier (a sergeant) marched up and came to attention with a loud stamp of boot and snap of uniform in a smartly delivered salute at the driver's window. He blurted out, almost like a delivered line "Welcome Sir Gordon, you are expected, your escort will take you to the facility." They can't possibly be mistaking Sir Gordon for theirs, can they? What about the ERV, haven't they noticed it's a bit different to other vehicles?

White and dayglo motorbikes appeared from nowhere, positioned front and back, and we were off. 70, 80, 90 mph. I was gripping my seat, too shit scared to notice much out of the windscreen, except for mile after mile of tents. The further we went the more people I saw.

Nearer the facility we encountered two further manned barriers and were waved straight through. We ended our journey at what appeared to be a factory, large industrial looking buildings and tall chimneys. We entered one of the buildings through a pair of huge sliding doors and immediately began to descend on an enormous spiral ramp, big enough to get several double decker buses side by side, I had no concept of how many spiral circles we went round but we kept on going further and further underground.

As we continued to spiral downwards we occasionally passed junctions in the massive, well-lit tunnel, judging by the curvature and inclination I guess the spiral is 50 to 100 metres in diameter, the tunnel itself could easily accommodate said double decker buses, travelling three abreast. The glimpses I saw down the intersecting tunnels were astounding, they appeared infinitely long, some empty, some containing machinery, vehicles and sectional buildings.

Sir Gordon suddenly began a commentary on the facility, so sudden in fact after all that silence, I nearly jumped out of my skin. Of course he knows the facility, he is in charge of it. Come to think of it I bet he knew about transit camps too, probably knew everything. Wish they'd told me.

More than a thousand metres to the bottom of the facility and almost a thousand kilometres of tunnels, that extend for many kilometres under the North Sea. This is/was a fully commercial working mine, one of Europe's largest potash mines, it also houses several physics and astrophysics laboratories plus other governmental facilities. The seat of government resides here in emergency conditions, shared with another, even larger facility in Cheshire .... His commentary was cut short as the next intersection came into view, we could see a 'Reception Committee' waiting to meet us. As we got closer I immediately recognised three of them, Sir Gordon, Colonel Smyth and Me2. There were other suited figures with them, including, I now noticed, Hendricks and Jerry, obviously this Reality's counterparts. Also with them were several armed soldiers, guns at the ready. We came to a halt, cut the motors, we are going out to meet them.

This is now recorded in retrospect, 11.00 pm, I'm sat on the edge of my bed in a small sectional building, my bedroom, part of the hotel complex. I feel completely exhausted, mentally as well as physically. I'm free to roam around the modular hotel, but they have requested I do not go further for my own safety.

They took almost no convincing that the story Me2 and the Colonel gave them was now factual. Sir Gordon was the first to be convinced when, earlier in the day, he saw the live stream from the observers of his and Me2s counterparts travelling, in a very futuristic vehicle in their general direction, apparently from the massacre site in Northampton.

ANTIGRAVITY DRIVE - THE DIARY OF AN INVENTION

Incidentally one of the insiders was Jerry's counterpart, they had made contact right at the start after the abduction and had been working together, hence it was an observer team on our tail and not a snatch squad. It seems Jerry had nearly got the job done without us.

Going back to earlier - We emerged slowly from the ERV, the guns gave me the impression I had to move slowly and carefully, no spooking of nervous fingers. Dave was, deliberately, the last to leave so that he could activate the return sequence. The ERV ceased to be in that place 10 seconds later. That was the deal clincher, the reception committee did a collective gasp, Sir Gordon stepped forward, arm extended to shake the hand of his counterpart. Me2 almost jumped on me and gave me a massive bear hug.

When Me2 eventually let go we were amazed to see the two Sir Gordons kissing, full lips and passionate, it was just a little discomforting to watch, the soldiers were obviously very embarrassed and didn't know where to look. They kept up with their passionate embrace for a full three minutes, by which time there was a lot of nervous shuffling and coughing. It wasn't so much the passionate kissing but that awkward feeling that it was akin to incest or something, it just didn't look right. Even the Colonel was shuffling his feet and giving the odd "Ahem". They stepped apart, still holding hands. There was a hushed sigh of relief, I hoped they could restrain themselves and get on with whatever we had to do next. Having said which, I remember my first meeting with Me2, we stopped short of kissing, but there was this huge connected feeling, a feeling of deep love, possibly, we were also reluctant to let go of each other's hand.

At that point we heard a strange noise behind us, like lots of very quiet whining electric motors. We turned around to witness Jerry and four of his men approaching on, what can only be described as trials bikes, proper off roaders, obviously designed by the same people who made our ERV. Fully electric, carbon fibre frame and polycarbonate panels. They had lots of little paniers and boxes attached, very streamlined boxes I might add. Any stealth materials had obviously been removed. They came to a halt next to us, dismounted, came to attention and saluted. Not sure which particular individual they were saluting but, nevertheless, it was impressive.

The Sir Gordons called us to order and we were asked to accompany them to a meeting room further down the tributary tunnel. The meeting room was a large rectangular sectional building, similar to all the others I had seen so far. The inside was furnished in a fairly standard, meeting room, kind of way. Sir Gordon1(usual Reality notation, this being Reality1) got things going. He started by saying that there was no one present that didn't know who everyone was, so he dispensed with introductions. He asked if I would take the floor and give a full, as briefly as possible, account of my entire journey, from concept to today.

The first thing I did was to give him a memory stick with my entire diary. He immediately inserted it into a notebook computer that he had with him. I asked that if there were questions, to ask them as I go along so that we may avoid any misunderstandings. I recounted the whole thing from dream to standing here, leaving out all the finer details, there were lots questions particularly around the time of my first abduction and the night of the massacre. Strangely I was asked to skirt past the details on construction and much of the experimentation, apparently there will be time for that later. I also left out details of my relationship with Jane2.

The whole monologue took well over an hour, I felt drained when I had finished, it was the first time I had recounted the whole thing in one go, I was actually very emotional when talking about the more dramatic aspects including the death of Jane. It also reminded me that even though it had been planned, we still had not had Jane's funeral or cremation yet.

The Sir Gordons sat at the head of the meeting table, I observed they held hands for the entire time, I could also see their thumbs were constantly making caressing motions. I tried really hard not to let it put me off but it was very distracting. Personally I think they should adjourn this meeting, get their initial fascination with each other over with and reconvene tomorrow, we will all be refreshed then. They carried on, next they asked Me2 to take up the story from where he thinks the Realities diverged. He did so from the point at which he chose not to lie about the rig to Jane and Tom and the quick relocation to Birmingham. He took it up to the point where he left to come here. Sir Gordon2 was next, he represented the governments of the United Kingdom, the USA and The European Community. He emphasised the offer of help to get right what has gone wrong here, to share the developments in science and technology resulting from the rig and to ultimately restore World peace here in this Reality. At this point we did adjourn, to meet again in the morning. We had an option to go for dinner and then retire or take a light meal back to our rooms. I chose the latter, I felt exhausted, I needed sleep.

Day 760 – 30th June 2018

I got up early, showered, dressed and went in search of breakfast. My room was a self-contained standard hotel room in its own sectional building. It was one of about a hundred such modules arranged two high facing each other across both sides of a tributary tunnel to the main arterial tunnel. Larger modules were restaurants (with kitchens), administration, conference and meeting rooms.

The hotel was designed for visitors to the scientific functions and other facilities in normal times and was now used for visitors of the emergency government.

I found breakfast and Me2, he was sitting at a table with Colonel Smyth, both Jerrys and both Smiths. They were chatting about the modified rig, the ERV and the trail bikes Jerry had used. They all greeted me cheerily as I sat down to eat my muesli, although the smell of their full English made my mouth water.

It turns out that the trail bikes were assembled in kit form before the rig modifications had been completed and had been used to do a lot of their scouting about gathering intelligence. It was because of these that the idea for the ERV had been developed. They were the pilot for the engine and the dustless engineering.

We all agreed that good progress was being made here and that in all likelihood the Colonel and Me2 will be allowed to return home. We also felt the Sir Gordon situation was a bit strange, we had not witnessed anything like that back in Reality2 including the larger number of people meeting their counterparts in Birmingham and Reality3. It was Jerry who posed the question, "Did we think he was homosexual in any case?" Really we didn't know nor did anyone mind, it was just a bit OTT.

An administrator from Sir Gordon's office walked over to tell us that the meeting was being delayed until the afternoon, we will be informed nearer the time. Both Sir Gordons are in a high level video conference and they will brief us at the meeting. Meanwhile, we can hang about here or it has been authorised for us to have an escorted tour of the facility.

The Colonel, the Jerrys and the Smiths were all fully acquainted with the facility, which left me and Me2 for the tour. Four hours later we had only seen a tiny fraction of the extent of the tunnels, even though we were zooming about in an open topped Jeep. We whistled by the scientific labs, on a level of the mine a few hundred metres above where we were staying. The labs were well established, having been there a number of years. They had other facilities in other tunnels and were carrying out astrophysics and particle physics research, something to do with dark matter and neutrinos and other mystifying stuff. You could easily get lost in these mines, the tunnels went on for miles and miles, most of them were working tunnels deep under the North Sea, connected by a network of railway and conveyor systems. Elsewhere tunnels were storage facilities, for undisclosed items. The emergency government was housed in several tunnels in hundreds of sectional buildings. It was easy to see why this mine was chosen for all these non-mine facilities. The sheer size of the tunnel complex was mind boggling huge, deep underground (and undersea), easily protected and defended. The whole time we were being driven around, our guide was rattling off all sorts of statistics, numbers and facts, most of which I have completely forgotten.

We were taken back to the restaurant and met up with the rest of the guys. After a spot of lunch we ambled off to the meeting room. We were not waiting long before both Sir Gordons joined us, along with a number of other very official looking men and women. They were all introduced by Sir Gordon1, an impressive list, I felt quite small amongst these very important people. The Prime Minister (Anne Simmonds), The Foreign Secretary (Sir Henry Pollock), The Minister for Home Security (Peter Thrange), The Minister for War (General Sir Mike Partington-Smyth), The Minister for Cultural, Economic and Agricultural Rescue (Dame Celia Longton) and The Chief Scientific Advisor (Professor Sir Adam Williams). The latter being Professor Rachel William's father.

Everyone else was introduced to the ministers by Colonel Smyth, The Jerrys and the Smiths were introduced by name only, the rest of us had some details given to put us in context. The agenda was simple, an overview of the proposal and next steps. This was all very good and positive but there was something I needed to know. Before Sir Gordon1 got the discussion going, I raised my hand to ask a question, everyone looked a little surprised if not alarmed that I would do such a thing. It did not stop me. I asked if someone would talk me through the events of the aftermath of the Mill Street Massacre and the following Nuclear war, where are all the people, what is happening elsewhere in the World? Surely this information is important to our understanding? After a brief pause and a few hushed conversations amongst the ministers, the Prime Minister, Anne Simmonds, stood up, coughed politely and said that this was very remiss of them, of course the information is crucial to developing a relationship. She said that they now have a better understanding of the events of the massacre after reading my diary, we should now be brought up to date on everything since. We will adjourn until tomorrow so that we can prepare and make a proper presentation. The meeting ended, we, the guys, all decamped to the restaurant and bar. The Ministers were shepherded off into the complex.

ANTIGRAVITY DRIVE - THE DIARY OF AN INVENTION

Day 761 – 1st July 2018

At breakfast today Me2 took me to one side and asked what was wrong, why am I not behaving normally with him. I assured him that all was OK, nothing wrong, just nervous and on edge about this whole thing. I pointed out that my home had been nuked here, it feels very strange. I could not admit my relationship with Jane, I know he will find out eventually but I cannot face it at this time.

We met in the meeting room at 09.30, there were lots more people present and more video and audio equipment installed. There were nine more people introduced to go through a programme of presentations, videos and live camera footage. The presentations, etc. would be in an approximately correct chronological order, starting with the massacre and finishing, by the end of today, with the present time. It is hoped we will finish by the end of today, if not reconvene tomorrow. All of the ministers were here too. I have been given the files on memory devices. I will not go into great detail here but give a summary for each.

1 **The Massacre** - (Commander Daniel Stevenson, Metropolitan Police -Presentation and video)

The emergency phone lines were overloaded with calls, extensive gunfire and explosions. Fire, police, ambulances and elite squads were all mobilised in minutes (In fact I remember hearing sirens as we crammed ourselves into the rig). The whole street and surrounding areas were sealed off, houses evacuated and major incident units set up. It was assumed it was a terrorist operation of some sort, failing that drug gang warfare. There was no prior intelligence to support either supposition. Everything went quiet. No one dared approach the direct scene of the incident, it was a softly, softly strategy.

30 minutes into the situation, the Incident Commander was contacted by the security services, they confessed it was an operation they were involved in, with cooperation from the CIA. Both organisations may have operatives involved at the scene, there was no current contact. A helicopter view directly over the scene (My house and garden) showed no activity but plenty of bodies. The scene was illuminated from the helicopter, adjoining houses and gardens.

A tight cordon was established, supported by marksmen in good vantage points. The cordon was slowly advanced until only my garden and house remained inside. A negotiator tried to establish contact with whoever was still alive. There was no movement. A full two hours into the operation, a crack team entered the garden, all Hell let loose, gunfire came from every direction, the team that entered the garden stood no chance, all were lost. Some of the gunfire came from the house, there were explosions as a sudden assault was made into the front of the house, lots of rapid fire continued. The house was ablaze in minutes, dark clad figures emerged into the back garden, it was the assault team, no other survivors. One lone gunman remained in the garage, he gave himself up, it was Gregori, the Russian researcher I had seen assassinating Rachel and the others.

The next day, the house appeared completely gutted, lost, nothing remained but a few walls. The garden and garage looked like a battlefield, bodies everywhere. There was nothing in the garage that gave any clue as to the reason for the massacre. They found the bodies of the scientists and Dave, also in the garage were three dead Russians, six more Russians were found either in the garden or the remains of the house. Eight Chinese, six Americans and four British operatives were also found shot to pieces in the garden. The bodies also included those lost in the assault of the previous evening. In short it was carnage. The sole survivor, Gregori, was taken into custody.

Immediate investigations showed that all members of the Charles family were missing, whereabouts unknown, no remains of them were found. Officials at Birmingham University had no knowledge or understanding why their team were there, including Bob from the Gravitational Waves project in the USA. Subsequent enquiries, found the link with Dave and discovered that Rachel and her team had gone to meet Bob and Gregori after a mysterious summons from him. The email communications from me were never found. The only chance they had of finding out what had happened came from interrogating Gregori.

2 **After the Massacre** - (Major Henry Bullement, UK Intelligence Services - Presentation only)

Suspect Gregori Ilyitchov (they were certain this was an alias, but never discovered if that was true or not) was taken to a high security unit for questioning, he said nothing, remaining silent during sixteen hours of interrogation. Forensic examination of the Mill Street incident site, produced plenty of information regarding, the victims in the garage, the deceased agents in the garage, garden and house. Exact details of some of the agents were never known. A whole mountain of information was documented on weaponry, ammunition, shots fired, by which weapon etc., etc.

ANTIGRAVITY DRIVE - THE DIARY OF AN INVENTION

China, Russia and USA claimed all of their agent's bodies, all were repatriated. No one accepted responsibility for the Incident, no one would give any details of their operation. Russia demanded the return of their countryman, claiming he had done nothing but survive a massacre, in fact he was a hero. Their claim was refused. The USA demanded Gregori be handed over to them, after all, his first crime must have been as an, illegally operating, agent in the USA. Their demands were refused. China said nothing except that their comrades were national heroes. The USA applied for extradition, stating his first crime, espionage, was in their country and they should have first claim on him. Their application was again refused.

The Charles family could not be located and were listed as missing. The reported burglary documentation was added to the case files. The documented surveillance of Richard Charles was added to the case files, no conclusions could be drawn from either, it was suspected that the cause of the massacre was hidden in the files, nothing could be found (Note: The copy of my diary was not with the files). Colonel Smyth, leader of the British surveillance team was also missing, no trace could be found.

A convoy of police and security vehicles was attacked during a transfer of Gregori between a high security unit to a higher security prison. Two policemen were killed, one attacker was killed, his body left at the scene. Gregori was abducted, or rescued, by agents unknown. It was initially thought to be the Russians, no one claimed responsibility. Relations with Russia became difficult as a result. It took three weeks to identify the attacker's body, it came to light that he was actually an American agent. There was outcry from both Russia and the UK. China remained silent, except to condemn the Americans. Initially, America denied involvement and said it had not been an authorized operation and the dead attacker was not one of their current agents. Subsequently, disaster struck for the USA, a video was leaked onto the internet of Gregori being horribly beaten, tortured and apparently killed. The voices of the perpetrators were American. America resolutely and strenuously denied involvement and claimed the video was a cleverly produced fake. They claimed it was the Russians who had taken Gregori and produced the intentionally misleading and provocative video. They also, embarrassingly, admitted that the body of the agent, left dead at the scene of the ambush, was indeed one of their operatives, but, who was previously listed as missing in China, only two weeks prior to the ambush. They claimed his body was planted as a distraction by the real perpetrators.

There was general, global disbelief and condemnation of the USA. Diplomatic efforts reached fever pitch, the UN was a vehicle which all countries tried to use to condemn their (The USA) illegal and highly inflammatory operations, a total disregard of supposed allies. All of this was under the intense scrutiny of the World's media, never afraid to whip up a storm, the story was continuous headline news throughout the developed World. There were anti American protests and riots, which themselves became headline news, in Russia, China, the Middle East and North Africa. Feelings were running very high. Some governments were suspected and accused of orchestrating the demonstrations and provoking the riots.

The actual involvement of the USA has never been officially verified, Gregori has never been located, dead or alive.

3 **Knee-Jerk Diplomacy** - (Sir Timothy Hartwell-Jones, Foreign Office - Video, media clips and presentation)

US diplomats and their staff were either expelled or withdrawn, for their own safety from Russia, China, UK, most Middle Eastern countries, 16 countries in Africa and a further 24 countries around the World. Many US embassies were attacked or overrun. The USA objected strongly at the UN. No one really listened. The U.S. embassy in an undisclosed, Middle Eastern country was taken over before any of the diplomats and staff could be evacuated, there were horrific scenes of the ransack of the building and of the captured diplomats and staff being publicly beaten, tortured and horrifically killed, there were no survivors. The USA reciprocated, expelling all staff from embassies of more than 60 countries. Additionally, all diplomats and staff from the offending Middle Eastern country were taken into "protective" custody. More outcry followed. A state of war was declared by the U.S. on all countries that had violated American territory by destroying and/or occupying their embassies. Diplomats and staff from 10 more countries were taken into custody in the US. More countries began withdrawing diplomats and staff from all over the globe. The original cause of this intense activity and violence appeared to get lost in the highly charged atmospheres that developed. Relations between the USA, UK, Russia, China and many other countries became extremely strained. The relationships in Europe seemed to get stronger as a result. Europe began to speak with one voice, supported strongly by The UK, Germany and France. NATO collapsed as an effective organisation when they expelled the US. Europe and the UK attempted to keep it going but it had lost its teeth.

It was only six weeks since the Mill Street Incident. Many European countries demanded that the USA withdraw all of their military operations, they felt vulnerable and did not want to appear to be military allies at this stage of intense diplomatic activity. The USA refused. More riots, more diplomatic standoff and failure.

ANTIGRAVITY DRIVE - THE DIARY OF AN INVENTION

4 **Show of Force, Threat and Counter Threat** - (General Sir Edward 'Jack' Dawe, Chief of Defence Staff, British Forces - Presentation)

In conjunction with the diplomatic crises, armies, navies, air forces and large weaponry were being mobilised, particularly in Russia and China. Russia began to move its vast army and mobile armaments along most of its borders, spreading their troops too thin to be fully effective on too many fronts. China did like-wise, but had plenty of boots on the ground and were fully equipped and prepared. The USA had their entire global forces on full alert, including its diverse Navy and Air force, much of which was already deployed around the globe. Russia made the first move, crossing the borders into almost all its former Soviet States. This was more than sabre rattling, they met tough resistance in many countries but pressed on, none of them gave in easily and were fully stretching the invading armies. Either by miscommunication or gross error of judgement they also began to advance on Chinese territory. China declared war and began a very swift rout of the Russian Forces, they made huge gains and advanced into Russia. There was a sudden and dramatic move, Russia deployed and targeted mobile nuclear missiles near the Chinese front in an attempt to halt their progress, targeting major cities and military bases within range. China deployed their own missiles, with reciprocal targeting. China also began moves to annex its own immediate neighbours, such as North and South Korea, Cambodia, Vietnam and Japan. Part of their strategy was to target larger nuclear missiles as a warning not to try what the Russians had done. These moves brought the USA and other countries directly into the standoff. All countries with nuclear weapons or bases for larger foreign powers were put on full nuclear war alert. The World held its breath in a huge, brain-tingling, standoff. In the UK it was estimated that a nuclear exchange was more than 80% likely, emergency plans were put into action. These included moving the seat of government, relocating VIPs to safe havens, mass civil evacuation from potential targets and declaration of martial law, with controlled curfews to avoid civil unrest, looting etc. Other European countries were also executing their emergency plans. They were on the brink of World War Three, only this time it felt inevitable that it would not be a war like any other. This would be a war with devastating consequences. The standoff lasted just over three weeks.

5 **First Nuclear Skirmish** - (Sir James Handys, permanent secretary to the War Office - video presentation, news clips)

There were news correspondents and journalists on many of the active fronts around the World, media coverage was extensive. Lots of news clips were shown of continued fighting on Russian and Chinese borders. The Chinese continued to advance into Russia. Russia began to lose ground on many of its other fronts too, particularly Kazakhstan Where they began to push back and encroach on Russian territory. In a desperate effort to halt the advances Russia launched five small, short range nuclear missiles, three into China aimed at military bases, one into Mongolia, the other at an American base in Afghanistan Only three were intercepted, two hit their mark, one in China which completely obliterated a military installation and adjoining small town, more than a hundred thousand people were killed, the scenes were too horrible to look at. The other destroyed the American base near Kabul, again hundreds of thousands lost their lives. There was no immediate retaliation, they were either too shocked or too scared of the ultimate consequences.

Russia, thinking they had made their point, continued their assault as if they had won a small battle. They attacked the Chinese front with renewed vigour, the Chinese were incensed and insulted, they belatedly retaliated with ten missiles, five were short range targeted at military bases, three were medium range, targeted at strategic towns and a city, two were long range, targeted at ports, one on the Baltic the other on the Black Sea. All ten found their mark, Russia's defences were caught short, either in use at other locations or plain non-existent. The devastation must have been immense, very few reports came out and only sparse video coverage. Needless to say, this was the beginning of the end. Every developed country in the World was put to the highest level of alert, emergency plans were accelerated, those that had nuclear weapons set into motion final battle sequences. A bigger standoff commenced, all were waiting to see what the Russians, the Chinese and the USA would do.

6 **Mass Evacuations** - (Ms. Helena Roxbury, Under Secretary, The Home Office - Presentation and film)

From the moment that nuclear weapons were observed in the field of battle, a well-oiled machine was started up and set in motion. 'Emergency Action in the event of Nuclear Conflict', first developed in the Cold War of the 60's, was formulated, simulated, practiced, rewritten, practiced, simulated over and over again, refined, computerised, digitised, simulated, put to bed, woken up, rewritten, simulated, practiced, but never used in anger. When the likelihood of nuclear conflict reached 80% it was once again awakened, dusted off and switched on for real, for the first time! It was like clockwork, everything worked, the years of refinement and practice paid off. It was highly efficient and effective, nothing, absolutely nothing went wrong. It was no surprise to those responsible, it was a huge surprise to those involved. A key element of the action plan was mass evacuation, the removal of the population from areas of high probability of targeting to areas of very low probability, the Safe Havens. The evacuation also included, The Government, Royalty, VIPs, contents of museums, art galleries and other National Treasures. Emergency power (energy), data backup and other infrastructure processes and systems were deployed. The whole thing was a marvel of ingenuity. Cities, towns, buildings and lands may be lost but the people and much of their history/legacy were saved.

Individuals, families, businesses, public organisations and educational establishments were all issued instructions and non-negotiable rules. All privately owned transport was forbidden, lots of them were requisitioned, only approved vehicles were on the roads in the right place at the right time, instructions were followed, the major part of the population was moved. Their first destination, preprepared transit camps, similar to the one surrounding this very facility. Their second destination, which happened at a much slower pace was to locations throughout the British Isles (including the whole of Ireland) that were very low risk, obviously the indigenous populations from these areas were not moved at all but were enlisted in the settlement and care of the evacuees, in hastily constructed, very large encampments. Another, and almost as equally large, operation was the requisitioning, movement and storage of food and other essentials. All of which was obtained from major supermarket organisations and other commercial entities in the evacuated areas. No recompense was given.

It was/is forbidden to travel to evacuated areas, in the event of lasting peace a controlled repatriation will take place where it is possible to do so, the remainder of the population will not move until new infrastructure and housing is developed. The emergency, planned evacuation saved countless lives, probably millions. The biggest challenge is yet to come, keeping them alive with a good quality of life.

7 **Unstoppable Nuclear War** - (General Sir Rodney Arbuthnot-Berridge-Simpson, Commander Tactical Weapon Deployment - Presentation, video, onboard footage)

The final standoff lasted fifteen days. Fifteen days of extreme tension and frantic diplomatic exchanges. Fifteen days of intense activity both planned and ad hoc, off the wall even. It was difficult to halt mass hysteria and in some countries, including some communities in the UK, there were lots of unimaginable, seemingly ridiculous, behaviours, such as, ritualistic warding off ceremonies and huge 'end of the world' orgies. Individual, family and mass suicides were like an epidemic, the police and other public services found it difficult to keep up with here, throughout Europe and USA. There were protests and riots across the World, news and video footage was alarming, if not horrific, there was general panic, everyone seemed to think total nuclear war was inevitable.

In the end it was. The urge to keep attacking, defending, holding on to what they had, became overriding for China and Russia, they targeted major cities and other facilities in their enemy's and their allies territories. This brought in, one way or another, all the remaining countries with nuclear weapons, fingers were on buttons, last ditch diplomacy failed, the first missile in the conflagration came from Russia aimed at Beijing. It is estimated that 80% of all missiles launched took to the skies within 10 minutes, that 80% represented at least half of the World's nuclear arsenal. Only video from one or two massive and destructive impacts were available as much of the media and communication systems collapsed around the globe.

No one knows exactly how many missiles were launched, how many were intercepted or how many reached their targets. Needless to say, a huge proportion hit their mark, the devastation was beyond comprehension. It is now more than two years since the last warhead wreaked its destruction and, still, little is known about the global picture, so bad was the impact on humanity's world and its infrastructure that we only really know our own situation. No one knows, globally, how many human lives were lost, how many cities, towns, villages, communities were destroyed, how many animals, birds, insects, plants flowers, trees, farmland and water courses are gone forever, maybe we will never know the exact figures. It will be many, many years before anything like the total picture is understood here, never mind elsewhere in the World. It is hard to imagine that it could ever be rebuilt, starting over would be almost impossible, we have to accept almost a third of the UK is a nuclear wasteland and will be for decades to come. It is possible there will be further mass extinctions, possibly there may have already been extinctions of some species of plants, animals and insects.

The planners just about got it right on targets and the evacuation sequences, before the first warheads struck, 90% of the evacuees were in transit camps, 5% were enroute, the remainder were in the lowest probable target status towns. Unfortunately some of those last 10% were caught in the fierce conditions during, or immediately after, the conflagration and suffered greatly from burns, radiation exposure, impact, and other injuries, a lot of which came from the hurricane-plus winds generated by each hellish, multimegaton detonation.

There is no real certainty about the origin of each missile that wrought destruction on the UK, but we played our part, our complete arsenal was launched along with many of the US warheads that were stationed here. It is estimated, details became sketchy as the exchange progressed, that 50 or more missiles, of varying megatonage, found their target here in the British Isles. As predicted none were targeted in Cornwall, Devon, 80% of Wales, the whole of Scotland, the whole of Ireland (North and South), much of the North of England (North of the M62 corridor), the Isle of Wight, the Isle of Man, the Channel Islands and the Scilly Isles. Consequently, transit camps or safe havens were developed in these locations. The targets in the UK were completely tactical, major ports, centres of industrialisation, military bases, airports and power stations.

The satellite towns, airports and cities surrounding London, including Northampton, but not London itself were the first to be hit, South Coast ports were next, followed by a series of other major cities, Birmingham, Coventry, Manchester, Liverpool, Leeds/Bradford, Hull, Sheffield, Doncaster, Bristol and Cardiff. Power stations and gas storage facilities were the last to go. The areas not targeted were not entirely unaffected, they suffered terribly from aftermath conditions, including, radiation and hellish winds. These areas evacuated but not suffering direct hits had no movement, no support, no help for the stragglers or few that remained it was hellish, few survived.

8 Land Battles, Land Grab, The Final Stand-off -
(Professor Dame Virginia Millington, Professor of International Strategic Studies, Oxford University and GCHQ - presentation and video)

Actual information from locations other than here in the UK and nearby Europe is sparse and sketchy, although some intelligence is beginning to find its way here via cobbled together media channels. Our part in any action following the nuclear conflagration was, and is, as support to NATO initiatives mainly using naval and air power. The initiatives have all been to defend territory for European Allies. We are not now equipped or have spare manpower to do otherwise, also we have no wish to enlarge our Sovereign Nation, merely to defend and recover.

The two superpowers in the initial conflict, however, are continuing with their attempted occupation of strategic neighbours, China has control of its Asian Peninsulas of North and South Korea and that of the huge Myanmar, Thailand, Vietnam land mass. they have made no moves on Malaysia, Indonesia or the Philippines, also they have abandoned any effort in taking Japan and any Russian territory. China, being content to hold their own borders, has allowed Russia the freedom to concentrate on returning to its historic USSR status. Europe has had to abandon its erstwhile members and watched helplessly as Russia completed their annexation of all former Soviet bloc countries, with the exception of East Germany. NATO has managed to get a forbidding presence along the entire border with New Russia. Both NATO and New Russia have retained a considerable nuclear arsenal and seem prepared to use them if either make a wrong move.

It appears that the USA has abandoned all efforts around the globe and has recalled all of its military operations home to concentrate on homeland defence and recovery. We do not have the full picture on the extent of damage to the U.S. and its major cities, we do know it is massive and they are deeply hurt. They also have a considerable nuclear arsenal at their disposal but have stated their intent of defence only.

A standoff remains but the probability of a further nuclear exchange has reduced to less than 50%. As time goes by it is becoming less likely that a second huge exchange will happen, as long as New Russia and China hold their ground. They too have to face a huge recovery programme, little is known of the extent of the devastation in either country, needless to say, it will be extensive and catastrophic, mirroring all other developed nations, that took part in the conflict.

9 **The Aftermath** - (Sir Selwyn Reynolds, Chief Undersecretary to the Home Office - Presentation and video)

There is now a huge amount of data, that is still growing, concerning the impact of the conflict. Survey teams have been busy assessing cities, agricultural land and open countryside in a bid to determine the extent and range of the damage suffered by the UK, even now the job is at best only half done. The total acreage that is now considered as wasteland is enormous, too big to contemplate here, the long term recovery plan takes into account different levels/categories of wasteland, from zero to fifteen, zero being not recoverable for more than 20 years and fifteen being suitable to recover and return to its original use in less than one year. This is alongside land and property suitable for immediate use, representing only 10% of available resource. Each category has different strategies and tactics for its recovery. It is estimated that the effect on the UK has reduced it to less than 25% capacity, compared to its output pre-conflict.

The effect on the populace is also alarming. In the region of 30 million people were evacuated to transit camps and safe havens, the sheer size of the operation was mind blowing and seemingly impossible, but the years of development and fine tuning of the plan paid dividends. The downside is that in less than one more year we will not have access to the food and water needed to sustain a population of its current size, unless categories 13 to 15 meet their recovery plans, it is estimated that there is only a 60% chance of success. This problem affects all countries that took part in the conflict and there are already moves to secure facilities and sources of supply from other countries. There is a greater than 80% probability that this issue will lead to further conflict as pressure mounts on meeting the needs of recovery and feeding and watering the World's population. In any case it is estimated that the overall population will decrease by a further third over the next five years leading to another more gradual decline to just over half the current population in a further ten years.

There is only a very little chance that these predictions can change as all countries are affected and involved, in fact it is predicted with a degree of certainty, the next World War will be on a larger scale bringing in those that seek to defend their own precious resources. The sheer size of the effort and timescale plus the staggering realisation that a further World War is inevitable brought the presentations to a very sombre close.

It is now 8.30 pm, the meeting is adjourned until tomorrow at 10.00 am.

I feel utterly drained by today's lengthy and very emotional presentations, I am having difficulty reconciling the whole thing, all of this because of my dream and my efforts to fulfil it.

Day 762 – 2nd July 2018

After a lengthy and relaxed breakfast the meeting got underway again. It was short and to the point. The Government accepts all of our story but, would like validation. It is agreed that two people, nominated by the Prime Minister, will return with us to Reality2, we must leave two key people behind as surety.

It is proposed that once validation has been confirmed that there will be a summit meeting between the Governments from Realities 1 and 2, this will determine the way forward. Sir Gordon and the Colonel are to stay behind, both Me2 and I are to return, along with Jerry and some of his men. I tried really hard to visualise that summit meeting with all those identical counterparts vying for position. It appears comical in my head, but obviously it's far from that. I, personally, am not sure what can be achieved. There must be an advantage to sharing and it will remain to be seen what, if anything, will happen as a result.

The Sir Gordons were very quick to volunteer Sir Gordon2 to remain behind, I wonder why? We are to depart tomorrow. Tonight is a formal dinner, of sorts, to celebrate a successful outcome. I got drunk very, very quickly to avoid any sensible discussions with anyone. I probably embarrassed myself and gained no favours but successfully put off talking to Me2.

Day 763 – 3rd July 2018

10.00 pm, I am back in my apartment in Reality2 on my own, Jane had the good sense to move out in anticipation of the possibility of Me2's return (I just knew she felt the same, it's not normal, we really have had an affair). I am feeling somewhat deflated, maybe it's a hangover. At such momentous times I should be elated, but having difficulty getting motivated. Bringing the diary up to date should fire me up a little, we will see.

First thing this morning, after a snatched breakfast, we were taken to the surface and to a fleet of limousines and, with a huge escort, were paraded between rows of tents and cheering refugees. It took me by surprise that anyone could be so enthusiastic about anything under the circumstances. We continued on for about another mile after the last row of tents to four waiting helicopters, gently ticking over at the ready.

The helicopters took us to an airstrip near Middlesbrough and a waiting small passenger aircraft, painted in RAF camouflage colours. The trip in the helicopter was fairly normal, the view was amazing, green open countryside and farmland, the only unusual sights were the acres and acres of tents in various locations on the way and the absence of traffic. I was in the lead helicopter with three other passengers, a close protection bodyguard and his two charges, Dame Celia Longton, The Minister for Cultural, Economic and Agricultural Rescue and Professor Sir Adam Williams, The Chief Scientific Advisor to the Government. They also happened to be the two representatives travelling to Reality2. The only conversation I had was with Sir Adam, he asked, or more accurately stated, that I witnessed the assassination of his daughter and was one of the last people to see her alive, all I could do was to agree with him with a nod of my head. He was about to ask more but was stopped in mid word by a sharp elbow in the ribs from Dame Celia. The rest of the journey was in conversational silence. In any case, there was not a lot I could add to that he already knew from my earlier presentation. I felt just a little uncomfortable for the remainder of the flight.

The passenger aircraft, possibly an Airbus of some sort, adapted for military use, which was more than likely for the movement of officers from base to base, easily accommodated all of the entourage. Half of the interior was made up of rows of large, comfortable seats, the other being chairs and tables set out as a meeting room. The view from my window, unlike the helicopter flight, was far from normal. As soon as we were airborne we were joined by an escort of two fully armed Eurofighter Typhoons. They kept their distance but were ever present in my field of view, a view that disturbed reality, a view that I truly wished I had never seen. At the height we cruised I could see many, huge, sometimes overlapping, circles of black devastation, a macabre pattern of black death, each one being the complete, malignant annihilation of all things human, of all things living, a massive work of art seemingly wrought by the devil himself.

Mile after mile of alternate devastation and green lushness was making my head spin, I felt nauseous and completely overwhelmed. It was difficult to concentrate or partake in any conversation. The view was irresistible, almost hypnotic, I didn't want to look but could not turn my head away from the compelling, sinister beauty of total destruction. I felt relieved when we began our descent to an airfield that was impossible to recognise, I was later told was Stansted, nothing much remained but the runway and a few blasted shells of buildings. When I felt able to drag my eyes away from the window I was amazed to see that, without exception, everyone looked shocked and downcast, some, including Dame Celia, had red eyes from the quiet shedding of tears. Dame Celia leaned across to me and whispered that although she had seen many photographs and videos she had not seen it with her own eyes before today and the stark reality was overwhelming.

We were met by another fleet of vehicles, this time in army camouflage colours, and quite a number of very smart but heavily armed soldiers. The Typhoons could be heard circling above us, leaving nothing to chance. We sped off along nondescript dusty highways in the general direction of Northampton. This time there was only Dame Celia and me in the back with her close protection officer in front with the driver. Again the journey was mostly in silence, the two of us gazing intently at the horrific surroundings of what were once heavily populated conurbations and verdant, productive farmlands. There was nothing we could say, it had all been said many times, silence seemed more appropriate, there would be plenty of time for talking later.

We were met by some of Jerry's men at the dusty remains of what was once my house on Mill Street, which was now the HQ for Reality2 here in Reality1. The field hangar was still almost impossible to see until you were right next to it, a marvel of the craft of the clandestine.

There were no formalities, a few handshakes, a few quietly spoken goodbyes, those that were going, entered the hangar, were shown their seats on the rig, the doors were closed and we travelled no distance at all, in no time at all, to Reality2. Now the formalities began! Waiting for us to arrive was the Prime Minister and her Cabinet, all the Dignitaries of the University, including Rachel, and many more that I don't have the patience to recall. The formal greeting and meeting was as you would expect, apart for the moment Rachel and her father met his counterpart. Adam Williams1 (Professor Sir) broke down in very noisy howls of grief as soon as he touched Rachel2's hand, he had to be helped to a seat, the proceedings came to a brief halt until he had managed to collect himself, with a lot of fussing from a cloud of people around him. When the formalities were over, Rachel and her two fathers went off to meet in private, Dame Celia disappeared with her counterpart and the rest of the cabinet, Me2 and I were left clicking our heels, Jane arrived and tearfully embraced the two of us, I felt really awkward and made the excuse that I needed a shower and sleep, lots of it, and beat a hasty retreat.

So here I am, 10.00 pm in my apartment, alone, no Tom, he has stayed in Birmingham, no Jane and distanced from Me2. Tomorrow we are to travel to the main campus in Birmingham with Dame Celia and Professor Williams.

I will finish this update here, there's someone at the door.

Day 764 – 4th July 2018

I never really got that sleep, I saw through the small opaque window in the door, that the knock was Me2 and Jane. I opened it and was immediately on my guard, Jane looked nervous and apologetic, shooting glances between the two versions of her husband. Me2 stepped inside and pushed past me to get to the kitchen and retrieved a beer from the fridge, tossing me one too, he said Jane had told him everything, what we did, where we did it, how often, what she felt like, everything. I said nothing, dared not even look at Jane or Me2. He asked how I felt, I could only shrug. Is that it, he said loudly, a shrug! I stammered and blurted out that I, we, couldn't help it, couldn't fight it, it was irresistible, even Clint said it was unavoidable, he suggested it would become the new normal. We tried not to, but in the end caved in, fell into, what felt like, a relationship we had always had, it was nothing new, a continuance, carrying on from where we left off, but at the same time new and exciting. Me2, emptied his beer and opened another, I had hardly touched mine. He sighed, heavily, several times, almost sobbing, looked up at me, tears in his eyes and said I wondered what was wrong with you, I knew you were keeping something from me, something you couldn't talk about, don't forget, I am you, you are me, I know how you feel, I know how you think, I know your every emotion and the way you behave, just the same as you know me. I am absolutely convinced I would have done the same, both Janes would have done the same, we are not different, we are the same people with the same history. Clint is right, it is unavoidable. It might feel strange but it would be cruel beyond belief not to be able to have a full relationship, we have to try our best to accept it as the new norm. The three of us, actually the five if us, have to live as one family, have proper relationships and develop new ways of behaving. From this moment on, if you are to stay in this Reality, we should all live together, as best we can, as one family, Jane has one husband, just in two versions, that's all.

Jane pulled us both to her in a group hug, we collapsed into tears, crying like babies, not wanting to leave go, I didn't want to be the first to release my grip, I clung on and on, tears soaking my shirt. Eventually the tears stopped and we slowly released our hold on each other. Jane wasted no time with talking or making up useless rules of engagement, she took our hands in hers and gently led us to the bedroom, kissing each in turn, she encouraged us to get undressed, she was taking the lead again. She too disrobed and got into the bed, we followed, now we were naked the only visible differences between us were my scars, red and ugly, constantly reminding me of their presence by having never-ending itchiness. The heat of the moment took over, it was very awkward, but, we made it up as we went along, both of us kissing and caressing different, delicious parts of Jane, I rediscovered her nipples for the umpteenth time, sucking, tweaking and caressing myself into a comforting but sexual frazzle. Me2 positioned himself so that he did not interfere with my activities and gently inserted his erection into that warm, moist pocket of delights between her legs. I don't know why I did it, but just at that point I chose to congratulate him on his elevation to honorary doctor of his own eponymous university, it had popped into my head that I kept forgetting to tell him and just had to do it there and then, it sort of broke the magic of the moment, we all stopped oohing and ahhing, grunting and groaning and collapsed into fits of laughter, real side splitting, rib aching, unstoppable laughter, it was like a release of emotion converse to crying but a release nevertheless. We laughed until we cried, laughed until we had no more energy. Exhausted we drifted off to sleep, clinging together like little pink piglets after a feed.

Twice in the night Jane aroused and coaxed me into making love, quietly and deliciously while Me2 gently snored on beside us. I am sure she did exactly the same with Me2, but, if she did I was oblivious to it, just as he was with me. That was probably the best way to proceed for now, separately but together, or individually when the other was not present, far less complicated for a novice like me, we will grow into two at a time eventually.

The three of us are scheduled to travel to Birmingham today with our two dignitaries from Reality1. They are to view the facilities and witness the Birmingham rig travelling to and fro between Reality2 and Reality3, even travelling there themselves to finally validate the whole scenario. We are to rendezvous in reception at the Mill Street entrance at 10.30 sharp.

An uneventful journey saw us safely to the Birmingham campus, we were taken straight to the newer of the two rig laboratories, where they have constructed and modified rigs of varying sizes. Again there was tiered seating for dignitaries and visitors to view proceedings. Before any formal tours or meetings we were to witness the opening of the first portal. Both Me2 and I were completely in the dark as to what this was, so it was exciting to sit and watch something new without knowing the outcome.

We were on the front row, Dame Celia between Me2 and I, Rachel was flanked by both of her fathers, holding hands with each of them. Jane was to my left, both Toms to her left. An amazing front row, full of people with fascinating relationships and back-stories, I was almost lost in a daydream thinking about it.

Before us was a huge rig, easily four times the size of anything built before, it was constructed very much like my modified rig, in that it had panels of polycarbonate, everything inside was visible, the core of the rig, the magnetic sphere cube, was still the same design as my own but much more sophisticated, this too was a modification of their original rig so that contact with Reality3 could be maintained. Two of the opposite sides were completely opened, drawbridge style, not the one facing us. The doors closed, we saw a few technicians and scientists inside, it disappeared, travelling to Reality3. On its return, some five minutes later, we were amazed to see that the rig contained another slightly smaller version of itself. The huge doors opened on either side as did the doors on the rig inside. A further, slightly smaller, version was wheeled in from the adjoining laboratory workshop, it was manouvered inside the other two, making three nested rigs. I had no idea what they were doing or what the result would be. Again all the doors closed and the huge rig, containing its nested versions, disappeared. On its return we could see a fourth rig was nested inside the other three. Four rigs, Two from this reality and two from Reality3, alternately nested.

There was a frenzy of activity inside the smaller of the four rigs (bearing in mind they were nested very closely together, with virtually no space between them), at the same time, on the outside, cabinets of electronics and communications equipment were all put in place and connected to each of the rigs and, I presume, Reality3.

ANTIGRAVITY DRIVE - THE DIARY OF AN INVENTION

Rachel was given a signal from one of the scientists that the work was complete and they were ready for the next stage. She stood and invited all of us from the front row to join her. We approached the nested rigs and the array of cabinets, one of which had a large, oversized switch at waist height. A microphone was brought out, Rachel made one of her typical short speeches and asked her fathers to press the switch together, in honour of her late and sorely missed counterpart from Reality1. From out of nowhere, there was a very loud blast of a fanfare that made most of us, including Rachel, jump out of our skins, the source was inside the rig. I saw, through the polycarbonate panels, two Heralds seemingly materialised in the centre of the rig and march towards the drawbridge exit nearest to us, they were followed by two more, they halted on the top of the ramp, two on each side, their long trumpets pointing in the air forming an archway, they blew another ear-bursting blast and Rachel's Reality3 counterpart materialised, along with her father, in the centre of the rig. They duly walked through the trumpet arch and descended the ramp, to meet Rachel2 and her two fathers. There were loud cheers from the audience behind us. I was almost too shocked for words, I needed to see more closely what was going on and attempted to get around to the ramp to see inside, Me2 gently held me back, asking me to be patient, we will see soon enough, let them have their moment. The five of them, Two Rachels and three of her fathers, ascended the ramp, walked to the centre of the construction, and from the viewpoint of the audience, disappeared. I could wait no longer and stepped on the end of the ramp, I could see the five of them descending the ramps on the other side, not into this Reality, but into Reality3. As they disappeared from view several more people began to ascend the ramp from Reality3, as they got closer I could see it was Me3, Jane3 and Tom3. They walked straight through the centre of the rig towards me, popping into existence for the audience, the three of them ran down the remainder of the ramp and almost knocked me off my feet in a ferocious group hug, we were immediately joined by Me2, Jane and both of our Toms. After a lot of hugging, back-slapping and laughter Me3 got us to ascend the ramp single file to make the journey into Reality3, at the centre we passed Team Rachel, also in single file, travelling in the opposite direction. There were a lot of witty remarks, giggles and snatched handshakes as we passed. We descended to cheers in Reality3 as they too descended to cheers in Reality2, I was lost in a daze of wonderment, trying to get in perspective what we were actually doing. The madness was added to by the presence of the four heralds at the top of each ramp, blowing an ear-busting fanfare each time a group passed through either of their trumpet arches. A deliciously wicked image popped into my head of two Janes and the three of me in an orgy of sexual frenzy, this was quickly followed by immense feelings of guilt and grief in the absence of my own Jane in these peculiar but spectacular events. That prickle of guilt served to remind me that Jane's funeral and memorial was my priority once this was over.

There was a lot more of this crossing backwards and forwards, Dame Celia joined in too, and seemed to want proof that the whole thing was real and not just a theatrical magic trick, as soon as she met Dame Celia3 she was convinced. I suddenly had a thought, I'd been through the, so called, portal several times, fanfares dulling my senses, I was not sure which Reality I was in, 2 or 3? I had this little moment of panic in the pit of my stomach. If they open this for wider use, someone really has to keep track of who is where, from which Reality and purpose of visit, how long staying and much more probably border control with passports and visas, it occurred to me that it was very necessary to control passage otherwise it could really get out of hand. What about mistaken identity in cases of the infinite ways people find to break the law. The trouble with numbering is that the population of each reality think they are the first. This really is a problem that needs solving. I will mention it to Rachel, but I do not have the answer.

Eventually we ended up where we began, everyone was buzzing and almost hyper with excitement, there was lots of noisy conversation regarding all the possibilities this offered. I was more relieved that the heralds and their fanfares had gone back to Reality3. The audience slowly dispersed, Rachel and the visitors from Reality1, went off to some meeting or other, which left me, Me2, Jane, both Toms and a few academics, including Graham, Tom's supervisor. Neither Me2 nor I knew how all this worked, but the Toms and Graham did, they offered to talk us through it, we readily agreed.

They talked us through the physics and the technology three times before we got even a glimmer of understanding, nesting the rigs and cycling them through from one reality to the other as a nested set, but very, very rapidly slightly out of phase, we are unable to see each rig is transitioning backwards and forwards between realities, the trick is it is almost in reverse, the rig nested first inside the largest is not squeezed until it is here in this Reality and the third rig inserted here, inside the other two, is not squeezed until it is in Reality3, the fourth is squeezed in Reality3 at the same time as the third rig is squeezed. The process of ultra-fast squeezing is taken care of by banks of computers in both Realities. The four nested rigs are flipping backwards and forwards so fast we cannot see it. Graham gave us two pieces of evidence, firstly, strobe lighting (also computer controlled) showed the four rigs to become blurred, appearing and disappearing inside the largest, it made me feel dizzy to watch. Secondly, playback from one of the ultrafast slow motion cameras, the video could be slowed to show the sequence of appearance and disappearance of each rig. It was fascinating to see, the physics was completely over my head, I really couldn't get it, no matter how much I tried to think it through. Apparently it was the two Toms who first postulated the process and even produced the equations to show it was possible, they are writing it all up as a dissertation for their doctorate. Graham believes that it could win them a Nobel Prize. Graham believes it is possible a similar bridge between here and Reality1 can be forged, facilitating Reality2's contribution to the recovery process. It would need to be even larger, allowing a transport link for trucks or even trains. I remain to be convinced, but kept quiet, not wanting to curb his enthusiasm.

The three of us got back to Northampton in the early hours and retired to our inviting, delicious and enticing king sized bed.

Day 765 – 5th July 2018

Today was a very quiet and reflexive day, not emerging from the warmth of our duvet until late morning, brunch in the cafeteria, lazing around, chatting and catching up on events, mostly for Jane's benefit. Early to bed in anticipation of our attempts to learn the mechanics of a threesome.

Day 766 – 6th July 2018

We ventured out into the campus at a more reasonable hour today, last minute preparations for Jane's memorial service and cremation taking place in two days. Everything is as it was planned, All Saints' Church in the heart of Northampton has agreed to host the ceremony, even though it will be a humanist service. Her body is now resting in a funeral parlour, anyone who wishes can go and say their goodbyes. A reception will be held at the Park Inn, in the Town centre afterwards, we will be catering for two hundred. Preparations have also been made for the invited media coverage, television, radio and a host of other media. There will be no press conference or interviews, despite the pressure to have them.

We will not witness her cremation, her ashes will be collected in two receptacles, the next day. One for each Reality. I will scatter one on the roses in the little garden here, the other to be scattered on what was our garden in Reality1. Late in the afternoon I went to the funeral parlour to say my own goodbyes. I was very surprised to find Colonel Smyth, on his own, chatting to the open coffin. I held back at the door, not wishing to interrupt or spoil his moment with Jane. I am certain he did not know I was there, I felt very rude, eavesdropping, but couldn't bring myself to tiptoe away. It would also be crass of me to record all that I heard here too, regardless of many things, he deserves some privacy and respect. What I did hear has really got me thinking differently about many things, not least the horrendous feelings of guilt I have had about Jane, the massacre and resulting death of millions of innocent people. Smyth confessed that he blames himself and his colleagues, he apologised to Jane for causing it, he said it wasn't me and my invention but the way they tried to deal with it, causing a frenzy of activity in the underworld of political subterfuge, if they had supported me just like in this Reality, everything would have been different, academia taking the lead, advancement in science, instead we got nuclear war.

I did tiptoe away after that and sat in the horrendously awful and dated waiting room, that had strong odours of disinfectant. I am sure this was disguising something distinctly worse. I sat there until he had finished, a full hour later. I was almost at my wits end with boredom and a sick feeling in the pit of my stomach, it felt like hours. I heard his footsteps pass the waiting room door and the outer door close before I emerged to say my farewell to Jane. I was with her, for nearly two hours, mostly in silence, staring, imprinting a mental image of her face on my memory. There was nothing I could say that I had not said before, nothing except my whispered words of love, silent thoughts felt more appropriate, channeling my thoughts to that once vibrant body, my forever soul mate.

Day 767 – 7th July 2018

Last night I slept alone, or more accurately, laid awake alone, lost in my thoughts, thinking of Jane, mulling over Smyth's confession, trying to come to terms with everything, Jane, my role in the outcomes in Reality1, my relationships here, Tom, Tom2, the enigma of Tom5, everything. It was a long, long night, hardly a wink of sleep. I emerged from my dark pits of memory at nine, much later than usual and stepped into the bright cheeriness of a Jane Full English Breakfast, delicious aromas of bacon and sausage on the grill, percolating coffee and a bright, cheery and very sexy smile.

Jane's funeral and memorial was today, so much has happened since she was shot during our dramatic escape from the massacre. Sadly, she was never aware that a parallel universe existed and would never have guessed in a million years that she would be cremated in one and her ashes scattered in the other.

Both Toms arrived at 10.30 and rather unceremoniously announced they wished it was over and done with, they were keen to get back to Birmingham and their joint thesis and their work on the portal. They meant no disrespect but felt it was almost an unnecessary distraction, after all this time, that and their continued exposure to Jane's counterparts. It started off like a typical family funeral, the hearse arrived with three black, shiny stretch limousines at 12.00 precisely, immediate family and closest friends climbed into the limos and we slowly embarked towards the centre of town.

I felt completely numb it was as if I was experiencing the whole thing in someone else's body. I was totally taken by surprise to see that the nearer we got to the church, the more that people had solemnly lined the route and threw flowers into the road and onto the vehicles. Their support overwhelmed me, and everyone with me. No one expected anything like that.

The outpouring of grief from all those around me and the waves of emotion from hundreds, if not thousands, of people lining the route, made me even more numb, I suppose I was in a deep state of shock, I could hardly breathe, it felt as if there was a ton weight pressing on my chest. I can't remember getting to the church or even getting into the church. I can only vaguely remember Jane and Me2 supporting me from both sides, without them I never would have made it. I was so ill I never went to the reception afterwards, they took me home instead, I was exhausted and needed peace and quiet. I needed my bed, on my own. I slept, unconscious, for more than four hours, only roused by Jane and Me2 returning from the reception. They roused me to check if I was OK, then left me to it for the rest of the night. I slept soundly and deeply until the alarm woke me at 7.00 am.

Day 772 - 12th July 2018

The last few days have been an emotional blur, I could only recall scant details, as evident from my entries. I felt rested but mentally drained. Today I purposefully closeted myself in the apartment, resting and building myself up, psychologically, for the next stage of Jane's final resting.

Jane's ashes arrived exactly on time, as planned. Two containers, one for each Reality, to be scattered in the garden of our house (or what was left of our garden). Although I felt OK in myself, I needed another day of reflection, so remained in the apartment all day. I need the scattering to be personal and not viewed by thousands or millions of spectators, no matter how well wishing and sympathetic they are. The date is set for tomorrow at 10.00 am. Just me and Jane, not even Tom, he understands, as does Me2.

Day 773 – 13th July 2018

We sat alone in the peace and quiet of the remembrance garden, holding onto each other, like cornered, frightened children, not really knowing what to do next. I couldn't think of anything succinct to say, I had lots of ideas but I would have rambled on for hours. After an hour of silently clinging to each other, Jane once again took the initiative, she helped me to take the top off the container, we both tipped it, allowing the entire contents to fall on one rose. I was relieved it was over, the penultimate action of the final resting of my Jane, my original Jane.

I still find it bizarre and extremely strange that Jane2 and I share the same memories of Jane, up to the point of Reality divergence. Before that point there was only one Reality that I was aware of and only one Jane.

(As an aside we found out today, by email, that the academics mapping Realities have announced that my reality was actually the first in this whole bizarre episode and that this reality, Reality2, is indeed the second. They have analysed diaries and carried out hundreds of interviews from the four known realities and found all the points of convergence and divergence. Apparently I had made a conscious decision to make a choice whereas in Reality2, Me2 did not. He only had one option whereas I had two, thus giving Reality1 the priority.

They have labelled them as in my diary Reality 1 and 2. Reality3 has become 2a and Reality4 is now labelled as 1b, they are making an assumption that Reality5 is 1a, the explanation was detailed in the e-mail but the logic, for the time being, escapes me. They are now proposing to issue identity numbers to counterparts and it is also proposed that legislation be introduced for all countries in all realities that this identification be mandatory on every passport and that any portal constructed includes passport control. I found this to be excellent news going someway to counteract the fears I have had about individual identity.

An extra, and surprising to me, complication is the difference in time between different realities and bridges. After detailed research, analysis and testing a team of academics led by Graham1 have developed a theory regarding time dilation and differences between Realities, their degree of overlap and their Reality Bridges. I really am unable to remember the equations and the detailed physics, but, here is the explanation as best as I can express it.

Reality1 (my reality) is the start point (as mentioned earlier) it's bridge is 480 times slower, making 1 day on the bridge equal to 480 days in my reality, it was expected that this would also be the same in Reality2, but, it is not the case. On return to Reality1 it was found that there was, coincidentally, exactly 2 years added to the date. My immediate assumption was that time was 'passing' twice as fast, that is also not the case, it's a factor of 1.000991 faster, it's not just the time we have been in Reality2 that's gone faster, it's all time that is faster by that factor. That in itself is mind boggling, that means the parallel universe came into being as a copy of my reality complete with its own history all the way back to the big bang but with time passing differently by a factor of 1.000991, how that is even possible blows my mind. This factor, apparently, reflects the fact that Reality 1 and 2 do not actually overlap and the degree of separation gives rise to the factor. They say it is best represented diagrammatically as circles of reality, if the circles touch (like a tangent) then time passes exactly the same, if they are not overlapping then the new reality has time passing slower, if they overlap then time passes quicker in the new reality, the more they overlap the faster it goes. They discovered that Reality 2 and 2a only differ by 1 day, but the difference between 2a and 1b is exactly the same as Reality 1 to 2 (f=1.000991). They are still working on why overlap and separation actually happen, but they are close to a good theory. They have also postulated, again I don't know how, that Reality 1 to 1b is at least + 5 years, f=>1.0025. I think this is mostly due to the forensic medical data from the death of Tom1b. In any case all these parallel universes are not all at the same date, some appear to be like stepping into the future, when I said this they chuckled a little, saying if only that were true, the truth is there is only now and past so any feeling of stepping into the future is only going from the past into the now. My head hurts just writing this, not so sure I have even described it as was explained to me, anyway let's hope it gives a reasonable picture and if anyone reading this wishes to know in more detail they can look up the published papers.

We left the garden in the early afternoon and made our way back to the apartment, Me2 was there, light lunch prepared. We sat about for the rest of the day chatting, reminiscing, wondering what the future will bring. We all agreed that such a lot has happened in such a short time in our respective realities, but we knew relatively little about the other two, how differentiated are they? We decided that soon, in the near future, we would investigate, if allowed.

Day 774 – 14th July 2018

Today we were briefed on the next steps in the development of the relationship between Reality 1 and 2. The existence of both Realities has been acknowledged by Dame Celia and, as such, the building of a portal can begin. Planning has commenced on what might be the practical assistance given to Reality1. Dame Celia and Professor Williams are to address the United Nations, accompanied by their counterparts from this Reality and Rachel. Once they return here, a week from today, we are all scheduled to return to Reality1. Jane and I are included so that Jane's ashes can be scattered in what remains of our garden.

Day 781 – 21st July 2018

Today is a big day, I am returning to my original home with the remaining half of Jane's ashes, Jane2 will be by my side, a great comfort. Dame Celia1 and Professor Williams1 are also scheduled to be passengers, returning to Reality1 to report their findings and the progress that they have made in Reality2.

Jane2, Me2 and I ate a healthy muesli breakfast in the cafe, chatted nervously about the impending return journey and the second scattering of Jane's ashes.

We assembled at the rig at 10.30 am, also accompanying us were Jerry and two of his team.

I am typing this as the doors closed, Jane to my left, Dame Celia to my right, Jane's ashes, in the receptacle, under my seat. I pressed the Mic button on my key pad to record the moment as an audio file too.

"Here we go"

ADDENDUM

EXCERPT FROM PROCEEDINGS

THE COURT OF ENQUIRY INTO THE 2017 NUCLEAR CONFLAGRATION, REALITY1

Location: THE UNITED WORLDS BUILDING, NEW YORK, REALITY2

Date: 3rd June 2022

In the Chair: Judges Lord Stevens1, 1b, 2 and 2a, United Kingdom

Panel: UN Representative Sir Peter Gregson1 and 2, United Kingdom

UN Representative Gray Meyerhouse2 and 2a, U. S. A.

UN Representative Rita Barndhoff1 and 2, Germany

UN Representative Brian Andrews1 and 1b, Australia

UN Representative Raju Gorinder-Gandhi1b and 2, India

UN Representative Ralph Schwartzman1 and 2, Switzerland

UN Representative Helen Jungmann1b and 2, South Africa

UN Representative Hans Bortzman1b and 2, Denmark

UN Representative Avril Render1 and 2, Argentina

UN Representative Michael Pochard1b and 2a, New Zealand

UN Representative Maria Perez1 and 2, Spain

UN Representative David Ferrier2 and 2a, France

Barry C Cunningham

CLOSING STATEMENT AND CONCLUSIONS

JUDGE LORD STEVENS1, 1b, 2 and 2a

READ BY JUDGE LORD STEVENS2

Good morning fellow Counterparts and Court of Enquiry Panel Members. I am honoured to address all those invited representatives from the United Worlds Organisation and the multiworld's press and media gathered here in the headquarters of the United Worlds Organisation, New York2.

This has been a long and thorough enquiry and my counterparts and I have been honoured to preside over the first court of enquiry for this organisation. We all acknowledge that this has been a long and arduous enquiry, hearing statements and interviews from more than a thousand individuals from all four connected Realities. We have, as you know, reviewed many documents and video material, not least the four diaries of each of the Richard Charles counterparts. We thank you for your patience and assistance. Copies of this closing statement are available in both hard copy and in electronic document format, available from the multiworld web:

mwww.UWO.com/mwenquiry001/report

Copies of the full report are only available to designated recipients or via freedom of information requests.

There were two main components to this enquiry, as such the conclusions are set out in the same way as follows:

1 - What or who was the cause of the nuclear conflagration in Reality1, 2017?

2 - The supplementary aim - Where is Richard Charles1?

I have not included, in this statement, the detail of any testimony or registered document. Those can be found in the full report itself. This statement is wholly concerned with the conclusions that this enquiry has reached.

In order to facilitate full and considered responses, we will not take questions, neither during nor at the end of this statement.

Questions will only be considered if they are submitted in writing or by email or via the appropriate links on the official website of this enquiry.

ANTIGRAVITY DRIVE - THE DIARY OF AN INVENTION

The first consideration of this enquiry was to assure a thorough and in-depth process, omitting nothing from scrutiny that was thought relevant by all individuals and organisations involved in the search for the truth. It was paramount that no individual, organisation, country or legal entity be excluded from this process in our quest for fairness to all Realities and all member countries for each of their United Nations Organisations.

I must emphasise that this enquiry is not a legal entity in itself, meaning that conclusions are not judicial in the sense that sentence, sanction, punishment or recompense may be awarded by those here assembled. That process, if thought necessary, is the responsibility of other international courts.

We will not be adjourning during the reading of this statement, in fact, at the conclusion of this statement the members and representatives of this panel will be relieved of their responsibility to attend the court. The Court of Enquiry will continue to exist only as a virtual entity in order to process questions that may arise as a result of the issuing of the report. The virtual nature of this Court of Enquiry will ultimately be disbanded after one full calendar year following the publishing of this statement. Any questions or appeals for further information and or process will not be considered by this court after that date. We are aware that there are joint projects in progress within the Dr Richard Charles Multiversity, any new findings made by them will not be the responsibility of this Court to scrutinise, draw conclusions or compare with current understanding, rather it will be up to them to present findings and compare them to conclusions presented here today.

In the case of Component One, we have concluded that there is a joint responsibility for each of the several stages of the nuclear conflagration as follows:

Stage one - The elevation of the original development and disappearance of the 'rig' to Classified level 4 in both the UK1 and USA1.

We conclude that the intelligence organisations for both countries behaved in a way that was out of control and not in accordance with governmental policies and practices. The treatment of Richard Charles1 would, under normal circumstances, have led to a full legal enquiry, that this court believes should have resulted in an apology and recompense. Their actions prevented the potential early involvement of appropriate academic and governmental bodies which ultimately led to other clandestine organisations becoming involved. It should be noted that at this stage no organisation involved knew what the rig was or even where it was. Several individuals, some of whom are not even now identified, take responsibility for this gross error of judgement and procedure and have admitted that they were operating under their own volition without higher government sanction. However, only one individual has publicly apologised, Colonel Smyth1, through necessity resident in Reality2, which in some way is a small penance to pay, never able to return to his own Reality.

It should be noted that Richard Charles1 befriended Colonel Smyth1 and accepted his apology for his actions prior to this enquiry and has, on several occasions, gone on record to say that this was the case. This, in itself, does not absolve Colonel Smyth1 of the responsibility for being one of the primary decision makers in the catalogue of poor judgements and mishandlings in stage one.

Stage Two - Clandestine and unauthorised surveillance, the intrusion and threats to Richard Charles1 and his family by both the UK1 and USA1.

We have concluded that this further amplified the apparent secrecy and hence international interest in the development of the rig, which in turn led to a series of "Chinese Whispers" amongst the clandestine fraternity. Many international organisations became competitively interested in whatever it was that the University was now getting involved with, this ultra-competitiveness, for something so big, but no one knew what it was, was the primary cause of the rapid chain reaction that led to Stage Three. All agencies, but principally the Russian and Chinese agencies, elevated stage two to unprecedented levels of illegal operations.

Stage Three - The Mill Street Massacre.

It was easy for us to conclude that once the agent, Gregori, planted in the American Gravity Wave Project, was briefed about the imminent secret meeting and an outline of the rig's properties, by his co-worker, Dr Robert Bayliss, he set off an unstoppable chain of events. The US agents were alerted by Dr Bayliss' security contingent, who in turn tipped off Colonel Smyth's team, who coincidentally had not yet managed to locate their leader. It appears that both the British and American teams blundered into the Chinese who were observing the Russians as they tried to take control of the rig. The ensuing gun fight resulted in the deaths of all agents and academics with only one survivor on the scene (Gregori). The survival of Richard1, Jane1 and Tom1 Charles was not known to the investigating authorities, nor was the actual existence of the rig at that time, the devastating fire which destroyed the house also destroyed any evidence of the rig and its development. Consequently we conclude that there was joint culpability by all clandestine teams and their controllers, principle amongst which where the Russians and in particular the agent Gregori, who, we further conclude, was responsible for the cold blooded murder of the academics and the neighbour, Mr. David Patterson, in the Richard Charles1 garage.

Stage 4 - Diplomatic Failure

We can only conclude that all parties involved with the arrest, the kidnapping and murder/disappearance of Gregori operated way outside of international law and that those involved were also determined to create escalating diplomatic stand-offs, with the intention of creating war or at least heightened tensions between nations. We will never know who really played what part, all that we can conclude is that the British Government appeared to be the pawn in this game.

We were unable to determine whether Gregori is dead or alive and if he did survive this episode, his whereabouts and ultimate status is indeterminate.

Stage 5 - Nuclear War

It is clear to us from the historical record, including the documents and statements within the Richard Charles1 diary, that all countries that developed and ultimately used their nuclear weapons bear a joint responsibility for the millions of souls that lost their lives during or post conflict. They equally bear the responsibility for their own people as well as those in other countries.

We concluded that the initial cause of the conflict were the heightened tensions between China and Russia brought about by the catalogue of errors and illegal operations in stages 1 to 4. We strongly recommend that the known Realities take heed of the needless and pointless loss of millions of lives we have witnessed in Reality1 where, in the end, there were no winners, only losers and that they urgently take steps to remove all nuclear weapons from active service. As many eminent politicians and philosophers had predicted, a nuclear conflict has no point, no winner and no place in human history. We have seen the results, let's not repeat them. This Organisation has been instrumental in building relationships between all known Realities since they were discovered post conflict, let us hope that this excellent work continues and that the rebuilding and restructure of Reality1 continues to be a success.

Richard Charles1 - The Whereabouts of Richard Charles1.

This has been the subject of much speculation since his failure to arrive in Reality1, unlike the other passengers, that accompanied him on that fateful journey to scatter the second half of his wife's ashes. His disappearance has been investigated on numerous occasions by a very wide range of individuals and organisations, both official and private, and has been the topic of many documentary films and programmes in all known Realities. The principle piece of evidence being his tablet computer left at the scene which, enigmatically, recorded his last moment in any known Reality. It should also be noted that the other passengers did not notice his moment of disappearance, nor did they hear or see anything to alert them to the fact.

We conclude that it is most probable he was taken to the Reality which, in his early days of rig development, was the source of the coded and mysterious card messages and were also responsible for the appearance of a very badly injured counterpart of Tom Charles, sadly that counterpart did not survive and was not able to give any information on his origin or demise. We further conclude that this Reality, labelled 1a by the academics, has potentially developed technologies that are hitherto undiscovered in the known Realities.

We also conclude that the voice heard welcoming Richard Charles1 was that of a counterpart of Colonel Smyth, the forensic voice analysis proves this beyond all reasonable doubt. We are unable to draw conclusions as to why other passengers did not witness any of the disappearance, except that what takes place on the, so called, Reality Bridge or Quantum Bridge is largely beyond current understanding. We can only hope that the active research programmes will ultimately deliver that knowledge. The full meaning of the brief recording of the very last entry of Richard Charles1 diary also remains a mystery. Why was he needed? Why were they waiting? It may be that we will never know.

As a closing remark here is the, all too brief, transcript of that recording. Goodbye and thank you for your support, patience and understanding during the entire proceedings of this Court of Enquiry.

"Welcome, Mr. Charles. We have been waiting for you Mr. Charles. Please accompany me to the reception. Leave everything, you will not need them here."

Appendix I

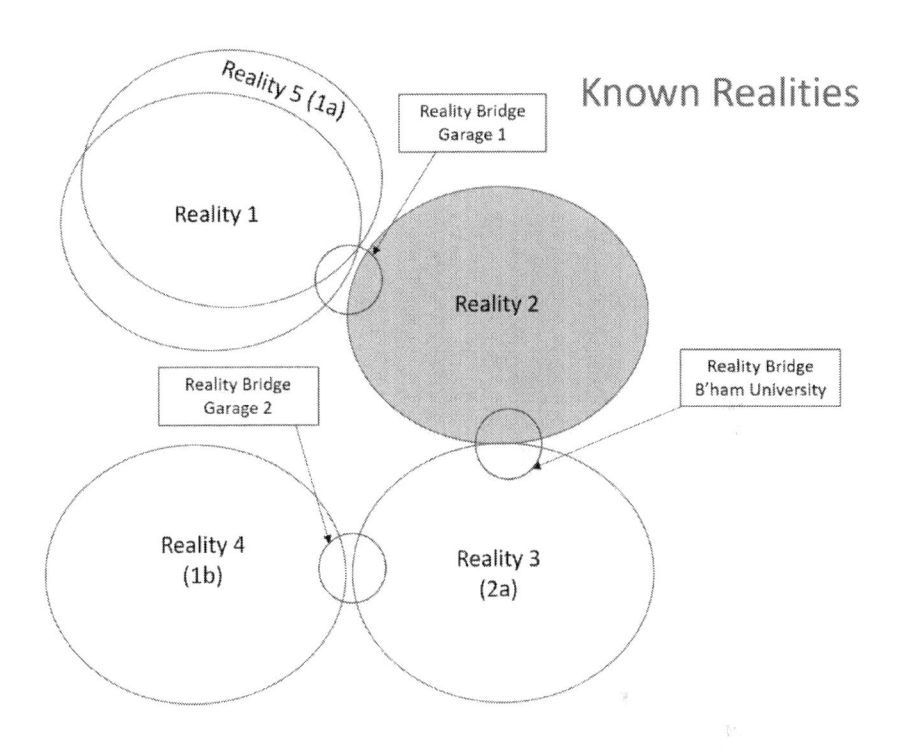

Known Realities

- Reality 5 (1a)
- Reality 1
- Reality Bridge Garage 1
- Reality 2
- Reality Bridge B'ham University
- Reality Bridge Garage 2
- Reality 4 (1b)
- Reality 3 (2a)

Appendix II

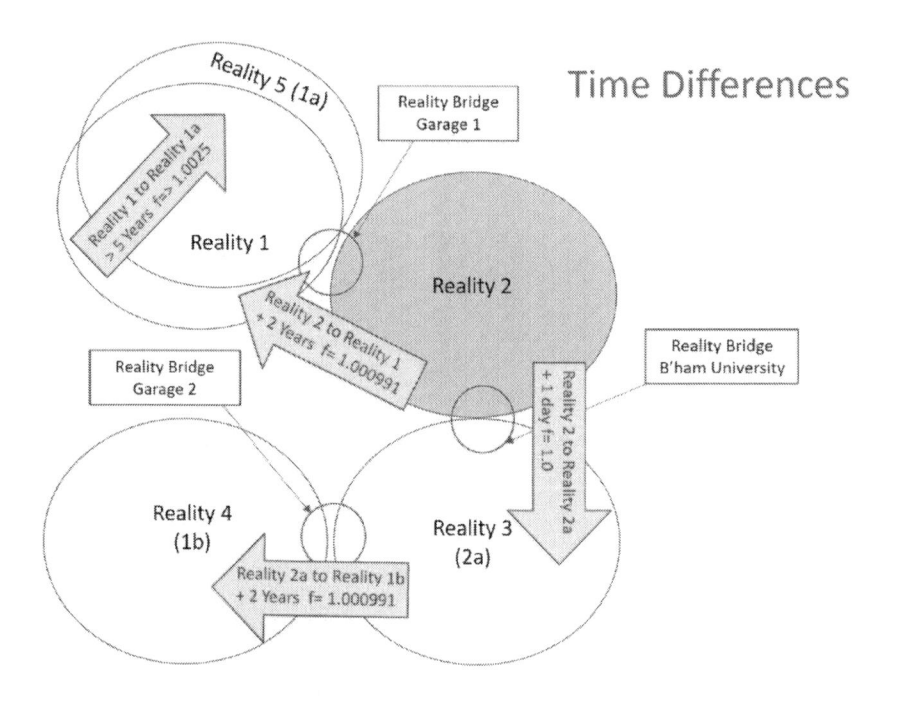

Time Differences

Reality 5 (1a)
Reality Bridge Garage 1
Reality 1 to Reality 1a
> 5 Years f=> 1.0025
Reality 1
Reality 2
Reality 2 to Reality 1
+ 2 Years f= 1.000991
Reality Bridge Garage 2
Reality Bridge B'ham University
Reality 2 to Reality 2a
+ 1 day f= 1.0
Reality 4 (1b)
Reality 3 (2a)
Reality 2a to Reality 1b
+ 2 Years f= 1.000991

Appendix III

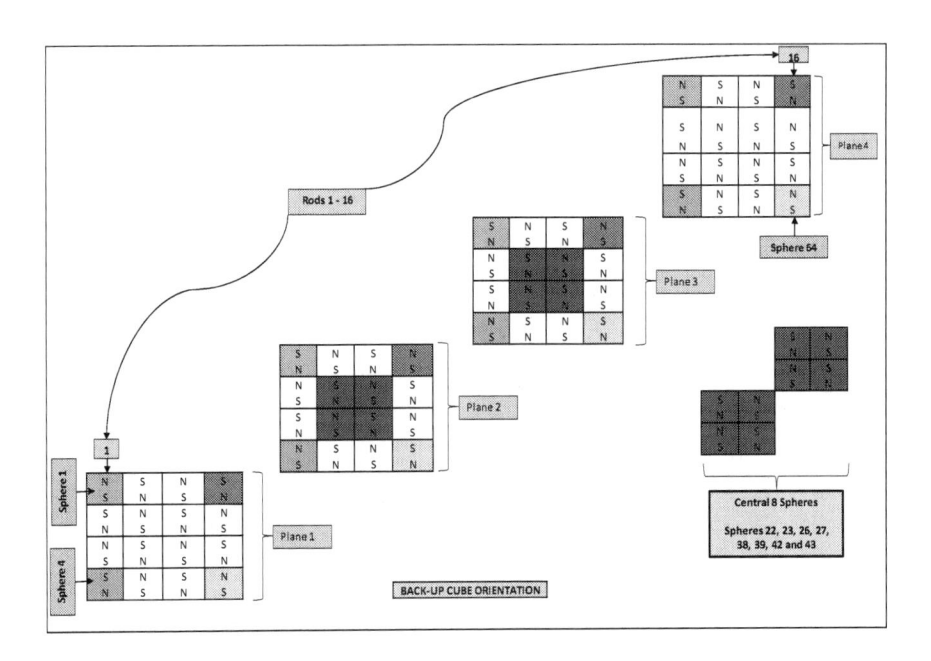

Appendix IV

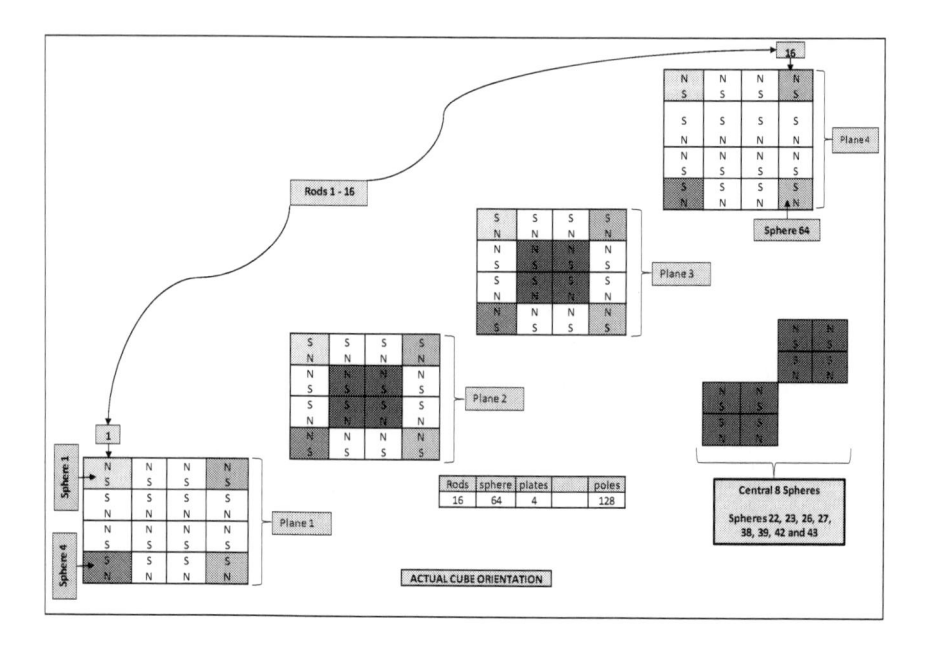

Appendix V

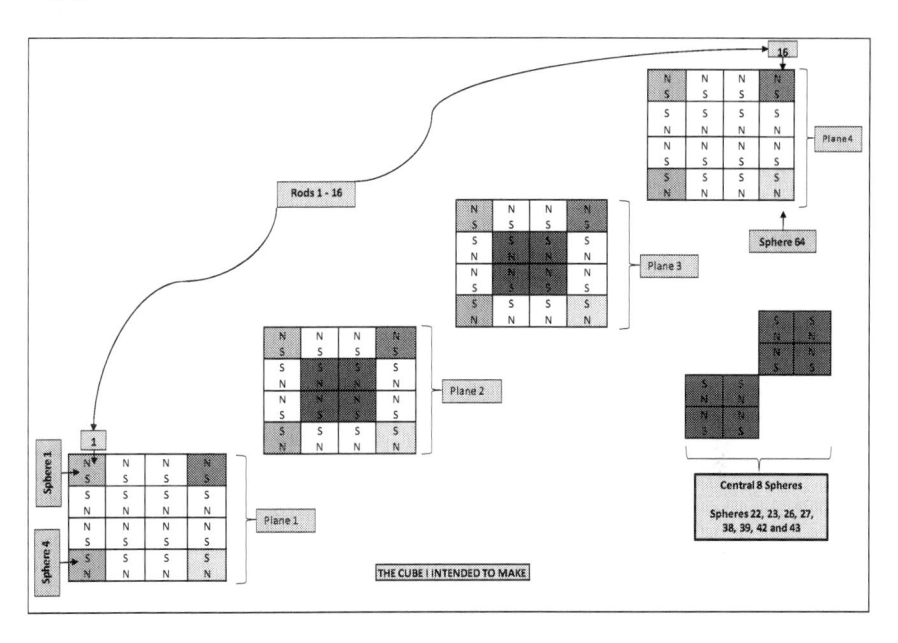

Barry C Cunningham

ABOUT THE AUTHOR

Barry is 66 and a retired chemist, not working in a shop (that would be a pharmacist), but someone who has spent his career immersed in the world of Industrial Laboratories and Product Development. He has been an active Rotarian for many years with The Rotary Club of Hull Kingston. He lives in the East Riding of Yorkshire, with his wife, Diane, two toy poodles, Tessie and Frankie, a tortoise named Daisy-May and several beautiful Koi Carp. He is a lifelong Science Fiction fan, which is just one of his many interests and passions, these include exploring the world of antiques and collectables, collecting and listening to music (He still buys vinyl, new and old and is developing an extensive 78rpm record collection). This is his first book, but has many more ideas, which may or may not come to fruition.

Made in the USA
Charleston, SC
11 February 2017